FOUR NOBLE TRUTHS

FOUR NOBLE TRUTHS

J D BUXTON

FOUR NOBLE TRUTHS

iUniverse books may be ordered through booksellers or by contacting:

iUniverse
1663 Liberty Drive
Bloomington, IN 47403
www.iuniverse.com
1-800-Authors (1-800-288-4677)

ISBN: 978-1-4917-4142-9 (sc)
ISBN: 978-1-4917-4143-6 (e)

Print information available on the last page.

iUniverse rev. date: 06/10/2015

"All that we are is the result of what we have thought.

The mind is everything.

What we think we become."

— Buddha

CHAPTER ONE

DRAGON

The blindfold didn't matter, he couldn't see but he knew anyway, the smell of the leather, the sound of its motion. He barely felt it anymore, barely felt anything anymore. Bound by his wrists strung above his head, it came as always, torturing his body until he had no feeling left. After, he lay shivering on the dirty floor, the smell of blood and stale cigarettes lingering, the blindfold protecting him from what he didn't want to see. He was bloody, his body marked and burning. He listened warily for the footsteps to return and as he heard them approach he hid in the corner, an attempt to disappear. The door pushed open and it was to no avail, the hatred gripped him again.

Dragon woke with a startled breath and looked quickly about the room, fully slipping out of the familiar nightmare. He slowed his breathing and remembered where he was. His long dark hair stuck to his face with the sweat of the dream. He sat up on the bed and reached for the 357 semi automatic, right by the pillow. The life he led was dangerous and one never knew. His distrust was engrained. The hotel room was small, grubby and dark and he looked around at the grim surroundings. The loneliness threatened to take over then, he had been fighting it but couldn't anymore. If he thought about her it distracted from the dark cold room and the memory of his receding nightmare. He took the gun and moved to the tiny bathroom, reaching for the shower. The mirror revealed him to himself as the water began to steam.

He was 6'2" and filled the small room. He pulled a hand thru the unruly black hair that hung too long. His dark, wide set eyes were large and deep and revealed his Asian heritage, but nothing more. As he methodically undressed, he eyed himself indifferently. An organized and regimented life had left him chiseled with muscle. His biceps bulged and the width of his shoulders would barely fit the shower. Naked now he turned and only the mirror could see the tattoo, inked forever on his back. It ran majestically from the base of his neck to where his back narrowed to the curve. Gleaming and shimmering in greens, browns and blues, to gold, outlined in black, eyes blazing red and orange, the mythical Dragon marked him with its identity. It coiled perfectly down his back. Its' tail curling, running down between his shoulder blades, it claws outstretched, wings poised, its' face a warning.

The hot water flowed over him and he relaxed thinking about the past days. The mission was completed successfully, no collateral damage and he and his team were safely there, awaiting retrieval. The violence that they engaged in meant nothing to him, it never had. Soon he would return to her and as the soapy water curled down his chest to his rippled stomach, his hands followed as he thought of her. He wanted to touch himself, but stopped from doing so. His body was begging him to; she was his everything and he wasn't right without her, he needed her and only her. In frustration he denied himself, rinsed the soap off and stepped out, reaching for a towel.

In the single dingy room, the towel now wrapped around his waist he stopped, aware of a small sound. It seemed familiar in some way but he reached for the Magnum, removing the safety. The window was open when it had not been and the dirty curtain swayed in the slight breeze. It was cold from the Stockholm winter outside and he tensed with the prickling intuition that someone was behind him. He resisted the urge to turn.

She laid the blade of her knife against the tattooed Dragon. Simultaneously he caught her scent, heady and alive, Jasmine soft in her hair. He froze and tried to still his breathing, looking for his voice. He felt the cold steel, electrifying him in contrast to the heat of her. She slowly ran the side of the blade down his back, tracing it with the finger tips of her left hand. He could feel her gentle touch on the soft smoothness of his skin, caressing the Dragon's body as it descended over the sculptured curves of his muscles. He knew she loved looking at it, she loved touching it and she loved him.

Like in a dream he released the gun to the small table and slowly turned to face her as she pulled the towel from him. He took her in with his eyes and his intenseness. He saw her beauty and saw her trembling for him. Her greenish blue eyes glowed with desire and his breath caught with how she affected him every time he laid eyes on her. Her thick mane of dark brown hair cascaded around her face, long down her back, full and soft. Her creamy skin and exotic eyes masked her lineage, confusing and compelling him at the same time. His hands curled into her hair pulling her against him, his hardness unbearable now. It had been too long since he'd had her and the need was now beyond control for him.

His eyes went to her lips, one of his favorite parts of her. He touched his to them, kissing her slowly at first but then deeply and sexually. He took the knife from her hand and laid it next to the gun and picked her up, laying her down on the bed. Looking down at her he paused for a moment to savor her. She was lost in a black winter jacket, fur hood competing with her hair. Her emerald ocean eyes were shining now, longing for him, begging for him and he loved her so much he thought he had never wanted her so badly.

He unzipped the billowing coat and pulled her free of it, pushing up her black T-shirt and removing it quickly. His hands found her soft skin, brushing over her breasts, gently feeling their fullness, making her moan. He kissed her everywhere now and moved his tongue across her nipples letting her know what he intended to do with her next. She arched her back into him as he found his way down her flat belly with his kisses.

He couldn't wait to get the rest of her clothes off, as he paused seductively on certain spots of her body with his lips, until finally she lay naked and open in front of him. His voice was soft and deep between his kisses, telling her and showing her how much he missed her. He pulled her by her hips to the edge of the bed so he could give her what she was now dying for. She let her thighs fall apart as far as she could and he pressed them open gently all the way. He ran his fingertips up the insides of them and stopped short. It made her gasp and caused a grin in the corner of his mouth. He smiled softly up to her begging impatient eyes. She was now a trembling mess for him.

He gave her what she needed and she responded to him, crying out with the feeling of it pulsing thru her body, her hands in his hair pressing his mouth down on her while it flooded over her in waves. It made him moan with her. She lay open and panting, her eyes a green glow in her arousal.

He flashed his perfect sexy smile, coaxing her response as he touched her with two fingers, gently pressing them into her. It drove him crazy that he could please her so readily and that she got so impatient for him. In no time he had her moaning again and moving against his fingers, wanting him inside her.

"Come here baby," he said. He pulled her up onto the bed to lie next to him and pressed himself against her. "I missed you." She moved into him wanting his hand again, pushing it down to her as he took her mouth in a smoldering French kiss. "Please baby, I need you so bad," she said. He rose to kneel over her.

She lay like a vision to him, loving and beautiful beneath him as he pressed her thighs open, her flexibility turning him on even more. Looking at her laying there like that for him made his heart swell, reminding him of why he even lived. Before he lost his mind, he pressed himself slowly into her. He was more than hard and careful to be gentle at first. He felt her tightness gripping him and had to resist the urge to fuck the living hell out of her.

Instead, he moved slowly and gently until she begged him for more. Bringing a slow sexy smile to his lips he gazed into the needing green pools, wanting to give it to her. Lost in it, dying for it, he pulled back, almost out of her and drove himself hard into her. She threw her head back, arching up to meet him and he nearly lost it, looking at her. He was almost beyond control now as he moved harder into her, building his orgasm with each stroke. Nearly there he could feel her tensing. His voice was deep and breathy as he worked himself closer, telling her to come with him. He felt her contract around him, her nails digging into his back and he let go, exploding inside her, stilling his motion as he flooded into her, breathing her name into her hair, collapsing down on her.

"Baby, my god I love you" he said.

He pulled her warmth around him, touching her everywhere and kissing her. She wrapped herself around him and as he felt her love he calmed. He wasn't clear how long they had stayed like that but became aware of the time.

"Baby, I want to lay here with you for the rest of the day and into forever, but I have retrieval now," he said. He reluctantly pulled out of her warm wetness. "Are you coming with me back to camp or do you have a mission?" "I have no mission," she said. "Except this one and I have completed it." He eyed her playfully, pulling on his pants. "It was your mission to sneak into my hotel room and fuck me?" he asked. She smiled her pretty smile at him. "Yes, as a matter of fact it was," she said. He nodded his approval, pulling his hair back, securing it into a pony tail with a hair tie. "And I can guess who sent you," Dragon said.

He knew Sensei was behind it. He was behind everything that had to do with them. Dragon finished dressing, pulling his boots on.

"Clothes on sweetheart, we have to go," he said. He eyed her sexy little body as she stood to dress. "Later I will lay you down and make love to you every way I know how, Ok?" he said.

He helped her with her shirt, dressing her had become something he enjoyed, making him feel close and protective over her. Her breasts were a perfect size and he had to control his urge to touch them again. He hadn't done it for awhile, but he used to be able to get her to lose it, just from that. Maybe tonight, as a starter, he thought to himself. He gave her his sexiest knowing smile.

After buttoning her pants, he wrapped her in his arms, kissing her lips softly, wondering how he had made it so long without her. He held her, loving her, a peace coming over him that hadn't been there earlier.

He focused then knowing they had to go. He shoved her coat back around her and they exited the room, heading for the stairs. Climbing the two floors up to the roof he could hear the Blackhawk's rotors. On the stairs ahead of them, the rest of his team also made their way to the roof. Emerging from the doors into the cold air, they followed to the helicopter.

The noise of it surrounded them, pulsing with anticipation. Snow swirled and a cold gray smoke was floating in the air as they made their way to the faithful sentry, waiting for them in the misty dawn. Instinctively ducking he lifted her in, followed closely and slid the door shut. Giving thumbs up to Sarge who was piloting, the Blackhawk's rotors pounded louder, forward and upward, deafening them as its engines drove them to full power. It lifted them off and away, the gentle movement of it freeing them of duty. Dragon nodded to the others and they strapped in.

Raven laid her head on Dragon's shoulder, intertwining her fingers into his much larger hand. Sensei was sitting across from her and smiled to her, mostly with his eyes, thinking she looked beautiful and happy and he was pleased. She and Dragon meant everything to him. What they were about and their devotion to it amazed him and tied him to them.

He had been worried about Dragon recently, as his nightmares seemed to be recurring more frequently and more vividly. It was part of the reason he had sent Raven to him. Whenever Dragon had to be away and especially when he slept without her, he had relapses, the chilling nightmares, pictures from his past that he had worked so hard to put behind him.

Sensei silently pondered Dragon's long journey of the past 7 years, since he had recovered him from a child pornography ring in Taiwan. He had been captive in it since a young child, just a teenager of 15 or so when Sensei found him. He was angry, full of hatred and distrust, scarred and wounded almost beyond repair. With determination and care Sensei had reached into his heart and helped him to find himself and know life for the first time. It floated into his mind again like it was yesterday.

He had taken Dragon to their camp to begin detoxification from a heroin addiction that had nearly claimed his young life. Sensei hadn't left his side for days as he suffered the painful withdrawal. When he felt Dragon had come out the other side enough, Sensei had helped him up and led him out to a new world. He knew Dragon was guarded so had taken it slowly, encouraging him. Nothing had been real in the boys' life and he wanted him to trust that what he was seeing was the truth finally.

Sensei smiled to himself, now looking across at Raven, leaning dreamily against Dragon's side. He recalled her appearing before them that day, out of nowhere, something she had a habit of doing which he always found amusing. She liked to be the first to meet new people in camp and make them feel welcome. The memory of their union always amazed him.

Sensei could see her smiling up at Dragon, who had been taken off guard. His anger and fear had come back into his eyes, as his only defenses. Sensei had reassured him and Dragon had chanced a look into her eyes. Her beautiful face and pretty smile had taken over. Sensei could feel Dragon's heart open, if only slightly, to allow her soft green gaze to see into him.

She had stood there dressed in a simple cotton dress, her hair everywhere around her. Her skin was glowing and she smelled like a flower or something growing. All of it had taken Dragon away. The flood of emotions came next; after all he was a teenage boy and she was beautiful. Sensei had watched and could see that something was happening to his little girl and this strange but compelling young man.

He had sensed Dragon quickly flee within himself when he became aware she could tell his thoughts like Sensei could. It was something they all shared. Sensei knew others had the gift but Dragon didn't. He thought it was something that haunted only him, until Sensei had explained it to him and reassured him in was not a devil's curse of some sort. They simply could see each other's thoughts and know them without speaking.

Her eyes had flashed to Sensei's and he had acknowledged her wonder that Dragon could see, as they could. They had all looked at one another, finding it strange but intimate and it had bonded them together.

While they smiled shyly at one another, Sensei was overcome with a feeling, as he was occasionally gifted with, that they were somehow interlocked together, in an impossible coincidence of meeting. He believed things happened for karmic reasons or purposes. None the less, there it was, and he would see to it they found each other when their ages permitted, even though he knew it was already done.

Still in his trance he allowed himself the peace of quiet meditation for the remainder of the flight to Munich. Inside the helicopter they sat silently as its powerful engines worked steadily to get them home. Sensei considered things as his mind relaxed. As Raven lay against Dragon's body, he felt her completeness now, he could see it. Needing each other physically had happened to them when they met and now that they were older it was very much a part of who they were. He knew being away from him was not good and she had died for him every minute.

Sensei had found her when she was 5 years old. A brief vision passed thru his mind as he meditated. She was holding out her arms to him and he had collected her from the dirty floor she lived on. She had told him she knew someone would come if she just waited and was good. It had gotten dark twice. Her mother's body was cold next to her and there was no one alive with her when he found her. She still had the knife in her hand and held it ready while she waited. He could see she was drifting in a dream world, the place she went to when she was scared.

Reading her thoughts he saw that the angry man that hurt her mother had been asleep face down on the dirty mattress when she had done it to him. She knew he had deserved it. The images of it had come to Sensei, breaking his heart. Blood had covered the knife, her tiny hand and the front of her. It had long since dried, while she had sat waiting for someone to come. She was wearing only a t-shirt. It was the only clothing she had ever worn. Something left over from one of her mother's dates that regularly frequented the dirty room they shared, supporting the drug habit.

She had wrapped her arms around Sensei's neck then, still holding her knife she had refused to put down when he had asked her to. Yet he still took her in his arms, knowing she wouldn't hurt him, carrying her to a helicopter much like the one they were in now. He had soothed her with his eyes, kind and concerned. She fell asleep on his lap, awakening when they had reached the camp. He was her rock, her father, her confidant and friend. He understood her implicitly, inside and out, as he did Dragon and the three of them had spent the most part of their lives since coming to camp, together.

As the rotors of the Blackhawk wound down, Sensei as always, magically returned from wherever he had been. In the seat across from Dragon and Raven was Wax. Wax was a mixture of Caribbean and Caucasian, light brown skin, dark eyes and long dreadlocked hair. A distant mixture of white and black he was usually eyed by women wherever they went. He was the same size as Dragon, tall, muscular and fit. He had become Dragon's right hand, a sharp shooter or sniper. He was deadly, never without his Desert Eagle magnum, making him a key player in every mission. He was like a brother, trusted, skilled and always good fun.

It seemed as though they had all been together forever, the only family any of them really had. Sarge had set them down on the rooftop of HQ Munich and they could feel solid ground again. He had climbed out and come around to open the side doors as they unstrapped. Sarge was Dragon's other right hand man. He flew, was a navigations expert and a devoted, loyal type that never faltered. He had longer wavy blonde hair and blue eyes, looking as if he belonged on a surf board rather than in a Helicopter. He had a wonderful sweet nature and spontaneous sense of humor and was also sought after by most women they came across.

He was Wax's wingman and they had a pretty good game going when it came to females. His name was Sergeant Willis, for a reason no one really remembered except Sensei because he had found him from somewhere long ago.

Raven smiled at him and he kissed her forehead, teasing her with his blue eyes. He was always bugging them about their passion for each other. So she gave him back a hard time with her sharp wit. It made things fun.

The helicopter steamed in the cold afternoon air, its blades drooping now like the swords of a weary warrior. They emerged from its' plume of whirling snow, exhaust and slowly swooping rotors, to enter the world of HQ Munich.

CHAPTER TWO

HQ MUNICH

They made a striking impression and were well respected at the Munich Head Quarters of the organization. It was officially HQ Munich and it was where everything of any importance took place. As they approached the doors an automatic sensor silently opened them, allowing passage directly into an elevator. Placing his hand on an opaque glass panel, a voice responded and the elevator began to descend. Wendy was the talking elevator voice that somehow knew everything and everyone and where you wanted to go. It was no doubt one of Chekov's programs that he spent endless time on, sitting surrounded by his computer screens 24 hours a day. Chekov was the resident computer geek and generally indispensable profiler at HQ Munich.

On cue the elevator doors slid apart and Wendy bid a computerized vocal "goodbye Dragon." He chose not to respond. Talking to Chekov's fake voices seemed weird to him. He wanted to focus on the de-briefing with the General. They travelled down the sterile grey hallway that led to the control centre. As they emerged into the large open room; all cement, steel and technology, it felt more underground than the top floors of a building.

The various bodies working at their screens turned all eyes on them. Sensei and the four of them were level-one operatives and out-ranked everyone except the General. They were respected and admired at HQ for their skills as operatives and their always successful missions. Dragon was aware of the many young men surrounding them in the room, eyeing Raven. It was always the same; he was used to it.

Chekov looked up from his computer lair to greet them. He had been smitten with Raven from the beginning of time and rather than reveal it by trying to enchant her, he displayed it in his obvious disdain for Dragon. Dragon enjoyed verbally sparing with the boy genius, who in spite of his geeky appearance, small stature and square glasses, was usually witty enough to give as good as he got. He had a narcissistic belief that he was smarter than anyone and he substituted it for confidence. And as if on cue it began immediately.

"Welcome Sensei, Raven, gentlemen," he said. Looking disgusted and disapproving he nodded at Dragon. It invoked smiles from them all. It lightened the otherwise sterile and regimented feel that was HQ Munich. Dragon out-ranked him and his disrespect was a risk so he was about to pay.

"Chekov," Dragon said. "Your elevator dream girl is almost as annoying as you, but has more personality. Did you invent her because that's as close as you'll ever get to being with a woman in an elevator? It's a common fantasy you know; I just didn't think you'd be that obvious about it."

The other various technicians and geeks smiled into their screens as Chekov gave Dragon an icy stare. Turning on his heel, he summoned them to follow. They were going to meet the General in his office. They reached another large door, this time Chekov laid a hand on the glass panel. The door opened into yet another elevator. Wendy's voice was heard again "Hello Vladimir," she said. Dragon, Wax and Sarge burst out laughing. Chekov responded cordially to his invention, silently cursing himself for not reprogramming her to use his surname instead.

It was too late then and Dragon couldn't resist the opportunity to mess with Chekov. "Vladimir! Where have you been all day? It was getting lonely in here," he said. His imitation of Wendy's voice had them all falling against the walls in laughter then. Even Sensei had a hard time controlling himself.

Unable to contain himself any further, just as the ride was over and the elevator doors mercifully opened, Chekov wheeled on Dragon. He face was blushing red and his voice raised to a shout. "You are a fucking dick!!" Laughter stopped and they fell silent as Chekov turned and stumbled directly into the General.

They stepped out silently; about to burst at the seams as Chekov gaped in flustered embarrassment at his clear loss of self-control. As General Strauss eyed him reproachfully Chekov momentarily regained composure and with a deep breath asked the General to forgive his foul language, apologizing profusely for running into him. General Strauss gazed at Chekov sternly, as he strictly prohibited the use of profanity.

"Well Chekov," he said. His German accent was thick and came across sternly. "I suggest you restrain yourself in the future and endeavor not to engage certain people if you are unable to take the heat of the flames that you yourself have fanned." Chekov nodded repeatedly. "Yes of course General," he said.

Shooting Dragon an enraged glance he stepped away and marched to a large computer screen and stepping behind it, was back in the protective glow of his machines.

Composed now as ever, Dragon stepped forward and extended his hand to the General. "Hello General," he said. Dragon had a calm confidence and charm about him that always made Raven a bit weak kneed. The General took Dragon's hand in both of his and warmly greeted him. His blue gray eyes sparkled into Dragon's deep dark pools, his fondness of him evident in his smile. "Welcome back in son. You look well and I want to hear all the details of course, but first things first," he said. He released Dragon's hand and moved to stand in front of Raven. "My dear, it is such a delight to have you here again, your beauty stuns me every time I see you," he said.

Blushing, she turned her green gaze up to his, smiling genuinely and sweetly at him, melting away his frosty German demeanor. "General Strauss, it is always my pleasure and if I may say, you look wonderful and are as charming as ever." It was the General's turn to blush, as she worked her magic on him. "Thank you my dear, you have made my day as usual," he said. He saw no point in hiding his adoration of her.

Ceremoniously he greeted Wax and Sarge and hugged Sensei to him. The four of them and Sensei were the General's creations, as he liked to think of them and he loved them. They were assets to him but he had developed love for them all, something he didn't allow himself to indulge in normally. They all sat dutifully and waited as the General sat at the head of the table.

Many years before, General Strauss was living a life of privilege and aristocracy, reserved for the very rich and the Royalty of old Europe. A genius himself with money and business, his fortune was flourishing. He was blissfully married to a wonderful capable woman and had a beautiful daughter they were raising together. Kathryn was her name; she was blonde, blue eyed and lovely in every way, the apple of his eye and the pride of him and his wife together.

It happened long ago now, and the General rarely relived it anymore, except in darker moments when his grief returned unbidden to haunt him. His assistant at the time approached his desk, visibly shaking and the General looked up in surprise, as this was not a man that could be flustered. Grimly he heard the news of his daughter's disappearance. She had been travelling in the Orient with her best friend, enjoying summer break from her studies at the University. She was a happy, smiling, 18 year old with the world at her feet. He had been against her going, but had relented as long as she allowed one security team member to accompany them. She had reluctantly agreed, knowing it useless to argue with him.

To this day he was unsure how it had happened, exhausting every resource to no avail, she had just simply vanished. The guard was found shot to death in their hotel room, the girls missing and presumed kidnapped for ransom. Sadly no contact was ever made with him for money for their safe return. It was the beginning of HQ Munich, but he did not know that then. Sources, private detectives, Interpol and the FBI were put to work to find her. Little did he know the trail they eventually followed would lead him into hell and onward to the man he would become.

It was the beginning of the General's education into the world of human trafficking and the sex trade. His privileged upbringing and sheltered background did not prepare him for what he would come to know of the world. A year had passed since the girls had disappeared and the news reached him on a fall day in late September. Kathryn's body had been found in a shallow grave and that of her friend next to her, in a rural area mainly used for farming rice, on a hillside outside Bangkok, Thailand. The short of it was, after many agencies delved into it, Kathryn and her friend were taken and sold into the sex trade. Her exact whereabouts was never learned, who had her was a mystery and who killed her, never known. It was speculated at best that she had been purchased, used and disposed of, taking all ties with her in her death.

The grief had been a monster in his life, eventually costing him the last thing money didn't buy. Consuming all of her sleeping pills while he was absent on business, his one remaining love had slipped blissfully out of her misery. Nothing left for him then, the enormity of it crushing him to the soul, the General began his quest for justice, devoting his money and resources to rid the world of the evil that had brought this terror upon him.

Slowly he built HQ Munich, training his teams to seek out the perpetrators and eliminate them. Yes illegally, but he had also taken care of that problem. In his secret world of today, he had agencies and law enforcement under control. And so it was. His empire, quietly marching on, unknown to the rest of the world, they worked together to eliminate the problem of human trafficking, child pornography, child abuse and the sex trade.

What was known on the inside as HQ Munich had quite a different façade to the outside world. As time had moved it forward, the General had cleverly disguised its entity in a number of legitimate ways. The building itself was a 32 story high rise located in the heart of Munich's industrial and financial district. Across the massive entrance spanned a glass wall of doors. Above them stretched the name "David Li Industries" in large chrome block letters on a background of black steely granite. The logos on the glass doors read DLI. David Li himself, in actuality, existed only as one of Chekov's cyber personalities. It was all just a clever front.

The first 15 floors of the building were leased office space, as one would assume it would be. The upper floors of the building were occupied by none other than David Li Industries, home to HQ Munich. While DLI could be accessed by a private elevator system from the ground, its' primary access was from the roof. Three helipads handled the incoming and outgoing. A civilian use Sikorsky sat there, the General's personal transportation and no-one questioned the Blackhawks' random appearances, as they came and went sometimes sitting like dark sentries guarding the secrets that lay beneath them.

Dragon finished his account of the final day of the last mission, describing his pleasure in shooting the target between the eyes and sending him into merciless oblivion. The aftermath was Chekov's domain and he picked up the story. The information he had retrieved from the targets computer facilitated the release of the twenty some odd children, ranging in ages from as young as three, and as old as ten. Some were returning to their families who thought they were lost to them, and the remainder who would not be claimed or able to return home were going to live in the camp with Sensei, Dragon, Raven, Wax, Sarge and all the others. The wheels of HQ Munich turned again, all according to the General's plan.

Leaving the General's office, not with Chekov, in the talking elevator, they headed to their respective rooms. It had been a long day after all and saying goodnight in the hallways, they each went to their beds. Sensei's room was next to Dragon and Raven as he needed to be near, just in case. Dragon suffered from the nightmares and sometimes Sensei was the only one that could wake him and calm him. His childhood had left him with many scars. They had been cleared to return to camp at 0800 hours.

Once again the hand on the opaque glass, the greeting from "Wendy" and Dragon and Raven were inside their room. Small but spacious, meticulously clean and modern it lacked the ambiance they loved about the jungle camp. None of this mattered now, as he took her by the arm and flattened her up against the now closed door. His mouth was on her as he let her know what would be.

Kissing her deeply and passionately she had melted for him. His sensuous lips, soft yet hard against hers, his tongue insistent and talented, teased hers and made her faintish at the memory of him earlier, drawing her to ecstasy so easily with it.

He released her lips from his and looked down to her, seeking into her with his eyes. He hadn't quite decided what he would do to her, there were so many choices. He had promised to give to her every way he knew how and he relished the idea of slowly making love to her, he had missed her so much. Sometimes when they were both in the same mood he could stay in her, bringing them off the edge, over and over again, until there was no more. She looked softly up to him and he decided it would be slow and continuous as she looked so vulnerable to him, taking away his heart.

He wanted to make up for the days he had been away from her. He could feel that she was in his world now, drifting in a sexual desire. He let her undress him, loving her touch on him, watching her eye his body with her hands trembling slightly as she unzipped his top. Smiling softly he let her take her time, unwrapping him like an unexpected gift.

As he watched her he thought how beautiful she was, her eyes almost blind with lust for him. He had on the usual regulation HQ uniform they all wore, black nylon mesh and leather. He knew she found it sexy on him as his flat muscular abs showed between the bottom of it and the top of his pants. She had made him leave it on once while he made love to her. As she removed it from him, he inhaled deeply at the feel of her hands on his chest, her kiss on his neck. He gazed at her body as she pulled off her top, peeling it away from her small muscular frame and falling into him.

His erection was becoming an issue in his ever tightening pants. He knelt down and unbuckled her boots at the sides and removed them. Then undoing the only button on her black tights, he pulled them down so she could step out of them. Her silk panties tempted him and he kissed the front of her through the fabric making her gasp. He decided to leave them on her for the moment, just to tease her a bit because he couldn't help it. Standing now he undid the top button on his own pants but left them on.

She knew to remove his boots and knelt to do so, releasing each one and peeling them off him. When he was barefoot she looked up at him and he knew what she wanted to do but was imploring his approval. He caught her ocean green eyes with his molten brown pools and watched as she followed a path with her lips, kissing the straining front of his pants, all the way up his erection. Lingering with her lips on him, feeling the outline of him through the soft nylon fabric she turned her face to the side rubbing her cheek against him, making him moan now. She moved to put kisses on the smooth skin of his lower abs below his belly button but above his hardness. When he smiled down at her with the corner of his mouth, she took a welcome breath and pulled his pants open. He let his head fall sideways and pulled the tie from his hair to let it fall freely down about his face as he watched her ruin him.

After, he pulled her down with him onto the bed, laying her on her back as he moved half over her, kissing her deeply. He made her ready and when she pulled him over her, he gently and slowly made it happen until their juices mingled and she lay spent and weak under him. She had wrapped herself around him, dug her nails into his back and bitten his neck as she died for him over and over again.

"There, my love," he whispered. "I missed you so much." "I know baby," she said. "You showed me how much, three times."

The want in her eyes had softened into a misty glow. In their usual way he took her by the hand to the bath. They waited for it to fill then fell into the hot scented water. She lay against his chest, her hair floating around her in the Jasmine scented water. He needed more but waited for her to be ready. The warm water was relaxing. When he felt her moving against him he pressed himself as far inside her as he could get. The feeling was overwhelming as he held her warmth around him. He was once again taken away by her sexiness, his powerful lust for her. Sometimes it was simply his mood and this was one of those days. He had missed her and was savoring every second of having her. And away in his world of Dragon, he gave her his love, as he came hot and desperately into her one last time, his head dropping back, his hair falling away and his eyes closing.

After he laid her warmly against his chest with him still inside her and in a quiet state of relaxed content he closed his eyes as she kissed his exposed neck softly. He circled his arms around her and held her gently, his fingers tangling in her floating hair. They settled and he brought his head forward returning to the moment. His lips touched the side of her head and he spoke softly in her ear. She wasn't expected to respond, he was just verbally connecting to her again. He watched her smile peacefully to herself, as she lay against him.

They'd had a long day and morning would come quickly enough. At 6:00 am, Sensei would appear with tea. Dragon could feel her weariness as much as she tried to push it away. He reached for the shampoo and holding it out to her gave her his sensible look. She obediently turned her back to him so he could wash her hair.

Rinsed and out of the bath now she sat on a small stool in front of the mirror, dry and wrapped in a fluffy white towel. She loved it when he brushed her hair out with his fingers, coated in smoothing oil they used to calm and detangle her unruly mane. She knew he liked to look after her that way and she needed it from him now.

He was everything to her, as he stood behind her pulling the tangles from her hair and smoothing it for her. Just his hands on her were enough to make her happy. She saw his reflection in the mirror and thought how she could hardly look at him sometimes. His dark hair hung long around his face and shoulders. His brow was strong, eyes that meant something but were soft to her. He was stunning to her and when he smiled it made her die for him. It was ever sexual and she couldn't resist his lips. His smile was full on sexy and disarming to everyone and it made her useless when he used it on her.

She stood now doing the same to him, pulling thru his dark black hair until it shone around his face in a sensuous haze of mystery. It was their way with each other that created the synchronized rhythm that was their life. She followed him to the bed, a modern platform with a mattress and pillows. She waited while he pulled the duvet back and lay half sitting, with his back propped against the wall.

She climbed on top of him, spreading her legs around his hips, lying against his chest as he covered them up. She always slept on top of him this way, making him feel safe and secure, knowing she was there when he was not awake. His hands trailed warmly over her back and he held her there, one hand resting on her lower back and the other caressing her cheek as she looked up at him.

She never got enough of looking at him, feeling him, needing him and loving him. Connected to him in his mind she closed her eyes silently hearing him tell her, "We need to sleep." She silently agreed and they lay like that together for a time, feeling warm and secure. Brief detached thoughts of the past day, their love making and their new day approaching, mused silently between them.

As she could feel them slip into the ethereal state, she lay her head on his chest and he slid down flat on the bed, holding her on top of him, her legs spread on either side of him, asleep like a child and he slipped away with her as the light faded from her minds' eye. In the safety of their secure surroundings they would achieve total freedom from the days' worries and hopefully from his dreams. Only when she was within his physical grasp like this could he be sure of them staying away.

CHAPTER THREE

CAMP

It was promptly 6:00 am, as Sensei was allowed by Wendy to enter Dragon's room, carrying his tray of Green tea and small cups. Wanting to wake Raven, Dragon turned to look down at her sleeping face. She lay uncovered from her waist up; her flat sculptured abdominal muscles framed her tiny waist, up to her breasts. They were full for her size and her nipples were perfect and pink. He pulled his mind away from his thoughts of what he would be doing to her very soon and leaned over her, taking her face gently in his hand. Turning her lips to his he kissed her, seeking her response.

In his mind he felt the warm light, the light they shared together that allowed them to 'see' each other's thoughts. Communicating without the need of speech connected the three of them. Bringing it to her, the same light that Sensei used to draw him from his own sleep, she came awake and joined them, happily hugging into Dragon's warm body. They discussed their day ahead, all of them looking forward to getting back to camp.

"Papa, will we be on leave for awhile?" she asked. "Maybe child," he said. "I don't think Chekov has anything for the moment, but we will wait and see. We have things to do in camp you know. There are new children and the younger boys to finish training. I know they are waiting for you to get back," Sensei said. Dragon eyed Sensei with a smirk. "Those boys better not have been fucking around while we were gone. When I get back they are going to prove some things to me," he said. Sensei smiled and sipped his tea. "Son, they want to make you proud. Don't be so hard on them," he said.

When their tea was done and they had caught up on everything Sensei decided to leave Dragon to his fate. Raven had been touching him under the duvet, wanting him. "Young lady, you have one hour, I suggest you use it wisely," Sensei said. He smiled at Dragon and stood to go. "Yes Papa, I promise," she said. As Wendy slid the door for Sensei, bidding him goodbye, he gave a smiling sideways glance to Dragon.

The door slid shut and in seconds he was on her. Pinning her to the bed, he held her arms back on either side of her, above her head. Spreading her legs with his thighs, he knelt between them, hard and on fire now. His eyes shone darkly into her and a smoldering smile came across his face. Dark hair falling around his eyes gave him a dangerous look. His biceps bulged as he held her arms apart. Dragon made love to her every morning one way or another and this would be no exception.

"Now little girl, if I'm not mistaken I think I have something you want," he said. His voice was deep and soft. "You want it hard now baby?" he asked. He let her go and sweetly kissed her, offering it to her playfully. She pulled him by his hair down to her mouth, not needing to speak, but giving him his answer.

He drove himself into her, gripping her underneath, his weight almost fully on her. He consumed her for as long as he could until he let himself go, driving them both into the universe with his final thrust. Her juices wet him and his hotness filled her, as he fell fully on her, moaning into her hair.

Spending the rest of the day, night and eternity like that would have been enough for them. However it was not to be, as he pushed her ahead of him into the shower. And miraculously twenty minutes later they appeared in the hallway to meet Sensei. Dragon had dressed her in the usual black tights, boots, and zipper top and flight jacket. They all wore the same thing. Her still damp hair was brushed back and lying in a long thick braid at the back.

Dragon pulled his own hair back and tied it. They proceeded down the hall, collecting Wax and Sarge, heading to the elevator together. Wendy chatted pleasantly until they had reached the roof. Waiting at the helipad was the General and Chekov. They had come to say goodbye, as was the protocol, but it was more of a friendly goodbye ritual. They shook hands and made the usual parting remarks. Dragon and Chekov were stoically staying in their own corners, displaying a level of mutual respect.

Raven hugged Chekov causing him to blush. "Goodbye Chekov," she said. "I'm sorry about them, but you only have to see them once or twice a year. I have to put up with it on a daily basis." She really did feel his pain sometimes at the hands of the others. Chekov smiled but looked at the ground. "It's Ok, I don't mind," he said.

Sarge couldn't keep quiet any longer, even though Sensei didn't allow them carry on in front of the General. "I'm the one that puts up with it," he said. "Chekov those two are at it continuously, as if there is no tomorrow." Chekov blushed furiously now and the General just smiled in amusement.

Raven glared at Sarge. "Sergeant Willis, what the fuck are you talking about!!?" Sensei stepped between them then and took the General's hand in his. "General, thank you again but we had best be going now," he said. The General nodded and winked at Sensei. He was well versed in the antics that sometimes played out between Raven and Sarge.

It was sometimes hard not to be sad about the goodbyes, as once it had been longer than a year that they had not returned to HQ Munich. Their relationships often existed on a cyber level, seeing each other and communicating thru screens and audio devices.

Then as if on cue, the waiting Blackhawk snorted to life. It was time to go. The latest UH-60M came alive now, its four rotors lazily beginning to turn, its engines spiraling up to a steely pitch. Now aboard, it lifted them off effortlessly and veered south for the short trip to Munich International Airport.

Awaiting them there was the DLI jet, fuelled and ready for the first leg of the 14 hours ahead that would get them ultimately to Kuala Lumpur. They climbed the steps to the cabin and took seats, fastening seat belts, obeying safety regulations. The captain's voice periodically sounded, advising them of flight times, weather predictions and normal in-flight pleasantries. As they moved through the sky, south east to home, it felt very familiar.

Shortly into the flight Wax got them some Scotch and Champagne and they toasted. It was still only morning and early to be drinking but they didn't care. They spent so much time in different time zones it became irrelevant. They moved to the small sitting area beside the bar. It was a U-shaped leather couch with a table in the centre and two side chairs facing it. Wax brought the two bottles to the table and they all sat. He took out his beloved iPod and chose some music. Their mood was light and relaxed and being 33,000 feet above all that was the world below, they were together with all that really mattered in their world.

Food was in the galley and eventually Sensei had the common sense to find it. He appeared with Smoked Salmon, some kind of flatbread, greens and vegetables. They sat together and ate, not realizing how hungry they were. According to Captain Simon, their flight plan involved a refueling at Jinnah International Airport in Pakistan. An hour stopover then they would finish the flight into Kuala Lumpur.

The flight had progressed as scheduled which had somehow rendered the Scotch bottle empty. Sarge was asleep now in his seat, laying back, his blonde hair loose. He looked like a Greek god.

Raven often wondered how it was that he hadn't found the right one. She laid her head against Dragon's chest and he breathed in her hair, holding her to him and drifting into the words of one of Wax's songs. Holding her close was all he needed and he relaxed into a romantic somber state. As the song played out he fell into the light of her and the overwhelming sweetness of how he loved her completely. In that moment and at times like this, he realized he was safe and secure. When the song ended, he didn't really have a choice of what would happen next.

Releasing her from his arms, he held her by the hands and stepped backwards toward the door of the aft cabin, pulling her with him. Her breath caught as his sexiness hit her. Looking into her eyes, without wavering, he drew her with him. His hair fell around his face as he pulled it loose letting it fall down to his shoulders. His lips trembled slightly, as he caught her reaction to him.

When he had reached the door, he turned her, so her back was against it. He pressed himself against her, hard yet gentle at the same time. He kissed her softly, her lips so vulnerable to him now. Then looking back over his shoulder to Wax and Sensei, he smiled his half smile and reaching behind her, turned the door handle.

The magic of them had taken over now. The door closed and he took her in his arms, wrapping one around behind her neck, stringing his hand into her hair and the other on the small of her back, pressing her into his mouth and his erection. She fell to him, reaching around and up his back, letting him take control of her. There were no words, as they kissed deeply, his tongue licking into her.

He tried to steady them knowing from the thoughts in her mind that she wanted it soft and slow. With his mouth still on hers, still wetly into her, they fell onto the bed. He smoothly pulled her to her back and laid himself against her, pushing his erection into her body in a slow teasing rhythm, never leaving her mouth. He continued in a French kiss dance, their lips seeking, his tongue responding and his hips pushing himself against her promising to take her into the next time zone.

Winds made for a rough landing but they finally stepped out of the plane and fetched their gear from the cargo hold, shaking hands with Captain Simon. Captain Simon was the General's personal pilot and Sensei was hoping he had not been too appalled by their cavalier behavior and somewhat profuse alcohol consumption. Just then, Sarge, who had lasted as long as he could, leaned over and proceeded to vomit on the tarmac. Sensei blanched with the resignation that this probably wouldn't go unreported, as Wax, Raven and Dragon burst out laughing. Dragon motioned to Wax, and they pulled him by his arms toward the waiting helicopter, their final conveyance. Raven and Sensei picked up his gear and followed, leaving Captain Simon gaping after them, a pool of vomit beside his plane.

The doors were open and they piled in, sitting Sarge up in a seat and strapping him in. "Put him by the window," Tom-Tom said. "Get us the fuck out of here," Dragon said. "I'm on it," Tom-Tom said. And promptly the engines pitched up and the rotors began to turn. It was a Medi-vac version Blackhawk from the Vietnam days, refitted with seats. It was Tom-Tom's baby, they called the War Horse. While waiting for their arrival he had refueled it himself, checked and rechecked its systems and hovered over the mechanics as they performed a regulation check on it. He had stocked it with the waiting supplies for the camp and then waited for the team to come in.

Tom-Tom was older than Dragon and the others. He was an American Army trained helicopter pilot that the General had recruited. Loyal and skilled he preferred the strange remote life in the jungle to the outside world. Airborne now and flying low over the jungle canopy, he motioned for Dragon to put on the headset. He pointed out the illegal logging. It had become a disturbing problem in the country's rainforests. It was widespread and had become a difficult problem for the Malaysian government, fraught with corruption and mishandling of resources. Instead of a direct line to camp, Tom-Tom took them a different route, away from the eyes of the logging camps. They would take the sight of the Blackhawk as a threat. So far their camp was secluded and safe and they wanted to keep it that way.

Using binoculars Dragon could see the forest devastation in the distance. It left a nagging voice in the back of his mind. They were too close. It was only a matter of time before their paths would inevitably cross. He flashed a thought to Sensei, to discuss this over tea the next morning. Sensei nodded.

Finding the clearing in the forest canopy, Tom-Tom set them down on the helipad, one of three. They were home. Raven squeezed his hand and he bent to kiss her forehead. They waited for the rotors to completely stop before exiting. Stepping out, it was an instantaneous assault on the senses. The average temperature was an agreeable 22 to 26 degrees Celsius, however there was a constant humidity of about 85 to 90 percent at all times. The monsoon season was from September to February. It was December now. It generally began raining in the morning and slowed by early afternoon, leaving the jungle wet and steaming. It was just about 1 pm and it looked like a scene from a prehistoric era. Green was everywhere they looked. The light was dim, but sunlight glowed through the canopy, reflecting off the rain soaked plants, the steam rising mysteriously up to nowhere. It smelled of trees, plants, rain and earth. Dragon thought it was beautiful even though he never paid much attention to that kind of thing. It meant home to him, his real and only home.

Together they headed off on the road to camp. It was walled by vegetation and they walked in peaceful silence, listening to the ever present sounds of the jungle. Birds squawked and insects chirped a pitched background medley. As they approached the end of the road, almost there now, a small figure appeared from the forest wall. She paused for a moment, attracting their attention, and then turned to run. Dragon took off after her.

Catching up to her immediately he scooped her up and tossed her above his head as she squealed. "Got you," he said. He swung her to him and perched her on his hip, as the others caught up. He looked at her little face, very seriously. "Did you think you could sneak up on us?" he asked. She hugged his neck fiercely. "I can run faster than you," she said. "I just 'let' you catch me." "Well, if you let me catch you, you must want something from me Princess Lily," he said. She grinned proudly at him. "I have a surprise for you," she said. Raven held out her arms and Lily fell to her in a hug. "I missed you too you know," Raven said. Lily kissed Raven's face and hugged her tightly. "I have a surprise for you too," Lily said.

Lily was 6 years old and had been in camp for about 8 months. She reminded Sensei exactly of Raven at that age; precocious, witty, naughty, intelligent and brutally honest, all at once. Also possessing a strange ability to appear from nowhere, unexpectedly, always intentionally and purposeful. She was a joy to them all and Sensei allowed her to help him with certain tasks in the kitchen and the infirmary. It was like Raven all over again.

Letting Lily to the ground, Raven took Dragon's hand again, Lily holding her other, as they walked into camp together. It was a large clearing, surrounded by the canopy. There were numerous buildings. An ammunitions warehouse of sorts that they simply called 'munitions', was the first one. Then they had a store house. It was a refrigerated place to store food, which they referred to as 'stores', and then barracks, and a common. The common was where the children slept, attended school and ate meals. There were gardens and a rice field, as they needed to grow some of their own food. Sensei preferred that. It was therapy for some of them.

At the far end was the main house. As they approached, they were greeted by the camp's inhabitants. Alerted by the Blackhawk's noisy calling card, they were waiting at the foot of the stairs to the main house, the boys stood lined neatly. To one side the children grouped together, closely huddled around the older girls, some of them teachers, some gardeners, all orphans. Sensei walked in front, and gave them his comforting friendly smile. Dragon nodded to them all, taking in their nervous shuffles and averted eyes. The older girls blushed at the sight of him which made him smile to himself thinking of a young Raven.

Stopping in front of the boys, Dragon paused. They were all about 17 or 18. They were training to become a team in the near future. They had all lived there for most of their lives, victims of common, unfortunate circumstances.

Dragon approached Damascus, who had always been the obvious choice as a leader for them. "Damascus," Dragon said. "Dragon," he said. He offered a cocky smile. It had become his trademark. Dragon kept a straight face with a direct unwavering stare. "I hope you are ready to work," he said. "Business as usual," Damascus said. He had a matter of fact, toneless voice that revealed no emotions. Dragon just smirked at him. "I trust you babies had plenty of fun playing with your toys while we were away," he said. Damascus pretended not to laugh. "If that's how you see it, then yes," he said. He eyed Dragon, holding back a smirk as he refused to be intimidated.

Nodding his head, mostly to himself, pretending to disregard Damascus' bravado, Dragon turned slightly and viewed the other five. As they felt his icy stare they mustered up the courage to look up and ahead, ready to take what he dished out. It was a pissing contest they routinely went through. He decided to cut them some slack, in too good a mood now. Turning back to Damascus, he relaxed his stance and smiled a teasing smile now, grabbing Damascus in a man bear hug.

Visibly relieved, Damascus embraced him briefly and pushed him away. "I see you are still a fucking asshole," he said. It was quiet but Dragon heard it. Dragon laughed. "You would be correct my friend."

With that, they all relaxed, the tension evaporating instantly. Damascus smiled then at Raven who nodded to him and he then in turn extended his hand to Wax and Sarge. Sensei gave him a casual pat on the shoulder and a proud smile. The boys dispersed, grateful at having expressed their greetings and gotten away without losing all their dignity, which Dragon could easily do to them if he wanted. Sensei had ordered them to the helipad to unload the War Horse.

Lily being 6 and unable to wait any longer clasped Dragon's hand in both of hers and pulled him up the stairs and into the main house. Her surprise was that she had prepared them food. One of the older girls had helped with some things but it had been her idea, thinking they would be hungry from their trip. In their usual way, they sat together, eating communally from large main dishes that were placed in the centre of the table. With traditional chopsticks they helped themselves. She had made a large fish that had been wrapped in a palm leaf to cook slowly on Cyprus coals. As always there was rice placed around it and fruit and edible root plants that grew indigenously.

Raven congratulated on her at being such a good cook and Lily had blushed, but looked pleased. She crawled up next to Sensei, now feeling shy. He put his arms around her letting her hide her face against him.

Dragon took a piece of fish and fed it to Raven, making her take it. He can't remember when it started or why, but he liked to feed her this way, feeling she would not eat enough if he didn't see to it himself. Eating, between putting things in her mouth, they devoured it all, not realizing it had been 8 or more hours since they last had anything, on the flight. Sarge inhaled it, casting off the final remnants of his hangover.

They talked animatedly amongst themselves, Raven laughing again at the memory of Sarge puking at pilot Simon's feet.

"You do realize we will hear about that and likely from Chekov," Sensei said. "Fuck him," Dragon said. "Dragon! Language!" Sensei said. Dragon glanced at Lily who had gone so quiet he had temporarily forgotten she was still there. "Hai Sensei," he said. Raven burst out laughing, which then incited them all into laughter.

When they had finished, Sensei and Raven cleaned up, and Dragon found Lily sweeping the outer porch. He took the broom from her, too big for her to use anyway and picked her up, taking her to a sitting area of the porch. She sat on his thigh in her little dress, her flip flopped feet dangling and wouldn't look at him.

"Lily, what's the matter?" he said. He lifted her chin and looked into her little face. She was Chinese and looked like a little doll. She peered at him from under her straight across bang. "I just miss all of you when you go away," she said. Her voice was tiny, speaking Mandarin. "Are you afraid we won't come back?" he asked. He used Mandarin, to make her more comfortable. "Sometimes people don't come back," she said. She could not look at him, as she struggled not to cry.

He hugged her, trying to gather his own thoughts. Her tears were now too close and she couldn't stop them anymore. It broke his heart, as they rolled down her tiny face. She had been abandoned in the streets of Beijing, girls being valued less in the Chinese culture. Dragon's team had recovered her and two others from a corrupt Christian Mission that helped orphans or abandoned children. It had been poorly run and fell prey to traffickers looking for young children. Lily had been a lucky one, but still bore the painful memories of her abandonment.

Victims of their pasts, the children were left with their pain, and it was everything that Dragon was about now.

"Lily," he said. "All of us here have pieces of our lives that are gone, or lost, or were taken from us. And sometimes the hurt of it comes back to remind us of it. But if you let it scare you too much, it will make you sad and blind you to what you have left to cherish in your life." His eyes looked to Raven then, not realizing it.

Looking at him now, her tears fading, he could tell she was trying hard to understand him. "Do you mean, like if a flower dies, you could stay with it, only seeing that flower, when if you just look away, you will see more flowers, still pretty and alive?" she asked. He nodded, not trusting his voice just then.

She sat thinking, playing with the zipper on his shirt. He sensed her mood lifting, "seeing" into her gently so he could reassure himself that she felt better and her fears had faded for the moment.

Then, typical of a child her age, she abruptly recovered. "Why do you have a dragon on your back?" she asked. He couldn't help but laugh then, thinking it ironic that she just cheered him up. He thought for a moment about how to answer her. "It's been there for a very long time. How do you think it got there?" he said. "I know," she said. She now whispered to him, using English again. "Tell me," he said.

He was playing along as if they were about to share an amazing secret that only they would know about. She got an excited knowing look in her eyes and in a low, 'this is meant for only you and I voice' answered him.

"It was when one time you were asleep. And the dragon was scared and lonely. It came in the night and lay on your back, falling asleep. And then when you woke up it was still there, staying on you forever so it could always be safe," she said.

His tears threatened to fall from his eyes, but he smiled at her. "Well then yes," he said. "That is probably exactly how it got there. And I think you are a very smart girl." She smiled up at him now, and was very pleased with herself.

She melted his heart with her grin, her two front teeth missing, typical of a 6 year old. As Wax and Sarge joined them now she jumped down and ran happily into the kitchen. Dragon got up and walked to the porch railing, leaning on his hands. He gazed out into the camp and beyond into the green abyss. Wax and Sarge sat but stayed silent, instinctively knowing Dragon was somewhere else for the moment.

Drifting in his mind, he thought that it was somehow strangely close to the truth, wishing the dragon really had gotten there that way. He had awoken with it on his back, but he had not really been asleep. He was in a heroin haze and while he was incapacitated by the drug, it had been put there to mark him. It made him more valuable, and gave him an identity that people would ask for by name, people who liked to pay for him, to use him, or to watch him perform the unspeakable acts. It would stay on him forever, but he was the one protected, by it. Being Dragon had kept him alive longer than he had wanted to be at the time.

He came back to the present, as Raven gently stroked his hair back from his face. Blinking, he pulled her into his arms, burying his face in her hair, breathing her in and settling himself. Then taking her face in his hands and looking into her eyes, he soothed her concern.

"Hey man," Wax said. "That was really special, what you did for that little girl there. These kids need you. You have a way with them." Dragon still looked into Raven's eyes, but shrugged. "She was just scared," he said. "She's fine now." He smiled at them. "She tells quite a story."

Sarge and Wax had watched, not wanting to intrude and had been touched by Dragon's ability to reach her. "You're a regular Doctor Phil," Wax said. "Who is that?" Dragon said. He flashed Wax a challenging look. "Man, what's up with you? It's called the real world," Wax said. Dragon rolled his eyes. "I don't give a fuck about that shit. Why do you care so much about what everyone in the world is doing every minute of every day?" Dragon said. "Sounds fucking gay to me dude." He knew he was probably going one step too far with Wax. "You think so? You want gay, I'll give you gay," Wax said. He launched at Dragon, dragging him over the railing and onto the muddy ground below.

Raven and Sarge looked to one another and rolled their eyes then. In the mud below, Wax and Dragon wrestled at first, each trying to pin the other. Wax just about had him, face down in a tap out hold, but the slippery mud now covering them completely allowed Dragon to slip free. He scrambled to his feet and spun to face Wax, and they assumed the stance to continue the battle with mixed martial arts.

Watching in amusement now, Damascus and the boys had returned to camp. Dragon slipped and fell at one point, when Wax got him hard with a roundhouse to the lower back thigh, taking his knee out from behind. Wax was on him in an instant, flattening him into the mud, once again nearly completing his hold to pin Dragon. Feeling seconds from succumbing to Wax's grip, he used every last bit of strength he could find in his right arm. The mud on his side now he forcefully slipped it through Wax's grip, and making a quick sharp right hook caught Wax on the side of his face, hard enough to stun him.

Wax fell sideways off Dragon, onto his back in the mud and they both lay gasping for air, spitting mud.

"Ouch," Wax said. He touched his cheek bone, making sure it was still there. "Sorry," Dragon said. They both started laughing at themselves. "Next time you want to give me Gay, you could just offer to suck my dick," Dragon said.

This got laughter from the boys, as Damascus reached a hand out to pull Dragon up. Sarge had joined them and hauled Waxy to his feet.

"You fucking idiots," he said.

The sound of Sensei clearing his throat stopped them, as they turned to see him standing at the top of the stairs looking quite annoyed. Sensei was never really annoyed but when he looked annoyed it was cause for concern.

"You two," he said. "Are you having trouble behaving in a civilized way?" Dragon and Wax exchanged glances, mutually deciding it best to say nothing. Damascus couldn't hide a grin so he looked at the ground, wishing to disappear into it. "Damascus?" Sensei said. "I see you find something amusing?" They were all holding their breath now, waiting for Sensei's final sword to fall on them.

"Dragon, seeing as you and Mr. Wax here are determined to set an example for the younger boys, I will give you the opportunity to do so," Sensei said. "Tomorrow, you will take them up to Makai."

It was a 25 km hike, with challenging uphill terrain. They normally used it for survival training. Dragon met Sensei's eyes and waited. Sensei narrowed his eyes to pierce into Dragon's own.

"You have 1 hour for every time I heard the word "Fuck" which comes to 5, I believe. You will leave at 8:00 am and have 5 hours. If you are not at the clearing by 01:00, you will miss your transport back down and, well, I think you may find that Gay?" he said. With a dismissing smirk he turned and walked back inside leaving them all gaping.

Turning back towards the silent group Dragon grinned through the mud covering his face and caking his hair. "Well, Sensei wants to see what you ladies are made of." They began to grin back and forth at each other, relieving the tension. "See you at 8:00 am," he said. They nodded and retreated to their barracks.

Wax and Dragon looked back and forth at each other and renewed their laughter, as they looked ridiculous covered in mud. "Come on man," Wax said. "Let's hit the showers." "Now you're inviting me to the showers?" Dragon asked. He stood back and gave Wax a very questioning look. "Go fuck yourself," Wax said.

Beside the laundry and supply building were two outdoor showers. They were used mainly for removing mud from things, like boots or equipment.

When the mud was finally gone, they left the showers and headed into the laundry room, depositing their discarded clothing. They grabbed clean towels from a nearby pile and dried off, slipping on woven flip flops from a supply shelf. They made their way back to the main house. Wanting to see what kind of music they were going to face from Sensei, they moved into the house.

There were no doors or windows; it was more like a pavilion, resembling a Buddhist shrine of sorts. Sensei had designed it, reminding him of his home in Japan. The large rectangular table claimed the centre of the large open main room. Long bench seating surrounded the table, accommodating their communal eating style. At the back, the kitchen stretched across the wall, separated from the room by a long counter, housing the sink and work surfaces. The cook top and fire pit were against the wall, set in more counter top. It was all native woods, hand done, warm and rustic. A small hallway at one end of the counter led to the back, into the small infirmary where Sensei worked his magic on their injuries and aliments.

On the other side of the room was a pillowed seating area, low table and a long chaise like bench. They used that area to gather and sit on the floor amongst the pillows to meet or talk or drink Sake. Sensei referred to it as a "reflection area". Another narrow hallway led back from that side of the kitchen down to a small bedroom, which used to be Sensei's but was now Dragon and Raven's. It was a bed, dresser, and closet and shower room, open to the jungle out the back. Overhanging roofs protected the porch in front and shower area out back from the rains.

Behind the long counter in the kitchen, Lily stood on a stool stirring something in a pot, likely one of Sensei's herbal concoctions he liked to use, made from the medicinal plants growing around in the forest. Sensei was beside Lily, overseeing her stirring, and when he sensed them approach he turned and came around to stand waiting.

Dragon stopped in front of Sensei, regarding him calmly and directly with his eyes. "Come on, it wasn't that bad," he said. Now smiling, Sensei touched his arm warmly. "No son, but you can't set that kind of example for the younger boys, you know that," he said. "Foul language, brawling and homophobia, all in one package. All things I do not tolerate. I just hope you are through now, having covered all the bases in one indiscretion."

"Ok, Ok," Dragon said. "I apologize for the language, but I can't help it if Wax can't keep his hands off me." Wax decided it best to play along. "Guilty as charged," he said. Sensei relented and laughed. "All this time, Wax, I never knew," he said. He was unable to resist their joviality. Wax smiled his handsome smile. "When you spend 24/7 with guys, anything starts to sound good," he said.

Sarge looked up then. "Speak for yourself," he said. It was Raven's turn to interject. "Wax, sorry but he's mine," she said.

Taking Dragon's hand she pulled him toward the bedroom. Sensei smiled but grumbled a final remark about them not being late for dinner. Wax and Sarge retreated with relief to the boy's barracks where they each had small rooms to themselves. Sensei returned to his stove, turning his attention to Lily and the steaming pot. Life in camp was always entertaining to him, to say the least.

Entering the hallway, Dragon scooped Raven up and she wrapped her legs around his waist, her arms around his neck, finding his mouth with hers as he carried her to the bed. The tiny room held so many memories for them, including their first time and many times after. Even though they had already made love again and again on the plane he couldn't wait to have her again on their bed, still missing her from the mission and loving being back in their jungle paradise with her. Holding her he broke off their kiss and licking her soft lips he moaned through his breath.

"I really want to fuck you into another dimension right now," he said. He pulled her clothes from her, not for the first time that day. Moving down her body, he kissed her breasts, squeezing them gently and kissing her nipples. "Get wet baby," he said. She moaned now, threading her fingers through his hair, resisting the urge to push his head lower. Letting him kiss down her belly was almost unbearable. He finally slid down to where she needed him.

Pausing to examine her, he tilted his head to the side, the most sensuous look crossing his face. "Let me see you," he said. He gently parted her, touching her vagina with his fingertip. "You're wet everywhere," he said.

She was moaning with the rhythm of her breathing now, as he slowly slid his middle finger in and out of her, holding her apart with his other thumb and forefinger. Taking his slick finger he put it to her lips for her to lick.

"Do you think you are ready yet?" he asked.

He raised his eyebrows to her, in question, his smoking hot half smile ever present. Teasing her was one of his favorite things to do, but he couldn't wait much longer himself as the little game was going to make him explode.

"Baby, yes, yes, please," she said, begging him now.

Sliding down on his stomach, supported by his elbows he lowered his lips to her. Licking up the middle of her, licking her wetness from inside her, he slid his tongue up to the apex of all her nerve endings, causing her to gasp and push herself into it. She begged him now not to stop. He slid two fingers into her, pressing gently into the front wall of her vagina. He knew exactly how to get her there and kept at it until he could feel her first shattering spasm hit her. He stilled his fingers hard into her and let up with his tongue as she writhed with it, squirming, panting and moaning through it.

He kissed her very softly, easing her down from her orgasm. He made his tongue soft and his lips softer on her until she was done.

"Stay like this," he said.

He positioned himself over her and let himself slide down into her. She threw her head back and arched up to him, gasping again as his size spread her apart. "Ok Sweetheart?" he asked.

When she managed a nod he put his arms on either side of her head leaning down, planting kisses on her forehead and cheeks.

"I have something for you baby?" he said.

He pulled out of her and drove himself back down into her hard, making her scream under him, digging her nails into his back. Losing himself in it, he got a rhythm and groaning now with every stroke he relentlessly drove into her over and over again, getting himself to the point of no return. Then, denying himself, not wanting it to end, he slowed. He held himself into her, all the way.

"Does that feel good baby?" he asked. "Yes, yes baby," she said. Her eyes were glazed and rolling back. "Tell me," he said. "Come on, tell me." She responded, taking it to another level, almost whimpering now. "Yes baby, fuck me, I want it so bad, give it to me hard, make me feel it."

Her words made his heart pound harder and he gave it to her deep and hard against her. She reached down and held his hard muscled butt, pulling him into her, driving him closer. She could taste his sweat now as he worked on her, breathing hard, getting them closer. "Oh my god baby, just fuck me, don't stop," she said. Seconds from his own demise he coaxed her. "Come baby, come with me," he breathed.

She stiffened and arched up to him, finally there for him as he collapsed on her, flooding himself into her. He gasped into her hair as his body wracked against hers, the waves of his orgasm carrying him into oblivion.

They lay entwined, gasping and clinging to each other, their shared euphoria making them float in and out of reality as they slowed their breathing. Their sweat mingled together, their come mingled together and their lips mingled together as they slowly came down out of their haze. He put sweet soft kisses on her lips and face, smoothing her wild hair away. Gently he slid out of her and moved off her, onto his side gazing down at her.

"Baby, I like that," he said. She looked at him playfully. "What do you like?" she asked. "When you talk dirty to me," he said. "I know," she said. "And I meant every word of it." "I believe you," he said. "And I think you're actually a naughty little thing that likes getting fucked." "And you would be right. As a matter of fact it's all I think about," she said.

CHAPTER FOUR

5 HOURS

When they arrived in Munitions, Damascus was already there. They would need some weapons and gear appropriate for the task at hand. They packed light, prepared water, and tested their GPS. Dragon strapped a Velcro armband to Ravens left bicep, containing two Japanese throwing stars then handed her a sheathed blade which she inserted in her right boot.

"Ready?" he asked. They all eyed each other in affirmation and headed to the meeting spot. The boys were waiting, looking eager to get going. "OK babies, we have 5 hours to do something that takes an average person 8. If any of you fuck this up, I'll personally kick the shit out of every one of you." They all nodded in approval of this.

Dragon let Raven lead because she was fast and small. It was easier for her to block the foliage and watch the terrain at the same time, making their job easier by simply having to follow her. She set a fast steady pace even though the initial ten kilometers or so were a gradual up-hill climb. The morning rains poured over them in the 26 degree heat. She, Dragon, Wax and Sarge had made this trip probably a hundred times. She knew the way like the back of her hand, and chose as many short cuts and familiar steps as she could recall. They had done this many times, but never in such a hurry. As they approached the end of the first segment, the sound of the cascading water became audible in the gloom, drowning out the constant sound of the rain.

Reaching the crest, they paused for all of them to get there. It was a magnificent view now, looking down. A jungle mountain river gorge faced them, swollen by the monsoons, it was beautiful yet dangerous. The jungle foliage reached the very edges, reaching out as if to feel the water's magic with long green arms. One wall held caves, home to scores of bats. Ancient rock caverns guided the water on its' journey, which at the moment was a tumultuous one.

Crossing it in this season was more difficult. A ten meter waterfall spilled down to a rocky basin below. Descending into the gorge, they continued on, to tackle the most difficult piece of the journey. Reaching a plateau, they stood in the clearing together, the rain beginning to let up. A climbing rope stretched across the gorge, secured there years ago and maintained by them. Secured to trees on either side of the gorge and pinioned into the granite rock face of the waterfall at intervals, it provided an adequate handhold. Water cascading over the falls, could drag a person away or a misstep or slip could result in a fatal fall. There was little room for error. The rope followed a rock ledge that provided enough of a foothold and at one point ran just under the waterfall.

The rock face was at an angle of about 85 degrees, the ledge as narrow as twenty centimeters in some spots. Dragon went first, climbing the rocks down and away from the side of the gorge and stepping onto the ledge. Giving him a five pace lead, Raven followed, and so on they went. The noise was overpowering, the thundering water magnified by the walls of the gorge and the insulation of the thick surrounding forest. They moved along in silent determination. The water was stronger than usual swelled by the recent rains. At a certain point Dragon came to a spot where it seemed to be pounding directly down on him from above, and his muscles strained hard to keep a grip on the rope and visibility became a challenge as water poured down over him.

He made it past the toughest spot and stopped, instinct cautioning him now. Raven was strong but he himself had found it more difficult than before, the volume of water far more of a consideration than he had experienced in the past. His biceps burned now from the exertion. He was past the falls, standing on a mossy out-crop, secured sure footedly on a large rock formation now, his left arm linked through the rope. He motioned for her to start through the torrent. She had it somewhat easier being smaller, she pressed closer to the rock so the main weight of the cascade didn't hit her as hard. He inwardly breathed a sigh of relief. Wax was following just a pace behind her now, also recognizing the risk to her.

Dragon wasn't sure what hit him first, as it all happened nearly simultaneously. As he watched her move toward him, her arms linked through the rope, moving hand over hand, one at a time, hugging the rock wall, she stopped, the heavy water cascading close behind her back. Her eyes pierced his and he was hit with a clear sense of fear from her, and a jolting order for him to freeze. In the same instance she released her grip with her right arm from the rope, and reaching for the star on her left bicep, retrieved it and drawing back her right arm in a lightning fast motion, she let it go, spinning it towards him as it sought its target. Feeling it pass his face, to quickly to see, his peripheral vision caught the scene, as it cleanly severed the snakes head. And then in slow motion horror to him, having made her throw, she had forced herself into the torrent of pounding water. It took her off the ledge, and hanging on by her left hand only, the weight of the water broke her grip and she slipped away.

His mind was a panicked blur now. Wax had seen from his angle behind her what was going to play out and had dove at her, the second he knew she was going to be washed away. He had let go of the rope and was flat down on his stomach on the foot wide ledge, hanging over the side, but he had her by her right arm. She was dangling in the pounding water from Wax's left arm.

"Fucking grab me man," Wax yelled. It was barely audible to Dragon through the raging noise. Dragon was already upon them, latching in a wrist-lock to Wax's right arm as he slipped off the ledge after her. "Jesus Fuck, Sarge! Help me!!" His left arm was looped through the rope, with Wax dangling from his right, as he clung to Raven. He wouldn't be able to hold on for long.

It took every bit of strength he had to hold them, the rope cutting into the crease of his left elbow. His chest muscles strained, trying to pull them up. Sarge had plowed his way to them now and with one arm through the rope he reached down, grabbing Wax anywhere he could get a hand on him, as Dragon managed to keep his grip, they pulled them back to the ledge, Wax scrambling to get upright and out of the raging water dragging Raven by her arm.

They all leaned, pressed against the rock face, water streaming everywhere, gasping for breath. Damascus and the others had frozen in place, witness to the near disaster. Dragon moved first, yanking Raven to him. He turned his back to the water and she was pressed against the wall has he shielded the downpour. He had her between his arms, between him and the rock, and moved them out of it to the safety of the rock formation, out of the torrent. Wax and Sarge came through next and Sarge motioned for Damascus to continue.

No one speaking they traversed the rest of the way, from rock to rock, climbing up again now to reach the upper bank of the gorge on the other side. The adrenalin had got them to the clearing, where the trail continued that would take them to their destination. When they were all finally safely there, Dragon ordered them to sit and rest. He needed to think.

It was then that he was able to make himself look at her, because he had to. She was standing off to the side. He could sense her terror from nearly falling, her love for him and something else she was blocking him from. He waited. She turned and going to Wax, she stood before him where he sat. Dragon could see he didn't want to look at her face because he wasn't in control of his emotions. He stared at a spot on the ground by her feet. She touched his face with the fingers of her left hand. Wax nodded, still looking down. She then moved past Sarge, letting her hand caress his face. He reached up for it and taking it he kissed her palm, his soft blue eyes following her.

Dragon felt the anguish, watching her go to them. It brought his emotions to the surface. As she turned to face him, in one step he had her in his arms. She buried her face in his chest and he could feel her crying.

"It's Ok baby," he said. "I'm sorry. I would have made it," she said. She was speaking to him silently as he held her, his heart still pounding out of his chest. "But that was a Malaysian pit viper, it would have killed you," she said. The thought of that brought more tears. He hugged her closer. "Do you know how much I love you?" he asked.

In the safety of his arms she let go of the block she had on his vision and he was hit by the wall of pain she had been hiding. When she was dangling by her right arm the water had been hitting her and in one twist too many had dislocated her right shoulder. She had blocked the pain, more from him than herself, but he needed to know now and she needed his help.

He would have done anything to take her pain away and gently smoothed her tears away. He knew there was a way to fix it temporarily but had never done it.

"Do you know what to do?" he asked. She nodded and he sensed it needed to be soon as the pain was becoming overwhelming for her. "Get Jacob," she said. "He knows." "Jacob!" Dragon said. "Get over here."

Jacob had taken an interest in medicine with Sensei and she thought he would be the most likely one to know how to put her shoulder back into place. Jacob inspected her shoulder and touched it gently, feeling for the problem.

"I think we can fix it well enough for now but it's going to hurt a lot," he said. "Now, do it," Dragon said. Jacob looked nervous but moved forward with what he knew to do. "OK, Dragon, sit down and hold on to her I guess," he said. "I need a strong hand, like Sarge?" He motioned for Sarge to come close. "Hold your hands here, on the bone, like this." Jacob demonstrated for Sarge, as Sarge paled but nodded. "I'm going to pull her arm hard and when I do press sharply until you feel it snap back into place," he said. He demonstrated the motion for Sarge to make. Sarge went from pale to green but he placed his palm on the protrusion, where Jacob indicated.

Dragon held her firmly to him, put a hand over her eyes, gave her everything he had to distract her and Jacob counted to three. She stopped her scream, nearly fainted from the pain, but it was done.

"It needs to be secured now," Jacob said. "Thank you," Dragon said. "Maybe you should go be a doctor or something."

Using their bandana headbands tied together he secured her shoulder in a figure 8 and fastened her arm to her body to immobilize it as best he could. They still had quite far to go to get out of there and not much time left. The boys were pacing and becoming eager again.

"Sarge! We need a faster way to the end," Dragon said. Sarge took out the GPS and began to input data. "There is a shorter way, 8.7kms shorter; we've just never been there before." "What's the terrain?" Dragon asked. "Same, a few ups and downs, maybe some wet areas where it gets lower, but see how it comes up a shorter way to the backside of the clearing?" Sarge said. "OK, it's our only chance of making it now. Ladies! We are going to improvise in order to finish this. All we have to do is make it to the pickup zone by a certain time. How we get there is up to us," Dragon said. They nodded and prepared to set out again.

Dragon turned to Raven. "Baby, is it better now?" She gave him a smile. "Yes. I can still do this. Shouldn't we be going?" she said. He flashed to her a sweet smile that made her feel warm inside and back on her game. "Come on, Sarge found us a short cut," Dragon said.

They took off running again, following the normal path for close to an hour until Sarge led them off it into the unknown. They had a half hour left now and according to Sarge's GPS only 4 kilometers left to go. The short cut had worked well, other than having to plow through a swamp which gave them all the creeps. Some of them had leeches in some not so nice places on them. But twenty minutes later they reached the open area. It was a barren patch with only low re-growth suitable for the War Horse to set down. The logging had left numerous bald patches throughout the rain forest.

Having made it with 10 minutes to spare and given the adversities, the boys were very pleased with themselves. They sat on the ground in a small group waiting to hear the rotors, joking about who had leeches in the grossest places and who had the worst wipeout in the mud. Dragon wanted to hold Raven in his arms but she had quietly dissuaded him, wanting to maintain herself as an individual person, a member of the team, rather than an extension of him. He knew that later when they talked privately about today, she would let him and he would fall apart to her.

On the dot of exactly 1 pm, Tom-Tom set the war horse down at Makai. They load in, looking like a bunch of swamp monsters. Tom-Tom looked back at them from his seat and laughed.

"Congratulations guys, I didn't want to doubt you but I half expected to be heading back empty," he said. "Not today," Dragon said. "Get us the fuck out of here, Ok?" Tom-Tom smiled turning back to his controls giving Dragon a half salute. "You got it," he said.

They all sat silently, resting. It had bonded them all together in some way that Dragon was sure had been Sensei's intention all along. In fifteen minutes they were back and on the ground. Dragon ordered Damascus to race his boys to the showers and the last one there had to do the laundry. So they disappeared in a tangle of pushing, tripping, cursing testosterone.

Dragon took Raven to meet Sensei in the infirmary. As successful as it had been, this whole thing had come too close to being his worst nightmare. Sensing Dragon's anxiety, Sensei reached to him, placing his hands on Dragon's bulging biceps.

"You are lucky she throws so well or you would surely have been at the bottom of that waterfall," he said. He silently, entered Dragon's racing mind, trying to calm him. "This is not your fault, she had no choice. A snake bite to the upper body would have killed you, even if the fall didn't. The snakes are there for the bats. With daylight they should have been gone. Sometimes they get trapped by the water."

Dragon allowed Sensei to try and placate him, but the images of the incident crept up, and as Sensei could see it replay from Dragon's eyes, his heart went out to him.

On the porch, Wax was sitting on the bench seats by the railing, and Sarge was leaning on it, his back to the camp, both had beers now. They were bare foot, and had removed their wet, muddy shirts. They looked bohemian, wild long hair everywhere, dirt smeared faces, shirtless and muscled. From behind Sarge, Damascus and they boys were returning to their barracks from the showers, clad in towels and flip flops. Wax nodded toward them and Sarge turned to see them as they approached the door to their quarters about 20 yards off.

"Hey, fuck-tards how was the jerk-off session?" he called to them.

They were laughing as they reached the door and scrambled inside to avoid his taunts. As they disappeared inside, Damascus raised a high middle finger to him, making a mental note to put a rubber snake in his bunk later. Wax was still laughing as Sarge turned back, grinning, to see Sensei standing there, crossing his arms.

"Sergeant Willis," Sensei said. "Perhaps this is an area of your own expertise? Maybe later it could be your assignment to show them how it's done properly?" Sarge, caught off guard, stumbled over his response. "Err sure, wait, um I mean NO, not happening," he said. They were all laughing now, Sensei nodding satisfaction at his ability to throw him off balance.

Smiling now Sensei looked at them, moving aside to let Dragon and Raven join them. "Beer man?" Wax asked Dragon. "Ya," he said. He took the cold bottle Wax had brought out for him.

They sat now, Raven finally curling onto Dragon's lap, letting him hold her at last. He shared his beer with her, holding it to her lips so she could sip it. Sensei returned to join them, carrying more cold beers. He opened one for himself and set the others on the table in the middle of them. Looking at them now, he tipped it toward them.

"Congratulations," he said. He had a playful glint in his eye. "Maybe you should have said 'Fuck' ten times instead of only five." They grinned at each other. "You really can be a dick Papa," Raven said.

She was the only one that was going to get away with saying such a thing to him. Finishing the beer, Dragon stood. He led Raven gently, her shoulder wrapped up for now.

"Is dinner at 5?" he asked. Sensei nodded. "We have a chat with Chekov tonight right after." "Good at least if I've already eaten he won't be able to ruin my appetite," Dragon said.

Leaving them smirking in agreement, he took her to their room. She was exhausted now. Sitting her down on the edge of the bed, he carefully removed her dirty clothes and took the muddy braid out of her hair. He turned to the dresser, removing the tie from his own hair, taking in his disheveled appearance. He then sat on a small chair and removed his mud caked boots, leaving him barefoot.

Looking at her now, his eagle like eyes met hers. Her eyes were green glowing pools now and her lips begged him. He stood and unbuttoned his pants. Her eyes ran up his frame, taking in his rippled abs above the open pants, his chiseled chest and broad thick shoulders. His head was tilted slightly on an angle, the unruly hair everywhere now, his dark eyes soft with a touch of amusement in them, seeing her watching him. His mouth turned up in the corner giving her his megawatt half smile, making her get up and come to him.

She only came to about chest level on him, being a full foot shorter than he and kissed him between his chest muscles. She slipped her only free left hand around his backside and down into the top of his pants, squeezing his butt.

"Get rid of these," she said. Inhaling, he resisted the urge to throw her on the bed. "I'm going to and then we are going in the shower, nothing more," he said.

He shook his head slowly at her. Stepping back she waited obediently as he peeled them down far enough to step free of them. Ignoring his now full erection, he took her gently and led her into the shower, where the warm soft water hit them. Her eyes half closed as he began to wash her body and shampoo her hair, soaping her gently everywhere with a big natural sponge.

He couldn't remember when the last time was that he had actually only showered in there. Catching his thoughts she gasped and entwined herself onto him.

"Baby, please," she said. He had to look up at the ceiling and take a deep breath to control himself. "If I throw you up against this wall, like I really want to, it's going to hurt you," he said. He ran his hand up her right arm to the tape holding her shoulder. "And besides, there are many other ways for me to give you what you want. I promise I have a very good one in mind."

He wanted to make love to her and erase the unpleasant memories of earlier, soothe her pain and make her safe. The jungle buzzed around them in the afternoon heat, mist rising in the green outside their open air room. Once again, the world outside would wait and time would stop for them.

Wrapped in towels now, he laid her back on the bed. She was looking at him, almost crazy for him, trying to control her breathing. He lay down next to her on her left side, propped on his elbow. He leaned over to kiss her and in his mind he soothed her, letting her "see" what he had in mind.

She was wracked now with desire, "seeing" the images he had in his private mind, only for her. Trailing his fingers down her flat belly he found her open wetness and she arched to his touch. Never taking his mouth off hers, his erection hard against her side he remembered their first time together. Letting her see the images from his mind, he took them back to the moment.

They were together. He knew what to do but was scared of hurting her.

She moaned into his lips, in the now, as the images of him poured into her mind, remembering them together, him kneeling over her, between her legs, his mouth taking her in a feeling she knew existed from only him, his fingers seeking her, their sweet innocence together. She had been moaning and writhing in her desire for him, as he came to lay over her, not able to stop himself any longer.

In the present he spoke to her, whispering. "Baby, easy," he said. "I'm going to make you feel it, just like the first time." Dragon held the thought for a moment, releasing her mouth for just seconds, to look into her eyes in the present moment. "I love you now, just as I did then," he said. Then touching his lips to hers again, he let his love reach into her. "Remember baby," he said.

Using his fingers he pressed them hard into her, taking her back instantly to him sliding into her for the first time, hard but gentle, breaking her, making her eyes roll back as he took her, falling against her, moving inside her, making them one, changing her permanently forever.

And as she came, he released her mouth, moving his fingers inside her so she could feel her orgasm in the present as the waves of it poured through her. Letting go himself, he pressed against her one final time, ejaculating hotly across her belly. He let his head fall back and his eyes close, as it washed over him, for now, for then, and every time in between.

He looked to her face now, and her tears fell gently from the corners of her eyes. He kissed them away. She looked up at him, loving him.

"Thank you baby, that was so beautiful, it just made me cry," she said. He kissed her softly. "You are the most amazing thing to me and that was just for you," he said. "For you to know how much I love you and will never forget one moment of everything you have given me, starting with yourself."

This brought more tears and he softly kissed her face everywhere, all her tears, her lips, her eyes, her hair and her neck until she was asleep in his arms. He folded her in the blanket, smoothing her hair aside and making sure she was breathing evenly. They had to be up for dinner soon but he wanted to watch her sleep.

CHAPTER FIVE

SECRETS

His mind had slipped on him a bit then, remembering the dragon tattoo, how it had really gotten there. He was tied face down on a bed. The dragon was on him now somehow. He vaguely recalled a woman's voice saying, 'don't worry, it be over soon.' Then, the heroin voided the details. He recalled someone was on top of him, using him and he felt the pain of it. He didn't remember but he must have done something wrong or he wouldn't be here.

Dragon awoke to Sensei's light and pulled himself to a sitting position. "Are you alright now son?" Sensei asked. Dragon's Post Traumatic Stress Disorder was always a concern to him. "Yes, just a little flashback dream or something, not a really bad one, from what I can recall," Dragon said. Sensei nodded. "Today had its' moments," he said. Dragon closed his eyes as he remembered. "I was scared today, and I don't like being scared," Dragon said. "That's likely why you regressed," Sensei said. Dragon smiled at him. "Thanks for being here." Sensei patted his hand and smiled. "Always son, but it is time to eat, so wake her and come, we will eat, talk to Chekov and then plan our days ahead," Sensei said. And with that he retreated to the kitchen to finish up their dinner.

They got dressed, he took her hand and they went to join the others, smiling at each other like they had a secret. In the kitchen, Sensei was un-wrapping a fish from palm leaves and Wax was tending to some rice on the stove and singing to some Reggae tune. It smelled delicious and Raven went to see if she could help them. Wax liked to cook and he often made them Caribbean dishes he could remember from his grandmother, most of them spicy.

They were vegetarians, and only ever ate fish as a protein, with vegetables, fruit and rice. Raven prepared the Sake and carried it to the table as best she could. They all looked clean and refreshed from the day's events and the mood was light and playful. Dragon made her eat more than she wanted to and in the end she was grateful, as she had been very hungry, after all. Sensei's fish was delicious and they consumed every last bit of it.

After two cups of Sake, Raven had become playful and her usual target was Sarge.

"Are you finally on page two of the Kama Sutra?" she said. Sarge eyed her sideways. "I've passed page two about fifty times, my favorite part is page 121," he said. Page 121 was the description and technique of fellatio. Dragon and Waxy were smiling now and shaking their heads, knowing this was probably going downhill fast. "Hmm, well," she said. But Dragon decided not to let this get to where he knew it was going and put his mouth on hers. "No, little girl," he said. "You need to behave, if you want to have a little fun save it for Chekov."

The Kama Sutra was a book Sensei had given to all of them, to introduce them to the ideology behind relationships and sexual contact. There were teachings on the priorities and needs of sexual relationships as well as sexual techniques. It was Sensei's intention to guide them into a healthy sexuality. It was a reprogramming for some of them, a trust building issue for others and an affirmation that sexuality was a healthy important part of being human.

The night had moved on and it was time to make contact with Chekov. Sensei logged in and eventually produced Chekov live on all three screens.

"Good evening, gentlemen," Chekov said. "Chekov," Sensei said. Dragon stood, arms crossed, waiting for it and Chekov got right to it. "Raven, you are looking well, all things considered," he said. Not waiting for a response he turned his attention to Sarge. "Sergeant Willis, how are you feeling? Apparently you had the flu when you got off the plane the other day." They all eyed each other, Sensei's jaw tightening.

"Now's about the time I tell you to suck my dick Chekov," Sarge said. Chekov shrugged, shaking his head condescendingly. Wax, getting impatient with Chekov's toying, snapped. "Enough Chekov, why did you need to talk to us?" Chekov gave him a dismissive eye but in an instant, two of the three screens changed to an aerial view of what looked like a factory building.

"This is a holding facility, on the north eastern border of Thailand and Taiwan. It's a temporary facility used to contain captives before they are dispersed. Intelligence shows it will be empty for the next two months, loosely guarded. Destroy it and eliminate any personnel. It's a minor job but we have no spare teams right now and you are closest. Dragon, I'm sending you the profile now, you will need explosives, and how you get in and out is your call. You have 60 days to complete. Are there any questions?" Chekov asked.

"Thank you Chekov," Sensei said. "We will be in touch." The screen went black. Dragon turned to Sensei. "Let's sit down with this in the morning, after Yoga maybe?" "Agreed," Sensei said. "Now I believe there's some scotch around here and some champagne." Feeling relaxed and free of any of the days tensions, they retired to the porch where a fire burned softly, raising smoke to rid them of mosquitoes.

Morning came, peaceful and green. They had passed the previous evening sharing conversation and had all called it a night early, just happy to be home. Dragon had woken and was sitting upright waiting for Sensei to appear with Tea. Raven slept beside him now, on her back like an exotic rag doll, hair everywhere, eyes closed serenely and breathing softly.

He hardened slightly, thinking about last night and how he had let her kneel before him and take him over the edge with her mouth. She had insisted, having driven him to the point where he knew he would let her do whatever she wanted to him, even though he had wanted her to rest. She had then pushed him back on the bed, put him inside her and fucked him until he didn't know his own name. She had looked like a dream, in the glowing candlelight.

He returned to the moment as Sensei quietly joined him. They discussed Chekov's latest profile. Sensei had brought the laptop and downloaded it while they drank tea.

"Looks pretty simple," Dragon said. "My immediate thought would be to have Tom-Tom drop us maybe 10 kilometers off, so they don't hear us. We can go in, eliminate the perimeter guards, and then move in on the rest. When it's secured, Tom-Tom can come right up and drop Damascus and his team and Sarge. They can run explosives from the back to the front. We will cover them till they reach us, then, we all get out before the timers blow the place off the map," he said.

Sensei nodded, pointing out an area on the topographical map. "There's an exposed area here that could handle the Blackhawk, looks like 100 meters or so from the front of the building." Dragon looked at what he was pointing at and agreed. "That will work. I need to brief Damascus and set a day and time. I'm thinking early, like dawn, that way we don't need night vision and we don't have to do 10 k's through the jungle in the dark. We will still have the element of surprise because they will just be thinking about their morning hard-on's about the time we hit the perimeter," Dragon said. Sensei smiled nodding, amused by Dragon's occasional lapse into frat house humor.

"And Raven?" Sensei said. "We can just wait for her shoulder to be good again, before we go. I need her because initially when we take the perimeter guards we will want the silence of her knives and I'll use a bow. If we come out of the jungle all AK 47, we won't have a jump on the guys inside. Once we are in, we can go automatic and get rid of them before they know what's happening," Dragon said.

Satisfied with their initial plans for the mission, they sat silently for a few minutes. Dragon organized his thoughts and moved on to another issue.

"That logging we saw on the way in," he said. "Yes, it's a concern now," Sensei said. "They are too close. It's only a matter of time before they find the camp. You realize that?" Dragon said. "Yes," Sensei said. Dragon could sense that Sensei was blocking him from this line of conversation. "What aren't you telling me?" He cut to the chase, giving Sensei a direct question that he expected to be answered.

Sensei stood now, running a hand through his hair and turning away from Dragon. "You may as well tell me Sensei," Dragon said. "I can see you are expending quite a bit of energy keeping this from me. What and why?"

Sensei paced away from Dragon for a moment, assessing his thoughts. He turned to face him with the honesty he had always given Dragon.

"The General has been aware for some time now that we are potentially not safe here any longer. Those people are dangerous and while it is not our priority to interfere in this concern, I can tell you two things. One is that we must eliminate their existing operation and two that we must then leave here," he said.

Dragon's eyes were fixed on Sensei's. And as his words turned over in his mind, he looked off toward the jungle, thinking and letting it sink in.

"OK," he said. "So you and the General have been discussing this for some time now?" he asked. "Yes," Sensei said.

Dragon now stood, grabbing a towel and tying it around his waist. He paced to the open wall, placing his arms above his head to hold onto the overhead beam, breathing in the jungle air. The tattoo on his back; the gleaming red and gold eyes seemed to be staring at Sensei, like it was glaring into his soul.

Dragon was confused as Sensei had never kept this kind of secret from him, something as personal and relevant to him. The fact that they were ultimately going to be leaving the jungle, probably permanently, was something he would have wanted to discuss with Sensei. It was important to Dragon to have control over what happened to him.

"You and the General have been planning my life and keeping it from me," he said. Looking a bit dangerous now, he reminded Sensei of who he used to be. "Dragon, this is not a betrayal. Everything I and the General do is with the greatest consideration for what is best for you and what will make you happy. This is just not the time to discuss it. You are aware that you don't have to do anything you don't want to do, but I assure you that any plans we have will be much to your liking. Please trust me, even though you now feel you can't," Sensei said.

Dragon turned his back to Sensei again, more to hide his expression and he gently and sadly blocked Sensei from his thoughts. He had never been mentally cut off from Sensei in the whole seven years that they had been together. It was like darkness had crept in and circled his heart.

He let Sensei pull him to face him. He could see Sensei's hurt and concern. To Dragon's surprise he felt Sensei open his mind to him and flash back to the day he first saw him.

Sensei and his team had taken the target in Taiwan, a particularly vile place that held children, some as young as four. It was a house of prostitution, ranging into very extreme things. Any age, any act, for any price, was what they claimed. Also, they were making child pornography and putting on live sex acts, for high paying customers.

As they had made their way through the hovel, eliminating every perpetrator, he had come into a room at the back, not knowing what he would find. Raising his weapon, he had shot the man, as he was about to administer a lethal dose of heroin, to a teenage boy.

Dragon saw himself as the needle hung from his arm, still in the vein. He was suffering badly from withdrawal, his long hair was caked with vomit and he was sweating and shaking. Making a decision, Sensei had taken the syringe and administered half of the dose into his arm. He would make it on that until Sensei could look after him later. He got him up and took him with them, the beginning of their lives together and Dragon's chance at living. Sensei had known from those first moments that he was special and for some reason he was meant to find him. If he had been seconds later in arriving in that room Dragon would have been dead from an overdose.

Dragon felt him beside him. He took a sighing breath and did not question it then but let Sensei feel the wall that he had put there to block him disappear, the light coming through gradually until any darkness was gone. It had sapped Dragon's energy to put it there and his eyes blinked out of focus again momentarily. The light flooded back to them both with a warm energy. Dragon turned to sit on the bed, next to Raven. His face was wet with tears that did not belong on his masculine features.

"Thank you for being there that day," Dragon said. Sensei sat down on the bottom of the bed and looked at Dragon with his passionate eyes. "I've been connected to you since then and I would never do anything to intentionally hurt you," Sensei said. "And I'm sorry Dragon, but I'm not always at liberty to tell you everything. The General likes you to stay focused on what's in front of you and not worry about future events."

Dragon nodded and accepted it. "So, it will be 'much to my liking' you think?" he asked. He was struggling with a smile that he lost the battle with. "Come here," Sensei said. He held Dragon's face to his chest and pressed his cheek to the top of his head. "If you ever want to know, know anything at all, just ask and I will let you see. You deserve it and sometimes I need to listen to that more than I need to worry about getting in trouble with the General," Sensei said. Dragon nodded and smiled, feeling peaceful again.

They sat reflecting and Dragon playfully eyed Raven who had been sound asleep. "You'd better wake her," Sensei said. "I have to go and explain the delay somehow, people are starving and I told them 8 am." It was now 8:15 am, not like Sensei to be late. He got up to leave. "I can only buy you half an hour. She's going to be pissed," he said. Looking amused with himself he left and left Dragon looking concerned.

After they ate they gathered on the porch and Sensei led their ritual Yoga session that they liked to begin their day with. Sensei had unwrapped Raven's shoulder, letting her use it to her discretion, not wanting the muscles to tighten too much. They started with basics and moved into advanced strength poses, testing their flexibility and balance, finishing with a sitting position, controlled breathing and relaxation. When they were done, Damascus appeared at the bottom of the steps. They were all going to head to the range and practice weapons.

They warmed up with straight target practice. Dragon's favorite weapon was a Compound Bow. Raven loved to watch him with it, his biceps flexing with the tension of the bow string as he drew it back. He was formidable with it and as a weapon, it suited him. He laced off a series of bulls eyes, before pausing, seeming satisfied. Wax was always fun to watch as well, his accuracy with almost any gun, remarkable. He had his 357 magnum desert eagle handgun to start, equipped with a laser scope. He nailed every wooden figure with accurate head shots, before switching to his other favorite, a Remington 700 series sniper rifle. Sarge preferred the automatic AK 47, and they all put on hearing protection while he fired off a number of rounds, shredding one of the wooden figures. They took turns, with Damascus and the boys and then all waited to watch Raven throw her knives.

She was restricted to the use of only her left arm for today, but could throw accurately with either arm. She used a 10 ¼ inch stainless blade, weighing only 7 ounces. She was proficient in both techniques of spinning throws and straight throws. She was deadly accurate and having this talent had been beneficial to them on many occasions. She had finished up her throws, as Dragon and Wax came out of the munitions shed walking and talking. Not being able to resist a little fun, she took aim.

The knife spun end over end reaching its mark, embedding itself into the ground directly in front of Dragon's boot as he walked with Wax. In the next second he was face down in the dirt, having tripped solidly over the protruding handle.

"What the fuck," Dragon said.

He shook his head, pushing himself to a sitting position, noticing the knife at the same time. Wax was taken off guard at first but quickly realized what had just happened.

"Dude, your woman is fucking with you," he said.

He offered his hand to pull Dragon to his feet. Dragon gave Wax a private knowing smile and moved toward her, stopping directly in front of her, inches away from her. He handed her the knife.

"I believe this belongs to you," he said. "Thank you," she said. "I was wondering where that went."

In his mind he told her she was in trouble. In response she flashed her eyes at him with a defiant glare. He had her attention, looking up at him and he made his move. Reaching for her he put one hand behind her head forcing her mouth on his and the other arm pulled her into his body. With his mind he forced his thoughts on her as she struggled to get free of him. He continued to kiss her, bombarding her with sexual images.

At first she had resisted, but feeling his kiss, combined with his very sexy thoughts, she had succumbed. It was a game she was going to lose this time. She had gotten close very quickly. His mental images of what he was going to do to her in bed later cascaded through her driving her hard into his sexual abyss as he held her against his thigh.

Finally falling limp in his embrace, he released her mouth as her breath caught and she struggled to hide the physical evidence of her contracting muscles. Her taught tummy muscles betrayed her and her clenching thighs gave it away, her breath almost lost from it.

Holding her gaze with his eyes, dark and triumphant, he stepped back from her leaving her breathless and trembling, a crimson flush in her cheeks as she felt the boys eyes on her.

She knew he would retaliate but didn't expect this. It always amazed her how quickly he could respond to situations. She regained her composure and smoothed herself, tossed her braid, and stepped around Dragon, giving him a sexy smile.

"Thank you very much for that, but now if you will excuse me," she said.

She marched to the munitions shed to put away her knives, giving them all a view of her very nice behind as she went. They all eyed each other and Sarge was the first to laugh out loud. She was ever amusing, if anything.

They made their way back to camp. Dragon advised Damascus they were briefing for the mission that night after dinner. Damascus nodded his understanding and he and the boys headed to the general communal area where everyone else went to eat.

Sensei was waiting for them, preparing them a soup of some sort and rice noodles that smelled delicious as they came up the steps. Raven had taken Dragon's hand and silently asked him if he would really do those things to her later. He just had his sexy half smile, and kept looking straight ahead as they walked.

After eating they sat feeling rejuvenated and serene. They were going to spend a few hours with the children, something Dragon loved to do. He and Raven had discussed having children of their own and had decided against it because they wanted to devote themselves to the children that came to them. And as they had agreed tearfully one night, they were not willing to share the love they had for each other in any other way. They had both been loveless for a formidable part of their lives and they had found each other, and that was enough. It had made up for everything and they didn't want that to change, treasuring their love and their connection to each other.

Spending the afternoon with Lily and some of the others had been endearing and exhausting. Back at the main house later, they had half an hour or so to shower and change for dinner. They stood under the water, washing away the day's sweat and dirt. She was beautiful as she leaned against him, letting him hold her while the water covered them.

"You made me come by kissing me," she said. He smiled to himself about it. "You know that can happen when I get in your head sweetheart," he said. She smiled. "I like that." "Me too, sunshine," he said. He wanted to do it to her again right then, but it would make him crazy and they had no time.

HQ MUNICH

The General sat in his darkened office, computer screens lighted around him, Chekov off to the side in his own cyber world. The time had come to invent David Li. The issue at hand was how to do it. The General had carefully managed things meticulously, to where Dragon was a very wealthy man, as were all of them. He had a vision a number of years back that was about to come to fruition. He just had to decide how to handle it. Sitting pondering was not his style and he quickly made the decision. He contacted Sensei and they discussed it.

CHAPTER SIX

THE MISSION

The War Horse carried them secretly through the dawn to the drop sight. It was 5 am and just getting light. They had armed themselves accordingly and sat unspeaking as it took them to their destination. Tom-Tom set it down and they exited it nodding to him and moving away quickly. Dragon, Raven and Wax had hit the ground and ran for cover in the jungle foliage. They moved quickly through the tangled heat, needing to cover 5 kilometers in 45 minutes.

Now, shining with sweat they waited, watching. Dragon adjusted the earpiece as they hid 15 yards from the nearest guard. "Do you have a visual?" Chekov asked. "Yes," Dragon said. "There's two together, take them out then hold," Chekov said.

They moved low through the never ending green thickness until they were ten paces from the two outer guards. The dawn light was dim and steamy as the condensation began to evaporate in the early morning heat. When they had their positions, Dragon took his bow and readied it. He nodded to Raven. She pulled a knife from a sheath on her leg and standing she drew back her arm. At this point he stood with his bow drawn, aiming to kill. Catching that he was ready she released the knife and it flew end over end in a spinning throw, embedding itself in the man's forehead. Dragon had let his arrow go seconds after her release, piercing through the back and into the heart of the man now gaping at the man with the knife in his head. They both fell silently to the ground.

"Move," Chekov said. They had an open space to cover now to reach the remaining outer guards. "Wax, go right, you'll see one. Dragon and Raven go left; there are two more by the doorway in," Chekov said.

Wax nodded to them and split off to the right. He crept along the ground now, invisible, until he had the target in his sight. He placed the laser red dot directly on the man's forehead and squeezed the trigger, eliminating him instantly. "Clear," he said.

Dragon and Raven ran out in the open now from one dark area to another until they came upon the remaining two guards, which Dragon shot directly with a 357.

"Good," Chekov said. "Now go in."

The War Horse had dropped Sarge and Damascus and the boys in a clearing behind the building. They had to rappel out of the helicopter due to foliage and were now silently lining the outer perimeter with explosives, as Dragon, Raven and Wax, took the interior. They could hear the automatic gunfire over the Blackhawks rotor noise.

Dragon led Raven and Wax down a long corridor that emerged into a large open room. There were five targets all sleeping on mattresses. They burst in and finished them off in seconds, before they knew what was happening. Then in perfect timing, Sarge and the boys were coming through with the explosives, and it was time to get out.

They all turned and ran out the way they had come in. Tom-Tom had come back around to the front, to the clearing for the retrieval and had set down lightly, rotors pulsing. The explosions had started to detonate in the back of the building and there wasn't much time to get clear. Then it hit Dragon, that Wax was no longer behind him. Sarge and Dragon connected immediately.

"I'm going back!" Dragon yelled. Raven moved to follow him and Dragon motioned back to Sarge to keep her. The smoke and the noise from the explosions now over took everything. Dragon disappeared in the smoke and dust, as Raven struggled in Sarge's grasp. Stopping her was like trying to hold on to a bag of feral cats. Tom-Tom had hit the throttles and the Blackhawk was about to leave or they would all be blown to hell in the impending explosion.

Dragon retraced his steps going about 20 yards back, running full out now and found Wax crawling towards him, his left lower leg a hanging mess. One of the guards had briefly survived their assault and raised his gun to hit Wax just above the ankle as they had fled in their retreat. Cursing, Dragon hauled Wax over his shoulder and carried his 225 pound frame back to the now leaving helicopter. Tom-Tom had no choice, the charges would take them all down and he had begun to lift off. Raven was screaming in Sarge's hold as Dragon appeared out of the dust from the rotors and Sarge released Raven long enough to alert Tom-Tom to hold for two seconds.

Dragon made it to the open doors, now five feet off the ground in ascent, throwing Wax's body off him into the open door and using every last ounce of strength he had left in his legs to jump, hanging half in and half out, as the War Horse breathed its way upward. Sarge dragged them both aboard with everything he had as the final explosions blew through the front of the building, the fall out hitting them full on in a heated blast. They careened sideways threatening to lose air.

Tom-Tom growled as he forced the War Horse to get them out of it. He pulled off a miracle as the Blackhawk struggled with the uneven air and hot buffeting aftershocks, managing to get them clear of the exploding devastation. They made it out and veered sharply away, rising above the tree line and heading home.

Tom-Tom, barked into his headset, reporting to an anxiously waiting Sensei and ever listening Chekov. When the War Horse finally set its' wheels down at the heliport in camp they were back to reality. The doors slid open and Sensei waited, helping to move Wax to a waiting Gator. Dragon and Sarge helped lift his now dead weight and they hurried him off to the infirmary.

Sensei immediately put Wax out and prepared him for surgery. It was informal and basic but all they had and the way they had always done it. He cleaned and examined the wound, which was a gunshot that had gone clean through his lower leg above the ankle and had broken both bones in the process. Sensei carefully plated and screwed the bones back together, leaving Raven to stitch the wound. Wax would be asleep now for a few hours and be off his feet for awhile.

Sarge and Dragon sat patiently watching while Raven washed the dirt and sweat from Wax, cleaning his face and his dreads with warm lightly soapy water. She finished off with the rest of him, leaving his light brown muscled body with a clean sheen, as Sensei completed a dressing on his leg. She then covered Wax with a light white sheet, giving him some modesty back. He looked peaceful and had a good glow to his skin again, handsome as any model in a magazine. When Sensei felt things were as good as they were going to be for the moment, he ordered them off to attend to their post mission duties.

The three of them walked in silence to the munitions shed to discard their weapons and gear. Damascus and his team where there still, finishing up cleaning and storing their things. They dutifully took the weapons from Dragon. Sarge handed them Wax's guns to clean.

"He's ok?" Damascus asked. "Ya, he'll be fine," Dragon said. Good job, you guys lit it up back there." "Ya," Damascus said. And with that the three of them left, walking slowly back to the main house, dirty, bloody and exhausted.

Taking Raven's hand he took her up the steps to the porch where Sensei now sat meditating. He acknowledged them with a nod, letting Dragon know he could have a few hours until dinner. Dragon nodded and they proceeded to the hallway and into their room. He knew she was questioning herself and was upset at the turn of events.

He didn't pry into her thoughts and she didn't bombard him with them. He could see she was feeling rather numb and couldn't put words to any of it at the moment. He took her and she welcomed his strong arms and lay against him. He led her to the shower so he could turn it on and let it warm while he undressed them. He sat her down on the bed and knelt down to unfasten her boots. He removed her clothes wordlessly and she sat there naked while he unbraided her hair, pulling it to cascade around her shoulders, covering her breasts in long curling waves, thick and everywhere.

He planned on spending the next couple of hours making her forget the day. They had just killed ten or so people and it had cost Wax the use of his leg for awhile. Taking them away together was the only thing on his mind.

The soothing water poured over them, as he held her against him now, getting hard as he felt her warmth against his skin and her sexy body in his hands. He rubbed soap up and down over his erection, teasing her with it.

Seeing his hand on himself made her flood with desire for him. "Baby, please," she whispered. He kissed her gently. "Touch yourself angel, show me," he said. "Don't think about anything, just how good it feels right here, right now."

His mind had entwined with hers and she instinctively gave him what he wanted. She was in another world now, their sexuality attacking her senses and driving her crazy. She wanted to turn herself inside out for him. He liked to watch her and she made it good for him.

He let out a deep moan and let himself get there, watching as his hot come flooded onto her as she lay back on the shower bench, open to him. He held himself so it coated her as his orgasm shook through him. It was white hot and everywhere on her smooth skin as he finished, dying with the pleasure of it.

He pressed himself into her then, falling onto her, moving in her, for her. Her eyes flashed into his, rolling back, the feel of him putting her over the edge. The waves of it hit her, knocking her into oblivion, gripping him inside her, the feeling of him making her come forever.

Gently he withdrew from her, leaving her breathless and panting. He stood to shut off the water and pulling her up to him, he kissed her deeply using his tongue against hers as she grasped his face in her hands trying to get more of him.

He spoke silently into her mind, not wanting to release her from his lips. He wrapped them in a big towel and pushed her to the bed. She lay back and he covered over her, pressing his mouth on hers even more urgently now, taking them into a passionate desperate kiss that he let slide down her body.

Afterward she moaned, as he released her from the torment of his persistent tongue and watched her contractions ebb away. He held her apart, kissing her softly, being careful to avoid her sensitive spots. He then lay between her legs, his head resting on her open thigh.

"That felt so good baby, the things you do to me," she said. She stroked his hair now as he lay quietly. "It's all I ever really want in life," he said. "You know that."

Dragon woke himself to his inner alarm around 4:30 pm so they could get clothes on for dinner at 5. They were so comfortable together he really didn't want to get up, but awakened her anyway.

He dressed her in little white cotton shorts and some woven sandals and a cropped pink tank top, suitable for the heat. He brushed her hair out, running the oil through his fingers and pulling it through her hair to calm the unruliness. She looked sexy and sweet and adorable all at the same time, making his heart melt at her reflection in the mirror. Her thick hair made her face look tiny and innocent, her green eyes captivated him and if he didn't stop thinking about her he wouldn't be leaving the bedroom.

When they walked into the main room, Sarge was just coming up the stairs, looking clean, rested and "California". His blonde hair was washed and hung in waves away from his forehead. He was built like Dragon, tall, sculptured and muscles everywhere, tight waist and defined quadriceps. Not to mention a butt that wouldn't quit. His icy blue eyes warmed at the sight of her, refreshed and adorable. He smiled at her, not being able to resist hugging her to him and kissing her forehead.

"Hey sweetheart," he said. "Want to go check on Wax with me?" He knocked fists with Dragon as they headed to the infirmary. "What happened to your face?" Dragon asked. There was a swollen purple mark under Sarge's left eye. "What do you think," he said. He glanced at Raven. "She left me with a little something to remember her by."

In his efforts to restrain her in the helicopter she had elbowed him under his eye, struggling to get her arms free of his bear hug and dominating weight he had needed to use to subdue her.

"I'm sorry Sarge," she said. She genuinely felt badly for not co-operating with him, but couldn't help giving him a teasing eye. "Just happened by accident I guess," she added. He smiled teasingly back at her. "Well we'll see what 'just might happen by accident' then won't we," he said.

She smiled coyly at him, knowing he was baiting her for later. They often got into little brawls, where she would tease him verbally until he came after her, using his strength to pin her down and make her give up. She would call him all kinds of bad words in French that Dragon would translate for him because he didn't speak it.

Sensei was with Wax and looked up to see them come in. "Chekov watched the satellite feed and the man was dead technically, with a knife straight through his forehead. You did not miss, Raven. It was a random involuntary muscle reaction; he pulled the trigger almost as a death throw reflex. You've seen this thing before," he said. "It was bad luck for Wax. Nothing more, it could have been any of you he hit." Her face seemed to clear somewhat, thanking Sensei for his words. She turned to Wax's sleeping figure, brushing her fingers tips down his cheek. "Will he be the same?" she asked. "Yes, my dear, he will be, with time," Sensei said. "We will see to it, right?"

CHAPTER SEVEN

FUN AND GAMES

They sat down together to eat. Sensei had prepared rice and a grilled fish of some kind and a blend of native greens that he grew in a small garden beside the house. "After this, I want to wake Wax up. He needs to eat too," he said. "Good," Raven said. "It will cheer him up when he finds out I gave Sarge a black eye." Sarge stopped eating and looked at Dragon with a warning eye. "If you don't deal with her, I will," Sarge said. Dragon just smiled at him, shaking his head. "Feed her something, so she shuts up for five minutes," Sarge said.

"Sarge," Raven said, "That girl in Moscow, the one I saw leaving your room in the morning. Was that the last time?" Sarge looked over at her, feigning exasperation. "What the fuck is the matter with you? I bet you can't stop thinking about what went on before you saw her leaving. That sort of stuff probably turns you on. When you aren't getting laid, all you can think about is other people getting laid," Sarge said. "I like getting laid," Dragon said. "I know you do baby," she said. But not missing a beat, she turned her attention back to Sarge. "You're right Sarge; I'd love to know what you did to that girl. It's one of my favorite fantasies and, I'm not going to apologize for having a sex drive."

"What are you calling 'a sex drive'?" he asked. "You drag 'sexy boy' into that room at least 3 times a day. I'd call it an addiction, wouldn't you agree Sensei? There's a chapter about it in the Kama Sutra. And as far as what I did to that girl, you can refer to chapters 7 through 20." Sensei raised an eyebrow then. "Leave me out of this please, but I will say, the amount of sex they have would be considered clinically, as obsessive. However, knowledge of their individual personalities, backgrounds and physiologies would allow me to grant, that for them, it is normal," he said.

"See!!" she flashed at Sarge. "I'm not such a freak after all." "Sexy boy??? Really??" Dragon said. Sarge eyed him and shrugged.

Raven kept at Sarge, wanting to push him to his limit. "Chapters 7 to 20 you say? Boring, boring, and boring," Raven said. "She was making a call on her phone when I saw her leave, probably calling someone else who actually knows how to fuck." She had finally pushed Sarge's last button and he looked across at Dragon.

She knew Sarge was going to try and grab her so she jumped up and ran. He caught her at the top of the steps, throwing her over his shoulder, bringing her back in and tossing her down on the pillows in the reflection area as she struggled, cursing him in French. Dragon and Sensei exchanged eye rolling glances at each other, watching the ever familiar scene play out between them.

Sarge sat astride her and held her arms back above her head. "Now, little brat," he said. "I got you now and you are going to repeat after me." To this she replied with a French hiss of insults. "Dragon, what did this little bad tempered, foul mouthed thing just say?" Sarge asked. "You are a huge fucking asshole," Dragon politely translated. Sarge laughed, looking down at her. He gave her a sexy pout. "That's right, I am, which is why you need to repeat after me. "Sarge is the sexiest guy in the whole world and I would do anything to have him," he said. He taunted her with his blue eyes.

This got Dragon and Sensei laughing. She was laughing now too. If she didn't give in he would keep it up until she had to. "Ok, OK, Sergeant Willis, you are the sexiest guy in the whole world and I would do anything to have you," she said. She managed it somehow between her laughter. "Very good," he said. "It's the truth and you know it. Don't forget it or I'll remind you." Still laughing she squirmed under him. "Ok, let me go, I'm not one of your bimbos that like you forcing yourself on them," she said.

He eyed her sexily. "You mean like this?" he said.

Leaning down, still holding her hands above her head, he kissed her lips, in a sexy, soft, Sarge kiss, his blonde hair falling around his face, giving her the idea of what it would be like to have him make love to her.

He broke it off leaving her eyeing him. "Very nice Sergeant Willis, maybe you do know how to kiss," she said. He let her arms go, nodding to her. "Yes I do, but behave yourself now, or you'll find out more about what I know how to do," he said. As he stood off of her, she jumped up and shoved him, cursing him again in French. "You're such a dick," Dragon translated obediently. Sarge grinned and held his hands up in a 'guilty as charged' fashion.

Raven retreated into Dragon's arms for a quick embrace of his warmth, flashing her green sharpness at Sarge. "Can we wake Waxy up now?" she asked. "Yes," Sensei said. "I was just waiting for you and Sergeant Willis to return to the adult world."

Sarge gave her his best 'fuck you' look to stop her from starting something again and with that Sensei turned and they all followed him back to the infirmary. He dosed Wax's IV with something to wake him up and waited, watching the heart rate monitor responding to the drug. Wax began to stir out of his anesthetic daze, blinking his eyes open and gathering his surroundings.

"Pain son?" Sensei asked. He looked at Wax to get his attention wanting to be sure he could understand him. "Ya," Wax said. He closed his eyes against the pain and nodded weakly. They watched the realization come over his face. "OK," Sensei said. He turned and went about preparing a morphine injection. Raven took Wax's hand in hers and he moved his eyes to her face.

"Hey baby girl," he said. "Hey Hollywood," she said.

She smiled to him. It was her nickname for him because of his resemblance to a stunning black actor she had seen in a magazine once. Normally it pissed him off when she called him by it, but he smiled at her now.

"You going to dance with me later kid?" he said. She kissed his hand and gave him happy eyes. "Sure Waxy, any time," she said.

Wax began to breathe a little easier as the morphine did its job. "Can you eat something for me Wax?" Sensei asked. Wax nodded, realizing he was actually very hungry.

Reading Sensei's mind, Raven went to find Wax something to wear and Dragon and Sarge retreated to find something to drink for them. She returned with some of his usual clothing and helped Sensei get him up and dressed and standing with the help of crutches.

"No weight, OK Wax?" Sensei said. Wax nodded and standing now on his good leg, balancing himself with the crutches he looked at them. He smiled his 'Hollywood' smile and tossed his dreads back, looking as good as new. "I think I'm good, let's go," he said.

He managed to get to the end of the bench and sit at the table, leaving his left leg resting off to the side. Raven pulled the food to where he could easily reach it and he ate.

Sarge had retrieved the scotch bottle from the kitchen cupboard and out of his pocket he retrieved Wax's iPod. He put it on the table beside Wax and gave him a pat on his shoulder. He then poured some scotch, neat, handing one to Dragon and one to Sensei.

They sat and talked and enjoyed their drinks, waiting for Wax to finish eating. Raven amused him with the earlier shenanigans between her and Sarge, and her version of Sarge's black eye.

They were interrupted by the screen as Chekov was contacting them. They moved over to the desk, Wax just turning on the bench so he could listen in.

"I gather you are Ok Wax?" Chekov said. "Ya I'm fine," Wax said. He was still eating and didn't even look at Chekov as he spoke.

Dragon pulled Raven into him, facing her at Chekov and circling her with his arms so she stayed still. In his mind he was teasing her. "You're going to be in trouble later, for being such a brat to Sarge." In acknowledgement of his thoughts she pressed her back into the front of his shorts, feeling him through the fabric, warning him just 'who' was going to be in trouble. Even soft he was big and visible. "If you get me hard I'm going to hit you hard." He mentally responded, backing himself off of her touch, which was all it would take if he didn't move. She flushed at his mention of the game they liked to play.

"Dragon!" Chekov snapped, pulling Dragon's focus back to the screen. "Yes, what?" he said. "I sent you a profile on the logging project. Go through it, decide how you want to proceed and update me." "Fine," Dragon said. "I'll look at it and see if we can manage without Wax." "Analyze it without Wax and add Damascus if you need him," Chekov said. "From my initial impression of it, a ground assault should take care of the personnel and you can finish it with an air strike, to destroy the operation. Your Blackhawks have guns don't they?" Chekov asked. He was looking at Dragon with his usual condescending stare. Dragon just nodded, running a hand through his hair. "I'll look at it," he said.

What was really entering his mind now more than anything was his past conversation with Sensei about the events that were to occur after eliminating the logging operation. Where were they going to go he wondered? He made a mental note to talk to Raven about it. As he thought this he realized she had turned in his arms and was looking up at him. He silently said to her he had something to discuss with her later. Chekov bid them farewell and the screens went blank again.

"It will be a good 8 weeks for Wax to be fully recovered," Sensei said. "Let's deal with this in the morning," Dragon said. He dismissed the subject and poured them another scotch. They managed to haul Wax out to the porch where he sat on the bench with his leg up and they gathered around, while Dragon relit the fire pit. Sitting together now, they reflected. "Dragon," Wax said. "It might be the morphine talking, but thanks." He toasted him with his scotch glass. "Wax for fuck sake, just get better," Dragon said. Wax smiled and sipped his Scotch. "You aren't going on that logging mission without me. Even if I have to sit somewhere and watch, I can still cover you guys," Wax said.

With that they all relaxed as the jungle darkness descended around them, the strange night sounds coming in from the trees enveloping them, making them grateful for their fire. They passed the evening hours talking.

Raven entertained them talking about her, Wax and Sarge's childhood in the camp, prior to Dragon's arrival. She had lived with the other girl's in their dorm and Wax and Sarge had been in the boys barracks, like Damascus and his group were now.

"You were so annoying back then," Sarge said. She grinned at him, giving him her sweet pretty smile. "You were just the easiest one to bug and still are," she said. Getting up and going to him, she jumped in his lap. He playfully wrestled with her for a few moments until she pulled his hair like she used to when they were young. "Ouch, let go you little viper," he said. She released his mane as he dug his fingers into her side to get her to drop her hands. "You two haven't changed in the least," Sensei said. "I used to worry about what I was going to do with the two of you; always at one another."

"You're right Sarge," Wax said. "She was annoying, and you spoiled her Sensei." "I did not," Sensei said. "She was just hard to resist and I found her entertaining to a fault."

Sarge finished his Scotch and eyed Sensei with feigned offense. "I'm happy to know my grief was so 'entertaining' for you," Sarge said. "I assure you it was not my intention to allow you to suffer at her hands, but half the time I didn't know what was going on until it was too late," Sensei said.

Dragon stood now and retrieved her from Sarge's grasp. "So," he said. He took her in his arms and held her off the ground. "It sounds like you've been getting away with things around here for a long time. You're going to come with me now and take a bit of punishment you have coming to you." He set her down, his eyes never leaving hers. She tossed her hair, flashing her eyes back at him. "Well, it's about fucking time," she said. "Oh boy," Sensei said. Dragon raised his eyebrows at her. "You'd better run," he said.

She took off in the direction of their bedroom. He gave her a two second head start, nodding at them as he turned and went after her. In seconds they heard a quick little scream, as he had caught her in the bedroom doorway.

He had grabbed her by her arm as they entered the room. "You're going to do something for me before I give you what you deserve," he said. With his other hand he unbuttoned his shorts. "On your knees," he said.

He pushed her down, grasped her by the back of her hair and tilted her head upwards. Taking himself out of his shorts, he rubbed the head of his erection across her lips. His breath caught slightly as he watched her lips and tongue on him, feeling her soft and wet gentleness on his sensitive glands.

"Don't make me come," he said.

She knew how he wanted it and let him guide himself at his own speed. She applied just enough pressure with her lips for him to feel it. As he worked himself up a bit more, he increased his motion and drove himself farther to the back of her throat holding himself into her, triggering her gag reflex. He backed off allowing her a breath, her lips wet with saliva which had begun to drip from him. Holding her head with both his hands now, he punished her with it a bit harder, sliding himself down the back of her throat, letting her breathe at intervals. Her saliva poured off him now and her eyes were glazed and moist from her efforts to please him.

He was ready now for what he really wanted and looked down at her, her lips puffy now from his abuse, her eyes watering, hair a tangled mess, and saliva coating her chin.

"Go and get what you need," he said. She obeyed, going to the dresser drawer. He removed his shorts completely and lay back on the bed. She returned to him with the items. "I'm all yours angel," he said. "Give me what you got."

She tied a blindfold around his eyes and positioned his arms above him. He would never allow her to tie him but he would keep his arms back where she put them. She moved next to him taking him in her mouth again. Working him up now, she made him rock hard and he was moaning with it. Pausing she kissed his mouth gently.

"Ok baby, be ready because I'm going to make it bad," she said.

He moaned and gasped as she worked on him again with her mouth and hand, driving him where he needed to go. Knowing the exact right timing as she could feel his orgasm building, she fastened the ring over him, pulling it down to the base of his erection and drawing it tightly closed just as he was about to release.

He groaned as it efficiently stifled his orgasm. Using her hand then, she tormented him. He was shaking from the feeling of it, the blindfold forcing him to experience the depth of his other senses.

"Baby, let me come, please," he said. He begged her to finish him now as the ring caused him to hover indefinitely on the brink of release. It was like an orgasm that went on and on without an end, until it became unbearable.

Watching him carefully now, she could feel the erotic pleasure he was getting but there was a fine line. "Ok I think you need to come now, do you want too?" she said. "My god," was all he managed and she knew he was exactly where he should be.

He was vibrating, moaning. She squeezed his now almost painful erection with her left hand. He was breathless now and he looked so sexy to her; his arms back with his fists clenched, his hair fallen over his blindfold and his body naked except for his shirt.

Then, all a matter of perfect timing, pushing him to the limit of the technique, she released the ring and he exploded onto himself. His orgasm was tenfold now and he gasped over and over again as it shook him. She freed his sight, sliding the blindfold up above his eyes. He lay completely spent, panting and glazed, his T shirt covered in himself.

"Baby," he said. "You just blew my fucking brains out with that."

It had taken her a long time to get him to accept all the steps of the technique. He liked the cock ring part but for many times initially, he wouldn't let her blindfold him or tie his arms. After what he endured in his earlier life he didn't ever want to be bound or blindfolded. She had gradually urged him and with trust and her skill he overcame his phobia, allowing the blindfold. It was now one of his favorite games to play. They didn't engage it in regularly but it was always special when they had nights where the mood was right.

In the aftermath, as he lay still, his breath returning to normal, she stroked his hair back from his face lovingly, happy that she had pleased him.

He looked at her, loving her. "That was unbelievable, baby." "I aim to please," she said. "And you do," he said. He kissed her, taking her chin and softly exploring her lips with his. "I hope some of that wasn't too uncomfortable for you," he whispered. He kissed the puffiness of her lips.

She kissed him back, softly responding to him. "No baby, I deserved you to be rough with me." She eyed him now letting him know she was more than ready for what he was going to do to her next. Responding, he tilted his head, taking her chin again. "And do you still think you deserve me to be rough with you?" She nodded. "How rough?" he asked. He looked at her with a knowing light in his eyes.

She stood and went to the dresser again. She withdrew some things and returned to him and held them out. He eyed them and then let his eyes go to hers. "I see," he said. He bit his lower lip now, pondering. "These things are for very bad girls." "Yes," she said, nodding. Her wetness was leaking out of her now. Instinctively he traced a middle finger between her legs, the wetness coming through. He licked it from his finger. "Well," he said. "This is very bad of you to be like this. I think I'm going to have to do something about it." She moaned now as he took the items from her trembling hands.

He got up, still wearing his shirt and removed it. He then removed her clothes one piece at a time laying them over the chair. She stood naked in the candlelight and he wanted to devour her. She had brought him silk rope and a cat of nine tails whip. This was her most secret fetish. She enjoyed it and he had mastered it for her even though he didn't enjoy hurting her, testing her pain, and did not ever want it for himself. He would please her however she wanted though and to the best of his ability.

Deliberately taking his time as she stood waiting, he picked up the rope. "Hold your hands out," he said. She complied, shaking slightly. He took her wrists placing her palms together and tied the rope tightly around them, then told her to lay face down on the bed. She did so and he pulled her arms up and tied her to the headboard. He took the blindfold she had used on him and covered her eyes. "Bye bye baby," he said.

She trembled and a slight whine escaped her now. He spread her legs all the way apart and knelt between them.

He gently caressed her back with his fingertips, down and over her sexy butt, stopping short of touching her where she needed it.

"You really do deserve this, now that I think about it. I warned you about making me hard, do you remember that?" he asked. "Yes," she said. His deep voice, quiet and calm was making her crazy. Tied and unable to see him she could only feel him in her mind and hear his sensual talk.

"And what did I warn you would happen?" he asked. "You would hit me hard," she said. "Exactly," he said.

And with that he began. He knew he had gotten her to that sexual oblivion state and needed to finish the game. He moved away from her and picked up the whip.

"Do you think I should fuck you?" he asked. She was rapidly trying to get air, turning her head from side to side, unable to see where he was or what he was doing now. "Yes, please," she begged.

He raised his arm and allowing the whip to spiral down putting the velocity into the tails, he laced her across her back with it. Stinging her to just before the point of intolerance, she cried out, panting with the bite of it.

"I don't know baby," he said. He moved around her, touching her inner thighs, making her moan for him. "You need a little more of this first I think." Teasing her was part of the game and he did it well.

He let it fall again hitting her lower this time. Crying out each time at its sting, she was mad with desire now. He inserted his fingers inside her and as she gasped at the feel of it he hit her again lower on her back now. She squirmed on his hand, fully thriving on the rush now.

He knew he only needed to hit her about twice more for it to be complete. He withdrew his fingers and grasping her hips he positioned her so he could slide her onto him. "You're almost done baby, you deserve a little bit now," he said.

He eased himself half way into her, spreading her open around him as he brought the whip down again. He let the tips of the tails lash her as close as he could get without catching any of her most sensitive spots. He was expert at getting it just right, using just the right amount of effect on her with it. She cried out again and knowing she was just about ready to explode he pulled out of her, lacing her hard, one final time with it.

Letting the whip go, quickly he lifted her blindfold, slipped the knots from her wrists and turned her onto her back.

"Hold me baby," he said. "I'm going to fuck your lights out for you."

She clung to him now, wrapping her legs around him, raking her nails down his back and biting his shoulder as he slammed into her making her come. He unleashed all his energy into her, moving in the rhythm he knew she needed to get there.

"Good girl," he said. "Give me all of it."

He needed one last one for himself and when he knew she was done he finished himself off, holding hard into her.

Afterward, she lay beneath him still clinging to him, trembling, her eyes closed, hair sweaty around her face. He kissed her eyelids gently. Complete and satisfied now, he covered them in their bed and took her in his arms again.

"Thank you," she said. "I know it's hard for you to be that person for me." He smiled. "It's not my favorite thing to do to you," he said. "You're very good at it though," she said. "Well, I aim to please," he said. She smiled and kissed his chest.

They continued to talk to each other and he filled her in on the talk he had with Sensei about the future. She listened and hugged him, understanding his hurt and Sensei's predicament at the same time.

"I don't care where we go," she said. "I will miss it here, but as long as I'm with you it won't matter where that is." He hugged her tightly and his emotions overwhelmed him as he felt his love for her overflow. "I need to make love to you again," he said.

She turned on her back and pulled him over her. He kissed her lips softly as he slid carefully into her. She moaned at the feeling of him inside her again. He moved slowly and gently, just enough for them to feel the sensation. In his mind he let his thoughts of love for her and his sexuality mingle together, making them warm and excited at the same time. He stayed inside her for a long time, edging them closer then taking it back losing them together in it. When the feeling of it had reached the right point he held her to him, asking her "Are you ready?" She responded with a silent nod.

CHAPTER EIGHT

DAVID LI

Dragon sat cross-legged on their bed, leaning back against the headboard, having woken himself early. Raven was asleep against his chest, sleeping beside him as always, her face against his collarbone, her hair a mass of curling softness down her back and around them. Sensei would be in soon with tea. He sat peacefully watching the palms outside the open air room waving gently in the trade winds Hawaii was known for. It had been 18 months since they left the jungle for the last time. He reflected back on their last mission, the logging mission which had gone badly.

During their retreat from their land assault, Raven had run straight into an ambush. Dragon had watched in gut wrenching anguish as she took a hit to the forehead from a gun stock. Then a cold steel gun barrel had pressed him hard behind his right ear rendering him motionless, unable to help her. He and Sarge were at gunpoint as she lay unconscious on the ground. As his racing mind grasped the situation, things unraveled quickly. In an instant he had seen the laser dot from Wax's Remington land on the forehead of the one holding Sarge. He remembered yelling 'Get down' to Sarge and simultaneously dropping to his knees. Wax had let his shots off killing both men in a matter of seconds. Dragon had then launched himself at the one who had hit Raven, who was then off guard, beating him to a pulp and snapping his neck.

Wax was supposed to have been waiting in a truck for them to return but had instinctively followed them, slowly in his walking cast that he had on by then, protecting his healing leg. They had eliminated all the targets and were retreating when they had come across three of them that they were not aware of. It had unfolded quickly then.

She was unconscious and he had picked her up in his arms like a ragdoll and they had fled to the truck. Wax had driven like hellfire, away to their retrieval spot where Tom-Tom sat waiting, the War Horse's rotors spinning and ready to lift them away. He had held her to him in the War Horse, willing her with everything he had, not to leave him. She had a nasty cut on her left eyebrow and swelling had closed both her eyes.

Later in the infirmary, Sensei had expertly stitched the deep laceration through her left brow and after what Dragon thought was forever she had slowly regained consciousness. Her eyes were purple, swollen shut and the whites had gone red with broken blood vessels behind them. She had turned to look at him as he held her hand and he knew instantly she was not alright.

He spoke softly to her, leaning close so she could hear. "Can you see me?" Weakly she had answered, "Yes." Using her "sight" she tried to reassure him. He knew what was wrong but dared the question, hoping it wasn't true. "Raven, can you see me with your eyes?" "No," she had answered. She had tried to smile at him, wanting him not to worry about her. It had broken his heart into a million pieces that she was trying not to scare him. His eyes darted to Sensei, panicked and frantic for her.

"Kai-Li?" she had said. She rarely used his given name. Her voice was quiet and even, tears now leaking from the corners of her sightless eyes. "Don't let go of my hand, Ok, because if you do I will be alone in the dark."

With this, he had come apart completely, taking her in his arms, sitting up on the bed and rocking her, burying his face in her hair, his own tears coming freely down his face. "Baby, don't be scared, I'm here, I'm right here and I will always be right here." He had wept openly then, not able to stop it.

They had all broken down then, Wax had turned away to hide his own tears and Sarge had slumped to the floor, hugging his knees and burying his face, his sobs shaking him. The moment had overwhelmed even Sensei, who through his own glistening eyes had fought to hold his composure. Placing his fingertips on her forehead he used his "sight" to feel what was happening in her injured brain.

"Son," he had said. "It's the swelling on and around the optic nerves." Knowing what he needed to do, he had taken a syringe and swabbing her inner arm had injected her with an anti inflammatory. "We wait now; it will take time for the swelling to go down," he said. He tried to put on a calm demeanor on the outside.

Dragon had died a thousand deaths over the next 24 hours, as her sight had slowly returned. Her headaches had been bad and her vision blurry but she was slowly returning to him. He had held her close to him and waited to see her beautiful green eyes, clear again. She had wanted him to make love to her then. With or without eyesight they could see each other, the feeling of it was their connection and she needed him that way more than ever right then.

For the first time in 7 or so years he had wanted to leave the jungle, leave the fight and live like a normal person. Sensei had been right when he had explained the General's plan. It was time to move on.

Sensei disrupted him from the rather unpleasant memory, with tea. It was yet another beautiful day and they had some plans for an adventure. "Hai Papa." Dragon greeted him, as he silently appeared around the bedroom door. "Son," Sensei said. Sensei sat, placed the tray and poured them tea, same as forever and it warmed Dragon every time.

Life had been good in spite of the strangeness, since becoming a real living version of David Li. In his mind and to everyone close to him he was still the same, but they still had a job to do and a purpose in life to fulfill. The entity itself meant nothing to him, but Sensei had been accurate when so long ago now, he had foreshadowed to Dragon, saying 'it would be to his liking.'

David Li had been a fictitious person created by Chekov and the General, but always with the plan that Dragon would put a life to him, when the time was right. There were companies in his name, charities, and foundations and Dragon was legitimately a very wealthy man. When Sensei had explained this all to him, he really hadn't understood. It had taken time to assimilate. The General had created a life for Dragon that he had been ready to assume. The time had come for them to leave the jungle and find a new place and so it had also become time for David Li to join the real world.

Sensei sipped tea and they discussed their plans for the day, as they had always done. Sensei had a few issues to deal with concerning some of the construction still going on, regarding the children's dwellings and the road maintenance. The property they had was a tip of the island of Lanai. It had been for sale when Sensei had first shown Dragon photos of it. There was a beautiful home on the ocean, and many facilities, which included a heliport, numerous vehicles, and a beach and ocean in almost every direction. It presented a kind of life style Dragon had never known about nor cared about. Initially to him the whole thing just seemed like another mission and he would carry it out if that's what he was asked to do. And in a sense it was. Being David Li served the General's purpose and was all part of the plan.

The General had wanted him and Raven to be married, for social reasons connected to his new identity. They had cared less for the ritual, but had agreed. Chekov had arranged the papers and records, and passports that identified them for the first time in their lives. Before, they had been a secret, untraceable, silent and invisible. Now, it had become public knowledge that David Li was who he was. It was all a clever front to what really went on behind the ever secret doors of HQ Munich. No one ever questioned where David Li had ever been. It was just of the utmost interest now, to the media and business world, as to whom and where he was now. Everything he did, or said, or where he went was news worthy. He was powerful and influential, exactly where the General had planned for him to be.

Today they had plans to take their boat along the south shore and find the river outlet to a waterfall they had seen while flying over one day. As a wedding gift, the General had equipped Dragon with the same Sikorsky he had. It accommodated 8 and was light to handle, fast and sleek. Dragon had learned to fly when Sarge had. It was mandatory in case something ever happened to Tom-Tom on a mission.

When they had first arrived they had seen it there, bright and shiny, the standard DLI in black, outlined in gold, on the side of its ebony finished body. They had gone flying in it the next day, to see the area from overhead. They had discovered a beautiful waterfall that lay maybe 6 kilometers inland. If they could find the opening to the sea, they could follow the riverbed upward and get to the waterfall. They had asked Kona, their caretaker and he had explained its religious meanings to the Hawaiian people. He advised it was beneficial to go there, but you must never disturb anything, remove anything or lay waste to anything there. It was believed that their gods had bathed there and it was sacred. It was only ancient myth, but nonetheless they would respect it.

He and Sensei sipped their tea and decided what they would all do after breakfast, starting with Yoga and a workout and then a swim in the ocean. Right after lunch, they would board the boat and go in search of their destination. Dragon woke Raven then, to include her in the discussion of the search for the waterfall. She was playful and good natured as always and when Sensei left them, she fell back pulling Dragon on top of her, clinging to him breathlessly while he woke her up properly.

After he had done a few very satisfying things to her, Dragon had pulled her with him into their shower. It was off the bedroom and was modern granite and glass but had incorporated natural elements in its design, consisting of a natural rock wall. It was large enough for 5 people, had 4 rain faucets and steam. They didn't have their bench but Dragon had found many ways to use the rock wall. There was also an oversized tub in the room they could lay in together.

The whole bedroom itself was unique and Raven had loved it immediately. The door was off the main room and when you entered, the king size bed was there. It had a carved wooden head board gave it a traditional Hawaiian feel but it had a modern frame and was covered in white sheets and pillows with a billowy feather duvet. The wall it was up against was a dark native wood, as were the floors. The bed faced a huge stone fire place that went 20 feet from floor to ceiling. And on both sides of it, were windows. There was a big furry white rug on the floor in front of the fireplace. Off to the right of it as you faced it was a large spa like hot tub, made of granite, built in to the floor that had an infinity edge that flowed over and down to a private swimming pool and the outdoors, surrounded by glass walls that could be opened, seeming to disappear somehow if you wanted them too. The ocean was visible from every vantage point. Stone steps led down to the private pool from the hardwood floor of the bedroom. Ceiling fans turned slowly to circulate the air and the overall size of the room was bigger than the whole main house in camp had been.

Dragon had done everything he knew how to do to his new wife in this room, on every surface and element. If it were up to Raven they would never leave it, but none the less they emerged as usual to join the others. The main room of the house reminded Raven of their past. The kitchen was on the back wall, with a long granite island creating separation from the main room, which held a long communal table. There was a comfortable seating area that looked out to the ocean, again open to the outside unless the glass panels were closed, which they almost never were. The floors were the same dark wood, the furniture was a warm white and it suited perfectly because the outdoors brought in every color of nature. The ocean's ever moving blues and the palm trees were a sea of green and the beautiful flowers in every exotic red.

On the other side of the entrance way, was an office area, again surrounded by glass, where Dragon felt Chekov spied on them from, as the computer screens stared toward them. He didn't really think that or care anyway, if Chekov was spying on them, but it amused Raven when he joked about it. A hallway led off the main entranceway from there, leading back to the whole other side of the house which was bedrooms, for Sarge, Wax and Sensei. Also the gym was at that end.

Sarge and Wax were already eating and they joined them at the table. Kona, a native Hawaiian had come with the place, so to speak. He was outside cleaning the main pool. After Dragon had seen the photos of the home and Sensei had outlined the plan, he had purchased it as a gift for Raven. She had cried when he gave her the key, as she had been led to believe it was just another stopover for them.

He had realized then that perhaps she had missed stability and having some sort of roots in life. He didn't care about marriage and neither did she, because between them something existed far deeper, but in the end, Sensei and the General had been correct. Something had touched him deeply about it, he just wasn't sure what. They had never owned anything except one another and he liked that she loved it and it symbolized their bond and commitment to move forward in their lives.

Kona's wife Marietta was in the kitchen with Lily. Marietta took care of the household needs inside and Kona the rest. They were discreet, kind and loyal, and Dragon liked them. Sensei was busy all the time with the building and organization of the children's facility which was located a kilometer farther down from the main house. The last 18 months had been full of change and happiness for all of them. Sensei and the General had planned it that way. Dragon had been on over 120 missions in the space of 4 years, with Wax and Sarge. They had never stopped moving around and they hadn't realized it but it was time to take a step back. Damascus and the boys had been sent to HQ Munich as fully fledged recruits and were now level 2 operatives. They were taking over the missions previously handled by Dragon's team.

Dragon's new role now involved his metamorphosis into the personality of David Li. Soon there would be higher level missions for them, involving more complicated jobs. They were well rested now, physically fit and assimilated. He knew instinctively it wouldn't be long before they would be hearing from Chekov. Sensei was busy these days with the children and the facilities, but they always had time together and Dragon had gotten that feeling again that Sensei was hiding something from him. He would wait to hear what it was, but for today, they were simply themselves, about to go have some fun.

At breakfast, Lily had come to sit on Dragon's knee. She was almost 8 now, still a tiny thing but she was growing up. "Did you know what Paulo did yesterday?" she said. "I guess you are going to tell me, right?" he said. He was looking amusedly at her. "Yes!" she went on. "I was driving the golf cart to come to the house to get Sensei and Paulo wasn't listening when I told him to push the brake and he made me drive into the acacia bushes."

Dragon was smiling now at the image of it. She had decided to learn to drive one of the golf carts that were around, as she had grown impatient waiting for Sensei one day. Being too short to reach the pedals, she had taken Paulo who was only 5 and made him sit on the floor and operate the gas and brakes for her. Her feet didn't touch the ground and he sat between her dangling legs and used his feet to press the pedals, as she commanded him to go forward or brake. He could see nothing from the floor and had to listen carefully. She bossed him around endlessly but he was her favorite friend and she took care of him. It amused them all to see them driving the cart this way and at first Sensei had scolded her, worrying for their safety but she had won him over, using similar techniques that had worked for Raven in the past.

"Well if you didn't have him to help you, then you couldn't drive at all," Dragon said. He was eyeing her now, watching her think this over. "I suppose not," she said. "But he needs to stop being so dumb." At this, Sensei cleared his throat, causing her to flash her almond shaped eyes in his direction.

"Miss Lily," Sensei said. "We don't refer to one another in negative, disrespectful terms. Paulo loves you and if he heard you call him a bad name it would hurt his feelings." "I don't mean it," she said. Then pausing momentarily to think, she continued. "But, yesterday Dragon called Waxy a 'fucking shitbag', right to his face." She was looking at Sensei with a questioning expression.

At this, Raven got up and walked behind the kitchen island, to hide her laughter. Dragon leaned his head back in a 'busted' resigned pain, barely holding his laughter. Sarge had gotten up when Raven had and gone out to the patio, so he could laugh un-noticed.

"I see," said Sensei. He turned his stare on Dragon and Wax. "Why don't the two of you explain this to Lily?"

Dragon recovered quickly. "First of all, that is not language for a young lady to be using, whether you are simply repeating it or not," he said. "And, also, I was unaware of your presence at the time, as you have a way of appearing unannounced." She looked down. "Yes that is true," she said.

He tilted her face to have her look at him. "But, Sensei is right about not using disrespectful terms when referring to one another. If you overhear one of us doing that, it is because we are older. And also, Waxy knows that he is 'one' and I was simply just stating a fact," he said. He was trying not laugh again now. "That's absolutely right," Wax said. He tried to appear serious, nodding in agreement.

She seemed puzzled as she thought it over and Sensei interrupted now, before she asked anymore questions. "Lily, come now and help Marietta." She jumped down from Dragon's knee and took Sensei's hand as he led her into the kitchen. "Dragon is right, you know," he said. "Let us not hear that kind of language from you for any reason. Understood?" She smiled up at him. "Ok Papa, I don't even know what those words mean anyway." "Good," he said.

With finality he gave Wax and Dragon a chastising glance. Raven hugged Lily to her and offered a word, whispering in her ear. "Boys are all dumb." Lily giggled at her private little joke and went off to help Marietta, as Raven went to replace her on Dragon's knee.

"Dumb are we now?" he asked. She just smiled at him and shrugged, her eyes flashing up to his, under her lashes. "You didn't think I was so dumb earlier when you ripped a few handfuls of my hair out, nor when you were leaving red lines down my back," he said. "Well yes, you are definitely not dumb about certain things," she agreed.

She gave him a naughty smile and pulled gently at a piece of his wayward hair. He brushed her hair back from her face and kissed her gently. She let the softness of his lips touch her and caught his vision of her earlier as she grasped handfuls of his hair. It made her eyes close and she weakened in his arms, having to leave his mouth to catch her breath. He smiled at his success at flooring her so easily.

"Let's go work out now and later I'll show you how dumb I am about some other things, OK?" he said.

Wax was standing with Sarge now, waiting for them to head to the weight room. "Why did you call me a fucking shitbag anyway?" Wax asked. "I can't even remember," Dragon said. "It was because you called him a horny fucking Asian," Sarge said. "Oh ya," Wax said. He started laughing again at the memory. "You two are lucky she didn't repeat that part in front of Sensei," Raven said. "I would have just admitted that I am," Dragon said. "Just like Wax admitted he's a fucking shitbag." "Ok, Ok, horny Asian guy and shitbag guy, behave now," she said. "Where was I when all this went on anyway?" she asked. "It was when we got back from the ride to town yesterday," Dragon said. "You were talking to Kona in the garage for a minute when Shitbag here started on about stuff." She blushed slightly, knowing what Wax was referring to.

She and Dragon had been ahead of Wax and Sarge, in the red Ferrari convertible. She couldn't really be in that car with Dragon without some sort of sexual act resulting. Since they had been there, he had fucked her in it, on it and around it, countless times. Yesterday was no exception. Dragon had put his arm around her as they sped down the road and pulled her mouth down on him while he drove. He had weaved over the line a couple of times as she had let him have the best head she could give him. Wax had been driving the Hummer behind them.

The hot cars, courtesy of the General, consisted of the red Ferrari convertible, a white Lamborghini and a Hummer. Also, floating 150 yards or so off the beach, at anchor, lay the yacht. It was registered to David Li, out of the port of Honolulu Hawaii, U.S.A., and Dragon did in fact own it. It kind of also had come with the property, although Dragon suspected the General had something to do with all the 'things' that 'came with' the property. It was some ninety feet long, gleaming white fiberglass, chrome, glass and wood, it was every ones favorite thing of all. Across the broad stern, in black lettering with gold trim, lay the name "Dream Weaver," written in English script.

It was new, state of the art in every way and could take them anywhere in the world they wanted to go. Sarge had devoted himself to its mechanics and had learned everything he could about its engines inside and out. He and Dragon had spent days and days aboard her, learning the navigation systems and communications systems, while Wax and Raven had fed them beers and entertained them with Wax's iPod. This afternoon would be no different as they were going to take her down shore to search for the river opening that would take them to the waterfall.

Kona waved and pulled away in the Zodiac, leaving them aboard the Dream Weaver. They climbed the stairs and prepared to set off. Raven and Sensei sat on the padded area that she had only just recently let Dragon make love to her on, while Sarge went to the bridge. Dragon and Wax studied the chart table, discussing the destination and the shoreline depths. They had auto piloting controls but were not going to program them, preferring to sail themselves, making themselves aware of the depths. Sarge pushed the engine ignition switches and the diesels groaned to life, one at a time. As they came up to temperature, they raised the anchor and Sarge hit the throttles, guiding them off the shore, heading south around the island.

It was a beautiful afternoon, sunny and slightly breezy. They had all climbed up to the flying bridge to sit and take it all in. The stairs came up the middle and on either side were padded benches curving around the cockpit area, and then there were two large seats that swiveled that had a front and a back area to sit in. Like double-sided lounge chairs. Raven's cheeks flushed as she remembered things Dragon had done to her on them. He caught her thought right then and leaned in and licked her lips. She flashed him a message to leave her alone unless he meant business. He smiled at her now shaking his head. She knew she better stop or he'd drag her into the bedroom and take her to pieces.

She climbed into his lap, and they shared a beer and listened to Wax's iPod. She had on a tiny bikini he had found in a drawer; it was navy blue with white Hawaiian flowers on it. He had tied the bottoms on her by the strings and fastened the top on her which was like a bandeau across her breasts with no straps. It was beyond sexy and he had been worried he would have a noticeable hard on for the entire trip.

He had found board shorts, also navy blue with a white stripe going from the back over his butt and down the sides. She had nodded her approval and he tugged them on while she groped him. In the end they had made it out of the bedroom to join the others but he had still had to try and conceal his hard on with a beach towel.

They had sailed for about two hours, finally reaching what they figured to be the river head for the waterfall. The water was stunning and mesmerizing to watch as they moved through it. The wonderful feeling of the warm soft air and the smell of the ocean was transcending. The hot sun hit them and the beauty of what was around them made them not believe. They anchored as close as possible and covered the distance to the shore on long boards. Raven sat cross-legged while Dragon paddled and Sarge and Wax had a faux sword fight with the paddles to see who would sit and who would paddle the other one. Wax lost so he sat and Dragon taunted him about being Sarge's bitch. They reached the beach and pulled the boards up to clear the tide when it came in and headed up along the river's edge. It was beautiful forest and the temperature was perfect. They were barefoot without fear of snakes, as there were none on the island. They were carefree, weaponless and free as children going on a hike together.

CHAPTER NINE

THE WATERFALL

It was a day they would all remember forever. They hiked uphill for about an hour, climbing gradually, enjoying the company and their surroundings. Sarge had brought a camera he had found at the house and had become quite good with. He often photographed their adventures. It was the first time they had really seen photographs of themselves. It was waterproof and state of the art digital. He captured some stunning shots along the way, of the flowing river, the moss on the rocks and the gleaming sunlight coming through the trees.

After about 45 minutes the black lava rocks got a bit steeper as the vegetation began to fall away, and they could hear the noise. They had stopped talking now and Raven had found the best path to lead them up. They followed her precisely as a team, as they had been doing for the past 5 years or more. She had been dead on in her choice of ascent and when she reached the top of the climb she moved aside for them to join her and they stood in utter silence.

It literally had stunned them and they stared around them in wordless awe. Looking down they were standing in hard black sand, clearly lava rock pulverized over centuries by the towering water. A large serene pool spanned out in front of them for another 300 meters or so, where the waterfall towered, cascading into it. The surroundings were a mixture of vegetation and lava rock walls that glistened with moisture. The sun shone down into the open area lighting the water a beautiful emerald green color. The waterfall itself must have been over 35 meters high, flowing lightly down in a spray of beauty. The water from the pool ran gently over and down the rocks they had just ascended, down the forest and out to the ocean, through the stream bed they had followed to get there.

The first sound they heard besides the water was Sarge's camera. It brought them back to awareness. Dragon said nothing but took Raven's hand and began to walk into the pool, drawn to the waterfall. Wax followed and Sarge went around the perimeter, snapping photos of them as they slowly walked into the gradual depths of the green glowing water. The whole aura of it reminded Dragon of Raven's eyes, green and blue all at once, glowing but serene, peaceful but alive. Something there was captivating his senses. They all felt it, as no one spoke again and they each descended into their own personal spiritual version of the magic of it.

Dragon swam toward the base of the waterfall, knowing she would be right behind him. He found a place to climb up on the rocks, the water cascading around them in a steamy mist. Wax had gone to another area where he had climbed up and was sitting on a ledge with Sarge, who was busy capturing everything he could. They sat together not speaking and Sarge took some shots of him looking like some kind of dark exotic god, his light brown skin glowing against the green and black background, his wet dreads falling back from his forehead.

Dragon and Raven had climbed a bit higher up the side of the waterfall now and had found an area of rock to lay on that was like a plateau in the rock face. The water was coming down over it partially and the rest was exposed, shrouded in rising mists. Dragon had felt the light in him begin to glow and he could clearly see her in his mind as a bright beacon. Something here was touching their inner sight and drawing it forth. He was no longer thinking in a conscious state and everything that happened now was completely directed by an inner source of some kind.

Feeling more relaxed and calm than he ever had in his entire life he sat down, spreading his legs apart in a yoga pose meant to open the heart and mind and soul. She sat closely in front of him then and did the same, her back to him, copying his pose, stretching upward through their bodies, and spreading their arms far apart reaching out with their finger tips to eternity. They were in another world now and Sarge had begun to photograph them. Dragon being taller and bigger was behind her, his arms stretched out, his head slightly back, his eyes focused upward. She sat between his outstretched legs the same way, her head at exactly the same angle as his and her eyes focused in the same direction. They sat straight and tall, and looked almost mythical in their beauty, tanned skin glistening, muscles shining and their wet hair slicked back from their faces.

Completing the pose, Dragon had then encircled her in his arms as she had brought hers down and she laid her cheek on his hands clasping hers over his in front of them. Connecting with her only in his mind now she could feel their love overwhelming her now. He stood now and she wasn't really even aware that she had knelt in front of him and removed her things. His back was to Wax and Sarge as he stood now legs slightly apart. She had clung to his leg, opening his shorts and pulling them down from the back, in a slow motion of erotic love for him. At some point he laid her on her back on the cool rock and was inside her. His warmth filling her, his mouth urgent on hers, they were partially concealed by the falling water and the rising mists.

He moved inside her in a slow powerful rhythm and the light of him was pulsing inside her, his love for her consuming them and their passion bringing them to a simultaneous orgasm like none they had ever experienced. She had let her head fall to the side, eyes closed, lips parted as the waves of it hit her, her soft moans heard only in her head. He had pushed himself up fully extending his arms, arching his back and pressing deep inside her, his head thrown back, water washing his hair back from his face, his eyes closed, as he came deeply inside her.

He had then gently come down to rest on his elbows over her, looking into her eyes now, loving her with every piece of him and wondering what they were feeling right then. Gradually he became aware again in a more conscious way that they were in a waterfall with Wax and Sarge. Afraid to look around too much he had put her bikini back on her and his shorts. They sat up, feet dangling from the ledge and only then did he consciously look around. Wax and Sarge were on another ledge above the green pool, talking and taking pictures. It truly was probably the most beautiful strange and exotic place they had ever been. Raven clung to him, kissing his skin on his arm that he had around her neck, holding her next to him. She still seemed to not be fully there and he mentally coaxed her from her reverie. He pulled her with him, jumping off the ledge into the pool, to swim back to the black sand. Wax dove off his perch to join them and Sarge took the dry route with his camera.

Once back on the black sand beach, they stood taking one last look. It definitely had a spiritual energy and it had affected them all in various ways. Dragon could feel Sensei reaching into his mind, gently urging him to return now. They retraced their steps, making their way back to the surf. It was early evening now but there would still be 4 or so more hours of light to get back in. They were going to have dinner on the boat anyway and have Kona pick them up when they were ready to retire. Sensei was waiting for them. He had stayed behind to watch the Yacht and meditate alone while they were gone.

They paddled out to the Dream Weaver and jumped aboard, full of stories for Sensei. The diesels had been idling in wait and once the boards were stowed and the anchor lifted, Dragon had hit the forward throttles and they moved off the shore again and northward back to their beach. Wax had produced beers and some Champagne for Raven. He and Raven were going to cook dinner tonight for everyone and they discussed their plans for it.

Sarge had connected his camera to the laptop in the main bridge and downloaded his photos. Then using the laptops battery power he brought it to the upper bridge for them all to see. There were beautiful shots of the landscape. He had a knack for catching the right light and angles. It was mesmerizing as the images came to life on the screen. There was a picture of Dragon and Raven from the back as they had begun to walk into the pond. The camera had focused on Dragon and Raven in the fore front, the waterfall and background less defined. It was stunning, the sun was gleaming off their backs as they were stepping simultaneously through the deepening water that shone like glass around them, Dragon's long hair fell shiny black on his shoulders, the dragon tattoo gleaming, glinting in the light, hers' a cascade of soft brown down her back, just beginning to float in the water.

There was some of Wax looking mysterious and sexy in the mist, looking like he lived there and had risen out of the waters somehow. His exotic looks captured in the right environment, made him beautiful and exciting to look at. Raven teased him, calling him by her 'Hollywood' nickname again to bug him. Then there came a series of pictures Sarge had taken of Raven and Dragon that captured their private moments. They all sat in silence as Sarge moved through them.

He had captured their moment when they had taken the yoga pose. It was a stunning photo of both of them but the most definitive thing was how he had captured the mood of the pose. The light had caught their faces evenly, their eyes were looking off in the same direction and their muscled arms were stunningly set off by the sunlight on their wet skin. It accurately portrayed the energy they were feeling then. It was peaceful yet powerful, full of passion and defined their spiritual connection to one another. The mist was around them, slick black lava rock behind them, their bodies glowing in the forefront. Water droplets had formed on their bodies and the look of love and innocence and belief was on their faces.

Next and most stunning, was the second one. Sarge had taken a shot when Dragon had stood, after the yoga pose, with his back to he and Wax. The sun was above them and the Dragon tattoo was reflecting all its colors, lying between the massive shoulders, alive on his back. There were so many things to notice in the shot it was hard to know where to look first. Dragons' head was turned toward his left shoulder, looking downward, his profile stunning and sexy, and his beautiful half smile revealing his white even teeth. His hair was slicked back from his face and curled around in a wet unruly shining mane. Water was splashing out of focus around them.

As the eye travelled down his back following his downward gaze, following the Dragon, to the lower half of his body, it became even more unbelievable. Raven was kneeling before him, naked in front of him, slightly to his left, holding his left thigh in an embrace. Her face was turned up to his, love covering her in a beautiful expression as she gazed up at him, with obvious desire. Her left hand was on his right inner thigh gripping the fabric of his shorts. Her right arm was around his butt and her hand was reaching up, grasping his shorts by the waist, which she had begun to pull down, to reveal a tan line at the top of his butt. Her knees were spread on either side of his leg, which blocked any indiscreet view, just showing her sexy, tanned, muscled thighs. Her tiny waist was visible as she arched her back into him. Her hair hung down wetly around her and her right arm reaching up had partially covered her right breast, leaving most of it to the imagination. It was absolutely breath taking and encompassed their physical beauty, their passion for each other and the spirituality of the moment. Raven had actually blushed as she looked at it. Dragon thought it was beyond sexy of her and they all agreed it had captured them completely on so many levels.

The third one was very emotional for them, as Sarge had captured their most private moment and it was clearly evident. It was only from the waist up; the water cascading had obscured anything inappropriate. It showed Dragon's head thrown back, eyes closed and lips parted, as he had arched his back into her in his orgasm. Raven had her face turned to the side towards the camera, which had captured her release. Her eyes were closed, her hair everywhere, stuck to her face, water glistening on her lips, her expression a look of total erotic escape. Her hands were on Dragon's forearms, which were blocking any view of her breasts. After looking at it for a minute they decided it went well with the other ones and made sense that Sarge had taken it.

Raven took his hand and kissed it. "Thanks Sarge, they're beautiful, and so are you," she said. He smiled and got up to refill their drinks. After another glass of Champagne, she had teased Sarge about being a voyeur.

"Any pictures of you two I get to take are going to be of you having sex because that's all you ever do," he said. "And besides, I have probably seen you having sex a million times, so by now it's like reading the same pages of the Kama Sutra too many times." "Poor Sarge, we really do have to get you laid soon," she said. "Me too," Waxy said. "Papa!" she said. "Can we find them some girls?" Sensei rolled his eyes at Dragon. "Leave me out of this my dear," he said. "Ok, well maybe tomorrow night we will go to that bar in town, like at night this time and I will find you some," she said. She was very pleased with her idea.

In the galley, which was equipped with everything they would ever need, Wax turned on his iPod, and poured them both some champagne. She had taken what they needed from the fridge and they had set to work. She cut vegetables and Wax started rice and seasoned their fish. Hawaii had so many wonderful types of fish available which suited them all perfectly and they had tried almost all of them to date. Tonight's was a Mahi Mahi. Wax liked to make things spicy and he was in charge of how things tasted and she was more the sous chef, preparing and monitoring while he crafted. They made a good pair and it gave Sensei a break. At home Marietta had assumed most of the cooking duties so they enjoyed this time together when it was just themselves, like old times.

Dragon, Sarge and Sensei had joined them below now, the food smells drawing them down. Sarge sat at the lower bridge helm and monitored their progress. They were heading to shore now, wanting to anchor before their food was ready. In twenty minutes they found their mooring spot. Dragon had set the anchor and Sarge powered off the diesels, leaving them rocking gently in the quiet tropical evening. It was a beautiful finish to a beautiful day.

They didn't have to clean up too much because that was Kona's job, to restore the yacht to its pristine condition, and replenish what they had consumed so it would be ready for their next adventure. They had sat on the stern deck for the rest of the evening watching the sun drop below the mountains.

By now, Wax and Sarge were intoxicated and dancing together to a cowboy song, something about having 'friends in low places'. They were so funny, even Sensei was laughing at them. Kona had arrived to pick them up and appeared on deck. They hadn't even heard him approach because of the music. He took in the scene, a grin enhancing his Hawaiian features.

They made it into the Zodiac somehow and were entertained on the short trip back to shore by Sarge; repeatedly explaining to Kona that he and Wax were just friends and that sometimes they danced together because of where they grew up there were no girls around. They were all laughing now as he dug himself deeper. He continued on, telling Kona that tomorrow they were going to find some girls and that Raven had promised to get them laid. Sensei shook his head in his hands, wondering what kind of explanation he was going to have to come up with for this one.

Dragon had tossed his arm around Sarge at this point, pulling his face to his, whispering "Ok bud enough; he already thinks we're fucking weird." "Ya, ya, we are weird as fuck man, I know," Sarge whispered loudly back to Dragon. They finally made it to the beach where Wax proceeded to fall out of the boat into the shallow water. Sensei had Sarge, propping him up and Dragon had to pull Wax out of the water. They hauled them up the lawn and stuffed them into their respective rooms. Sensei made sure they were safely on top of their beds and left water bottles for each of them. "My fuck," he said. "Papa," Raven said. "Since when do you swear?" "Since I have to put two drunks to bed," he said.

They said good night and Dragon took Raven by the hand to their bedroom. She stood watching him passively as he prepared things for what he was going to do. He put towels down on the furry rug to cover it. Then took some things from a special cupboard they had. The fire was burning evenly but he lit some candles as well. There was no other light and the room glowed warmly. He came to her, and removed the cover-up tied to her waist and then her bikini. He pulled her to the mirror of their dresser. Standing behind her, he removed his shorts then pulled her against him, still facing the mirror. They gazed at each other through their reflections. He reached for a bottle of oil he had removed from the cupboard and pouring it in his hand he massaged it onto her breasts. Her breath caught at the feel and look of his hands on her, sensually teasing oil onto her nipples. His eyes watched in the mirrored candle light. He was so gorgeous taking in her reactions, her beauty and the sight of her now shiny body under his hands.

He turned her then, he still facing the mirror, she with her back to it. He put some more oil in his hand and mentally asked her to watch over her shoulder. She turned her head to the side as far as she could and with one eye she could see his hands on her butt, rubbing oil onto her, gripping her, his big hands able to cup her, sliding under her and then upwards. She stopped watching and leaned her forehead against his chest and let the feeling of it take her away. He rhythmically let his hands slide down, his fingers coming so close to her where she wanted them, then sliding back up. His erection was hard against her belly now. His eyes were on her in the mirror, watching his own hands on her perfect butt. He let out a quiet moan.

He released her and took her hand again adding some oil and then placed it on his erection. "Make me slippery baby," he said. He softly looked in her eyes now. He was so gorgeous right now she thought she was going to come just looking at his face. Sensing her quaking, he placed her hand on him, and she took a breath in and began smoothing the oil over his hardness, up his lower belly and around over his butt, feeling him everywhere with her hands. "Ok," he said. "Now turn around." She obeyed and faced the mirror with him once again. They were shiny and glowing in the candle light. He looked wild and sexy, like he was about to devour her and she looked vulnerable but cat like and exotic at the same time.

"Watch, baby," he said. He pulled her leg back, exposing her to herself in the mirror. "This is what I see, sweetheart," he said. "Do you see what this would do to me?" She gasped as his fingers slid between her openness and slightly into her. She could see herself; wet and pink and moaned as she watched his fingers enter her. He watched her eyes in the reflection. "Does it make you want to come when you see this angel? It always makes 'me' want to come and it makes me want to do things to you and it makes me want every inch of you and it makes me want to drive myself into you and never stop." He moaned to her now, his eyes tearing through her in the mirror. "Watch what you do to me now." He pushed himself into her from behind and she watched as he moved inside her. "Look at me baby," he said.

He closed his eyes and drove himself hard into her, holding there. In seconds his orgasm overtook him and he opened his eyes so she could see him. She could see his pleasure, his emotion, his love, his pain, his needs and his vulnerability, all at once as he let her look right into him. His dark eyes were deep moist pools now as his orgasm enveloped him and finally he closed them slowly, catching his breath, leaning his cheek against her hair.

She kept her eyes on him, as he released her leg. He kissed her shoulder as her tears began to slip down her cheeks. "Baby," she said. "You are the most amazing thing." She turned to him now and he took her in his arms and pulled her to the rug, laying her down and kissing her deeply. "Don't cry angel," he said. "I just love you so much there aren't words. I wanted you to see it inside me, feel how you feel to me." She had clung to him then. Their passion for each other an ever present thing, he needed her then, wanted to please her, felt vulnerable to her.

"Come for me now," he said. He made love to her in front of the fire, sweet and soft, hard and wanting, all at the same time. He had made her reach every plateau she had ever had, taking her there as many times as she needed.

After, as they slept entwined, she didn't normally dream but it seemed to be happening. The waterfall, and their love and then they were in camp. They were leaving the next day for HQ Munich. Sensei had come to their bed, after they were asleep, which was unusual and was talking to them. He spoke quietly to them.

"I have something for you Dragon," he had said. His voice was like a whisper now in her dream. "Before we leave here, I must give you this." He had placed a beautiful jade ring in Dragon's hand. They looked at him wondering and waiting. "I have had a love like yours. I met her when she would come to water the plants at the monastery. People would come to visit the shrine but never anyone like her. I would wait for her every day and see her. She was beautiful," he said. Raven had crawled into Dragon's arms, tears flowing, knowing.

"We became one, like you are; she was my life and my love," he said. "I had to leave the monastery to be with her, and I did. We were to be together forever, I thought my life was perfect." He had paused for a long time, trying to get his breath and his composure, as Raven cried uncontrollably on Dragons chest. "She died, of cancer. A disease I couldn't cure, a disease I couldn't fix," he said. Sadly he told them. He had hung his head in the grief of it.

"I had time with her for three and a half years and I loved her with all my heart. There will never be another. That's why I understand you and why we are together now. It is what she would have wanted for me." Raven had fallen to pieces, crying desperately into

Dragon's chest. He gripped her tightly, his own tears falling now, for Sensei and for her. "No, No please Papa," she had cried. "Don't tell me this is your life, alone. How do you go on without her?"

"Because I have a reason to and a purpose to fulfill, please, you must not let your heart break for me. She is here with me all the time. I'm sorry to have kept this from you; I just didn't want you to hurt for me. I want you to have the ring, it was ours and now it would make me happy if it could be yours. Come Raven and hold my hand now," he said. He tried to relieve her pain.

He grasped her hand and held it to his chest as she wept. Sensei relaxed and using all his strength he calmed her, pulling her into him, he let her 'see' through him, what he felt, for the first time. Raven relaxed and lay against him, tears still falling from her eyes. Dragon held her other hand and together they were in his world. Sensei brought his own true love to them in the light, a vision of sweetness and beauty. She was Mariko, long dark raven hair, tiny and beautiful. It was like a warm feeling falling over them, reminding them of their own love.

Raven awoke gasping, startling Dragon awake. "Baby, I'm here, baby hold on to me I'm here, what's the matter angel?" he said. She clung to him, her tears wet on his chest. It had come to him then as she calmed and he held her close, wondering about it. Sensei's story had come back to her in a dream.

"Baby," he said. "It's ok you don't have to worry about Papa, you know that."

She seemed dazed and hid into his body, not knowing what she felt. She eyed the ring on her finger that had been there since that day. He stroked her hair and kissed her forehead, sending her gently back to sleep.

In the morning, Dragon awoke, feeling as if it had all been a dream himself. Sensei had brought the Tea. Raven still slept peacefully. He moved her to lie on her stomach, face to the side and he pulled her hair away. As he did that, a feeling crept into him and he turned to face Sensei, who was looking straight into him. "There's a mission Kai Li, in Mexico," he said. They drank tea and did not speak of it again at that time.

CHAPTER TEN

MEXICO

" My dear it is that time again," Sensei said. Mariko had died of ovarian cancer and Sensei had always wondered if he had detected it sooner she would have survived. Now he was compulsive about it with Raven. Dragon sat beside her and watched Sensei carry out his inspection of her, used to the ritual.

He routinely conducted a pelvic exam now paranoid about losing her to the disease. He examined her outer areas, gently holding her apart. His touch was gentle and almost imperceptible to her. "Ok," Sensei said. He seemed satisfied once again that she was perfectly healthy. "I hope you are doing what I showed you to do Dragon," Sensei said. "She isn't built for someone your size." "Yes Sensei," Dragon said. "Papa, stop please," Raven said. She was laughing now, like she always did. "Well, you can't put something ten inches into a space meant for something five, without properly preparing," Sensei explained. It was for the hundredth time. Dragon rolled his eyes, for the hundredth time. "Your mixed blood has given you a pleasurable gift, but you must use it correctly." Sensei went on like he had never had this conversation before. "Yes, Sensei," Dragon said.

The ritual was nearly complete as Sensei finished the internal examination and Raven was now in a very playful mood, their banter amusing her to no end. Sensei had then administered her hormone shot in her left butt cheek and she let out a little cry at the sting of it, just to tease him. He patted her little butt softly.

"It's a small price to pay for your pleasure. Without this, you would likely be pregnant simply at the sight of him," he said. She smiled coyly at Sensei and crawled into Dragon, reaching under the duvet and sliding her hand along him. Sensei shook his head at her.

"Papa," she said. She looked in his eyes, more seriously now. "You shouldn't worry so much that I will get, um, you know, like Mariko." "I know," Sensei said. "But there was a long time that I did not forgive myself for not paying enough attention to her this way. I blamed myself. I am over that now, but I can take care of you this way now." She smiled warmly at him. "I like that you take care of me, Papa." "Well good then, because I'm not going to stop," he said.

They drank their tea and talked, avoiding the Mexico thing. Chekov would take care of that soon enough. They had all been so happy over the last 18 months. Dragon was around 25 years old now, his exact birth date not known, and Raven about 23. They didn't acknowledge birthdates anyway; it was one of those things that didn't matter.

"I'm sorry about my dream, Papa," Raven said. She brought up the subject, knowing he would have 'seen' it anyway. "It's OK my dear," Sensei said. "I just hope you are not subconsciously hurting for me." Raven looked inwardly. "I think it was just something about the waterfall," she said. He nodded and got up to leave, pausing. "Take as long as you like this morning, Sarge and Wax may be awhile."

Dragon let her see into him that there was a mission of some sort, to Mexico. "Did Sensei tell you about it?" she asked. "No, but I have a feeling there's a good and a bad. Let's wait and see, because right now…" he rolled on top of her. "I need to be sure you are ready," he said.

"Don't be smart now Mr. Li, you need to do your job," she said. "Well then Mrs. Li, if it is 'ready' you want to be then I know exactly what you need." "I just want you baby," she said. "Oh you're going to want me, and want me bad," he said.

He put two fingers inside her and began his assault on her. It felt like heaven to her, his fingers stroking her most sensitive spots that he knew all about, making her crazy with his ability to bring her to her limits. He could feel her orgasm threatening, so he withdrew his touch.

She gasped. "No baby, please I was just about there." He smiled, turning her over onto her tummy and moving behind her now. "Face down, on your knees baby," he said. She obeyed and, on her knees, as far apart as they could be, her face on the duvet she opened herself to him, begging him now to take her.

"Now I can see if you are ready baby," he said. He ran his thumb over her vagina. She gasped, absolutely crazy now, she begged him again. "Please baby, make me come I'm so close, Please." "I don't know," he said. Taking both thumbs he spread her open, exposing her. She was beyond ready, a creamy wetness dripping from her. He took a sharp breath in. "You should see this." He leaned in and licked her sweetness with his tongue, making her cry out and arch into his lips.

She was begging him again. "Please let me come, don't do this to me baby, I want you." He put a kiss on her and sat back, still sliding his thumb through her wetness. "Do you think you want me enough yet?" he asked. "Do you think you are ready?" She moaned as he held her apart, watching her vagina contract with every tease he gave her. "I think you want me now baby, maybe just a bit?" he said. She was just moaning then as he positioned himself behind her. "I need to fuck you," he said.

Grasping her hips he slid into her hard and full making her cry out. The feeling of it was mind blowing for both of them. He gasped, feeling her tightness gripping him, her wetness allowing him, his size dominating her. He held her hips and drove into her again and again, building his orgasm, watching as he sunk inside her, all of him, coated in her wetness. She arched her back, moaning. "Fuck me, fuck me, please baby, and don't stop. Make me come."

He was waiting for her now and as she reached her turning point, he finished it. She cried out to him as her orgasm went through her, with him buried all the way in her, his come filling her with its heat. She flattened out on the bed under him and he lay over her, inside her, moving slowly to calm them from it.

They softened into an embrace, as he withdrew from her, rolling onto his back and pulling her into his side, still breathing heavily.

She coiled over him, pressing herself against his hip, caressing his chest, kissing his neck. She smoothed his hair back and let her lips softly fall onto his. She kissed him sweetly, biting his lower lip gently, telling him with her mind how much she desired him, how sexy he is and how crazy he makes her.

Seeing as they had extra time he responded by taking them everywhere they could go and as many times as he could.

He had finally led her to the shower. They dried off in fluffy towels and he smoothed and brushed out her hair, braiding it down her back. He gave her a tiny red bikini with gold colored pieces at the hips and one in the middle of the top, which tied behind her neck and clasped at the back. She put little white shorts over the bottoms and he thought she looked adorable.

He pulled on black board shorts with a white Hawaiian flower on the left front leg and pulled on a tight white T shirt with a V neck. She brushed his hair for him and tied the top section back from his forehead with a hair tie, leaving the bottom section hanging loosely over his shoulders.

They went out to the patio, hand in hand to find Sensei sitting. Wax and Sarge lay like dead carcasses on the chaise lounges. Sarge had dark glasses on and appeared to be comatose. Wax looked up at them as they approached. "Hey baby girl," he said. He smiled to her, very 'Hollywood'. "You have that 'well fucked before lunch' look that always suits you." She beamed at him. "Thanks Waxy, I am quite well fucked, as a matter of fact. You look fairly shitty though, sorry," she said. "Well, I happen to be really extra fucked, but not the same way as you unfortunately," Wax said.

Dragon grinned at him, shaking his head. "Man do you remember falling out of the Zodiac on the beach?" "No, Really?" he said. "Really really," Dragon said. "Shit fuck," Wax said. "Well you better recover man because as I recall, you and Sarge are supposed to get fucked the right way tonight," Dragon said. Dragon then noticed Sarge. "What's with him?"

Sensei eyed Dragon and sighed. "What do you think is 'with' him?" he said. "Likely second stage alcohol poisoning, if I was to be clinical."

They all looked at Sarge then. "Fuck off all of you, I'm fine," he growled. Raven couldn't resist now and going to him climbed on top of him, straddling his hips. Tipping his dark shades up so she could see his eyes, she teased him. "Pretty grumpy, for someone who's 'fine'". He pulled the glasses back down and sighed in resignation, unable to fend her off. "Come on Sarge, you have to perform tonight," she said. It was making them all laugh now as she motioned her hips on him, imitating sex. "You remember how to do it, don't you?" "Get the fuck off me or I will show you what I've forgotten that you haven't even heard of," he said. "Baby?" she said. "Did you hear that? Sarge is going to fuck me some crazy Sarge way we've never heard of."

They were all laughing now, except Sarge and Sensei had heard enough. "Children, please, your inappropriateness never ceases to amaze me. Raven, behave before Kona sees you. He already thinks you're fucking them all, as it is," Sensei said. He shocked them into more laughter with his own language now.

She put a fake pout on her face and climbed off Sarge. "So what if I am. I can fuck whoever I want," she said. Dragon eyed her. "Is that so Mrs. Li?" he said. "Do I need to drag you back in that room and remind you of exactly who it is that you fuck?" She grinned and circled his waist pulling her into him. "Mmmm, that would be nice." They were all distracted then by Chekov's summons from the screens inside. "Thank god," muttered Sensei, as they all stood and went to receive his call.

Chekov faced them, looking his usual self, pale, spectacled and ever serious. "Hello, everyone," he said. "I see you had quite the day yesterday." They all glanced at each other, wondering what he knew. "Spare me Chekov," Dragon said. "You can lurk all you want if that's what get's you off, but we don't need your opinion." Chekov kept at his screens, not bothering to look at Dragon. "I have quite an opinion Dragon, especially of these," he said. In an instant the photos of them at the waterfall appeared across the other screens. Before anyone could react Dragon was quick in his anger. "Chekov, you're such a fucking dick. You jerk off to thoughts of my wife anyway, now you have real pictures to go along with your fantasies. Have you cropped me out of them yet and added your face?" He glared into the screen at Chekov. Chekov just smirked and shrugged. "Think what you like Dragon, but I think they are quite touching, of both of you."

"Where are you going with this Chekov?" Sensei said. "No-where, I'm being candid. They are nice shots, well done Sergeant Willis. You have a gift," Chekov said. Dragon hissed slightly under his breath and turned away for a moment. Chekov was odd enough as it was, but 'nice' Chekov brought a slight nauseous feeling to him. "Get on with it Chekov, before I puke," he said.

Unfazed, Chekov looked almost amused. "Speaking of vomit, how are you today Sergeant Willis?" Sarge was in no mood for this and looking at the others quickly reacted. "I'll show you Chekov. Do you want to know how I am? Here, see for yourself."

He moved in a flash and knelt up on the computer table, grasping himself through his shorts, gripping the length of him through the fabric so the outline of his penis was visible, which was semi erect from Raven grinding into it. He shoved it into the camera lens at the top of the screen. They all burst out laughing, doubled over, and falling away. Raven thought she was going to pee her pants. Sensei blanched but couldn't help laughing as Chekov wheeled back from his screen in his chair, visibly abhorred. The image of Sarge would have filled his screen right in front of his face.

"There Chekov," Sarge said. He was thrusting his hips into the camera. "See, I'm eight inches of fucking great." And with that he climbed off the table, muttering 'fucking asshole' under his breath.

Dragon and Wax were laughing out of control now. "Fuck Sarge," Wax said. "That was hilarious." Dragon tried to stop laughing but the sight of Chekov's face as he rolled backwards was too much. "What's the matter Chekov, Sarge was just showing you what you look like to us," he said. And with that they all started up again. Chekov had moved back into focus now, visibly trying to regain his composure. "Point taken…Yes very funny, whatever," he said. "If I could get your attention back please, you've had enough fun and I have a profile." "Do you have a hard on?" Sarge said. "No," Chekov said. He was shaking his head, wanting to escape somewhere. "You mean not anymore," Dragon said.

Chekov looked at Dragon, with his best 'how do I tolerate morons like you' look, making Dragon smile at him with his 'because you have to and I can' look. Sighing defeat, Chekov took a deep breath and continued.

"Download the profile later, I have sent you the link. Basically you are to travel to Mexico via Dream Weaver and make contact with this man." A new image appeared on the other screen and Chekov continued. "Juan Carlos Guerrera. He is a higher up general in the cartel there. This isn't about drugs of course, but prostitution, child prostitution. He is charge of that end of their business. Befriend him anyway you see fit Dragon, find out what he has going on. We haven't been able to get intelligence on their operation, it's too tight. You need to get inside. Ultimately you will eliminate him and anyone else involved. He has a weakness. Besides young girls, he's a heroin junky. Functioning but addicted. The details are in the download, but when you arrive at the marina in Mexico you will be moored next to him. He lives on his boat. The rest is up to you. Plan to be away from Hawaii indefinitely. Are there any questions?" Chekov said. "Time?" Dragon asked. "Make your preparations and go," Chekov said. "And if that is all, have a good day." The screen went black.

They all stood silently now, finally Raven turned to Sensei, now knowing what the 'bad' was. "You are not coming with us are you," she said. She looked into his eyes, her own filling with tears. He looked wrenched to see her hurt, "No, little one, I am not," he said. "But why, Papa?" She asked the question but she knew the answer. "I can't leave here just now; someone has to oversee the children. You know that," he said. He brushed tears from her cheeks. "Besides, you are all grown up now and don't need me with you all the time. All of you will be fine, and I will be fine and sooner or later you will be back."

Sarge, who had been quiet since his banter with Chekov, pulled her braid. "Come on sexy, you better get me laid tonight or you're going to be on a boat with me for weeks and well I don't know," he said. He let her have his whitest California smile and honest ocean blue eyes. She laughed now, letting go of Dragon and playfully shoving Sarge away. "You better not try it, because you're not getting any of your page 423 shit." She teased him back, referring to the section of the Kama Sutra that focused on group sex. With that they went back to the patio and the sun.

"That was some funny fucking shit man," Wax said. Sarge just tipped his shades back over his eyes and fell back onto the chaise. "No kidding," Dragon said. "Fucking Chekov just about fainted. Can you imagine how that would have looked to him right in his face?" They all laughed about it again.

"That will be recorded, you realize," Sensei said. "We can only hope the General won't see it." "How did he get the pictures Papa?" Raven asked. "He is linked to all our systems, I would imagine when Sarge downloaded them to the files he saw them then. Oh, and Raven, there is a surprise for you in Mexico, call it another 'wedding gift' from the General," Sensei said. "Can we look at the profile now? I'm curious," Raven said. "Sure," Sensei said. He went to get a laptop.

The profile consisted of travel instructions, regarding how to sail from Hawaii to Mexico. Weather charts and predictions, routes and coast guard regulations. They would have a bit of studying to do. There were pictures of the marinas they would come to, hotels they were to stay in and vehicles they would drive. Also, there was a beautiful Hacienda at their final destination. Sensei explained that it was leased by DLI in David Li's name and they would live there, while the Dream Weaver was moored next to their target.

It looked beautiful and exciting, making Raven feel somewhat better. She didn't care so much for nice things, as long as she was with Dragon, but it looked like a new adventure for them all to share.

After dinner, they had sat by the pool and around 8 pm decided to head to town to their favorite bar, Bobby's, a local hangout. Usually they just went for lunch to sit by the ocean, watch surfers and have a beer, but they had a specific mission on this night, which they kept joking about.

They didn't make a habit of going out much as the image of David Li was such that they were elusive and selective as to where and when they went anywhere. Everyone knew who they were and that they lived on the island, rumor having, that they preferred their privacy, which was true. In the end they had a fun night, a few beers, a few dances, and a few girls for Wax and Sarge.

Dragon had pulled Raven out and headed for home, leaving them in the charming hands of two very cute tourist girls. On the drive home they had messed up the Lamborghini and he had carried her to bed, messing up the room as well. Mexico was on the horizon and they wanted to have a good farewell.

The morning sun was warm and fabulous and tingled Raven's skin as they sat by the pool after breakfast, waiting for Sarge and Wax to return from the night at Bobby's. She reached for sunscreen and began smoothing it on her arms, as Dragon eyed her. She had a tiny bright pink bikini on that tied with strings at the hips as well as the neck and back. Her hair was loose and tendrils of it blew gently about her face in the breezy morning. Dark sunglasses protected her green eyes from the sun.

He rose and came to sit at the foot of her chaise, unable to keep his hands off her; he loved to put sunscreen on her. Sensei was waiting for Kona to discuss their preparations but he was not there yet, so Dragon undid her top at the neck, exposing her breasts. He then enjoyed every second of smoothing sunscreen on her chest.

"Those parts are covered up you know," she said. He was massaging it into her nipples. "Not right now," he answered comically. His cuteness made her smile at him.

He loved her breasts, their firmness and size perfectly suited her tiny frame, sexy but not overly so, in a way that they were the first things you would notice about her. She was athletic and had a physique like a gymnast, only with nice breasts, he thought. She took in his erection, straining the front of his shorts now, as he re-tied the string of her top. She eyed Sensei approaching them with Kona.

Dragon, moved her to sit between his legs on the chaise, to hide his shorts which were about to rip. He leaned back and she leaned against him successfully covering him until he could compose himself. Sensei sent him a disapproving grunt in his mind and something about using restraint.

Sensei and Kona sat and were about to begin the conversation when Wax and Sarge came through the front door. Seeing Kona there, they used discretion and simply said hello and sat. Raven eyed Sarge using all her will power to not bug him. It would wait until they were done.

Dragon gently let his fingers graze her jaw line and brush her lips distracting her. She took his hand and kissed the back of it, eyeing his fingers and remembering what they had done to her earlier, causing her tummy muscles to clench. Sensing her, he responded silently, 'Baby, just wait.'

They discussed the options for the journey and decided they would head to Honolulu to a Marina there, where Kona knew the manager. There was a competent mechanic who would perform a service check on the engines and systems. They would refuel then depart Honolulu Harbor for San Diego California. That would take about 5 days at sea, for which they would require supplies.

As far as Kona knew they were going on a trip in the yacht for something to do, it was after all what the rich would do, not having to work for a living. Sensei had walked Kona to the door, finalizing his duties. He was to stock the food and water for them and they would leave in the morning, the weather forecasts clear for the next number of days. Closing the door, he then went to the computer table and summoned Chekov.

They all joined him as Chekov's image glowed in the room. "We will be arriving at this San Diego Marina in about 6 days," Dragon said. "I have made arrangements there for you," Chekov said. Immediately images of the Marina appeared on the two other screens. "There is a five star hotel attached to it and I will book you a Suite for two nights. It will be expected that you will want off the boat and also you should be seen in the restaurants and bars, taking in night life and such." Dragon grunted his disapproval of this part of it, but knew it was part of the cover.

"I will see to it that appropriate wardrobe is available there, as well," Chekov said. "Depart after you've restocked and refueled and proceed south to Puerto Vallarta Marina. It will take approximately 2 days if you keep it to 15 knots. They will be expecting you and you will be escorted to the mooring next to the target. Vehicles will be waiting to take you to the Hacienda. Dragon you will figure out how to meet Mr. Guerrara."

Dragon nodded, removing his sunglasses and looked at Chekov. "I already have a pretty good idea of how I'm going to do that. According to your profile Chekov, Juan Carlos is a heroin junky pedophile. I'm assuming he prefers females, so he will enjoy my wife. And what my wife enjoys is watching me, with younger girls. And me being the loving husband that I am will see to it her fantasies are realized. We are going to have a lot in common with our new friend."

"Excellent idea, Dragon, and it won't matter if he thinks the famous David Li and his wife are sexual predators like him, because he will be dead," Chekov said. He grinned at the plan. Dragon nodded to him. "Exactly, and just for the fun of it, I'm going to kill him myself by injecting him with a nice overdose of his favorite poison," Dragon said. "I'll arrange the delivery of that for you; to the Marina I would think. I'll use a delivery company and disguise it as something else," Chekov said. "It sounds as though a successful mission is in the offing and I look forward to watching you execute this. The General will be pleased I'm sure. He is away at the moment, but I will forward him this feed and he can hear it from you himself." "Sure," Dragon said.

"One last thing," Chekov said. "Keep in mind that people are watching you, and media will be present likely when you arrive in San Diego, especially as California is huge on celebrities. Take it in stride please. And be sure to do regular bug scans on the yacht and your vehicles and hotel rooms. Use the current passports Sensei has and take as many weapons as you can manage discreetly. The coast guard may approach you but it is unlikely they would come aboard, but if they do I will distract them somehow with a fake emergency somewhere," Chekov said. "Is there anything else?"

"No!" Raven said, "We have to go now Chekov because Wax and Sarge got laid last night and I have to hear all about it." "Congratulations," Chekov said. The screens went black.

"You brat," Sarge said. "You just can't wait to piss me off now, can you? I'm not going to tell you anything, how's that." "Oh yes you are," she said. She jumped on his back. "Get off me," he said. He stumbled out to the pool as she pulled his hair. "You're going for a swim now. And I'm not talking so give it up." He proceeded to fall with her attached to him into the deep end of the pool.

Dragon and Wax and Sensei had followed them outside, amused as usual by their antics. Dragon then shoved Wax in on top of them, catching him off guard, which started a huge brawl between them, ending with them wrestling on the lawn until they had to stop because they had started laughing and had no strength left.

The morning had passed, and Sensei had prepared lunch, which they ate on the patio. "You all need a workout after this," he said. They would not have the same facilities on the yacht for their workouts. Reading his thoughts, Raven went to him, hugging him. "Papa, you know I'm going to cry my eyes out tomorrow when we leave." "Yes my dear, and so will I, but until then, you will allow me to boss you around and take care of you ok?" he said. He kissed her forehead, and she followed him down the hallway to the gym.

After working out together, Dragon and Raven had spent a wonderful afternoon making a mess of each other all over the Ferrari and all over the island, as they had decided to go for a drive and have some fun before they had to leave.

Sarge was just retrieving beers from the fridge when they came through the front door. "Hey buddy," he said. "Want a beer?" "Absolutely," Dragon said. Raven went to help Sarge, and with a free hand he lifted her sundress at the back, checking out her naked butt.

"I thought so," he said. She flashed him a fake angry glare. "Hey, behave Sergeant Willis," she said. "Give me a minute Ok babe," she said to Dragon. "I need to change so Sergeant Willis can relax." "Yes you do," he said. He stood watching her little butt as she retreated to the bedroom to put on a bikini.

"Cheers," Dragon said. He touched his beer to Sarge and Wax's. "How'd it go with the, um supplies?" He was referring to the weapons they planned to bring along. "Good," Wax said. "Everything's on board. Kona's been stocking the freezers all afternoon, we should be ready I think."

Raven reappeared in the navy blue and Hawaiian flowered bikini Dragon had figured was his favorite. Sarge eyed her in it and stepping next to her, put his arm around her and touched his cold beer to her cleavage. She squirmed away from him, scolding him.

"Sarge what the hell is the matter with you, get your hands off me. I thought after last night you would be stable for awhile," she said. He laughed to her. "You're just so cute when you're pissed at me, I can't resist." "Well, resist, because in a minute I'm going to make you wish you didn't have a dick," she said.

He knew what that meant. Sometimes when they were having one of their little fights she would tease him with dirty talk, trying to make him horny. Dragon and Waxy would laugh and bug him about not having control of it, even though any one of them would have succumbed to her.

"Ok you. We don't need a hornier than usual Sarge and you need to behave yourself," Dragon said. "He started it," she said.

Sensei gave Sarge his warning look and they all moved to the patio to sit and enjoy their drinks, leaving Marietta to start dinner, sparing her from their strange behavior.

Raven eyed Sarge, thinking he was adorable and hoped that the girl from last night appreciated having him in her bed. She knew Sarge would be a sweet lover and deserved to find someone to share that with.

Dragon caught her thoughts and smiled to her, he liked that she cared so much for Sarge and Wax. It made them who they were together. She sat between his legs, leaning back on him as he circled her in his arms letting his left hand rest on her flat tummy, sipping his beer with the other. It was lovely and hot and breezy as they sat catching the late sun. This would be their final night here for awhile and none of them wanted to talk about it.

CHAPTER ELEVEN

DREAM WEAVER

In the morning, Sensei had arrived at 6 am with tea, waking Dragon alone first. "I want you to be careful with these people son," Sensei said. "I will Papa," Dragon said. "I'll try to avoid reminders, but it may be hard considering the nature of the mission." "Yes. Keep your mind as clear as you can and take time to refocus if you have any flashbacks, no matter how slight," Sensei said.

Sending them off alone weighed on him. Dragon's Post Traumatic Stress Disorder concerned him constantly and he needed managing in order for him to be the Operative that he was.

"Wake her now please," Sensei said. She responded to his mouth on hers, crawling into his warm body. "Good morning baby," he said. She smiled at them both and sat up taking tea from Sensei. "Papa, please don't worry about us, I will look after us while we are away from you," she said.

She had cried in Dragon's arms that night for what seemed like forever and he had soothed her the best way he knew how, by making love to her slowly and softly on the furry rug in front of the fire, wanting to hold on to their last night there for as long as possible. She had fallen into his sensual trance eventually, letting him take her over the edge as many times as he could, her heart and her body giving in to him again and again, until she had been softly asleep in his arms. He had carried her to bed.

On the beach, Kona was preparing to take them to the Dream Weaver, and Raven lay in Sensei's arms. Tears ran silently down his handsome face as he held her. Dragon gently pulled her from his hold and embracing him himself, his eyes filled. "Keep in touch," was all he managed. Sensei hugged Wax and Sarge respectively, telling them to be careful and stick together. And they left.

Later, after making port in Honolulu they set out for San Diego. Sarge set the engines for 20 knots and they were at sea. The Dream Weaver was a dream and it had everything they needed to be comfortable and they settled in for five days aboard her. The GPS was set and they sailed on auto pilot, away from the islands out into the Pacific Ocean. The yacht was magnificent as it surged through the ocean waters taking them where they needed to go. The weather forecast was good and they expected no problems on the journey.

Together they sat on the upper bridge moving on to their destination, the first mission in almost two years. They had looked amongst themselves and agreed, drinks were in order. Sarge and Raven climbed down into the main cabin and retrieved beers and Champagne. The warm wind blowing their hair, the sun on their skin, they drank to their futures. The ocean was blue around them and the Dream Weaver secured them in warmth and serenity. The open ocean was beautiful but empty and daunting at the same time. They passed the first day and Dragon had taken first watch.

They had all come a long way from their unfortunate backgrounds, to this. In the dark, as they moved forward through the sea, Dragon thought back on it. Raven was asleep under a soft blanket beside him as the yacht powered on through the surf, through the night. Dragon drifted, thinking of his life now, the love he had and the commitment he had. He felt he owed his life, his happiness and his freedom to Sensei and the General. Even though it had been a nightmare, he felt now that he wouldn't change it if he could. It had made him who he was and he liked who he was. At 5 am Wax relieved him and he carried Raven to their cabin. He let her sleep even though he wanted her badly and consoled himself by hugging her soft body tightly to him, kissing her face and finally sleeping himself. The dream came back to haunt him then, unbidden and unwelcome.

Wanting to die he had finally cried. They had taken everything from him and he was helpless. They could hurt him when they wanted and he had no way to stop them. His will was failing him now. He wanted to die and make it stop. He was 13, which was when they came with the needle. They had broken him finally, sending him into oblivion with the drug. It was a way to control him and it had worked. He had taken the abuse and the beatings, for as long as he could remember. He thought for awhile that he was being punished for something. He had fought back always, but that was just another nightmare for another time. Now, tied to a beam by his wrists above his head, he had protected his face. When he regained consciousness, he was crumpled in the dirt. He was hurting everywhere and bleeding from another torturous rape, blood running down his inner thighs. He had hung from his wrists until he had passed out, he guessed. Someone must have let him down.

The dream was sometimes the same and sometimes different, always unpleasant visions and images. Sometimes he would only see scenes and sometimes entire years of events.

Raven had awoken as his distress came to her mind and she had pulled him free, drawing him to the warmth of her light. He emerged sweating and breathing, but shaking as if he was cold. She held his face to her breasts gripping handfuls of his hair whispering to him to calm him. He let her hold him, slowly feeling her warmth around him. The engines droned in the background bringing him back to where he was. A tear fell from his eyes as he remembered what he once was.

She kissed his face and held him to her, loving him. She knew that he had secrets and things he held inside that haunted him. He sat on the side of the bed and she let her hand caress the dragon on his back as he composed himself.

"Baby, lay with me, I know what you need," she said. He turned to look at her, his eyes soft, his heart vulnerable and it crushed her to think that anyone had actually ever hurt him.

He crawled to lie beside her and she covered him with the blanket. "Just love me baby," he whispered. Kissing him deeply, she guided him into her and enveloped him in her warmth and love, bringing him back to her.

His need for her was intense and it would take him numerous times before he would be able to sleep peacefully. She had lain under him letting him release his demons as much as he needed. In the end, he had exhausted himself, falling beside her, a light sweat coating him, his hair everywhere.

She had taken a warm facecloth and cleaned his face, pulling his hair back for him and wiping the sweat from his brow and neck. She ignored the discomfort she was in as a result of his use of her.

They slept for three hours and Dragon woke them, not wanting to miss the day. He turned on the shower to warm the water and went to her as she lay folded in the blankets still. Kissing down her belly he wanted to know if he had been too rough on her.

He was not entirely satisfied with her condition. Sensei's reminding words echoed in his mind. He picked her up and carried her to the shower. It was tiny by their standards now, but roomy enough for them both, which was all they cared about. The warm water felt wonderful and washed away the tension in Dragon's neck he was sometimes left with after a bad dream. They soaped each other clean from head to toe and wrapping her in a big white beach towel he laid her beside him on the bed.

He took her fingers and kissed them, gently licking one with his soft tongue. "This is all you are going to get today I think baby," he said. She raised her eyebrows at him, pretending to look shocked. "I can't survive all day with only your tongue," she said. "Yes you can, and you will, and I promise you, I will make it very nice for you," he said. He kissed her neck, letting his fingertips brush her nipples. "You were nice to me last night and I'm going to be nice to you now," he said. He pulled open her towel. She moaned softly as he sucked each nipple, biting her gently, making them hard. He held her breasts, kissing them, tasting them, teasing her with his tongue.

"You know I can make you crazy just with my tongue, don't you?" he said. "Yes baby, kiss me everywhere." She moaned now, his sensual mouth pushing her desire for him. She had spread her legs apart now, wanting him lower.

Responding, he moved down. Her knees were flat on the bed and he turned her hips upward, making her fully open to him. He kissed the insides of her thighs, teasing her further as she begged him with her hands, pulling his hair, wanting his mouth on her.

"Baby, I know what you want and I know how to give it to you," he said. He finally let his lips reach her nerve endings.

He moaned now, feeling like he might come just from doing it to her. He pushed his hard-on into the bed as he lay against it, suddenly urgently needing his own release.

He let up on her as she climaxed and holding her apart he watched her contractions hit her, pressing his tongue inside her at the end to finish her off. She was perfect for him every time, lying squirming and moaning and completely undone because of him. He moved to his knees and taking himself in his hand, his muscles flexing he brought himself there, coming hotly onto her.

He fell next to her breathing hard, his lips still wet from her. She turned to him and taking him in her hand she squeezed upwards to the tip, licking the bead of come that leaked from him. Then she licked his lips, kissing her taste from his mouth.

"I watched you come, did it feel nice?" he asked. He smiled to her between her kisses. "Yes baby, I love your tongue on me and you did make it very nice for me," she said.

The orgasms he gave her from oral sex were different than the vaginal ones she had from him being inside her. They were acute and intense in different ways, having been achieved by different techniques. He knew the finesse lay in working her to it at a certain pace, sustaining it with the right pressure in the right place, and backing off at the right time. He had perfected this with her, understanding her body and its reactions, knowing exactly where she was in the process.

He ran his fingers in the come he had left on her. "Sorry I made a mess of you angel. I needed to let go," he said. She smiled at him, brushing his cheek with her hand. "Poor baby, next time, we can do it together," she said.

He raised an eyebrow at her, thinking that was a good idea. They hadn't used that position in a long time for some reason. The challenge was being able to come at the same time and it was actually intense because of the focus it took to manage your own orgasm at the same time as being tuned in to the one you were providing.

"Well I will look forward to that," he said. "But we need to get up now, I told Sarge and Waxy 10 am for Yoga."

They made their way to the main deck; Wax had some fruit for them and tea. Sarge was sitting cross legged reading the GPS manual. They discussed their schedule for night watch, deciding to keep them to 3 hour periods each, starting at mid-night, so none of them would lose a whole night of sleep like Dragon just did. They would stay up together until 12 am then Sarge would watch until 3 am, Wax until 6 am, and Dragon until 9am and Raven would have breakfast for them all. They figured it would work best. Finishing their food, they relaxed into an hour of Yoga.

Dragon led them, in the absence of Sensei, and he pushed them to the limits of their flexibility and strength, taking a hand standing pose and letting his legs flex as far apart as possible and holding it. Incorporating balance and strength he then lowered to his forearms, bringing his legs together and bending at the knees, he flexed his back, bringing his toes toward the dragon. The difficulty was extreme but they had all completed this many times, Raven having no difficulty whatsoever, with her tiny flexible frame. It was far harder for the large framed men. They followed him, making it look effortless and graceful even. After, they stretched and breathed and completed their routine. They had been doing this together for many years, as Sensei had insisted they become proficient in the art, for spiritual and psychological reasons. They were kind of addicted to it now and tried to start every day they could that way. They could only do it on the boat when the surf was calm, as balancing poses was nearly impossible if it was rolling at all.

Climbing to the flying bridge, they sat, enjoying the sun. Dragon and Sarge studied the navigation system and determined their position, satisfied that they were indeed cruising on the charted route. The ever turning radar scanned the sky for weather readings and they regularly checked the updates. Nothing was in the immediate forecast that concerned them and the radio had remained silent since Sarge had plotted their course to the US Coast Guard back in Honolulu. They likely wouldn't make any contact again until they re-entered US waters, approaching San Diego.

They appeared to have the vast Pacific to themselves. The Dream Weaver was steadily cutting the surf at 20 knots, even though she was capable of 32. Sarge had decidedly set her for 20, feeling that was pressure enough and based on his calculations would put them into Port during early evening of the fifth day, well before dark.

Raven chose sunbathing as the next activity and removed her bikini top. She lay on her tummy on the white padded cushioned seat, and Dragon rubbed sunscreen on her back for her, pulling her long thick braid out of the way.

"Why don't you take the bottom part off too?" Sarge said. "No tan lines then?" She eyed him and smirked. "You'd like that wouldn't you, if I got sunburn on my butt. Why don't you take your shorts off and fry your dick?" They all laughed. "You two better not start already," Waxy said. "It's not even lunch time, which reminds me baby girl, should I thaw something for dinner tonight?" Wax and Raven were in charge of cooking. "Ya Waxy, want me to come and look with you, see what there is?" she asked. Dragon had finished sun screening her and she sat up to go with Wax to the galley.

They decided on lobsters and rice and some greens Sensei had grown in his organic Hawaiian garden. They set the lobsters on some ice in the sink to thaw, then went back up to continue doing a whole lot of nothing. She lay back down, still topless and Dragon knew if she had it her way she would be naked.

She cared less about it, but he had told her she had to keep the bottom on or he would have a raging hard-on all day. He knew Sarge and Wax didn't look at her in a sexual way, but they were men and they were victims of their hormones and she was sexy, especially naked. It was bad enough he had a hard-on most of the time without it happening to them as well. He could at least do something about it when he wanted.

He admired her little butt now, demurely covered in a sweet pink fabric, tied with strings at the sides, a white Hawaiian flower on one cheek.

Seeing Dragon's gaze and expression, Wax teased him. "Easy man, we have five days to go here, if you don't cool down, she's not going to be able to walk by the time we hit San Diego."

Dragon knew Wax was right after the condition he had put her in last night already. But it was because of the dream and he had needed her to take him until he was over it. He eyed her back, reminding her of the position they were saving for later. She squirmed slightly feeling her inner thighs clench softly.

"Don't worry, its business as usual," Dragon said. "Well, what you call 'business as usual', I call Horny Fucking Asian," Sarge said. Dragon just smiled at him and nodded in agreement.

"Hey baby," Raven said. "If you're in the mood to piss someone off, you could summon Chekov, that's always fun." They all laughed, thinking about it. "I could, but you would have to put a top on, Chekov would blow his load on his keyboard if he saw you topless," Dragon said. She looked at him curiously. "He would not," she said. "Fucking right he would," Sarge said. "Can we do it just to see his reaction?" "No," Dragon said. "It would be fun to see his face, but he records everything and he would play it back in his room later, a thousand times."

As they mused over more ways to annoy Chekov, the laptop screen signaled them and Dragon signed in, allowing Sensei to appear before them. Dragon brought it to Raven knowing no one would be able to communicate until she had seen him first. She sat up and crossed her legs as he handed it to her.

"Thank you baby," she said. She gave him a big smile, her eyes happy and alive. "Papa!" She smiled to him, touching his face on the screen. "Hello child," he said. He eyed her lovingly. "How are you?" he asked. "We're fine Papa," she said. "It's beautiful and sunny and we just finished Yoga. I think we are heading in the right direction, and Sarge hasn't been too irritating, so far." She managed it all before having to get a breath. He smiled at her now. "That's good my dear, anything else?" He raised his left eyebrow to her.

Dragon sighed and reached for the laptop, with a resigned look. "I'm sure you are aware of 'what else' Papa," he said. Sarge and Wax eyed each other, having no clue what he meant. "And you are fine now?" Sensei said. "Yes I am. You know, it was the same as always and after awhile I was fine," Dragon said.

He left out how he had pushed her to the point of soreness in his need of her. With his mind Sensei let Dragon know that he knew about 'that' and it was of a slight concern to him. The fact that he was not aware he was doing it to her was his concern.

Dragon answered verbally. "I knew, I just needed her, um more than normal, I guess," he said. Sensei nodded to him. "Just be honest with yourself son because if you weren't aware and you were 'somewhere' you could really hurt her." "I understand Papa, it wasn't like that, but I know what you are worried about," Dragon said. "Good," Sensei said. He seemed to be satisfied for the moment.

Sensei had been in Dragon's head and there were things that made him cringe. There were no limits to what he had been made to do and if some of those things should happen to surface it would not be good. In particular he was worried about a dream Dragon had once before, having been in camp only a short time. Dragon was caught up in it like it was happening all over again. He was made to do things, pale and scared; there had been brutality beyond comprehension. It had come to an end when he had strangled the girl to death and the life had faded from her frightened eyes as his hands had closed on her neck. Later he had been beaten senseless for not making it last long enough. They wanted a 30 minute video.

He had dreamed of it in a subconscious state, common to PTSD sufferers. Sensei had awoken him from it, but he had remained in the dream, angry and strong and fighting and scared. It had taken all of Sensei's strength at the time to subdue him until it passed. Dragon was too strong now and if he got hung up in a subconscious state Raven would have no chance. She could fight but he outweighed her by more than double and out powered her immeasurably. He had to trust that she could reach him if the worst was to happen. Dragon's past was truly what nightmares were made of.

He still had nightmares sometimes, but nothing as bad as the ones those many years ago and never that one again. They had discussed it at length at the time; Dragon had shaken uncontrollably in Sensei's arms as the memory of it went back to its hiding place. He had cried into Sensei's loving embrace, reliving it. He had tried to make the girl go away as quickly as he could after what he had done to her. He hated hurting her, hated himself, and hated everyone and everything. Sensei had held him for hours putting him to sleep finally in a peaceful dreamless bliss and had guarded him ever since from his demons and their horrors.

CHAPTER TWELVE

THE PAST

It was late afternoon as they fell together onto the middle of the bed. She curled into his arm, her head on his chest. It was quiet, except for the low white noise of the engines and the sound of the surf against the sides of the yacht, coming through the open window. She wanted to ask him about his dream and was considering how to approach it.

Aware of her thoughts as always he began. "I'm sorry I hurt you baby," he said. He turned on his side to face her now, her head resting on his arm. She met his eyes. "I don't mind that you hurt me because you didn't mean to, but I don't know why you need me like that. I couldn't connect with you to tell you it was hurting me. I tried to, but you weren't there," she said.

Her eyes had filled with tears now as she sadly told him what she had not wanted him to know. It had hurt her more that he was lost to her than anything he could do to her physically. He had never hurt her in any way and it had scared her.

He pulled her into him, enveloping her in his hold, kissing her hair, kissing her tears. Sensei's words flooded his mind at the same time, 'be honest with yourself son,' and Dragon knew now, this was Sensei's way of letting him know it was time to tell her the truth, by himself in his own way, because she was ready. She was the one person he needed to share it with, if he were to move forward in his battle to leave his past. He would need her help and she needed to understand. She knew about his past but they did not discuss it because he had not wanted to and she would never question him. But she was now, as he had scared her and left her. He would answer her because he loved her and could see he was hurting her with it now, emotionally and physically. That was worse for him than confronting any demons from the past.

He kissed her salty tears on her cheeks, taking her little face in his hands, his own tears threatening to flood him now as his heart broke for her.

"Baby," he said. "I'm sorry, I never ever want to hurt you, in any way, please know that." Her tears continued to fall slowly from her beautiful eyes, sad now as she looked to him. "I know Kai Li, but you can't leave me, please, it doesn't matter how bad it is, you have to let me see every bit of you, not just the good parts. I know you need me. Let yourself free of this and share with me what scares you, what haunts you and what makes you vulnerable," she said.

His own tears fell now, feeling her pain for him and wanting to soothe her and wanting desperately to let his secrets be known to her. He looked into her eyes, his lips trembled with his emotion and she kissed them.

He pressed his forehead against hers and taking a deep breath, he tried. "Baby, after I have a dream, I hide, I hide in my mind. That's why you can't reach me; I don't want you to see what's there. I don't want you to feel how afraid I was, how much hate I felt and see the pictures that are there." She wept now for him, forcing herself to look at him. "I know you want to protect me from that, but I am with you now and you don't have to be alone with it anymore," she said.

He began to tell her; to let it out, pouring himself into her like a wall had come down spilling his emotions out for her to see.

"Baby, I did awful things, they made me, they raped me, they beat me, and they controlled me. They sold me to others, over and over again. It never stopped. When I dream about it, afterward I need you; I need you physically, to make it go away. Sometimes after I did something they wanted, I would be alone, always tied so I couldn't get away. There was a woman, she was older and she would come. She would touch me with her hands. I didn't want her to touch me but she did. I think she tried to make it feel good for me, what it was supposed to feel like. When she did, that would make it stop and I could sleep. When I hurt you, sexually, that's where I was, using the only way I know to make the images fade. Sometimes it takes a lot. It takes me longer to make it stop." He paused now, not knowing how it would make her feel to hear his pain, hoping she would understand and not find him disgusting.

Seeing she wasn't sure, he continued. "She wasn't supposed to help me but sometimes she did I guess, because she felt sorry for me. If they caught her it was bad for her. Sometimes she would untie me if they had left me. They would tie me by my wrists above my head and leave me like that for a long time. Sometimes, she would come and let me down, or give me water, it was like she cared. And other times she would touch me. It was all I had," he said.

He felt out of himself now, anger surfacing then disappearing within moments. She sat up, crossing her legs and took his hands. He sat up then too, facing her, waiting now. When she didn't look at him, he took her chin and tilted her face up to his, needing her to respond. He dared not pry into her mind, afraid of what he might find out.

His heart pounded in his chest, his fear of her rejection nearly consuming him. His hand brushed her wet cheek and he pleaded with his eyes for her to speak. And she did, seeing he was falling to pieces.

"Baby, it is true I can barely stand to hear this, the thought of anyone hurting you ever, is unbearable for me to think of. But I don't want you to use me as a release, the way you did. I 'want' to give you what you need, if you need it, whenever you need it, but because it is me giving it to you. When you need to make your nightmares go away I want you to be in my mind, with me, in the present. Do you understand the difference?" she said.

He reached to her and hugged her to him now, sobbing into her hair. "Yes, Yes I know," he said. "I was just afraid. I never wanted you to 'see' it." She held him tightly, holding him to her, hands in his hair. "Baby," she said. "I don't want you to leave me anymore. I need all of you and if you need me, if you need to tear me apart with it, you can. I don't care what you do to me, as long as you are with me when you do it and not back there, not back then and not hiding it from me. You've never done anything that could make me not love you."

He heard the words he had needed to hear and still hugging her to him he fell sideways to the bed taking her with him, holding her into him, pressing his body against her. He was overcome by a wave of emotion as he could feel his final walls completely crumbling, freeing him finally to completely be who he was to her. Only Sensei had ever known him this deeply and he hadn't realized the freedom it would give him to let it out to her. They had something so special and he had connected with her so completely on every level. He had wanted desperately to be free of the fear that she could ever not love him if she knew everything.

They clung to each other. She held him, gently stroking his hair back now, trying to get him to calm to her touch. "Baby, it's OK. Loving you with everything I have is all my life is about," she said. "There is nothing about you and nothing you could ever do that will change that. All I want is for every minute of every day to be all that you want it to be. We can't change what happened to you, I wish I could, so badly. But let me make the rest of your life a dream you will love. I've had no choice since the minute I met you, it's all I am about," she said.

He let her pull his mouth to hers, kiss his still trembling lips, brush his tears away. Her words rolled over him like a warm wave, soothing his heart and pulling him from his despair.

"I know we have been in love since we first saw each other and you have been everything to me since. You have been patient with me and I would be lost without you," he said. "Can you trust me now?" he asked. Looking into her eyes with his pleading wet dark pools, he risked it for her. "Kai Li, the person I met, I could trust then and I will love you endlessly and forever as the person I will always trust. Don't ever doubt that," she said.

"Baby I love you," he moaned. She pulled him onto her as he hardened and she guided him inside her. "Make love to me Kai Li, please now," she said. He gasped as he entered her. "Baby, baby, it's all I want," he whispered.

Gently and sweetly he let himself become one with her. Letting their tears fall away to be replaced with their passion and desire for each other. He was gentle and slow and they drifted in their minds together, feeling the excitement of it, the warmth of it and the release of it, blending their pleasure together until they had no more.

After, they lay together, facing each other, tangled and damp. He smiled at her now, his beautiful sexy look making her blush. They had demolished an invisible wall that he had around him and felt peaceful and happy in the aftermath.

"There's my sexy lover," she said. She smiled up at his handsome face, kissing the corner of his mouth. "And you my love are a sweet adorable mess," he said. He smoothed her wild hair. "Why don't you fix that and we can go make dinner. Wax will be wondering where I am," she said. She got up and pulled him with her. He followed her to the bathroom, and they showered. They were lost together in their love as they dressed and kissed their way back to join Wax and Sarge.

When they came into the galley, Wax was just starting dinner and Sarge was opening a beer. She had on a tiny short pair of white shorts and a red bandeau top with a little white hoodie over it that was short and revealed her tanned tight stomach. She had pushed the sleeves up and zipped it tight around her waist and she looked sexy, sparkling clean and happy. Her hair was left long, still damp. She made Dragon wear the dark blue board shorts with the white strip down the side that made his butt irresistible to her and a white cotton T shirt that was tight across his chest and arms but roomier as it hung over the top of his shorts. She had smoothed his hair back from his forehead and it now curled around his face still wet, draping over his shoulders.

"Hey," Waxy said. "Hey Hollywood," Raven said. "Are you going to help me cook?" Wax asked. "I sure am. Baby you want a beer?" she said to Dragon. He kissed her lips. "Ya babe, I'll get it, give Wax a hand and I'll get you some Champagne," Dragon said.

Not wanting to leave her, he kissed her again, hugging her to him. He and Sarge were going to the upper bridge to check their position and have their beers.

Working together, getting things prepared, Wax had asked her. "Everything OK baby girl?" "Ya Waxy," she said. Leaning up, she gave him a quick kiss on his Hollywood lips. "You know Dragon, there's a lot of stuff and he dreams it sometimes." "Ya I figured," he said. "Is he OK?" "He is now," she said. "Don't worry Waxy." He smiled at her now and pulled her toward him, hugging her. "Ok, I know you got this baby girl." She smiled up at him. "Yes I do, now let's eat, before I end up drunk."

After they were done eating and a few more drinks later, Dragon and Sarge were cleaning up the galley and Sarge was in fine form, entertaining them with stories from camp when they were young.

"Waxy, remember when we had to do kitchen duty for a month?" he said. "Yes I do my friend, that was your entire fault if I recall," Wax said. "You were supposed to be watching for Sensei and instead you had that pretty dark haired one in the corner."

When they were around fourteen or fifteen they had liked to sneak out at night and see some of the girls. They would make it to the girl's dormitory and find hiding places with their current crushes.

"Well, so like, I'm standing there with a fucking hard-on and he's waiting for me to say something," Sarge said.

They were laughing again picturing Sensei taking in Sarge's predicament. It was one of Sensei's favorite techniques he liked to use on them, making them extremely uncomfortable in a polite way.

"What's her name disappeared behind me so I'm left there with him. I just said like "Hi Sensei, to him." "Man, you have no game," Waxy said. Sarge glared at Wax. "Well, where in the fuck were you? You got off easy appearing all innocent later, after I had to face the shit on my own," Sarge said. "So what did you finally do?" Raven said. "Well you know how it's useless to bullshit Sensei, I learned that way before, so I just said 'sorry Sensei, I was horny.'" Sarge said. They all laughed their heads off at this.

"That's what you said to him?" Dragon asked. "You broke all his rules and got caught by him doing it, all because you were horny." Sarge laughed, remembering it. "Well for fuck sake, back then, being horny was a good enough reason to do almost anything I guess," Sarge said.

"Damn right it was," Wax said. "And those girls didn't help, they were like all smiling and eyeing us and shit, you remember that Raven?" "Ya in all fairness, you guys were whispered about a lot, late at night in that dorm," she said. "They used to all envy me because we were so close."

Having finished in the galley now, they took the Scotch bottle and Champagne to the flying bridge to enjoy the evening before the sun set. The breeze was warm still and the sun was beginning to glow orange on the ocean behind them in their wake. It was vast and beautiful and the Dream Weaver moved through it smoothly, the ocean's loneliness contrasting with their togetherness. Dragon sat on the back side of the helm seat and rested his feet on the padded bench and let her crawl into him. She curled into a ball on his lap and sipped her champagne in his arms.

Sarge sat in the co-pilot chair and Wax stretched out on the opposite bench. He found his iPod and they listened to his music and sailed on into night two. They discussed their activities for the next day, deciding to lift some weights after Yoga. They had made one of the four state rooms into a makeshift gym, not nearly as equipped as the one at home but enough for them to work out.

"What ever happened to that girl I got in shit for," Sarge asked. "Her name was Sophia, Sarge," she said. "And she went to University somewhere; she's probably like a rocket scientist by now." "Ya, all I remember is that she was Thai or something and wouldn't let me do anything but kiss her, no wonder I was so horny." They all laughed at him.

"Sarge, none of the girls let you do anything, we weren't allowed," Raven said. "Sensei was super strict about that, even I wasn't allowed to be with Dragon until we were older, like I was 18." "Well I would have been happy with like page 114 even," Sarge said. He was referring to the page of the Kama Sutra that taught hand jobs.

"Well, too bad, so you had to be happy practicing page 114 on yourself, join the club." Wax said.

"Sarge, you finally got what you wanted that week we were in Munich on a stopover, remember?" Raven said. "I did indeed and it was about time," he said. "An older woman, no less," Raven said. She gave Sarge a playful smile. "Erika," Sarge said.

"I remember Erika," Wax said. "What!!" Raven said. "Not you too! The same week we were there?" "No, another time, before," Wax said. "See, you don't know everything about me, I still have some secrets." They all laughed now. "Nice one man," Dragon said. "Wow that must have been her thing. Getting all the virgin hotties that came through the door," Raven said.

Sarge just shrugged. "It doesn't matter to me. I was more than old enough and she was good at it, if I recall," he said. Wax was nodding in agreement. "She's probably got Damascus with her right now, showing him what her desk is for," Wax said.

Raven's eyes flashed anger. "He's a sweet heart, she better not fuck with him," she snapped. Defensive as always of her boys, she recalled Damascus's still cute boyishness in her mind.

"Raven, don't be fooled by Damascus's innocent smile, he's a naughty boy," Dragon said. "What are you talking about, Damascus is all business, the mention of sex makes him blush," she said. She wasn't so sure what she had missed along the way. Dragon eyed her, giving her his sexy smile. "Baby, Damascus has a very clever disguise. He's good at keeping his thoughts in check around you, but I've caught more than the odd idea from him when he likely didn't think I was paying attention." "Really?" she asked.

Dragon nodded. "And he won't need Erika's services anyway. Chantelle; I believe was her name, already dealt with that for him," Dragon said. "Oh, well I knew she always had a thing for him, but I never knew it went that far," Raven said. "He hides it well, especially from you. I won't tell you what he has in his mind on that subject," Dragon said.

"Damascus has a huge crush on you," Wax said. "What the fuck, do you mean all of you knew this and never told me?" She glared at them all now. "It's a guy thing," Sarge said. He was getting ready to really piss her off.

"Don't give me that 'guy thing' shit, Sergeant Willis. I should come over there and we can discuss personally your 'guy thing'," she said. Sarge laughed at her now. "Look how pissed you are, because you didn't know everything about Damascus' sex life. You can't stand not knowing what other people do in the bedroom, because you're a little sex freak," he said. Probably pushing her final button he got ready for her. She launched at him, not quite making it to him as Dragon's arm caught her around the waist.

"No, no, no, you're going to leave Sarge alone tonight." He laughed, pulling her down on top of him onto the padded bench. She squirmed in his arms. "Fine, I can beat you up instead," she said. "Ya," Sarge said. "Blame him for not telling you all the sexy details."

Dragon lay back with her sitting on him now and held her arms by the wrists, eyeing her playfully. "What are you going to do little girl?" Dragon said, disabling her with his grip on her wrists. She narrowed her eyes at him. "Maybe it's what I won't do, that you won't like," she said. Sarge rolled his eyes at Wax. "Oh for fuck sakes. That I'd like to see. You can't resist him any more than Wax could resist a set of twins," Sarge said. They all laughed now at Sarge's humor. "That's the truth," Wax said. "Ok Ok," she said. She leaned down kissing Dragon like a sailor, making him release his grip and circle her in his arms. "I rest my case," Sarge said. He eyed her moving her hips against Dragons.

"Later boys," Dragon said.

Picking her up, he stood and she was all over him, kissing his neck, wrapping her legs around his waist. He carried her to their room feeling her biting his neck. Pushing open the door to the room and kicking it shut behind him, he fell with her onto the bed on top of him. He rolled her over onto her back, brushing her hair away from her face, looking into her eyes.

She looked up at him and he was taken away by her beauty in the dimly lit cabin. Her green eyes glowed softly, full of love for him, with an innocence that always made him die for her. It took his breath away and he pasted his lips to hers, moving against her, his hands around her back and through her hair holding her to him as his desire for her took over them.

She had taken him out of his shorts and he was hot and hard in her hand. He moaned and rolled onto his back. She got up and he moved himself to the edge of the bed so she could kneel on the floor in front of him, pulling his shorts all the way off. She wrapped her hand around him, making him groan as she licked the head of his erection, before fully enveloping him with her mouth. He lay back and closed his eyes and let her work on him until he could no longer hold it back.

Gasping, he sat forward, taking her hair at the back in his left hand and as the first wave of it hit him, she removed her mouth, clasped her hand around him and got him to finish. She tilted her head back to let his come flow onto her lips and cheeks, licking it with her tongue. He watched as he coated her face. He moaned, thinking she was unbelievable.

He caught his breath, wiping it off her cheeks with his thumb and letting her lick it. She looked up at him, her lips puffy from the work she had put into pleasing him, her eyes wet and glowing. It pushed his senses to their limits and right now he was going to devour her.

"Come here baby, I'm going to make you scream," he said.

He pulled her up and practically tossed her onto her back on the bed. He pulled her clothes from her and pressed her thighs open as far as they would go as she grasped his hair and pulled his mouth down onto her. And scream she did, his fingers inside her and his tongue blowing her senses off the map.

Afterwards he moved over her and entered her gently. Still careful of her soreness he made love to her, eventually taking them to the end again, filling her with his wetness and his love, holding her to him, her orgasm leaving her trembling in his arms. Later, he had held her as they talked softly together. Dragon had finally made her sleep, drifting off with her as she lay on his chest.

The next day fell together as they had planned, completing their night watches, they had all met for Yoga and then had worked out for the rest of the morning. After lunch they had nothing to do but spend the afternoon in the sun, drinking beers and talking. Wax and Sarge had just completed an epic chess battle, leaving Wax the victor and they joined Dragon and Raven on the front deck, with some fresh cold ones. Raven lay topless on her back, her now dark body glowing in the sun and Dragon lay bedside her, also on his back, his hair pulled back and tied, sunglasses glinting in the light, the sun darkening his chiseled muscles. They sat up as Wax and Sarge found a spot.

Earlier they had spoken with Sensei and learned some sad news that Damascus had lost two team members in an ambush during a mission and he himself had suffered a serious gunshot wound to the chest. He was recovering, but sadly two young members of his team had not made it. It was being looked at by an overview team at HQ Munich.

Dragon and his team had been ordered back to HQ Munich immediately upon the completion of the Mexico mission to pay their respects and offer support to Damascus whom they hadn't seen in person for nearly two years. It had been Sensei's idea, feeling Damascus may need them right now and in the upcoming grief period. They all knew the lost members well; having seen them grow up in camp. They were a small family and it touched them all. They reminisced about them sadly, as they drank their beers.

"Do any of you remember your real name?" Wax asked. He had been affected strongly by the loss as he had become closest with one of the boys, back in camp. "No," Raven said. "Sensei always called me Raven, after the color of his wife's hair." "I didn't know he had a wife," Wax said. Raven had just looked at him, and he knew not to pry further.

"I can remember mine," Wax said. They all looked up at him. "Maybe I don't want to remember, maybe it doesn't matter now, I don't know," he said, seeming to be arguing with himself more than anything.

When Sensei found Wax in a brothel in Manila, he had said he was called Wax, it was a slang from the dialect spoken there and had no meaning in an English translation. Dragon put a hand on Wax's shoulder now and looked into his eyes, using his sight to try and reassure Wax that it was Ok to go back if he wanted too.

"You can tell us your real name if you want to Waxy, it's all good," he said.

Wax looked back at him and Dragon's heart broke for him as he could see with his senses that Wax was deeply hurting, for the lost boy from Damascus' team and for the lost boy that he had been.

"My name was Lester," he said. With his statement, tears fell from his eyes. Raven had almost never seen Wax cry and her own tears fell unbidden from her now. Dragon leaned over to him and with both arms pulled him into a hug. "Come here man," he said. Wax let Dragon embrace him. It was unusual for him to have emotional moments; he was always strong and saw life simply.

"I haven't thought of it for years," Wax said. He sat back from Dragon, thinking. Sarge was quiet; more easily moved to emotion and couldn't find words. "It reminds me of my Mother," Wax said. He looked beyond sad now. They all knew this feeling and understood his avoidance of it. "That's Ok Waxy," Raven said. "We all know what it feels like, unfortunately."

Wax kept looking down but nodded. "Sensei knows I don't like the memory so he's always called me Wax," he said. "Understood man," Dragon said. "At least you can remember it," Sarge said. "Ya I guess you could look at it like that," Wax said. Sarge just shrugged, wanting to cheer Wax up. "Look at me, I'm Sergeant Willis, and I don't even know why," Sarge said.

Sensei had found Sarge hiding in a cardboard box, in a blown out city in Croatia. It was freezing out and he had surrounded himself in a US Marine serviceman's jacket, likely from a fallen soldier who went by the surname of Willis. The rank on the jacket was that of a Sergeant. He had refused to take the coat off, and since then had been known only as Sergeant Willis.

Sarge didn't know these details and Sensei had seen no purpose in telling him the story. Sarge suffered from a complete memory loss of his life prior to the age of about six or so when he was recovered. It was a common but unfortunate thing, with children who have suffered extreme trauma or prolonged abuse, both of which Sensei had suspected applied to Sarge.

Raven touched Wax's hand, gently taking it in hers. "Wax do you remember why you came to live in camp?" she asked. Wax paused, but nodded. "We used to live with my grandma, me and my mother. One day my grandma was gone. At the time I didn't know why but I'm guessing she passed away. After that we had no home. My mother took me and we moved to the place Sensei found me. My mother worked there and I did chores. I would clean the rooms, take customers to the women. I swept the floors, that kind of thing. One day my Mother was gone too. I don't know why, probably drugs took her. They let me stay because I worked. Sometimes there were children there, that got used, but I never did. It was mostly girls that were wanted. Then Sensei came one day and I went with him."

They all sat silently, picturing Wax's early life. "I'm sorry Waxy," Raven said. Wax nodded. "I know, but I had it good compared to Dragon or you or some of the others. I was just poor and lonely," he said. She kissed his hand then and released it. "Not anymore Waxy, right?" she asked. He gave her half a 'Hollywood' and she knew he would be alright.

Dragon pulled his discarded T-shirt over Raven's head, to cover her from the now intense afternoon sun. The breeze was cooling, the sun warming and the beer soothing as they passed the afternoon enjoying all three. They listened to the music Waxy played but didn't have the joviality needed to engage in dancing. They used whatever strength they had to not succumb to the unspoken sadness they were all feeling.

"I just want to get back to work or something, I don't know, like I want to meet this prick for some reason," Wax said. "Don't worry, we will," Dragon said. He gave them his 210 percent smile. Wax made it all the way to a full on smile back at Dragon. "Well, I'm all yours man, just tell me what you want me to do and consider it done," Wax said.

Dragon knew he meant every word of it. Wax was devoted to his position within the team, completely committed and possessed invaluable skills. They all did and together they teamed up perfectly and he had no doubts the people they were going to meet wouldn't know what hit them.

CHAPTER THIRTEEN

SAN DIEGO

They passed the remaining days on the open ocean in relatively the same way and when they began their approach into San Diego Harbor they were happy to see land again. The endless California coastline was beautiful, long sandy beaches and a desert mountain back drop, different from Hawaii the way it went on forever in either direction. The city sprawled out from the shoreline and shimmered in the heat of the late afternoon. The Marina was massive, a little world in and of itself, providing a secure home to hundreds of yachts, protected from the open ocean by an inland water system.

Arrangements had been made for their mooring and it was somewhat tedious, but eventually their lines were secured by the numerous dockhands, which were obviously skilled at their jobs and likely were used to receiving large tips for their efforts. Chekov's profile had detailed these sorts of things for Dragon and over the journey he had read and re-read the etiquette and protocols of such situations so he would be aware and act accordingly. They had reluctantly exchanged their bohemian clothing and lifestyle for one more suited to the rich and famous. They were to depart the yacht and check in to the suite at the Hotel adjacent to the Marina.

Dragon had dressed Raven in a clinging white halter dress, just the right shortness, made of a silk and cotton blend that clung to her shape and showed off her tan. He brushed her long wavy hair down her back, off her face and handed her some sunglasses. She looked stunning, as he touched some shiny gloss on her lips from something he found in the bathroom drawer.

"Later angel, it's going to be you, me and these," he said. He smiled sexily as he tied a pair of gold colored sandals with heels around her ankles. "Fuck," he said. "How am I supposed to see you in this outfit, my pants are going to rip." "I hope they do. That will make it easier for me. I've wanted to rip them off you since you put them on," she said. She eyed the front of his pants, then the rest of him.

He had on black cotton and linen pants that clung to his thighs fitting him perfectly everywhere. They were belted with a black soft leather belt with a beautiful buckle in Platinum that formed the letters DLI. He had a black tight silk knit V-neck T-shirt and a cream colored linen jacket, left open. He had pulled his hair back and tied it. He put his glasses on and smiling his beautiful white smile at her, he looked unbelievably sexy, sophisticated and intimidating all at once. Seeing her thoughts, he shook his finger at her. In the cabin he opened the safe and folded two thousand dollars in US cash into his jacket pocket from a manila envelope containing fifty thousand, Sensei had sent them with and obtained two credit cards, one in the name of David Li and the other David Li Industries.

Wax and Sarge joined them now, looking equally stunning. They had both tied their hair back and wore crisply ironed dress shirts and some sort of dress pants in black. Wax looked very Hollywood, in dark burgundy and Sarge very sexy in dark Navy blue, his tanned skin stunning with his blonde hair and blue eyes.

Raven eyed them and licked her lips. "Well, I'm the luckiest girl on earth, I'd say. You two look delicious," she said. "Behave baby girl," Wax said. He gave her his sexy Wax smile that he only used as a closer usually.

"Look at you," Sarge said. "You really are a 'girl' after all, who knew?" He eyed her seductively in her heels. "Ready?" Dragon said. He turned his attention to them now.

They stepped out of the main cabin. Waiting for them was the Marina Manager. He greeted them from the dock. "Welcome, Mr. and Mrs. Li, it is my pleasure to have you here," he said. "I am Rodrigo DeSousa; please allow me to escort you to your car." And with that he gestured to a waiting six passenger golf cart. A young attractive Latino boy was waiting in the driver's seat. Dragon shook Rodrigo's hand and Raven nodded politely. "Of course, and thank you," Dragon said.

The four of them sat, Dragon taking Raven's hand in his as they made their way through the maze of docks, to a waiting limousine. Rodrigo enquired about their trip and details of their stay in San Diego.

"A couple of days," Dragon said. "Refuel and restock please, I will let you know our exact departure time later."

Rodrigo seemed satisfied with this and also with Raven. He was eyeing her, barely able to listen to what Dragon had been saying. Dragon waved a hand in front of his face. "Mr. DeSousa? Are you with me?" he asked. Rodrigo paled and turned his eyes up to Dragon's. "If I may say Mr. Li, your wife is stunning, excuse me Mrs. Li," he said. Dragon lowered his glasses eyeing Rodrigo. He gave him his half smile that curled up on one side more than the other. "I am aware of that Mr. DeSousa," he said. He pushed his glasses back over his eyes.

Rodrigo swallowed and looked away, leaving Dragon with his thoughts that David Li was the most intimidating man he ever saw. Dragon passed the driver kid a twenty and they climbed into a Limo's open door, its' driver nodding politely.

They arrived at the hotel entrance and that was when the fun began, as they departed the luxurious car. Cameras began to flash and voices came from everywhere. Dragon became instantly aware of the media issue Chekov had warned them about. The hotel had put up a rope to keep the entrance clear, but they lined it. Taking Raven's hand they went up some steps to the two huge doors, as flashes went off and reporters threw questions. 'Mr. Li what brings you to San Diego, Mr. Li can we have a shot of you and your wife, Mr. Li do you have business here', and on it went. Making a decision, Dragon paused, pulling Raven against him, he removed his glasses, smiling a breathtaking smile at her. "My wife and I are stopping by on a trip to Mexico; we are looking forward to a few days here, as we have never been to the city before," he said.

They avidly flashed their cameras capturing his voluminous good looks and Ravens adoring gaze. They wanted more, but Dragon had turned and with his arm around Raven now, moved through the opened doors into the hotel lobby, dismissing them.

They were escorted to a back elevator by the manager, a middle aged woman who could barely take her eyes off Dragon and then could barely speak as Wax winked at her, making them all want to burst out laughing in the elevator. She made apologies for the media problem and assured them they would have complete privacy during their stay.

They had arrived at the Penthouse suite and their mood was alive. They looked around the spacious dwelling, taking in its setting. Sarge had moved to a desk and set his back pack down. It contained their guns, a laptop and the bug scanner. He activated it and proceeded to scan the room for devices as they all silently walked about idly checking it out, without speaking until he was finished. Raven had found the master suite and had pulled Dragon onto the bed and they were making out as Sarge scanned the room.

"Baby, no, I'm not going to mess you up right now," Dragon said. He sat up and pulled her hands off his erection, making her pout. Sarge just shook his head, well used to their constant sexuality, as he completed the scan.

"All clear, I just need to reach Chekov to confirm and we're good I think," Sarge said. They communicated with Munich via a satellite and his image streamed to them in a matter of seconds. Chekov's usual coldness chilled the sunny room. "Dragon, go to dinner, all four of you, there's a reservation at the Surf Restaurant on the Mezzanine level for 8 pm.

Afterward ask the concierge for a decent nightclub and contact me with your phone by text message and I will check it out. If it is legitimate then go to it, be seen and do whatever it is you do in one of those places then return to the hotel. Clear?" Chekov said. "Got it, thanks Chekov," Dragon said. "Take it easy guys; let's make this a good one, OK?" Chekov said. "That's how it's going to be Chekov, trust me," Dragon said. Chekov nodded back and the screen went black.

"Ok," Sarge said. Closing the laptop and putting it back in the bag, he crossed the room to a bar area and found a chilling bottle of Champagne and four glasses. He deftly removed its cork and poured. They raised their glasses together, in a toast. "Cheers, guys, let's do this," Dragon said.

They had a short time to relax, before they had to change and get ready to go for dinner. "Come here you," Dragon said. Pulling Raven to him he kissed her wetly. "Right now, I just want you and those shoes," he said. He breathed into her hair as she circled his waist and held him against her, feeling him harden. Sarge downed his Champagne and eyed them. "Didn't you two just spend all afternoon fucking," he asked. "Well that was three hours ago. How long am I supposed to last?" Raven said. "I don't fucking know. It doesn't matter because in reality you can't last five minutes anyway," Sarge said. He was in a good mood and wanted to bug her. She turned on him, taking his bait. "You're the one who probably can't 'last' five minutes," she said. Dragon and Wax laughed then. "Fuck off, you have no idea, page 78 is my specialty," Sarge said. It taught ejaculation control and orgasm denial.

"Ok you two," Dragon said. "We have all night and you two need to 'last' not causing World War 3." "But baby, he's full of shit," she said. She looked up at Dragon, innocently stating her mind. "I can always prove it to you Miss Raven," Sarge said. "So, stop it or I'll let him," Dragon said.

It made her quiet for the moment. Sarge caught her eye and grinned at her and she gave him back her best expression of 'vomiting', sticking her finger in her mouth as if to make herself throw up.

In the master suite there was a large walk-in closet that held the things they would need to wear while there. Dragon decided all he needed was to change his jacket to black, a fine wool Armani, perfectly tailored to his physique, fitting his shoulders and arms and narrowing down from there. He brushed his hair loose. He laid the jacket on a chair and went to her. He eyed her like a tiger about to spring. Her breath caught as she realized his restraint had failed him.

He pulled her little white dress from her and she stood naked except for a pair of white lace panties that had nothing in the back and showed off her sexy butt and the sexy heels. He pulled her to the bathroom and they stood in front of the mirror.

"We have time for me to take the edge off you sweetheart, OK?" he said. He reached down and touched her through the lace, watching in the mirror, feeling her wetness on his fingers. "Baby, I need to fuck you, you are so wet." His voice was soft and sexy, like his eyes and she melted for him. "Please baby, I'm going crazy," she begged.

She turned to him and undid his belt and pants and let his erection free so he could enter her. He pulled her panties down so she could step out of them and then standing he sat her on the counter, taking her ankles in his hands and pulling her legs up and apart. She supported herself with her hands behind her on the bathroom counter as he held her apart by her ankles. He kissed the inside of her left ankle by the thin leather strap of the sexy heels he had left on her. She gasped, as he leaned in and pressed his erection against her wetness.

He moaned deep and low as he slid himself into her. His hands went to her hips so he could hold her still and drive himself into her. He made it quick and hard and she came intensely, her head falling back as the waves of it rocked her. And before she was done he held her against him, deep inside her, coming hard into her, his eyes closing at the feel of it, his arms folding around her holding her into his body as the spasms shook him.

He rested like that for a time, getting his breath, still holding her to him, "There baby, all better now?" he asked. "Ya baby," she said. She rested her head against his chest while they calmed from it. He slowly pulled out of her, his come dripping liberally from her onto the edge of the counter. "Stay there a second angel," he said.

He turned the faucet on warm. He took a cloth and cleaned himself off and put himself back inside his open pants. Rinsing another cloth in the warm water he cleaned his come from her, tasting her briefly with his tongue to be sure she was sweet again, the way he liked her. She moaned as his tongue touched her sensitive openness.

"Baby, I will give you some of that later," he said. "But now, come and put something on before I lose it again."

In the closet he found a black cocktail dress. It was strapless and tight, made of nylon and spandex. It had a heart shaped edge in the front that had an inch wide band of soft leather trim and her cleavage looked amazing. It smoothed down over her body like an expensive driving glove. He admired her for a moment.

"My god that's hot," he said. "Leave it to Chekov; he probably jerked off thinking about this one."

He removed the gold sandals and found a pair of black leather shoes that were like little ankle boots with a solid heel. They had an inner side zipper and a ring of sparkling rhinestones around the top edge, covering her foot up to just below her narrow ankles.

There was a jewelry drawer with a glass top, and he pulled open the drawer and found her a necklace. "I don't know much about this stuff," he said. He held up a silver colored necklace, a fine thread of white gold with a diamond centre in the letters DLI. "Sure," she said. Those diamond letters match those shiny things on the shoes," she giggled to him. "I agree, I guess," he said. "Lift your hair."

She did so and he managed to clip it on her, his hands not cut out for tiny objects. There were matching 2 ct. diamond studs as well which she put on herself. He brushed her hair again, untangling it where he had messed her up a bit before. He pulled back the top section from her face and brow and put a black clip in it behind her head, the rest fell down her back in a warm sexy curling fall, smelling like Jasmine.

"You are absolutely beautiful my love," he said. "And so are you, Mr. Li," she said. She couldn't resist kissing his soft sexy mouth.

He put on his jacket, put the money and cards and his phone into the inner pocket and they joined Wax and Sarge in the main room. His Blackberry alerted him there was a text message from Chekov and he retrieved it. 'Those diamonds are real and you should take everything when you leave.' was all it said. 'Thanks and nice job', he replied, and put the phone back into his jacket.

Wax and Sarge were sitting waiting. Sarge had brushed his hair down as well and had put a dark navy jacket on that appeared to be the same tone as his shirt and Wax had a black jacket similar to Dragon's but a different cut by a different designer.

They took the elevator to the Mezzanine to find the restaurant. They went through the expansive carpeted area to a dark doorway of huge double doors, covered in a gleaming stainless steel with the word SURF embossed onto them. Inside they were greeted by a male host. The restaurant was not really a restaurant of traditional nature, but another world within a world. It encompassed half the side of the building itself and was a wall of windows overlooking the pools and palms and beach and ocean. The sun was setting just then and it was stunning.

The interior was modern and clean, dark woods, soft fabrics, crystal lighting in a soft glow, and candles. It smelled of something delicious and made them all realize they were starved. There were tables spaced apart for privacy, occupied by a number of patrons who eyed them as they made their way to the table. Wax clearly heard a whisper from someone, to the effect of 'oh my god that's David and Raven Li'. He turned to note where it had come from and spied a couple of nouveau riche girls about twenty years old or so, sipping wine and staring. He paused slightly and raised an eyebrow at them as if to say 'really?' which caused them to blush and look away.

Dinner proceeded and was delicious; they had a fish soup followed by a salad with nuts and fruit in it, then salmon and rice. The music was low and pleasant and they watched the lights of the inner harbor, the lovers walking and the ocean sparkling in what was now moonlight. It was pleasant and uneventful other than one incident where the two girls Wax had shut down earlier appeared to be approaching the table.

Wax immediately rose and intercepted them. "I wouldn't if I were you ladies," he said. They looked guiltily at him and the braver one finally spoke. "Well we were wondering if you and your friend were doing anything later," she said. Wax smiled his 'Hollywood' smile then, shaking his head. "Not now ladies, but we are heading to a club after this, maybe if I see you there," he said. He turned his back on them. They paused for a moment then retreated, afraid to ask where.

"Why'd you blow them off?" Sarge asked. Raven giggled, "Ya Waxy, Sarge needs to get laid again." "Damn right I do," Sarge said. Wax just eyed him. "Easy sailor, the night is young," he said. Dragon smirked at them, shaking his head. He summoned the waiter and asked about clubs in the area.

"There are a few," he said. "Lately the most popular place is 'Venus', its near here." "Can you get a car for us?" Dragon asked. The man nodded. "Of course, Mr. Li, give me a minute, I can have one meet you out front," he said. He was not supposed to leave the restaurant, but had been ordered to do whatever Mr. Li wanted. "Thank you," Dragon said.

Once in the lobby again they were aware of stares and whispers. As they waited the few minutes for the car, Dragon resisted the urge to strangle a leering intoxicated bar patron, who was clearly undressing Raven with his eyes. There was an open air lobby bar full of them and he was relieved when they finally proceeded to the waiting limo.

Inside the club they were seated and attended to instantly and annoyingly Dragon thought. Wax spoke for him, sensing Dragon wished he could tell everyone to fuck-off.

"Beers for us and Champagne for the lady," Wax said. "This shit is just not me," Dragon said. "Baby, it's OK, we don't have to stay long. Chekov said it was fine and it might be fun for Wax and Sarge," she said. She was rubbing his inner thigh under the table.

Dragon was just glad he had told the car to wait for them. The bar was filled mostly with girls at least a two to one ratio. A male waiter arrived shortly with their drinks and Dragon downed half his beer at once, advising the waiter to keep them coming. He poured Raven a glass of Champagne.

In due time Wax and Sarge had left them and blended into the subculture of the dance club scene, drinking beer and indulging in a never ending supply of wanting girls. Raven had distracted Dragon by getting him to make out with her but she made him promise to dance with her if a slow song came on. He had agreed, thinking he was safe because it would never happen.

In the end, it had gone her way and she pulled him to the floor. He held her amongst the sweaty, squishy confines. Sarge had a girl pinned against the wall, devouring her, as she visibly rubbed his erection through his pants and Wax was still the dance floor king, groping yet another hot thing as the slow song progressed. Raven wasn't sure when it all fell apart, what happened first or last for that matter, but only that it did. It was more like a sixth sense overwhelming her and the actions that followed were instinctual.

In the middle of their dance Dragon had suddenly pulled her by her hand through the crowd. She hadn't seen what happened, but Sarge was cornered up against the wall, wiping blood from the corner of his mouth with the back of his hand. A group of Latino's had surrounded him, as Wax and Dragon shoved through them.

"This better be good," Dragon said. The bravest one of them responded, acting cool and looking ridiculous. "What's it to you. Step aside and let us teach you're gringo friend here about touching another man's woman." Dragon and Wax and Sarge were outnumbered, but the men were a lot smaller than them. "He just hit me out of nowhere," growled Sarge. "You little fucker, let's go when I can see it coming."

Dragon put a hand on Sarge and the mouthy Latino fuelled the fire some more. "Come on Muchacho," he said. Dragon couldn't believe it; this guy was full of himself and stupid. He'd had enough and in a second he was on him, pinning him in a hold, his arms pulled behind him, in Dragon's grasp. Dragon turned him to face his friends. "Here's how this ends. If any of you makes a move, I break his arms," Dragon said.

For emphasis he wrenched the man's arms in the hold, nearly to the breaking point, making him wince from the pain of it. The five or six of them postured but backed off slightly. That was when Raven heard the unmistakable sound of a switch blade opening.

Seeing it in the hand of the nearest guy, she reached out, like lightening, grasping his wrist just behind his hand in a pressure point grip, bending his hand back against his will and removing the knife from it. He glared at her, stunned and humiliated.

"You people seem to have a problem fighting fair," she said. She looked at him in disgust and then with barely a glance she threw it, sending it end over end into the wall right next to the face of the cowering girl Sarge had been kissing moments before.

Dragon nodded at Wax, who stepped up and sent a hard right hook into the side of the guy's face as Dragon held him, splitting his eyebrow and knocking him out cold. "That's what it feels like to get hit when you aren't looking my friend," Dragon said. He eyed the others. Then in one hard swift move he snapped both his forearms and let him fall to the floor. "You fucked with the wrong guys," he said. Giving them a flat dark stare, he took Raven's hand and they went back to their table. He tossed money down and they headed for the back door, out to the waiting car.

They sat in silence for a minute or so. When they all eyed each other at the same time, Sarge was the first to laugh. And in a moment it was over and they were good again. "What the fuck is that matter with these people?" Dragon said. "That's more stupid in one room than I've seen in my lifetime." They returned to the hotel. The driver dropped them at the back entrance and finding the elevators they went to their floor and gratefully flopped on the couches in the main room. "Scotch?" Sarge asked. Dragon and Wax nodded and Raven helped Sarge bring them. She found a glass for some Champagne from the bottle they opened earlier, ice cold in a bucket and still bubbling.

"You hit that guy pretty hard Waxy," she said. "He needed it," Wax said.

"What went on Sarge?" Dragon asked. "I just saw this guy hit you." "Ya, one second I was kissing this girl and then someone tapped me on the shoulder, like saying "excuse me" all polite and I turned and then he totally hit me without me seeing it coming," Sarge said. Dragon shook his head, not understanding it. "What a dick. I should have snapped his neck, but I guess around here you get jail time for that. Oh well, he'll have trouble jerking off for the next 6 weeks anyway." They all laughed at that.

Eventually Dragon let Raven pull him to the bedroom. She could sense his weariness. "I think for once, you are actually tired baby. I'm going to undress you and rub your back," she said.

He looked grateful and sat down on the bed. She was right, he was tired. She decided to run a bath in the oversized tub and turned it on. As the hot water flowed, she added a fresh scented bubble bath. Returning to him she removed his jacket, laying it over the chair back, then his shoes, then pulled his shirt over his head. She told him to lie back so she could undo his belt and his pants. He lay there looking at her and she thought he was the sexiest thing she had ever seen. Something about him partially clothed always made her nuts. His perfect body, with the top of his pants open made her want it. She stilled her urges and pulled him up so he could step out of his pants and be naked. She was still fully dressed as she led him to the bathroom.

She shut the water off now, as the tub was full and bubbly. It was built-in to a tiled wall and surround and she sat him on the edge of it. She turned her back to him so he could unzip the dress. He did so, slowly sliding the zipper down her back. She turned to face him, holding the dress up at the front. He took her hands away one at a time and the dress slid off her. He breathed in the sight of her now hardening nipples. He moaned and gently took her breasts in his hands, leaning in and kissing her nipples. She stroked his hair as he licked them and sucked them gently, making her want him badly.

She pulled his chin up and kissed his mouth. Tiny black silk panties just barely covered her in the front and the outline of her showed through the soft silk. He closed his eyes slowly at the sight of her.

"Baby I can't stand this," he begged her now. He gently touched her through the silk making her moan. "I need you," he said. She knew he meant it. "Ok baby and she turned away so he could get a view of her sexy little butt as she bent over and undid the little black shoes.

That just about blew his mind and he had a hard time resisting grabbing her hips and slamming himself into her right then. Barefoot she turned back to him and he looped his fingers into the top of the panties and slid them down.

She stepped out of them and into the tub, pulling him in with her. He sat down and she immediately climbed on him, sliding him inside her, slowly taking him all the way into her. He held her to him, feeling her breasts against him and her tight warmth around him.

"Lay back baby and let me fuck you," she said. He smiled a slow sexy half smile at her, liking that idea a lot. "I'm all yours baby," he said.

He let his head fall back to lean against the edge of the tub. He could feel her and it was exquisite, he was going to come but it would be slow and sweet and intense. It was actually making him crazy, as she slowly used her body to get him to climax. She had done this to him many times and each time it was like the first. He would forget what it felt like and feel it newly every time. He closed his eyes as she rocked his world and made it happen for him.

After on the bed he lay flat on his stomach and she had sat on him and massaged him. There was some oil on the bathroom counter that smelled nice and she used that. She poured a small amount over the dragon and massaged it in, making the colors of it glow and intensify. She loved to touch the tattoo, tracing its body with her fingers, massaging it as well as him. She did each shoulder and up his neck, massaging out his knots of stress that he got because he was a worrier. Then the tightness between his shoulder blades because he was intense about everything, then down his spine, easing the tension in the long muscles running down either side of his backbone, because he was strong. His back told a story about him and she loved to read it.

CHAPTER FOURTEEN

DUSTY

Their morning came all too soon, sunlight pouring in the bedroom windows. Dragon had brought her awake and they had made love until the time was up.

"Did I fuck you enough?" he asked. "Yes, baby, I just woke up extra, you know," she said. "Yes, and it was very nice for me that you did," he said.

He gave her his sexy smile, feeling happy, and content. She grinned at his sexiness and climbed into his arms for him to carry her to the shower. After, they dressed in work-out clothes, as the plan was to use the gym facilities and take a run down the beach.

Sarge and Wax were on the terrace, some kind of breakfast had arrived and they had tea waiting. Sarge looked good as new and Wax's hand was bruised but otherwise there were no signs of the previous night's altercation.

When they were through with their breakfast Dragon retrieved the laptop from Sarge's bag. "I need to talk to Sensei," Dragon said. "I want some answers about why Damascus's mission went badly."

Sensei appeared on the screen and Raven was glad to see him again. They filled him in on the events of the night before and then Dragon moved on asking about the details of the mission which had cost Damascus his team members.

Sensei explained that after they had eliminated their targets and were withdrawing, they were overwhelmed by an additional group they were not expecting to encounter and Chekov had only been able to warn them when it was too late, the exits to the building were compromised and they had been trapped. They had been outnumbered and it was a miracle that only two had been lost. It appeared to be random and bad luck. Had HQ been aware, they would have sent two teams. A satellite connection had randomly failed at the worst possible moment and there were 45 seconds that Chekov did not have eyes on the building, before he was able to reroute. In the end, the mission had been classified as a success; they had intercepted a shipment of young girls, bound for Thailand's sex trade.

"I have to talk to him today," Dragon said. "Yes I know," Sensei replied. "He needs you, from what I am hearing. He took a hit covering Jacob. Just talk to him Dragon." "I will Sensei," Dragon said. "Anything else?" Sensei asked. "I miss our morning talks," Dragon said. "I do to," Sensei said. He smiled at Dragon, always proud of him, showing it in his eyes. "Well, go and work out and enjoy your day son. You leave tomorrow morning from what I gather." Dragon nodded. "I guess I will talk to Damascus first and I don't care what Chekov says, I'm not going to anymore fucking night clubs in this place," Dragon said. "I don't blame you," Sensei said. He smiled, looking mischievous. "Sarge and Wax will have to get laid some other way."

Raven giggled at him. Sensei was rarely crude and when he was she found it really funny. He smiled at her, wishing he could hug her. "Contact me tomorrow, maybe after you are on your way, Ok?" he said. With that they said their goodbyes. Raven had tears again. "It's Ok sweetheart, this will be over at some point and we can go home," Dragon said. Feeling the same way, he wanted to get on with it.

She went to join Wax and Sarge, allowing Dragon to talk to Damascus alone, knowing Damascus would be more open if she were not present.

Dragon was somewhat shocked when he finally saw him. Chekov had taken a laptop to him as he was still stuck in the infirmary, hooked up to things. He looked older and he was, but somehow looked younger at the same time. His hair was longer and his features sharper, his eyes still masking but expressive and tired now. He was only 21 and Dragon's heart went out to him.

They greeted each other and Dragon told him he looked like shit, just to lighten the mood. "If you say so," Damascus said. "I take it you are still a fucking asshole." "I make a point of it," Dragon said. "I'm heading there in awhile, after I take care of a couple of shitbags, so you can see firsthand." "I can't wait," Damascus said. "There's not enough of them around here already or anything," he said. He tipped his head, nodding slightly in the direction of Chekov who remained nearby. Dragon laughed at that. "I hear you."

Dragon decided it was time to get to the point, enough dancing around the elephant in the room. "Damascus," he said. "I'm really sorry. It's a tough thing to go through." Damascus met his eyes, and nodded, looking angry and sad at the same time. "I couldn't get to them," he said. Dragon continued to hold his gaze, willing him to continue. "They were ahead of us," Damascus said.

Dragon was familiar with the tactic, they were on point, to secure ground and provide cover for the others to proceed. It was standard tactics. Point men were always at the most risk.

"We heard the gunfire, we moved, but they were already down," he said. He was visibly trying to hold back his emotion as he told Dragon the story.

Dragon had to fight his own emotions with all he had then, to not fall apart for him. "Damascus, that's the way it goes sometimes. There was nothing you could have done. There were unavoidable issues going on in the background you were in no way able to be aware of. Had it gone down differently we may have lost all of you."

Damascus looked away, angry. "I would have rather it been me," he said. Dragon pushed on, wanting to help him. "Damascus, it wasn't you and no amount of wishing it was will change that. And they wouldn't have wished it was you and you know that." Dragon knew he needed to be tough now. "Listen, I know you don't see it right now because you can't, but try and believe me when I tell you; you will get over this, you have to get over this and if you don't I'm going to kick your ass. You have to Honor them by continuing with your job, being the best you can be and remembering them when you're doing it," he said. Damascus glared at Dragon through the screen, defiance and pride coming, if only slightly back to his face.

"You need to find it within yourself to move forward, recover physically and mentally and get back in the game. We need you," he said. He smiled at Damascus now, sensing he had mended some tiny bit of the brokenness in his heart.

Damascus gave him a slight nod. "When are you coming here?" he asked. "Soon, a month maybe," Dragon said. "Ok, well by then I promise I will be out of this room and I'll kick your ass at flags," Damascus said. Dragon breathed a sigh of relief, seeing a glimpse of the old Damascus. "You'll never kick my ass at flags, but you can try for amusement's sake," Dragon said. "If that's what you think," Damascus said. He was managing a cocky smile now. Dragon smirked at him shaking his head. "Ok, so get the fuck out of that bed and off your ass and I'll see you at flags." He left Damascus with a brighter expression and a bit of relief in his own heart.

Dragon joined the others, leaning and kissing Raven's cheek. "How was that baby?" she said. "He thinks he's going to kick my ass at flags," Dragon said. "So does that mean you got through to him?" she said. "He was really fucked up, it worried me, but ya I guess so, a little bit, it will take time," Dragon said. "Kick your ass at flags?" Sarge said. "I don't think so." "That's what I told him, but he can try, he's looking forward to it at least," Dragon said. "Let's go work out, I can kick your asses right now with the bench press," Dragon said. "Like fuck you can," Wax said, getting up. "You haven't got it left man, you fuck too much," Sarge said. "There's no such thing as fucking too much, my friend," Dragon said. Raven laughed and took his hand. "Maybe, if you're Sarge," she said.

They all laughed now, heading for the elevator. "You're just so funny, aren't you?" Sarge said. He grabbed her in a fake choke hold. She elbowed him playfully in the ribs. "I read once that someone had a heart attack and died from fucking," she said. "I hope that doesn't happen to you Sarge. You should practice more, then you'd be able to fuck all morning too and still bench 425." "Why don't you shut the fuck up now," he said. She eyed him innocently. "Ok, I was just saying."

His playful expression made her laugh and she shoved him against the wall as they were leaving the elevator. "Man, you get away with shit," he said. She walked away ahead of him, her pony tail waving and her little butt sexy as ever in her spandex shorts. Dragon eyed him and shrugged, trying not to laugh.

Later, they had run on the beach and after lunch they were headed for the Dream Weaver to make a check on things. They found their way down to the Marina and made their way uninterrupted to their mooring. Things changed as they realized someone was aboard. Wax pulled his gun and led in as they approached. The covers of the engines were open and a figure was semi-hidden.

"You have five seconds, make it good," Wax said. "I'm Dusty, Dusty McLean, the mechanic," he said. He immediately raised his hands, his back to them.

"I didn't request a mechanic," Dragon said. Raven took his wallet and handed it to Dragon. He tossed it to Sarge, who immediately scanned it to Chekov. "Standard procedure man, you pay the fee, I check your engines, it's how I make a living," Dusty said. He sounded bored and annoyed. The data came back from Chekov; Dusty McLean was indeed a mechanic there, prior criminal history for possession of marijuana, unlawful conduct, protesting, misdemeanors, drunk driving, he owned a bar south of there, just above the Mexican border. He is 58 years old.

Dragon nodded to Wax to lower his gun. "Well Dusty McLean, I'd say sorry about that, but I'm not. I don't like finding strangers on my boat messing with the engines no less, I'm sure you understand that." Dusty turned to eye him. "Its fine I'm used to it, you fuckers are all the same." This was interesting, a person who spoke their mind. Dragon grinned, challenging him. "How so Mr. Mclean, tell me?"

Dusty had turned to face Dragon now and looking him in the eye answered him. "You rich bastards come here, thinking you own the place. You enjoy throwing your money around to all the fucking ass kissers dying to get their hands on it and maybe just for fun you even beat up a few shitheads in a bar just because you can. The more attention the better, the more money you blow the better, you're all the same. And I don't care if you want to go get me fired, I've been fired 100 times and they always call me back to this fuck hole of a place. I'm just not taking any of your shit because I could care less."

Dragon was smiling at him. He glanced at his phone. "92 times to be exact Mr. Mclean and I hope I don't disappoint you if I don't live up to your expectations. Want a beer?" he said. Dragon turned to the fridge. Dusty eyed them. "Help yourself." Dragon gestured as he sat. Dusty got a beer from the fridge and also sat, eyeing them noncommittally. "You people are fucking weird," he said. He drank his beer.

"That's the first real statement I've heard since we got here," Dragon said. "You see Dusty; I don't enjoy throwing money around and those that do disgust me. I prefer to help someone who deserves it, which is the only good purpose I see for my money; money that I somehow have but couldn't give a fuck about. I dislike attention almost more than I dislike stupidity and assholes and yes I did enjoy messing up some shitheads in a bar, but not because 'I can', but because they needed it."

Dusty appeared to consider this, taking long gulps of his beer. Dragon could get a sense of him, seeing an honest man, a troubled man, an addicted man but a man in touch with reality almost to a fault.

Finally seeming satisfied, Dusty replied. "Well I hope you are who you say you are. It would be a nice change around here. Who the fuck are you anyway?" he asked. He sat drinking and looking at each one of them now. This made Dragon laugh.

"David Li and this is my wife Raven, friends, Wax and Sarge," he said. Dusty shrugged and got himself another beer. "Why do all you guys look like Arnold fucking Schwarzenegger?" "Who???" Dragon looked at Raven and the others for help. "It's just a habit," Wax answered.

Raven answered Dragon in her mind, explaining the body building actor and political figure. He gave her a wide eyed 'what' look, making her giggle. She went to him and leaned into him where he sat, wrapping her arms around him. Dusty eyed her now, seeming to only notice her just then.

"Where did you two meet?" he asked. Dragon heard his real thoughts which were, 'Holy fuck where did he find you?' "We grew up together," Raven said.

He seemed satisfied with that and it was a slight relief to Dragon that he didn't engage in pornographic thoughts about her like most assholes did. He simply thought she was hot which was fair enough to Dragon, because she was.

"We're heading to Mexico tomorrow morning, Puerto Vallarta. Ever sailed there?" Dragon asked. "Many times, it's a nice ride, two and a half days, nice coast line, except when you cross the channel opening to the Sea of Cortez. Moor for the night in one of the bays, Turtle Bay is nice, cuz you don't want to be crossing that in the dark. It can get rough with the tides and the wind. Watch your weather, specifically wind," Dusty said. Sarge and Dragon exchanged glances; they would plot their course later.

"So what do normal people do around here for fun at night?" Wax asked. "Nothing fun here as far as I'm concerned, especially if you're normal. Just a bunch of neon dance bars, greasy locals, fake tits and STD's," Dusty said. He finished his second beer. "True," Wax said. Suddenly he was glad he didn't get laid last night. "If you want to kick back and have a couple, hear some decent music, head down to my place. I got a bar. It's on the water about 5 miles down the coastal highway. You'll see it," Dusty said. He rose to leave. Dragon nodded to him. "Later," Dusty said. He departed, giving them a wave behind him as he sauntered away.

"Interesting guy," Wax said. "We should go there tonight." Dragon shrugged. "I don't care either way as long as it isn't anything like the place we went last night." "Somehow I doubt that babe," Raven said. "I like that guy," Dragon said. "He says it like it is and doesn't waste words."

Raven tugged at Wax's arm. "Hey Wax, Google Arnold Schwarzenegger so Dragon can see," she said. She had a naughty glint in her eye. "Ya, come on," Wax said. He pulled her inside the cabin to find the laptop.

Dragon and Sarge eyed each other. "After you," Sarge said. "You're the one who failed 'pop culture 101'." "I never failed it," Dragon said. "I never learned it; I couldn't give a shit about half the crap the world thinks is interesting." "Ya but you have to know what Coca Cola is, or who the Rolling Stones are or you're going to look like a retard," Sarge said. Dragon just smirked at him. "Fuck that," he said. "Then I'd look like you." He shoved Sarge ahead of him into the cabin.

Wax had pulled up images of Arnold from his body building days and they all laughed like a bunch of kids. "I don't fucking look like that," Dragon said. Sarge cracked them up even more, imitating the poses, making Raven roll onto the couch trying not to pee her pants.

Shortly they were interrupted by the Marina Manager, whom they had met earlier last night. "Excuse me Mr. Li," he called from the edge of the dock. They went out to the stern deck to see what he wanted. "Mr. Li, pardon my interruption, but I wanted to tell you, the Dream Weaver was guarded last night by hotel security and there were no unusual events." Dragon eyed him, shifting his eyes to Wax and Sarge, who both shrugged.

"Mr. DeSousa, I didn't request extra security so what the fuck are you talking about?" he asked. Rodrigo hurried with his answer. "I should tell you Mr. Li, there was a car, belonging to the, err um 'people' that may not be happy with you right now. It was seen passing the gates. I would caution you to be careful," he said. Dragon eyed Sarge and Wax again. "What have I got to worry about Mr. DeSousa? Get to the point." Rodrigo looked visibly nervous. "Ah, well, you know, gangs in this city are a problem, they retaliate, that kind of thing," he said. "We normally don't see them around here but uh…" He seemed to run out of words.

"Mr. DeSousa, as far as I'm concerned the matter is closed, they assaulted my friend and they faced the consequences. The score is even from the way I see it," Dragon said. "Mr. Li, with all due respect I must tell you, that is not how these people will see it," Rodrigo said.

Dragon completely lost his patience now with the conversation and Raven tensed slightly, warning him in her mind not to lose his temper. Dragon stepped to the edge of the stern facing Rodrigo, his eyes dark and piercing into the other man.

"Mr. DeSousa, listen to me carefully, I don't give a fuck. If you want me to be intimidated by a bunch of shithead cowards, you're a poor judge of character," he said. His voice was low and firm. Rodrigo met his stare, sweat beading on his forehead. Before he could think of a response Raven interjected. "Excuse me," she said. Touching Dragon's arm, getting his attention, she passed him an idea that they should leave and moor down the coast by this Dusty persons bar and stay there overnight. "Maybe we should just leave a little earlier than tomorrow baby. What do you think?" she asked.

Dragon instantly processed the idea and agreed it would be best, and more fun. "My wife as usual is correct. We're out of here Mr. DeSousa, that will solve the problem wouldn't you say. Give us an hour, and then make it happen," Dragon said. "It is not necessary Mr. Li," Rodrigo said. "But if that is what you would like to do I will see to it."

Dragon dismissed him, turning to Wax and Sarge, cueing them to follow him into the cabin. Raven eyed Rodrigo somewhat sympathetically, as Dragon took her hand and pulled her with him.

Rodrigo nodded to her and left, as he had his work cut out for him just to round up the staff it would require to cast the yacht from the mooring and position it to leave the inner harbor in one hour's time.

Inside, Dragon outlined the idea to Wax and Sarge. "She's right, let's get the fuck out of here and sail down to where Dusty's bar is and moor there until the morning. That way we avoid any more trouble with these shitheads that everyone's so nervous about and we are out of this fucked up scene," he said.

They all agreed it was a better plan. They locked up and went back to the hotel to get their things. On the way out of the marina they ran into Dusty who was leaving in an old rusty pickup truck.

"Hey man," Dragon said. Dusty braked as they saw each other. His window was down and he was smoking a joint. He stopped next to them. "What's up?" Dusty said. "We've had enough of this place and are going to head down the coast in about an hour. Can we moor near your bar for the night?" Dragon asked. "Sure, there's plenty of water, just stay back from the surf line, there's a nice sandy bottom for your anchor. Just wave when you want to come in and I'll pick you up," Dusty said. "Hope you like Tequila." He gave Dragon a hazy stoned grin and drove off.

They went to the Suite, got their things together and left, avoiding any conversation with staff or otherwise. In the elevator Raven hugged him then leaned up and kissed him.

"If these two guys weren't here I'd give you a little elevator love baby," he said. "Well after we get going you can give me a little boat love instead." She fit the words in between his kisses. "Oh you're going to get boat love alright, I already have that planned," he said.

He sent her a private brief visual of what he planned on doing to her in their cabin. Her breath caught as she saw a flash of a silk rope, his hands tying it around her wrists.

They were interrupted by Sarge's wit. "You know, you're so rich now you should just get your own private elevator," he said. "You could just ride up and down in it all day, fucking."

Back at the Marina, they boarded the Dream Weaver, more than happy now to be moving on. A fun evening and their mission still awaited them on the horizon. They decided to simply depart and make their way to where they could see Dusty's bar from the water, then anchor. They had the whole afternoon so Sarge and Dragon could plot the course to Mexico then and register it with the Coast Guard. After that they were free and clear to relax and Dragon planned on making his 'boat love' a reality, before dinner.

Dock hands appeared and cast the Yacht off, releasing her lines and rolling them neatly aboard, while a tow boat secured a line to her stern and pulled her free. Sarge had the engines idling and when they were turned and pointing outwards, the tow line released, he put them in forward and they cruised out of the harbor into the cool coastal waters. They didn't look back as they all sat on the flying bridge again, sunglasses on, hair blowing and thinking about nothing in particular.

Raven was eventually thinking about something in particular and Dragon eyed her over his shades and winked at her, making her laugh. The Dream Weaver suited him, she thought. She loved the way he looked, his sunglasses, his masculine cheek bones and strong jaw line, his long hair blowing back from his face. He wore the light blue cotton T shirt she loved and dark grey board shorts, with bare feet. His skin lightly tanned made his hot sexy smile look even whiter.

He caught her squirming and pulled her onto his lap.

"What's the matter little girl?" he asked. Wax and Sarge rolled their eyes at each other. "For fuck sakes you two. Go and fuck or not, but can you spare me the googly eyes and tongues?" Sarge said. "I can't help it Sarge," Raven said. "He's teasing me in my head, you have no idea." Sarge and Wax rolled their eyes at each other again. "Ya it's his entire fault. Give me a break, you can't wait to rip his clothes off 24/7 and you know it," Sarge said.

"It's all good baby-girl. You can be horny for your man," Wax said. "And I am," she said. "Is that so Mrs. Li?" Dragon asked sweetly. Sarge eyed them in frustration. "Would anyone like a beer?" Would that help?" he asked. "I know it would help me."

Dragon laughed pulling her hand off him. "Yes please Sarge and you behave," he said. "Making me rip these shorts isn't going to get you anything any sooner." Wax laughed. "Easy big boy, there are some things I don't need to see," he said. Sarge fled to the galley to get a bucket of beers for them.

Raven moved to the padded seat and removed her shorts, leaving her in a tiny black bikini. She stretched out, her head propped on a cushion so she could drink her beer. She had to try and stop touching Dragon or she was going to explode. She rarely would have beer but felt like it now, it was cold and she was thirsty.

It didn't take long; maybe an hour and they spotted the bar. Sarge had the throttles open to about 10 knots and he pulled them back to a forward idle. The Dream Weaver slowed and flattened out into a smooth approach, as Dragon monitored the depth sounder. They felt 5 meters was good and Wax dropped anchor and they waited to feel it catch. It held, as the wind and the current turned the Yacht to pull the line taught. Sarge let the diesels fall silent and silent it was, just the breeze and the small sounds of the ocean against the hull. They drank beers and sunbathed and put any of the unpleasantness of the past night out of their minds.

They decided on a late dinner to watch the sunset and then they would go to Dusty's bar. Wax and Sarge were asleep in the sun and Raven was still lying on the padded bench when Dragon had stood and cast his shadow on her, causing her to open her eyes and see him standing above her. She parted her lips slightly as her breath escaped her. He held out his hand for her to take, his sexy half smile curving up in one corner of his mouth, his head tilted slightly sideways.

"Come now Angel, I have some things I need to do to you," he said.

He pulled her up into his embrace, putting kisses down the side of her neck, pushing her hand to his erection. She couldn't speak and trembled under his spell now. She rubbed his erection through his shorts as he slipped his hand into her bikini bottom to touch her wetness.

"You're a good girl," he said. It had only taken seconds for him to make her completely overcome with desire for him.

She let his mind work on her, thoughts of the game he was playing now in her mind. It was one of her favorite games. She would be completely at his mercy and the thought of it now was making her weak in the knees.

"Are you ready?" he asked. "Yes baby." She looked into his eyes, loving him with all her heart, loving how he loved to please her. "We'll see. Come with me now," he said. He led her down the steps to the main cabin and into their bedroom.

Closing the door he turned her to face him and he undid her bikini strings so she stood naked. She eyed the front of his shorts which looked like they would tear at any moment. He followed her line of sight, and tilted her chin up.

"Look at me," he said. "You're not allowed to look there and I'm going to make sure you don't do it again. I'm going to deprive you of something so you remember for next time, do you understand," he said. "Yes," she whispered.

Holding her chin he leaned down and kissed her hard, weakening her more. He eased up sensing she would come if he didn't back off a bit for the moment. "Wait here," he said. He removed his shirt now, testing her, but her eyes remained looking at his face. "I have some things to play with that you might like," he said.

Opening the top drawer of a built-in cabinet, he took only one thing, as he didn't want her to see the rest. Moving back to her, he held a silk scarf and taking it he moved behind her and tied it securely around her eyes. "Now you won't look where you don't have permission to look, will you?" "No," she moaned now.

Dragon smiled to himself, loving to play her favorite games for her. "Now," he said. "I'm going to tie you up so you can't move." She looked towards the sound of his voice, her lips full and wet, her hands shaking. He picked her up and laid her gently in the middle of the bed. "Just a minute, don't move," he said.

He took the white silk rope from the drawer. She felt him taking her left hand and knotting the rope around her wrist and pulling it to the corner of the bed. He tied the end of the rope to the bed frame. He tied her other arm next, spreading her across the bed tightly. Her breasts were vulnerable to him and he desperately wanted to kiss them, but he continued with restraining her instead.

"Almost done Angel, be a good girl and spread your legs, all the way," he said. She obeyed; her flexibility always made him crazy and his breath caught as she let her legs fall completely open to each side of her. Now he was afraid he was going to come.

"Baby, that's good, you should see how sweet you look, you're making this hard for me you know," he said. He controlled himself and managed to finish tying her.

"Baby," she whispered. She was falling completely into his sexual abyss.

He removed his shorts now because they were cutting off his circulation at this point. He knelt below her and took her by the hips tilting her upward, which tightened the ropes on her ankles, holding her legs apart for him to willingly and freely torment her. Her wetness was everywhere, the insides of her thighs were wet and she glistened with it. She was already spread open for him but using his middle finger he smoothed her inner lips away so he could see her.

She gasped at his touch, her hips involuntarily trying to move into him, but she was prohibited by the ropes and it made her whimper to him now. He would do nothing to her until he was ready, as part of the game, but she begged him anyway. He leaned down and gently kissed her openness, his lips just a whisper on her, making her cry out and try to arch her back. She pulled hard on the restraints, her involuntary movements straining them.

"I warned you I would deprive you of something to remind you not to stare at certain things. You remember that don't you," he said. He enjoyed toying with her and continued it. "I think we should get that over with and when you promise never to do it again I will think about letting you come." "No, No, baby," she begged him. "Yes yes, baby," he said.

Holding her apart with his thumb and forefinger of his left hand, he slid his two middle fingers of his right hand inside her, hard, and all the way. She cried out at the feel of it. She was so wet, his fingers were coated in her moisture and he moved them into her, making her crazy. He urged her with his sexy voice, as he increased the motion and pressed harder into her favorite spot. He had her nearly there, she was resisting him, knowing he wouldn't let her finish, but her body was compromising her will and he was taking her to the peak of her climax, making her give in to him.

"That's it baby," he said. He withdrew his fingers, leaving her gasping and straining, and out of her mind.

He would never torment her like this in reality and when they had first practiced this technique it had been hard for him to want to complete the denial part of it. But he had learned to trust that she would gain the pleasure from him following through and gratifying her afterwards. The Kama Sutra was a good book. He also had become expert at sensing her orgasms and was able to deprive her at exactly the right second, making it as intense as it could be.

He kissed her lips, still leaving her blindfolded. "Now what do you want to tell me?" he prompted her. He waited until she was able to speak, her breathing evening out finally. "I promise not look without your permission," she said. Her blindfold was wet from tears of frustration and desire. "Good girl," he said. He then touched her lips with his creamy wet fingers. "Taste yourself baby, because that's what I want to taste in a minute," he said. She licked his fingers, as he put them one at a time in her mouth.

"Now, let's see if I can get you back to where you want to be," he said. "You are so sexy right now baby, I can't wait to fuck you."

He tried to be slow and nonchalant, to draw it out and make her wait but his eyes took in the sight of her tied and spread open to him. The sexiness of it was bringing him too close himself.

"Baby please let me come, please," she said.

He touched her again gently, parting her and exposing her completely. He loved seeing her like this and he examined her, kissing her inner pinkness again, watching her contract at the feel of it.

"Oh God Baby I need to do this," he said.

He ran his whole tongue up the middle of her, to her nerve centre in a French kiss that made her senses scream in response to him. He worked on her that way, making her go crazy. He had a lot of talent when it came to this and she lost it to him when he didn't quit, pushing her hard into it. She let the waves hit her, making her scream as he held her apart, watching her spasms, his tongue touching on her gently, feeling it with her.

He was more than ready now and he moved over her as she finished and pressed himself hard down into her.

"My god I'm going to fuck you, I want you so bad," he said. He was lost in it now. He moved himself into her hard, over and over again, just needing to come.

She cried out under him from the feel of him nearly splitting her in half. She moaned louder now as his movement was making her crazy again. Feeling it building, barely over her last orgasm, she begged him once more.

Holding himself up by his arms on either side of her, he looked down at her stretched out under him, her breasts sweet, her sexy lips apart and her body open and taking him. He watched as he buried it with each stroke.

"Baby I'm going to explode," he said. He pushed it even harder, closing his eyes. "Come for me baby, I'm almost there," he said.

She cried out, doing it for him and he let go, falling forward over her, pressing hard and holding tightly against her, as the heat of him filled her. His cheek was pressed against hers and they moaned to one another in the ecstasy of it. Breathing hard from his efforts, laying over her he stayed inside her waiting for his orgasm to subside. He pulled her blindfold up and let each of her arms loose, still laying on her. He wanted her arms around him.

His hair fell forward around his face and she brushed it out of his eyes and kissed his mouth. "Baby, that felt so good, you make me crazy for you," she said. "That's good baby," he said. "I need to untie you angel, so I can hold you."

He reluctantly moved out of her so he could free her ankles. And when he did, he lay next to her and they tangled up together. She kissed him everywhere, tasting his saltiness from the light sweat on his skin and the salt air of the ocean.

"Baby," he said. "I hope I didn't hurt you, I just wanted you so bad. You looked so sexy like that I almost didn't make it a couple of times." He could sense she was close to tears with her emotion for him and he hugged her to him, their bodies connecting.

When they had both calmed enough, he lay back and let her kiss his neck and chest. Warm and content together they kissed and talked about the rest of their night. It would be the one last free night they would have before they reached their target and would get to work. He felt they had just made a perfect start to it.

CHAPTER FIFTEEN

DUSTY ROADS

After dinner, they had a scotch on the stern deck, it was a soft moonlit night and they were feeling happy about their decision to leave San Diego when they did. Giving Dusty a wave that they were ready, shortly they were boarding his Boston Whaler and heading to the dock in front of his bar. They made it through the surf and walked the long dock and up a traversing flight of stairs to Dusty's bar. There was an immediate sense of comfort.

Dusty's was basically a wooden shack, wood walls, and wood floors, standing on pillars to accommodate the tide. It was homey, warm, and smelled like Tequila and the ocean. There was a deck, overlooking the water and they followed Dusty to a table. The surf in the background was pleasant, the breeze was salty and the music was old.

"Nice," Wax said. Always one to appreciate music and atmosphere, he looked around, nodding his approval. Raven was entranced, it was so normal and comfortable and Dragon as usual was not sure. Sarge was checking out girls.

"Welcome," Dusty said. "Tequila?" Dragon smiled and nodded, and Dusty eyed a waitress.

Dusty was a different man from the one they had encountered at the Marina. He was relaxed and there was no wariness or judgment in his eyes. Dusty was high on Marijuana all the time and oddly it made it hard for Dragon to see his thoughts. Dragon found this amusing and decided to let it go.

They sat together at a round table on the deck of the bar overlooking the surf. The bar lights were dim and yellowy, hiding what was in the corners. The tables were cheap but wooden and so were the chairs. A small platform was in the main bar area, to accommodate the bands that would bother to play there and a bar on the far wall. It was stocked with basic, but top shelf liquor and a vast array of Tequilas. The waitress arrived with a large tall bottle and five shot glasses.

"Maria, this is David and Raven, Sarge and Wax." Dusty had miraculously recalled their names, impressing himself. She smiled shyly, unloading her tray. "Welcome to 1942," Dusty said. He grinned and poured them each a shot of the beautiful Tequila. They had not had this one before and it was fine.

"That is 'very' nice," Wax said. It took him one second to empty the shot glass. "Yes it is," Sarge said. He wanted to down the whole bottle.

"My sister's band is playing later," Dusty said. "Hope you're going to stick around for it, she's good." Dragon already knew Dusty's story but tested him to see if he wanted to talk. "So how'd you get here?" Dragon asked. He let his eyes travel around at the casual scene. Dusty just shrugged and did another shot. "Living the dream," he said.

Dragon could tell he was the kind of man like Dragon himself, that didn't feel the need to explain his story to everyone. He didn't care what people thought or read between the lines. Dragon's own fears hovered; that someone would read between his lines and see what was there. He calmed himself and was able to see that Dusty's 'between the lines' only involved bad decisions and hard luck. Raven took his hand and climbed onto his lap and he embraced her, kissing her soft lips.

Dusty eyed them, taking another shot. "You two are tighter than… I don't know," he said. Dragon looked at him as if to say, 'can you blame me?' "I fell for her a long time ago and I'm still falling," he said. "That's nice, not something you see every day," Dusty said. "I fucking see it, every fucking day, what the fuck," Sarge said. They all laughed. "Cheers to that," Wax said. And their night began.

They had a few more shots of the 1942 and Dragon decided they needed to stock it on the boat, it was so good. Raven had gotten a laid back buzz from it and lay against Dragon's chest, her hair everywhere on him, as he held her there. Dusty had lit up a joint and sat smoking it at the table. He had offered it to them but they declined.

Sensei had discussed its use with them all, a long time ago. It had medicinal qualities, used practically for chronic pain control, but otherwise it was potentially damaging to brain cells and the lungs. Dragon had no desire for either and had never bothered with it. He could tell it was largely responsible for the haze Dusty was in for the most part.

Sitting around the bar were obviously locals, guys having beers and talking. They were mostly older and Dusty knew them all well. He had told them he was having friends drop by, so they paid no mind to it, which Dragon had noted and liked.

"Dusty, do any girls come in here?" Raven asked. She nodded slightly at Sarge and Wax. Dusty was in the middle of doing another shot. "There'll be a few from around here," Dusty said. He placed his empty shot glass down and looked about as if some would magically appear.

Sarge gave her a look and she eyed him back. "What Sarge? I'm just looking out for you, maybe tonight will go better for you than last night and you can go to bed with more than that Tequila bottle and your left hand," she said.

Dusty eyed the two of them; a look of amusement creased his face. Dragon could see him wondering if there had ever been anything between Sarge and Raven. Raven had caught his thought as well and smoothly addressed it.

"Sarge and I grew up together too, Dusty, we all did, so he talks shit to me because he thinks he can," she said. "I talk shit to you because you deserve it," Sarge said. "Does your sister annoy you Dusty? Not only do I have to tolerate them fucking every half hour, but she gets on my last nerve every chance she gets." Raven gave him an evil glare. "You are full of shit, Sergeant Willis," she said.

Dusty eyed them, sparking up another joint. "I get the gist here," he said. "My sister's cool I guess, if she pissed me off ever, I can't remember." They all laughed now. Dusty's way of not giving a shit about anything was infectious.

"We don't fuck every half hour," Dragon said. "Wouldn't blame you if you did," Dusty said. "You can fuck me every half hour if you want to baby, you know that," Raven said. Sarge looked pleadingly at Dusty for sympathy. "For fuck sakes, do you see what I mean?"

Wax sat back, looking amused. "It's just business as usual. They've been like this since they met," he said to Dusty. Dusty just grinned at them, finding them a refreshing change. "Like I said before, you people are fucking weird," he said. "I'll drink to that," Dragon said, and did a shot. "Me too," Sarge said, and did one with him.

The bar door had opened then and a group of girls came in. "Fuck, save me ladies," Sarge said. Dusty looked over to them. "That's my sister and a few of her friends. Her band must be here, give me a minute," he said. He got up from the table and went to greet them. The girls moved to the bar, greeting the other men, it was clear they all knew each other. Shortly Dusty returned to the table with his sister and made informal introductions.

"This is Anne Marie; David, Raven, Wax and Sarge," he said. She smiled to them, speaking with a slight Texas drawl. "It's nice to meet you all. Not bad," she added. She was eyeing Dragon, Wax and Sarge. "What I mean is, my brother usually brings home the strays, but you all are more like a herd of fine breeding stock. Haven't I seen you somewhere before?" She paused for a moment. "David, David Li?!" She looked at Dusty, impressed and a bit speechless.

He shrugged. "I don't know who they are, I just met them," he said. "At first I thought they were assholes, like everyone else." She looked shocked and flashed her exasperation at him. "Dusty! Honestly, how much shit are you smoking? They're only the hottest thing in every magazine these days," she said.

Sarge liked the sounds of that. "It's nice to meet you," he said. He gave her a flash of his blue eyes and perfect smile. She nodded at Sarge, thinking her friends were going to be really pleased, and then turned her gaze on Wax. "I hope I can get you boys dancing tonight, I brought a few friends in need of partners," Anne Marie said. "I will be all about that then," Wax said. She smiled at him. "I'm thinking you could be all about a lot of things," she drawled. Her slight Texas accent suited her look.

She turned then to Dragon and Raven. "Got a few love songs in the back of my guitar case for you two," she said to them. Dragon smiled politely. Unable to ever be void of his sex appeal it made Anne Marie blush, his good looks overriding her cool nature. Recovering and gathering her wits she turned to Raven. "I will do what I can to get this handsome thing to dance with you," she said. "The other guys in this place won't be happy if he doesn't let them get a glimpse of you." Dragon looked at Raven and then back at Anne Marie. "Bring it on," he said. She smiled back at him, thinking he was smoking hot like nothing she had ever seen before.

With that she had moved off as the band had begun to set up. Three guys had come in with their equipment and were going about their business, talking with her friends and setting things up.

Dragon sent the name Anne Marie McLean to Chekov, appearing to be absentmindedly checking messages. Dusty had lit another joint while they had been exchanging pleasantries and was leaning back in his chair against the deck railing, smoking it. Dragon's Blackberry vibrated and he glanced at it. Chekov was calling him so he picked up.

"Ya go ahead," was all he could say to Chekov. "Good evening Dragon," Chekov said. "You're ruining my Tequila buzz," Dragon replied. Chekov made a hissing sound into the phone. "That's bad when that happens. Try and pay attention now. Anne Marie McLean, also Anne Marie Watson, divorced from Wade Watson, Houston Texas, married for 12 years, no children. Brother Dusty, as you know, parents deceased. Criminal includes possession, prostitution, fraud, and a few other minors. You really know how to pick them Dragon."

"Suck my dick. Anything else?" Dragon said. "Nope, can't help you there, but you are in good hands if you really do need a blowjob," Chekov said. Knowing Dragon was unable to respond effectively at the moment, he was enjoying being extra flip with him. "I'll keep that in mind," Dragon said, and disconnected.

So Dusty's little sister had a few skeletons in her closet. Dragon decided he couldn't care less; her skeleton's paled in comparison to his.

He offered Raven another shot, she had just had the two earlier, so another was due. She didn't drink much and he was careful not to push her or he'd be holding her hair back while she threw up later. Dragon never got drunk himself either. Losing control of anything, especially himself, was definitely not his style.

Sarge on the other hand was always game. "I'm going to the bar for a beer," he said. "Me to brother, excuse us," Wax said. Raven grinned at them as their intentions were obvious. "Go get em Waxy," she said. "I'm on it Baby girl." He smiled hotly at her as he followed Sarge from the table. Dusty shook his head and did a shot.

Anne Marie's band finished tuning up and she spoke into the microphone announcing them. They were called Dusty Roads and they launched into their first set. Out on the deck, the breeze carried the sound off and it wasn't too loud to have conversation. The waitress Maria had lit the candle lanterns on their table and the surrounding ones, and more people had filled the bar.

"Is it like this every night?" Raven asked. "My sister's band draws it; they all know her, the people from around here. It depends, I get bikers stopping, that are coming through, there's not much between San Diego and the Mexican border but illegal's and drug runners," he said. "None of my business, they get their drink on, get in a few fights, satisfy the women, and move on."

The band played country rock, moving from some classics to new stuff. Her voice was good and suited the style of music well. Wax and Sarge seemed to be doing their thing, as girls vied for their attention. Watching Sarge and Wax, knowing they enjoyed casual sex with any willing recipient was a concept Dragon could never grasp, other than it was their release in some way. He had only ever craved Raven. He needed her 'being' around him, he needed her body to be there for him and he needed to please her with his own. It was how his world turned. She caught his thoughts and moved to sit astride him, kissing him wetly. He ran his hands in her hair, holding her mouth down on his as he responded to her tongue.

"Baby, I wish you could bend me over that railing and fuck me right now," she said. She whispered just loud enough for him to hear. It made him gasp in her kiss, then laugh at her. "No more Tequila for you. But later in bed I want to remember us again, Ok," he told her silently. She flashed her green eyes at him. "Ok baby." She moved off of his erection she had caused him and sat next to him in her own chair again. Dusty was eyeing them now. "You two are madly in fucking love or something," he said. His marijuana high was coming out in his tone. "Ya, I'm sorry Dusty, I can't resist him I guess," Raven said. Dusty eyed Dragon, "Lucky," he said.

"What about you Dusty? Any love life?" she asked. Dusty shifted his eyes to her, then off to nowhere. "Once, long time ago. I'm not cut out for it," he said. He did another shot, looking at her. She could feel his quiet acceptance of things, blurred by the Tequila and marijuana. Dusty looked back at his empty glass. "It's just easier this way," he said.

Raven thought he had been an attractive man in his day. He had let booze and dope erode him into a functioning addict, keeping life simple and the wheels turning fast enough to keep him going but slow enough that he didn't fall off completely.

Anne Marie was just finishing up a song. "You know you broke the wrong heart baby, you drove me red neck crazy." The line finished as the band completed the last bars. Sarge and Wax were with girls on the dance floor, along with many others, filling the small space with warm bodies. Anne Marie eyed Dusty's table.

"I promised a pretty lady a song, to get her man to show her off to you boys and I think it's about time," she said. Some eyes turned their way and there were a few cheers from over-served boys in the crowd. Dragon looked at Raven then at Anne Marie and smiled his 210 percent sexy grin, standing and pulling her up with him.

He led her to the dance floor, and nodded to Anne Marie. "As I said, bring it on." He turned and pulled Raven's lips to his, kissing her deeply, causing whistles and cheers from the drunks. "Get all close, all you lovers out there, while we steam it up for you," she said. And with that the band began a slow Johnny Reid version of a song, "Dance with me." They did their own take on it, which she sang well.

Raven fell into Dragon and they floated in their minds together like a long slow kiss. She was so small in his arms and he enveloped her, laying his face against the top of her head. The song ended but he didn't want to let her go and they stood like that for a few moments. The set had ended and the band was taking a break. Wax was making out with someone right next to them, also not leaving the floor immediately.

Raven slapped his butt to get his attention. "Having a good time Waxy?" she asked. "Living the dream," he said. Dusty's blanket explanation of life phrase came in handy. The girl blushed, taking in Raven and Dragon. "Hi I'm Selena," she said. Wax was relieved because he couldn't remember her name, to introduce her. They said hello to her, as she held Wax's arm, taking possession of him. "Where's Sarge?" Raven asked. Looking around they couldn't see him anywhere. "He's with Angie. Back of her pick-up truck I'd imagine," Selena said. Raven loved it; she would bug the shit out of him about it tomorrow.

"We're heading back pretty soon," Dragon said. "Don't worry, I'll take good care of him," Selena said. She looked pleadingly at Wax. "You can't go now." Her eyes let him know exactly why he shouldn't leave just then. Her low cut top, bulging cleavage and painted on jeans did the rest of the talking for her. She was pretty and dark, a Mexican blend of exotic, voluptuous and petite, very much Wax's type.

Wax looked at Dragon. "You heard the lady." Dragon smirked at him. "Sure buddy, just be back by 7 am, we need to head out. Text Sarge, and make sure he's OK." Dragon eyed Wax, who understood him completely. They looked out for each other instinctively and Wax would have to find Sarge and see he was OK before he would continue with his own agenda. Raven leaned up and kissed his cheek, avoiding his lips which were Selena's territory for now. "Later Waxy, have fun."

Back at the table, Anne Marie sat with Dusty, having a conversation and doing some shots. Dragon sat again and pulled Raven on top of him to sit with him again. "You want another shot?" Dusty said. "No, I'm good thanks," Dragon said. "We need to get back." "You're headed for Mexico?" Anne Marie said. "Yes," Dragon said. "I need to get my boys back first thing Dusty so we can get going." "Sure man I'll be here, I might be fucked up but I'll be here," he said. "Your girlfriends seem to like them," Raven said to Anne Marie. "Darn right they do, almost had a girl fight on my hands," she said. "Those are some nice looking boys, just not enough of them to go around." "Waxy will look after that problem," Dragon said. He was referring to Wax's passion for threesomes and group sex.

"Come on then," Dusty said. They said their goodbyes to his sister, admiring her voice and the entertainment. "We'll stop in on our way back probably, maybe catch you again then," Dragon said politely.

They left then, following Dusty to the Whaler. The Dream Weaver floated silently offshore, her lights glowing for them to see her as they approached her stern. It was a calm night and the ocean shone black in the moonlight. Raven though it was beautiful and the glow of it made Dragon look like pure sex to her and she felt herself getting wet.

Dusty pulled alongside the stern and they got out, holding his bow rail off, and they said goodbye. "We will stop in on our way back up, I just don't know when. But you'll see us," Dragon said. Dusty nodded, and then he oddly asked them. "Why are you going to Mexico anyway?" Dragon didn't know how Dusty could suspect them of anything so he answered as truthfully as he could. "There's something I need to do there," he said. Dusty took that in, then simply nodded, and departed, not looking back.

Dragon and Raven looked at each other then. "Weird," Raven said. "Ya, like he doesn't see, so I don't know, maybe it's just his way of asking a question, plain and simple," Dragon said. "True," Raven said. And now I have a question." She leaned into him, her hand pressing the outline of him through his shorts. "Yes Mrs. Li?" He smiled to her, thinking she was so beautiful in the moonlight. She squeezed him. "How much longer do I have to wait before you give me some of this?" she said. He eyed her and then the stairs. "30 seconds," he said.

He pulled her into their room and she fell to her knees in front of him. He gasped when he felt the heat of her mouth on him. She held him with her hands, stroking him and using her lips on the sensitive glands below the head of his erection, her saliva wetting him. He moaned, watching himself between her sexy lips. She kept at him, tightening on him then softening, letting him relax into the pleasure. The soft slow build achieved through oral sex was exquisite for the male and she wanted him to experience it perfectly. She released her hands and using only her mouth on him, she gripped his thighs, feeling his muscles beneath her fingers; she pressed her thumbs into them, running them up the inside, making him moan.

He held himself now, as he pressed himself as far into her mouth as he could fit, becoming more urgent for it. She reached around him and pulled his shorts down more so she could grip his butt, pulling him in to the back of her throat now.

"Oh god baby, don't stop," he moaned to her, his orgasm building now.

He was almost there. Moaning with every stroke now, clutching her hair, she could feel his come about to cover her. She squeezed his length with the movement of her hand tight on him and tightened her lips around him.

"Now baby," he gasped, shuddering. He let his head fall back, blinking as if he had been in a coma. He looked down at her then, taking in her sexiness as she licked his white wetness from her lips.

"Come here baby," he said. He looked adoringly to her. "You are so good at that. It just sent me off the fucking charts." He pulled her to the bed and she lay back and he climbed on top of her straddling her. He pulled her top off so he could squeeze her breasts. His hands slid over her nipples making her moan. "I'm going to make a nice mess of you tonight baby. Remember what that was like?" he said. He was referring to their foreplay they were restricted to before Sensei let them have intercourse. So many times he had done things to her. "I've been thinking it about it all night," he said, hardening again.

"I know baby, the thought of it is making me wet baby, touch me." She begged him now, wanting her clothes off, wanting his clothes off. He undid the button on her shorts and pulled them down her sexy tanned legs and off of her. He let his shorts fall and lay on his side next to her, pulling her thigh open across him and pushing the other one to her other side, spreading her legs.

"You want me to touch you sweetheart? It used to drive me crazy when I got to do things to you," he said. She took his fingers and put them in her mouth to wet them. "I couldn't get enough of it then baby and I can't now," she said. Grasping his wrist she shoved his wet fingers into her, fucking his hand with her hips. "You wanted it badly, didn't you?" he said. "Yes yes it's all I thought of." She moaned, and twisted under his now pressuring fingers. "Come on baby, fuck my hand, you're going to come," he said. "You remember how you used to come for me?"

She was crazy now, as she dug her nails into his arm, her nerve endings rubbing against his palm as she held him hard into her. He found her mouth with his, to finish her off, sending her an image of their bodies, together on his small bed when she had come this way for him for the first time. It had made him ejaculate all over her belly it was so erotic to him. The images flooded their minds and he was close himself, picturing it again.

Unable to stand it any longer, she fell into her orgasm for him, grinding against his hand, arching her back, as she held herself still while the waves of it pulsed through her, making her moan his name. He smoothed his other hand over himself in two strokes, coming hotly across her body.

"Baby," she whispered, lying open and moaning. "There, baby. Easy angel," he said. He withdrew his soaked fingers. "Remember how many times we did that? And I can think of the other ways I made you scream," he said.

When he was first learning about her body and her needs and the way it worked he had developed his love of exploring her intimately, forever fascinated by her. "Mmmm baby you used to make me crazy for you, and you still do," she said. He smiled, biting her neck now. "I think I spent most of my years in camp with a hard-on," he said. He remembered reading the Kama Sutra with her and they would explore the techniques with each other. He had learned to please her with his tongue, and it became their favorite thing to do.

"Baby, you were so sweet to me," she said, catching his thoughts. He had never touched her with his tongue there before and he had desperately wanted to, it was all he had been thinking about. "Do you remember that time?" she said. "Like it was yesterday," he said. He looked into the greenness of her eyes, the images of it entering the forefront of his mind now. "Baby, you blew my mind when you came for me," he said. He was falling into the feeling of it. "Let me, baby," he said.

Bringing back his words from that moment he let the memories come through. Sensei had left them alone in the main camp house, knowing they needed the bed yet again. In the tiny back room Dragon had gotten his wish.

"Baby, do it for me please," she begged now. "Remember it baby," he said.

He proceeded to bring it to her, laying his tongue on her, holding her apart, reliving the feeling of it, the taste of her and the sensation of stimulating her sexually with just his mouth. He kept at her, and she squirmed under his forceful tongue, running her fingers into his hair and arching into his mouth. It didn't take him long, her sensitivity alive and responsive. She found it wildly erotic to have him take her this way, then and now. She was completely at his mercy as he led her to a mind blowing orgasm that racked her body and made her nearly cry with the pleasure of it.

He recalled he had moved up to lay beside her, hoping she was happy and she had taken his face and kissed his mouth licking her taste from him. He did so now, resting beside her, kissing her shoulder waiting for her breath to come back to her. He had pushed her then, to another level she had not achieved before and it had amazed her. Now it was something she couldn't live without.

"Baby, I can't ever get enough of that," she said. "Neither can I baby. You know it's still my favorite way to do things," he said. "Stop it Mr. Li or I'm going to need it again," she said playfully to him. "I seem to recall that being the case on more than one occasion," he said.

He held her close to him, promising her that in the morning they could swim and then he would make a new mess of her on the chart table afterwards. The night was quiet, a light music sound drifted in the open window from Dusty's bar and Dragon hoped Wax and Sarge would be back on time in the morning. They were due to leave at 9 am. Hopefully Dusty would be coherent enough to get them there. Sarge would probably be hung-over but it didn't matter, he could sleep it off all day if he wanted to. Satisfied with all his thoughts, his lips brushed hers, and they were gone. No dreams plagued him that night.

CHAPTER SIXTEEN
PUERTO VALLARTA

Sarge and Wax arrived more or less on time in the morning. Dusty had left them on the stern platform. He looked like hell as he drove off.

"Welcome back," Raven said. Sarge looked groggy and disheveled and Wax looked cool as usual. "Good night?" Dragon asked. Wax nodded, grinning. "I'm thinking," he said. His expression said it all and they laughed. Sarge grimaced and moved uneasily. "My back hurts." He moaned and fell over on the sofa. Raven went to him. "What did you do to yourself?" she asked. "That girl had an appetite," Sarge said. He looked pained. "Did she wear you out?" Raven said. "Ya," he said. He winced and rolled onto his back on the sofa. His knees had abrasions and he was a mess. "Let's get him to bed," Wax said. He and Dragon pulled Sarge to his feet. "When you've showered, I'll fix your back for you," she said. He moaned a thank you and they hauled him to his cabin.

"That little Latino he was with rode him a bit too hard I think," Wax said. They sat and had tea and some fruit. "You look fine Waxy," Raven said. "Did that little Selena rock your world?" Waxy eyed her. "Yes and two of her friends, baby girl. You know me, go big or go home." Raven laughed. "Waxy how do you fuck three girls at once?" Wax just smiled at her. "That's not how it goes down sunshine." He was thinking it sweet that she was naïve in the subject of group sex. Dragon explained to her then. "Girl on girl," he said. Wax nodded. "It's just a big old hot party; you can join in or watch."

Raven looked at them and then thought about it in her head. For some reason she had never considered the idea that men liked to watch women together, even though she had seen it in the Kama Sutra

"See that's what I find weird about you two," Wax said. Dragon looked at him and shrugged. "I just don't feel attraction for other females," he said. "I can notice what they look like and things, but it has no effect on me." Wax shook his head, he knew they were deeply connected but it was incomprehensible to him. "See, I find every single one of them attractive," he said. "I mean I know how you two are, but it's hard for me to understand how you wouldn't like to see her make out with another girl." Dragon considered it. "In my book, that's sharing her and I don't share," he said. Wax looked bewildered, even though he already knew this about them it was the first time they had discussed it and it boggled his mind. Raven sensed his confusion, and teased him. "Don't worry Waxy; it's not a disease you're going to catch from us. You can go out and slay the masses with your sexy 'Hollywood' self for as long as you're able." He grinned at her, satisfied with that.

They weighed anchor and Dragon radioed the Coast Guard their position, sending them officially off on the last leg of their journey. It was uneventful, they stayed the night in a cove Dusty had told them about, and rounded the tip of the Baja Peninsula on the second day. Crossing the passage of the Sea of Cortez was as Dusty had said, high winds, rolling surf and a departure from the sight of land. They sat on the flying bridge and the Dream Weaver cut through the 6 foot waves. Sarge had slowed back to 12 knots as she took the hits from the rolling sea. Spray from her bow washed them in sea water as they made their way to the Mexican coast. Her autopilot kept them on course and they stayed alert watching the rough sea as they hit the rollers one after another. It was the only concern they'd had the whole time and eventually they sailed into smoother water, seeing land again and proceeding south.

Moving them to 20 knots again, they completed the journey making their way into the harbor of their destination, two and a half days after leaving Dusty's. Puerto Vallarta Marina was a vast array of moorings, inland from the open ocean. There were hundreds of docks all housing beautiful yachts, clearly a lifestyle choice for some, with the money to do it. The tourist city opened beyond it on the land, and beaches surrounded it. They cruised in and then were guided into their moorage. Raven thought it looked like a magical fantasy place which conflicted with the dark reason they were there.

Waiting for them, dressed in some sort of official nautical uniform was the Marina Manager, Jose Chavez. Chekov had instructed Dragon, there would be cars waiting for them and they were to go to the Hacienda. As they left the dock Dragon eyed the dark figure on the neighboring Yacht.

Finally Jose handed them off to an employee, driving a golf cart that would take them to their waiting transportation. He was very annoying. His weak humor was wasted on them and even more concerning was his inability to control his attraction for Raven. Dragon was ready to snap. They finally reached the parking lot and waiting for them were two vehicles. The first was a white Mazerati, with a red leather interior and the other a silver Hummer, shiny and solid.

They had almost made it until the golf cart driver, an Australian, older and smelling like liquor, stepped over the line.

"Here you go mates," he said. "One for pleasure and one for function, and you my lady are built for both." He was nearly drooling and eyeing Raven like she was Friday night on a stripper pole. Dragon finally lost it. He grabbed him by the throat, suddenly angry beyond reason.

"Listen you asshole, the last guy that fucked my wife in his mind got his face rearranged and you're way beyond that now. Lucky for you, I'm in a good mood." He drove him hard in the rib cage, knocking the wind out of him, cracking three ribs, before taking his head and smashing it on the steering wheel of the golf cart, knocking him out.

"Let's go," he said. They grabbed their stuff and left the golf cart with the slumped figure lying against the steering wheel. "Hey man, it's cool, if you hadn't done that I would have," Sarge said.

Dragon caught Sarge's blue eyes, and nodded. He held the door while Raven got into the Mazerati. Sarge and Wax loaded their gear into the Hummer. He knew she questioned his anger and he didn't have an answer. He wasn't familiar with the feelings he had suddenly had.

"It makes me angry sometimes," he said.

She somehow understood and nodded to him. They were not jealous of each other; it was an emotion they didn't experience.

Men's advances on Raven were useless and ridiculous, but yet it had angered him now.

"Sorry, but that guy just pissed me off for some reason," Dragon said.

She realized then that he had a vulnerability surfacing and squeezed his hand in hers. "You know when you see me sometimes and you tell me I look so vulnerable to you? Well that's how you look to me now, beautiful, soft, concerned, and in love. You don't need to be sorry for that," she said.

He took his eyes off the road to glance at her, love everywhere on his face. She always explained him to himself perfectly and loved everything about him, right or wrong. They watched the road after that, as it wound upwards, in the early darkness. Their duty called them in the morning and Dragon recalled the cold eyes he had seen from the deck of the neighboring Yacht.

After the glitz of the tourist region, it turned to poverty. Shacks, with no hydro or water were everywhere and desert conditions. Yet the Mexican people were native to their land and had existed there for hundreds and hundreds of years, learning how to live in the environment. Tourism was an economy booster but Dragon saw it as an intrusion on a culture that had thrived within its own existence long and forever before that. While tourism helped, it seemed to Dragon to be a curse against the true heritage of the country and a reason for the corruption that existed.

Dragon spoke to Chekov hands-free on his blackberry as they neared their new home. "You will meet Jose and Isabella, the couple that care for the place," he said. "They have a son, he keeps the grounds. They are trustworthy, try not to scare them." "Understood," Dragon said. He disconnected.

The Mazerati made Raven recall the Ferrari and the Lamborghini. She reached to Dragon's thigh and the rest of the drive was breathless and wet. By the time they arrived, Dragon was in a much better mood. They had travelled about 35 minutes, uphill mostly from the Marina. The road had become pretty much deserted now as they neared the end of it. They pulled into the drive of the Hacienda, it was a large horseshoe shape and lined with cactus and palms. The greenery was unexpected as they had just travelled through primarily monochromatic desert.

Dragon pulled in and stopped them in front. It was a beautiful structure, clearly restored and refurbished to its original beauty. The house was long, one story only. The stucco was a deep clay red color, with five white archways supporting a covered veranda that spanned the length of the front and continued around the entire outer structure. Rustic furniture was placed in groups, in the shaded area, looking casual and inviting. In the middle, the third archway led to the door. It was a massive wooden arched door, polished and oiled, fitted with handmade wrought iron hinges and a heavy latch.

"This is beautiful," Raven said. Her sixth sense took in a feeling of history and mystique. Wax and Sarge had joined them, standing on the driveway, taking in the vision together. "Damn," Waxy said. "Chekov hit a home run with this. Dragon nodded at him, eyeing the doorway now, as it had opened and two people, whom he presumed were Jose and Isabella had emerged. They looked nervous, so Dragon approached them, pulling Raven with him. "David Li," he said. He extended his hand to Jose. "And my wife Raven, my friends, Wax and Sarge. You must be Jose." "Hola Mr. Li and this is Isabella," he said. He shook Dragon's hand.

Dragon smiled at her and she looked like she was going to faint. Raven liked her instantly, she was so cute. It was hard to tell their ages, they were Mexican natives, short in stature and of slight builds. Isabella was more Raven's size, but matronly and Jose was only slightly taller and had a small pot belly and wore a mustache. His thick dark hair had silvered in places. They both had full, friendly smiles.

"Welcome Mr. Li, we are here for whatever you need. Please come in." Jose said. Politely and somewhat proudly he moved aside and allowed them to follow Isabella into the Hacienda.

Inside was like walking into the pages of history. The traditional setting was charming and authentic. The entrance came straight into the kitchen area. The ceilings were twenty or more feet high, lined with dark wooden beams against white stucco. The walls were colorful tones from the Mexican pallet of blues, reds, yellows and greens. The kitchen or living space really, was expansive. The cooking area was done in traditional tiling mostly blues and yellows, with modern appliances. There was a huge table, made of wood, heavy and rustic, with ten matching chairs, adorned with a hand woven runner in many colors, and native pottery. There were two seating areas; one was a large U shaped bench like sofa, in a terra cotta fabric, which blended with the terra cotta tiles on the floors. Then there was another casual area with four chairs around a small table, again rustic and in keeping with the era of the house. The overall décor was stunning, with native art and historical pieces lining the walls creating interest. Plants were around in large pottery containers, bringing the outside in. The room opened to a huge square courtyard. It was evident what the lay out was now; the house was square mostly with a courtyard in the middle and the rooms lining the perimeter. Archways again provided a shaded veranda running around the interior walls framing the courtyard. A beautiful pool glimmered. Hammocks and comfortable outdoor furniture sat invitingly in the shade. It was 38 degrees Celsius most of the time.

"This is beautiful," Raven said.

Dragon smiled at her, happy she liked it. She had a way of looking at new things with the eyes of a child and he found it adorable. He turned her to him, tilting her chin and kissing her lips. She gave him a pretty smile and adored him back with her eyes and his breath caught for a second as he recalled what she had done to him in the car on the way there.

Isabella flushed at Dragon's passion, but managed to smile at Raven. "Come Mrs. Li," she said. "I will show you the other rooms."

Raven wanted Dragon to come too but somehow felt that it was only appropriate for her to be interested in such things and he should stay with the men. She followed Isabella down a hallway, again high ceilings open air on one side, tiles and stucco. The interior stucco was a warm cactus like green with white archways. It was a tranquil color, exuding the naturalness present in the environment.

Dragon watched her go and then turned his attention to Jose. "Mr. Li, Senor Strauss has provided a surprise for your wife, a wedding gift I believe he said." Dragon recalled Sensei saying something about that. The General was so pleased they had agreed to appear legally married he wouldn't stop lavishing them with gifts. "I was aware, but have no idea what it is," Dragon said. "They are horses Mr. Li," Jose said. Dragon's jaw nearly dropped and he eyed Wax and Sarge. "What?" he said.

Raven adored all animals and to his knowledge he didn't think she had ever even seen a horse in real life, he knew he hadn't. She was going to be floored. "They are the finest Arabians," Jose said. "My son cares for them. Senor Strauss imported them from Egypt; they have been here for a few months now, waiting for her." Dragon ran a hand through his hair. "She's going to love them, where are they?" he asked. "There are stables on the property; we can go there when Isabella is through with the house. My son is waiting with them to show her," Jose said.

Isabella opened another large handmade wooden door and led Raven into the master bedroom. It was as stunning as the rest of the house. A huge four poster bed stood against one wall, again in the rustic wood. It was adorned with wrought iron detailing and crisp white bedding. Matching pieces stood against other walls, a dressing table and a wardrobe and bedside tables. A tall floor mirror stood in the corner reflecting the room and she knew exactly what Dragon would think about it when he saw it. He was going to love this for sure anyway, knowing he would make good use of the four posters on the bed as well. Isabella was explaining where everything was, and opened a wardrobe that contained clothing, clearly sent there from HQ Munich.

"You're clothes are here, Mrs. Li, and your husbands are there," she said. She indicated another wardrobe. Raven looked at the items, obviously chosen to suit the culture there and the climate. "I can show you the en-suite and then you can change if you'd like," Isabella said. Her voice pulled Raven out of her reverie. "Please, call me Raven, and um, my husband likes to choose what I wear," she said. She blushed slightly, thinking of Dragon's need to take care of her that way. "It is clear he adores you. Senor Strauss said you and your husband have a great love, and I can see that," she said.

The bathroom was amazing, it consisted of a large tiled free standing tub with steps built in to enter it, and a separate huge tiled shower, with rain spouts, and a built in bench, which once again Raven took note of, thinking of Dragon's enjoyment of the one they had at camp. It opened onto its own private courtyard, with a smaller square spa pool, surrounded in intricate Mexican tiling and plants everywhere. It was beautiful and tranquil and she loved it. One wall was mirrored with an intricate wooden vanity, tiled on top with two hand painted sinks.

"This is lovely Isabella," Raven said. She then turned as Dragon had entered the room to find her.

He eyed them, smiling as she came to him. "Maybe your wife would like to freshen up Mr. Li," Isabella said. Dragon didn't know what that meant, but gathered it had something to do with the clothing in the wardrobe. "Sure and baby then we have some more to see, Ok?" he said. Isabella nodded. "Yes I will leave you and show the others to their rooms while you change." And with that she retreated, closing the door behind her.

"Baby, look at this room. We could make love in here for months and never do the same thing twice," Raven said. His eyes went immediately to the mirror in the corner and he kissed her forehead. "Yes, I see what you mean, and we will," he said. "But we will save that for later. Right now you need to undress."

She stood in front of the mirror, in a tiny white lace thong waiting for him. He found a small skirt that tied at the side of her hip. It was woven cotton, with turquoise and greens and whites and yellows knitted into it. He kissed her nipples, unable to resist the opportunity before he pulled a bright green top over her head, close to the color of her eyes. It had an elastic neckline that he pulled down, revealing her tanned shoulders, the sleeves were short, just bands around her upper arms. It was cropped and elastic at the bottom, leaving her sweet flat muscular tanned tummy visible.

He looked at her reflection in the mirror now. "I must be crazy," he said. "I'm going to have a fucking hard-on till next Tuesday with you wearing this." She giggled at him and pulled him against her. "Don't laugh Mrs. Li, I'll tie you to that bed and fuck the living hell out of you," he said. "That's the idea baby," she said. She smiled up at him from under her lashes and rubbed his erection. He exhaled and let his head fall back, rolling his eyes to the ceiling. He forced himself to remove her hand from him. Thankfully his shirt hung long enough to more or less hide his predicament. "Behave now. Remember what Chekov said about not scaring these people. Not yet anyway," he said. She did as he asked, letting him tie some flat stringy sandals at her ankles and pull her out of the room.

They followed Jose back out the front door and around the veranda, which surrounded the house. There were steps down to a lower elevation at the back and a wide stone path meandered off, through foliage. They followed him, taking in the scenery wondering where they were going. The pathway emerged to a paved area, where there was a small open shelter that housed two golf carts and other gardening related items. Jose motioned for them to join him in one cart and Wax and Sarge could use the other.

Raven giggled as she could see Sarge and Wax were arguing about Sarge's driving. "Idiots," Dragon said. They couldn't help their testosterone and competed fiercely over everything, from fighting, shooting, weights, Chess games and also driving. Dragon was just as bad.

"Where are we going baby?" Raven said. "You'll see," Dragon said. The pavement had ended and they were on a dirt path now. They had come up a small incline and were descending now before coming to a halt finally. "Ok, we are here," Jose said. Raven then instantly caught on to something and looked at Dragon. "What are you hiding?" she said. "Come on," he said and pulled her with him.

It began to hit her senses right away. There was a smell of something she didn't know and as she turned, Dragon pushing her ahead of him, she saw. She stopped dead, staring. Jose stood grinning, waiting. There was a small barn, hay stacked beside it and fences going off as far as the eye could see. The terrain had changed back to desert, dusty ground, low growing plants and cactus. A boy stood, looking nervous waiting for them. He had dusty blue jeans on and cowboy boots, no shirt, and a large Mexican cowboy hat hung down his back from a leather cord at his neck.

"What is this?" Raven asked. She was looking wide eyed at Dragon, then Jose. "Come," Jose said. "This is my son Diego." Diego smiled shyly. "Hola Senor Li, err I mean hello," he said. Dragon nodded, smiling at him. "Hey Diego," he said. "This is Raven, Sarge and Wax." Dragon made his customary introductions. Sarge and Wax waved a hello to him and Raven smiled at him, making him look down at his feet.

"Um Senora Li," Diego said. "Senor Strauss has something for you that I am to show you." "Really?" It was all she could manage, clutching Dragon's hand.

They had moved to the edge of the fence now, Dragon pulling her closer as she seemed unable to move on her own. Diego turned, looking out to the desert pasture. He tossed his lithe figure up and over the fence and landed easily on the ground on the other side of it. He made a high pitched whistle somehow. He did it a couple of times and then the sound could be heard, hooves pounding on the hard dry ground.

Four stunning horses appeared, coming at a run from below a rise, dodging each other and tossing their manes as they galloped towards the sound. Raven's breath caught as she saw them. "Horses," she whispered. Dragon could feel her start to tremble. "Shit would you look at that," Sarge said.

Three of them took the forefront and another followed and when they arrived in a cloud of dust, nostrils flaring, eyes afire, the one came from behind and blocked the other three from getting to the fence. "Easy boy," Diego said. "Horses," Raven said again. Her eyes were wide and her jaw had dropped. "Baby," Dragon said. His voice brought her out of it enough to swallow and look at him. "What is this?" she asked. She did not believe her eyes. "A gift for you Senora," Diego said. "This is Raj and these are his ladies."

He stroked the Stallions neck. Raj was white, with large dark eyes, his nostrils flaring pink, his long white mane blowing in the breeze. He snorted the dust from his nose and calmed to Diego's touch. He eyed the new people and Diego soothed him.

"It's alright Raj, let them see," he said.

The mares were pawing impatiently wanting to get to Diego as well. Raj decided in unspoken horse language that it was safe and he dropped his head, moving around Diego to let the mares come forward, still eyeing the strangers. The mares crowded Diego, searching him with their sensitive nostrils for treats he sometimes had for them. They were the most beautiful things Raven had ever seen. "This is Sasha and that is Chivas," he said. "And the shy one is Venetia, she's only two."

"They're wonderful," Raven said. She was trying not to cry, they were so beautiful. "Come," said Diego. "Climb through the fence, they won't hurt you." Dragon and Raven looked at each other. "Go baby, I'm right behind you," he said. She climbed through the rails, followed by Dragon. "Don't be scared Senora, they can sense you. Here," he said. Taking her hand and turning it, Sasha leaned her nose forward, flaring her nostrils into Raven's palm, testing her scent. The mare bravely took a step closer. "Now, here like this," Diego said. He took Raven's hand and placed it in the centre of the mare's forehead. "Just stroke her face," he said. Raven couldn't believe the feeling, the smooth hair and soft muzzle as she gently ran her hand down the mares face. Sasha dropped her head, asking for more. "See, you are a friend now," Diego said.

Dragon looked to his left, as Raj had approached him now, and his eyes darted to Diego's. Raj was larger than the mares and muscled, his neck arched as he leaned forward, his nostrils flaring, touching his muzzle to the side of Dragon's face, breathing in his scent. "Let him smell you," Diego said. "It is his way, he is, how do you say, knowing you." Dragon had no intentions of moving and waited for the Stallion to finish his inspection. It was amazing to him how gentle of a touch the horse had and the softness of it. Raj took a few short breaths through his nostrils, blowing out and ruffling Dragon's hair. "Ok, now pat his neck," Diego said. Dragon reached up to the Stallions neck and ran his hand along it, feeling the muscles and smoothness of his coat. Raj seemed satisfied and relaxing his posture, he too lowered his head, allowing Dragon to stroke him, his large passionate eyes calming. "He would probably do anything for you now Senor Li; see in his eye?" Diego said. Dragon wasn't sure of any of it, but the horse was magnificent and he had an immediate sense of its nobility.

"This is incredible. They are so beautiful Diego," Raven said. Having taken turns paying attention to each one of them, she beamed at Diego. Raj clearly had Dragon in his sights and now nuzzled him, pushing at him with his nose, trying for more affection. "Raj," Diego said. "Don't be pushy." Diego took a step towards him, causing Raj to take a step back, tossing his head and flashing his eyes. The whole thing was amazing to them, the way Diego seemed to speak their language and use himself in a way they understood. Diego grinned at Raj's antics. "Ok Ok, my friend, but behave," he said. Stepping back he let Raj draw forward again.

Dragon had easily become comfortable and now stroked his neck and face, thinking the General had really done it this time. Raven eyed him with Raj and thought he looked so sexy. He caught her thought and pulled her to him. "So do you like them?" he asked. "I love them," she said. She had been so overwhelmed; she needed to be in his arms for a moment. Raj nudged Raven then. "You have three girls of your own, this one's mine," Dragon said. He pushed his nose away. Raj gave a slight squeal and tossed his head. "Shit, I'm talking to a horse," Dragon said. He looked at Sarge and Wax. "Looks good on you man. That horse reminds me of you, all muscle, goggle eyed and blowing smoke," Wax said. Dragon wanted to tell him to fuck off but remembered Chekov's words and kept silent.

"Tomorrow we will go for a ride," Diego said. He had begun to pull hay for them and they had flocked around him, wanting their food now. "Ride!" Raven said. "You ride them?" Diego laughed at her now. "Of course, I will show you how, don't worry," he said.

Dragon sent her a mental comment. "I'm not getting on that horse, don't ask me too." "Oh yes you are," she said, giving him a defiant flash. "Shit," he said.

They climbed back through the fence. It would be dark soon. The light was beginning to fade and they were starving. Jose had driven them back and when they entered the hacienda they could smell food. Isabella was in the kitchen with things cooking on the stove top.

"Senor Li, dinner is nearly ready," she said. "Thanks," he said.

Sarge was already opening the fridge to find them beer. They gathered in one of the seating areas outside by the pool gratefully downing them, as it was hot and humid and they had been in the sun for an hour, seeing the horses. The cold beer and the shade were welcome. Isabella announced that dinner was ready and they went to the table. She had made a large pitcher of something icy and green, and poured them all some. It was delicious and clearly laced with Tequila. Sensing Dragon's uncertainty Wax leaned over and whispered to him. "It's a Marguerite, cowboy," he said. "Tequila, orange liquor and lime juice."

"Thanks asshole," Dragon whispered back.

They ate their food. It was a delicious change of pace as Isabella had prepared things in a traditional Mexican way. It was the same stuff they always ate only with a completely new and different flavor.

"This is so good Isabella," Raven said. "You have to show Waxy and I how to cook with these spices." Isabella smiled with pride. "I will Senora Li, now if you will excuse me, just leave the dishes for me for tomorrow and I will go now so you can enjoy your evening. What time would you like breakfast?" she asked. "Nine is good, and thank you," Raven said.

Day one wound down and they sat after dinner, taking stock of things. "Tomorrow we will go down early and see what's happening and take it from there. I hope to make contact," Dragon said. They sipped 1942, talking about the mission. Dragon looked authoritative, cold, decisive and dark. It was where he went when he needed to do what he needed to do. "Tomorrow guys, we have a job to do." They all nodded, a seriousness covering them. "Cheers," he said. They finished their drinks, aware that time had caught up with them and things needed to be done. He stood then, taking Raven's hand and pulling her up. "Goodnight guys," he said. He proceeded to their bedroom.

She was aware of his serious mood and decided to run a bath. "Baby, let me rub your back, in the warm water, it will feel good," she said. He just looked at her with a softening glow in his eyes. She felt for him as she could see the weight of the mission landing on him now.

"We're going to make this happen baby, don't forget you have me, and Wax and Sarge. We can do this," she said. She knew Dragon would accomplish everything they had set out to do, but could tell it bothered him in some way. "Baby, I know you are worried about what you might have to do and what I might have to do," she said. "Think of it as a game that we can play, nothing more." He sighed, giving in to her babying him. "Make me forget it for tonight OK," he said. He kissed her hard. She pulled his shirt from him.

CHAPTER SEVENTEEN

JUAN CARLOS GUERRERA

In the morning, they went in the Hummer to the Marina. The manager had intercepted them and apologized profusely for yesterday's incident, assuring them he had fired the man and there would be no further problems. Dragon just ignored him, turning to business.

"Did you get the cases of Tequila?" Dragon asked. As per Dragon's request, Chekov had ordered four cases of the 1942, posing as David Li's assistant. It was part of one of Dragon's strategies to attract the attention of Juan Carlos Guerrera, not to mention enjoy drinking. "It will be here shortly Senor Li," he said. "And you have been refueled already as well." "Good," Dragon said. Then dismissing him he took Raven's hand and they proceeded to the Dream Weaver.

They were there to collect their weapons for target practice later and also as a ploy to attract the attention of their target. Dragon had three main ideas, guns, alcohol and women. If that didn't draw his eye, he didn't know what would, stopping short of waving a bag of Heroin at him. He had dressed Raven in the tiny red bikini with the gold rings. She wore a white cover-up tied at her hip and white wedge sandals. Her hair was loose and she wore sunglasses and looked like she just stepped out of the pages of a men's magazine. Dragon wore black board shorts and a black V neck clingy t shirt. He had tied his hair back in a pony tail, his glasses hung around his neck on a thin rubber string.

Before they rounded the line of docks that would take them to the Dream Weaver, Dragon stopped, turning to them. "Ok, we talked about this, are you all clear on how to play it?" he asked. "Ya baby, don't worry," Raven said. "We got it," Sarge said. "Ok, let's go," Dragon said.

They went to their mooring, attracting the glances of other patrons on the Yachts that filled the berths along the way. Juan Carlos Guerrera's boat sat silently like an ominous marker. Unlike most of the shining white hulls that surrounded them, it was black. The name Diablo was flourished in red lettering across its stern. The bow was long, sleek and nosing downward, built for speed, it was 50 or so feet of ocean ready prowess. Its inner deck space was white with red and white leather seating. Dragon's sixth sense told him they were being casually eyed by its occupants.

Sarge unlocked their cabin doors and quickly scanned for bugs or wires, before any of them spoke. Now waiting on the stern deck, Raven removed the white tied cover-up from her narrow hips, revealing her perfect sexy figure. Dragon moved to face her, posturing himself provocatively. He traced his fingers along her jaw line, running them down her neck and over her cleavage. It was a deliberate move to display their sexuality to the now curious eyes across the dock.

Wax and Sarge, according to plan, joined them, bringing 2 large black duffel bags, setting them on the padding of the stern seat. Drawing his attention away from Raven then, they removed their weapons, laying them in full view. They consisted of Dragon's compound bow, numerous large caliber hand guns, Wax's Remington sniper rifle, three Uzi sub machine guns and Raven's knives.

She took one from a black leather sheath, examining it. She turned to Dragon and looking up at him with a seductive smile she ran the blade on its side down his chest from his neck to the top of his shorts. He eyed her like a hungry tiger. Taking her hand that held the knife, he brought it to his lips, kissing the back of it. Sarge moved around behind her now and she followed him with her gaze, still facing Dragon. Sarge, close and touching her with his thigh, traced his fingers across her bare middle and then up, pulling her hair away. She let her head fall aside, leaving her sexy shoulder and neck open to him. He kissed her waiting skin, holding her against himself, pressing her into his hips.

Dragon stood, watching, appearing to enjoy the sight of another man's lips on her. She let her eyes flutter slightly, looking about to come undone. Then Sarge let her hair fall back and he stepped away again, turning his attention back to the guns. Dragon leaned in and kissed her long and wet, savoring her mouth and letting his hands trail down her back, cupping her perfect butt. He then released her, leaving her lips wet and parted, making her truly want him then, nearly forgetting for a moment what they were supposed to be doing.

She turned, replacing the knife and sat up on the stern seat, leaning back on her hands, showing off her breasts and flat tummy and sexy legs. Sarge looked at her and licked his lips, eyeing her up and down as she distracted him from the guns.

After inspecting their weapons, they replaced them in the bags. Just then, Dragon could see a dock hand approaching pushing a cart stacked with the cases of Tequila.

"Perfect timing" he said. He jumped down to the dock to meet him. "Senor Li, where would you like me to put these?" the boy said. "Just here, we can load them on board," he said.

He did not want the boy to see their weapons but wanted to be within speaking distance of Juan Carlos. He sent him off with 100 US dollars. He could see Juan Carlos now from the corner of his eye, watching them from his own deck. Hopefully he had taken in their entire show and now his curiosity would get the better of him. The boy had removed the cases from the cart before he left and Dragon stood looking at them, pretending to be thinking of what to do.

When he knew it was right, Dragon turned and met the eyes of Juan Carlos Guerrera. Now standing in the open area of his stern deck watching, Dragon's prediction about his curiosity getting the better of him had come true.

"That is some nice Tequila," Juan Carlos said. Dragon stepped toward him, stopping at the edge of Diablo's gleaming hull. His direct dark eyes were on Juan Carlos' as he smiled. "I'm David Li," he said. "And you are?" "I know who you are Mr. Li," he said. He leaned forward and offered Dragon his hand. "Juan Carlos Guerrera. Welcome to Puerto Vallarta Mr. Li."

He was typically Mexican, shorter stature, olive skinned, black smoothed hair with a wide smile and even white teeth. He was dressed in black loose fitting linen pants and a white linen short sleeved button down shirt. He was muscular and well built in a compact way. He wore gold, a large chain, and a ring on his little finger, thick with a large diamond glinting from it and another large diamond stud in his right earlobe.

Dragon shook his hand, nodding to his welcome. "Do you have a taste for Tequila Mr. Guerrera?" he asked. "I wouldn't be a self respecting Mexican if I didn't. Please, call me Juan Carlos." Dragon smiled. "I'm not Mexican and sometimes I'm not self respecting, but it goes down just fine anyway." Juan Carlos laughed. "Good point Senor Li." "David," Dragon said. Juan Carlos eyed Raven and Wax and Sarge now. "Are you staying long?" he asked. "Maybe," Dragon said.

"You should stay long enough to get a feel for my country Senor Li, maybe do some business here." He gestured to the yacht. "This is my home. It's not much, but I have simple needs," he said. Dragon smiled and nodded his agreement. "Simple needs are the best kind. My simple need is right there," he said. He turned his gaze to Raven. Juan Carlos smiled broadly, liking this. "I would be honored to meet her, if I may," he said. "Of course," Dragon said. He eyed her but knew already she was waiting.

He took her hand and stepped her down from the yacht, bringing her to the edge of the Diablo. She had taken off her sandals and was barefoot; it was perfect, as she looked young, tiny and vulnerable.

"Raven," he said. "This is Juan Carlos." She smiled at him with her most innocent look, her green eyes soft. "Hello," she said. She blinked at him and looked up at Dragon seemingly for his approval. He put his arm around her. Juan Carlos was speechless but for only a moment.

"Senora, it is my pleasure. I was just welcoming your husband and couldn't continue our conversation until I had met you," he said. He made Raven's skin crawl with his vulture grin and penetrating stare. But, she licked her lips and almost tried to look up, playing young and innocent and controlled. "Thank you, it's nice to meet you," she said. She winced internally as he blatantly eyed her breasts and body.

Not even looking at Dragon when he was speaking, he nodded and ran a hand through his hair. "David, you are a fortunate man," Juan Carlos said. Shrugging like it was nothing, Dragon smiled at him. "Like I said, simple needs," he said. "Indeed," Juan Carlos said.

Raven shuffled uneasily and finally flashed her eyes at Juan Carlos, making him grin to himself, as if he had just laid eyes on the best Heroin money could buy. Before anything else happened Dragon motioned to Wax and Sarge.

"Well, that Tequila isn't going to put itself away anymore than it's going to drink itself. We are having dinner tonight on board, perhaps I can tempt you with a shot or two later?" Dragon asked. "A very good idea David, but please join me here and bring your friends," Juan Carlos said. Dragon smiled to him, nodding. "It was very exciting to meet you Raven," Juan Carlos said. She smiled sexily at him, pretending to enjoy his flirting eyes. "And you as well," she said.

Dragon raised an eyebrow at Juan Carlos for effect. He had clearly planted the seed that he shares her with his friends and also that she has a sexual appetite for things. He knew Juan Carlos would be very curious about those things.

With that, he handed her back aboard their yacht and he and Wax and Sarge loaded the Tequila into the cabin. They locked up, taking the duffel bags. Dragon waved a hand to Juan Carlos as he stood watching them go. There were three other male figures with him now, which had been there the whole time but unseen during their conversation. Dragon gathered they were his heat. Juan Carlos nodded to him, smiling, eyeing them as they proceeded down the dock. Dragon could feel him questioning the guns, questioning him, questioning his friends and lusting for Raven. It had all gone exactly according to plan. A man with questions would want answers.

They didn't speak until they were back in the Hummer and Sarge had scanned it clean. Finally Dragon broke the silence, driving back to the Hacienda. He kept his eyes on the road and they could see he was replaying the events and thinking about his next move.

"He fell for it," he said. Raven turned then, grinning at Sarge. "Nice moves Sergeant Willis," she said. "Your lips were nice and soft." "Ya, well there was something else that wasn't so soft after that," he said. She laughed. "Did that make you hard?" "Everything about you makes us hard baby girl," Wax said. "Did it make you hard too Waxy? I know how you like watching," she said. "Damn right it did," he said. "OK you two assholes," Dragon said.

They were going to eat something then do some shooting that afternoon. When they returned, Isabella had left them lunch but was not present. They ate and then Raven needed to change before they went. She pulled Dragon behind her to their room. "Just go guys, we'll be there in a minute," Dragon said. "Yea right," Sarge said, rolling his eyes.

Closing the door behind them, she turned to face him. "Are you alright baby?" She was concerned for his mental state, knowing how intensely he dealt with things. He gazed down at her, loving that she understood him so entirely. He freed his hair from the tie and ran a hand through it. "Ya, that was annoying and I just need to shoot some guns or something now," he said. She undid her bikini top and let it fall to the floor, then removed the bottom and walked naked to the bed. Laying back on it, she spread her legs apart.

"Or that," he said.

They made it to the shooting range, walking hand in hand in the warm sun. They had seen it the day before when they were heading to the stables. Wax and Sarge were already there. They all practiced their accuracy and timing, taking turns with the different weapons until they were satisfied no one had lost their touch. Afterwards they sat together at a wooden picnic style table, cleaning the weapons and talking in the now very warm afternoon. They figured they would relax and swim in the pool when they returned to the Hacienda. Jose had joined them, talking about the weapons with them. He had been mesmerized by Raven's knife throwing.

They were about ready to head back when they heard the unmistakable sound of hooves. Coming towards them down the dirt road was Diego. He sat astride the black mare Sasha, bareback. She wore only an ornately hand tooled soft leather halter, with a single thick braided rope Diego held in his left hand. In his other hand he led Raj, also wearing only a halter. Raj pranced along beside the mare, his mane flowing long, his nostrils snorting in the dust, eyes everywhere. The mare moved gracefully at a prancing trotting step, her neck arched and her small ears flicking back and forth listening to Diego's words. They came to a stop before them. Raven just stared, wondering what was next.

"Senor Li," Diego said. "We can go for a short ride." Turning the mare's body sideways beside her, he looked down at Raven with a happy smile on his face. She looked up at him, staring. "Where? On her? With you?" Raven asked. "Yes!" he laughed. "Senor Li, here, take Raj," he said. He offered him Raj's lead rope.

Dragon rolled his eyes at her, but stood and took the rope. "Take a few steps backwards Senor Li, so he knows to follow you," Diego said. Dragon did so, looking into the Stallions large eyes. Raj flared his nostrils taking in his scent, then lowered his head and followed to him. "There, see, he is yours now and he will serve you as you ask him to," Diego said. "Serve me?" Dragon asked. "How?"

Wax and Sarge were smirking at him now, hoping he would fuck up and amuse them. He looked at them, knowing full well they wanted to have a laugh on him.

"Senor Li," Diego said. "You have to get on him. Then you will see."

He then spoke to Jose in Spanish and Jose moved to Raven explaining what he was going to do. She complied and he gave her a leg up onto the mares back.

She never in a million years would have seen herself on a horse. Dragon watched her, thinking he had never seen her look so sexy. She was up against Diego, her sexy legs against the horse's side as she curled her arms around Diego's shirtless, lithely muscled young body. Sarge had his camera along and he took some random shots that she was unaware of, completely immersed in balancing herself. Diego imperceptibly cued the mare and she walked forward, turning and walking in the other direction so Raven could get the feel of it. She had amazing balance anyway, from Yoga and had no trouble keeping centered, her abdominal muscles holding her steady.

"Mr. Li, he is waiting, just jump on him," Diego said. He instructed Dragon to place his left hand with the rope on Raj's withers then straddle up on him. Dragon eyed Sarge and Wax. "I can do this, you fucking assholes," he said. Then in one smooth athletic move he was on the Stallions back. Raj adjusted his balance to Dragon's weight. "Nice," Diego said. "Now move him with your lower leg, like this." He demonstrated, making the mare go forward and turn in either direction. Dragon cued Raj, who cooperated instantly, moving off his leg. The horse felt powerful under him, its muscles strong and hard and it had a balanced pace and smooth rhythm.

"Now, he will serve you," Diego said. "Take him first." He motioned for Dragon to proceed back up the dirt road. Raven held onto Diego as the mare moved to follow them. "We can just take a short path for today," Diego said. "Tomorrow we can go on a longer ride, down to the ocean."

"I didn't know you could get there from here," Dragon said. He was shirtless as he had removed his sweaty T-shirt after shooting. The dragon tattoo shone back at them in the sunlight, glowing off of his tanned back, making it impossible for Diego not to notice it.

"That's a great tattoo Senor Li," Diego said. "Thanks Diego," he said. "It's been a part of me for a long time. Sometimes I forget it's there."

They had come to a flat sandy area on the path. "Here we can go a little faster, Senor Li," Diego said. "Just ask him with your lower left leg." Dragon eyed him. "How much faster?" he asked. "Just enough to change his stride," Diego said. "Give him the cue, he will know." Dragon looked ahead and gently applied his left leg to Raj's side. On cue Raj picked up a bouncing canter stride, perfectly balanced, his neck arched, creating just the slightest tension on the rope. Dragon adjusted his balance to the new pace. Sasha responded to Diego and matched Raj's pace. They moved steadily along for another few minutes until the ground changed again and Dragon figured out when to slow. Raj came back to the walk, blowing his wind from the exertion and dust.

"Very good Senor Li, the ground up ahead is uneven and has rocks. We must walk so they can pick their way safely," Diego said.

They meandered downwards, eventually coming into sight of the stables, passing Diego's home along the way. They waved to Isabella who was hanging wash. Waiting for them, were Sarge and Wax with a golf cart. They walked up to them and Diego let Raven down, holding her arm as she got her leg over so he could let her land on her feet. He then showed Dragon how to get off without falling on his ass. Dragon stood now, stroking the Stallion's neck and face having developed a new affection for him.

Diego took Raj's rope. "Thank you Diego," Raven said. "You're welcome Senora Raven. Tomorrow you can ride her yourself and I will bring Chivas." They said their goodbyes and Diego turned and proceeded to the barn.

Dragon stood posturing, looking at Wax and Sarge. "Sorry to disappoint you two shit-bags," Dragon said. He climbed onto the back of the golf cart, with Raven. "If I can ride a horse you can drive a fucking golf cart without fucking up I hope," he said, to Sarge. "I don't know if I can," Sarge said. They all laughed and Sarge sped off, weaving all over the dirt road, nearly dumping them a few times.

Wax made them a pitcher of Marguerites and they sat in the shade by the pool. "Tonight, when we get on his boat with him, I'm going to pry into his business," Dragon said. "And Raven, flirt with Wax, he's already seen Sarge on you. Play it like you have one thing on your mind." "That won't be an act," Sarge said. "Asshole," Raven said.

Giving Sarge a superior eye she moved to Wax, around behind him, caressing his shoulders. "I get to flirt with you Waxy." "Go easy on me baby-girl," Wax said. He smiled to her, all 'Hollywood' hot.

They drank the cooling drinks and swam in the pool, cooling out the hottest part of the day, until it was time to head back down to the Marina. Sarge remembered his camera and went and got it so they could see the pictures of the horses. He loaded them on the laptop and they watched.

The first few were of Wax shooting at the range earlier, cleverly done, catching the line of his sight, his eyes and his muscled upper body, holding his gun in a two handed grip. Raven teased him about looking like a 'Hollywood' movie poster. Then there was one of Raven, she had just gotten up behind Diego. It was a side view of the left side of the black mare and Raven was pressed against Diego, her arms loosely around the flat of his stomach, their legs bent together at the same angle. He had his wide brimmed Stetson hat on and was looking down, to his left, his arm bent with the colorful rope running through his hand. Only his smile was visible under the hat brim. His skin was a tanned dark brown and his straight white teeth in his smile made him look like an exotic teenage dream. She had on her black spandex shorts and cropped yoga top, her middle bare with her toned core muscles flexing, as she balanced. Her braid hung over her shoulder and wisps of her hair blew about her face, her lips were apart and her eyes were green and staring at Diego as he appeared to be smiling back at her.

"That is some sexy shit," Waxy said. "That boy knew what he was doing all along." "The thought occurred to me," Dragon said. "It's nice Sarge," Raven said. The next was one of Dragon, sitting on Raj's back, that was equally stunning. Sarge had caught the horse turning back to the left, its arching neck bent and its head down, so that the front of his face was turned to the camera. Dragon was looking over his left shoulder, presumably at Diego and Raven, his hair blowing back, with his sexy smile, his muscled, shirtless body glowing in the sun. It captured an expression on his face that was truly happy and made him and the horse look like one.

"Baby, that's amazing, look at you," Raven said. Dragon smiled at her, not really comfortable with his good looks, especially in pictures. "There you go man, that's a Cover shot right there," Wax said. "I swear to god you're gay," Dragon said.

"Hey baby, maybe we can get Chekov to show the pictures to the General, to thank him for the gift," Raven said. "Sure, he's probably drooling over the one of you right now and photo shopping himself over Diego," Dragon said. "What do you suppose Chekov does about women anyway?" Sarge asked. "Who knows, but stuff definitely goes on there behind closed doors," Wax said. He was drifting then, remembering his visits with Erika.

"Next time we see him in person, I will try to see in his mind," Raven said. "Seeing into Chekov's mind? I don't know baby, all I ever get from him is his desire for you and he hides that pretty well," Dragon said. "He guards his perimeter like Damascus does."

And with that they decided it was time to get ready to go. Dragon had advised them to dress somewhat more formally and he now eyed Raven's closet looking for what he had envisioned for her. She sat cross legged on the bed in a pink satin thong waiting. He was trying to decide on innocent or temptress. He chose innocent. In keeping with her pink thong, he chose a baby pink dress. It had thin satin spaghetti straps and a heart shaped bust line that would show off her breasts. It was a silk and cotton blend that fit her shape perfectly as he zipped it up at the back. It was appropriately short. She slipped into silver wedge sandals with a four inch heal height. He found a solid silver arm band, shiny and intricately tooled, definitely native. He clasped it to the narrowing part of her right bicep. He brushed out her hair, leaving it down, full and curling thick down her back.

He pulled on a pair of black linen and silk blend pants that accentuated his sexy butt, draped his muscular thighs but hung sexily from his waist and a silk and microfiber T shirt style V neck that was a subtle light blue, a color she loved him in. It fitted over his muscled body revealing his sexy physique, his wide shoulders accented by the short sleeves stretched around his biceps. He found the black belt, with the familiar platinum DLI belt buckle.

Meeting Wax and Sarge at 5 pm they grabbed the food Isabella had gotten ready for them and manned the Hummer again.

"Baby, let Wax drive, so we can make out in the back," she said. Dragon tossed Wax the keys. "Works for me," he said. Wax shook his head, catching the keys and leading the way. Wax drove the 35 or so minutes back to town, as they took in the scenery again.

The tourist part of the town was busy and alive with the evening as they found their way to the Marina. Getting their things, they proceeded to the Dream Weaver, game faces back on. They settled in, sitting shaded, sipping Tequila, while Wax and Raven played in the galley, making a delicious dinner. In spite of the circumstances, they really did enjoy being on the boat together. Wax had his music on and they cooked. Dragon and Sarge had summoned Chekov and were getting any relevant updates, including Chekov's comments on Sarge's latest photography. They ate in the open air of the stern deck area, taking in the Marina sounds and sights. It had a community feel to it that was interesting. People really did this, Dragon thought.

The Diablo was deserted and he wondered if his plans were going to be changed. They sat, enjoying an after dinner cocktail, as Juan Carlos finally appeared, coming down the dock with his men in tow. Dragon noted him eyeing Raven so he thought a forked tongue would slither out his mouth.

Juan Carlos waved to Dragon and he nodded at him, tipping his glass toward him. They all found it very amusing, knowing what was to come. It would have been nice to have simply killed them that night. They were an annoying means to an end that had to be dealt with. Dragon could see Juan Carlos was high and liked the advantage. His clouded straying mind would be easy to pry into.

"Ok, you two, put on a little show first, then we'll go," Dragon said. Music was playing quietly in the background and Raven got an idea. "Wax, turn it up a bit," she said. Wax picked up a remote and used it to raise the volume, just loud enough. Raven stood, moving out of Dragon's embrace and approached Wax where he sat. She stood in front of him, moving slightly to the music. "Sorry about this Wax," she said. Taking his hands she placed them on her hips and straddled him. Knowing he had no choice, he pulled her down onto him. Her dress slipped up her thighs but didn't quite reveal anything from the back.

Dragon and Sarge pretended to watch like it was Saturday afternoon in the local strip club, as Raven delivered Wax a steaming lap dance. She felt his hands on her waist and lower as she moved on him, making him harden under her. She closed her eyes as she felt his lips on hers, his hands in her hair. She let him complete his share of the job, allowing his tongue to explore her. His lips left hers and he moved down her neck as she let her head fall back, feeling his finger tips tracing the top of her breasts above her dress. She wondered what it would feel like to a normal girl. The song ended finally, freeing them from further violation of their friendship. Hopefully the only residual side effect was Wax's hard on.

When it was over he looked at her and taking her face in his hands, he whispered to her. "Sorry baby girl, I'm only human." His erection pressed against her inner thigh. He was big like Dragon and it was impossible for her not to feel it. "Well, you kiss nice, 'Hollywood'," she said. Gracefully removing herself from him, she turned back to Dragon.

She eyed him and moved to him, completing the display, as she stood in front of him. He was leaning back and eyeing her seductively as she presented herself to him as though it was his turn now. He sat up finally, as she stood between his legs. He pulled her into him, kissing her, but meaning it. 'Baby, good job, you can do that for me later.' he said to her silently. She felt instantly better in his arms, his warm lips on hers, his real love soothing her.

Juan Carlos had taken in the entire scene. Dragon assessed him as having the type of personality that would see this behavior as enviable, if not admirable. Juan Carlos' narcissism allowed for him to feel that self indulgence was an entitlement and something a man deserved. He would also experience some level of sexual gratification from the demoralization of a woman or a child, whom he definitely considered inferior and subordinate to himself. It was the classic formula that when blended together created the kind of animal that he was. Dragon was hoping he could kill him sooner rather than later.

One of Juan Carlos' gorillas allowed them on board, as Juan Carlos stood to greet them. Dragon introduced Wax and Sarge, as his 'friends' and Juan Carlos greeted them graciously, eyeing their hardware. But all of his men were armed, it was normal and expected.

Dragon placed a bottle of Tequila he had brought on a nearby table. "Shall we," he said. "Senor, I like your enthusiasm," Juan Carlos said. He eyed one of the minions, who proffered small heavy glasses, double shot sized. Juan Carlos poured five doubles and motioning for them to take one, he raised his. "To new friends," he toasted. Dragon nodded, touching his glass against his then downing it. Raven managed to down hers, but she would not be having another. Dragon would make sure, handling it for her.

"Please sit, gentlemen," Juan Carlos said. He eyed the minion again, who left and then returned with a cooler full of some sort of Mexican beer. "Refresh yourselves my friends, it is the Mexican way of how you say 'pacing yourself'," he said.

They had beers, allowing the effects of the tequila to ease into their blood stream with a feeling very unlike other alcohol. They settled into conversation, Juan Carlos beginning with the questions Dragon had expected from him.

"You have an impressive collection of weapons," he said. "It's a hobby. We all shoot, there's a range at the Hacienda and we had a little fun this afternoon," Dragon replied. Juan Carlos nodded, satisfied with that. "The coast guard around here is 'picky' shall I say, should you be searched," he said. Dragon just looked away, playing a game. "I don't get searched," he said. It was bullshit but he wanted to see the reaction. Juan Carlos raised an eyebrow and grinned, tipping his beer in Dragon's direction. "Understood Senor, this is Mexico, there are many ways around the rocks in the road," he said. Dragon nodded, saying nothing else, but satisfied that Juan Carlos readily bought into the theory that being David Li made him untouchable.

Juan Carlos turned his attention to Raven, making small talk. He feigned interest in how she liked life on a boat. She expressed that she found it boring except for the diversions her husband had provided her. She had eyed Sarge and Wax, and looked shyly at the floor. She fanned the flames while Dragon waited for him. He had let a glint in his eye show to Dragon as he smoothly moved to Wax and Sarge. He discussed guns with them, and cars and boats, until finally, after they had done another shot, he directed his sights to Dragon again.

He had set the Tequila bottle in front of them, poured shots and held up his glass. "David, do you have business here in my country?" he asked. Dragon eyed him, the intimidating Dragon. He smirked, picking up his shot. "Juan Carlos, you know that I don't. I'm sure you know most of what there is to know about me. Let's not waste each other's time," Dragon said. Juan Carlos eyed him back, knowing the game had begun and Dragon had made the first move.

"So, you are here on a vacation, shall we say," he said. Dragon kept a poker face and looked indifferent. "I love my wife Juan Carlos and I like to indulge my wife. She has, shall we say some specific things that she likes and I enjoy spending my money on them," he said. It was a vague remark meant to pique the man's curiosity. For effect, Dragon eyed Wax and Sarge and then smiled at Raven, kissing her softly. "I like to show her how much I love her, you understand," he said.

Dragon figured the combination of sexual curiosity, the smell of money, and a potential business proposal would surely push him into revealing something. He could see some things in Juan Carlos' head. His Heroin high was softening but his Tequila buzz was replacing it. He could 'see' that he was very interested in the specific things Raven liked and his dark side was very close to the surface now.

"Of course, she is very beautiful and very desirable," Juan Carlos said. He was speaking of Raven as if she was no longer present. "Where did you 'find' her Senor?" he asked. He chose the word specifically. It could be taken harmlessly. Dragon took a sip of beer and shrugged nonchalantly. "Where one finds beautiful things, when you have the money to pay for them. I just happened to fall in love with her," he said.

Juan Carlos leaned back in his chair, appearing to be thinking or wondering something. "So what exactly do you like to spend your money on, if you don't mind me asking?" he said. Raven looked down submissively and Dragon eyed Juan Carlos. He lowered his voice and leaned forward to Juan Carlos, responding as though he was revealing a secret. "My wife likes certain things." He nodded toward Sarge and Wax. "Looking at them I'm sure it is obvious, however specifically sometimes her appetite leans towards something different." He paused, letting Juan Carlos' imagination work. To help him out, he continued. "Female, younger and forgive me but seeing as you asked, expendable. She likes to watch, while the boys and I take turns." He felt Raven's skin crawl as she heard him say the words out loud. It made her feel angry even though it wasn't true.

Juan Carlos sat back now, placing his shot glass on the table and putting his hands on his knees. This was when it could get ugly. In his line of business, revealing information could get you dead. He knew how this kind of negotiation went. David Li had revealed a very dark secret and would kill him if there had been any kind of a misunderstanding.

They could all sense the turning point in the situation. Juan Carlos responded with a knowing glint in his eyes. "Well, I may have exactly what you are looking for Senor," he said. He looked Dragon in the eye. "I have everything." Dragon smiled, giving Juan Carlos a dark, knowing, devious eye back. Pouring himself another shot and Juan Carlos one, he raised the glass. "Cheers," he said. They drank. A Mexican hand shake. "I'm beginning to grow very fond of your country."

They sat in a moment's silence and then Dragon felt it was his turn to ask a question, that Juan Carlos now owed him some answers. There was no turning back now.

"Is this your own personal business, Juan Carlos?" he asked. "I'm extremely concerned about discretion and like to know well who I am dealing with." Juan Carlos answered him readily. "I'm involved in certain things and this is something my organization is developing. Your privacy as well as mine is of the utmost importance."

Privacy of no issue actually, Dragon had gotten Juan Carlos to answer the real question he had wanted an answer to and then knew exactly what he would do next. He changed the subject.

"Juan Carlos, do you fish?" he asked. "Most certainly, there is wonderful Marlin and Swordfish, only a few kilometers off shore," Juan Carlos replied. "Would you take us? The boys here enjoy it and we haven't been out for awhile," Dragon said. He was making up the easy lie as a plan had come to him while they were talking. "Absolutely, how's tomorrow evening? It's best a few hours before sunset," Juan Carlos said. Dragon nodded and raised his beer tipping it toward Juan Carlos in agreement.

Raven on a silent cue from Dragon coiled herself around him, looking bored and pouty. "Well I need to call it a night," Dragon said. "Juan Carlos, perhaps tomorrow when we are fishing, we can discuss our business further." "Of course, and please rest assured that what happens on this boat stays on this boat David Li, I guarantee it," he said. Dragon nodded, smiling to himself thinking about what would happen on that boat very soon.

They had locked the Dream Weaver already so they proceeded straight to the Hummer. Raven would have to drive as they had all had five or six drinks, except her. No one spoke the whole way back. Dragon was quiet, Raven was hiding for the moment as she drove, and Wax and Sarge just waited. They arrived back, parking out front and headed inside. It was late.

"Good job guys," Dragon said. "Sure man," Sarge said. "Can we talk about this in the morning?" Dragon asked. "Easy man whatever, go to bed," Wax said. Dragon nodded and took Raven's hand and pulled her after him. He would use the remainder of his energy telling her his plan then let her take him down as only she could.

CHAPTER EIGHTEEN

DIABLO

Dropping into first gear Dragon spun the tires of the Mazerati out of the driveway, heading out on the road. His eyes were covered by his glasses, his hair tied back, but his jaw clenched as he pushed the car to its limits. Having left Raven crying in Sarge's arms, he and Waxy made their way to the Marina. The events of his entire life and the last 24 hours had led him to the final actions. He and Wax pulled into the Marina in a record 25 minutes. Wax picked up his pack and they headed to the dock and the final chapter of Juan Carlos Guerrera.

They arrived at the mooring and Dragon and Wax eyed each other, steeling themselves, moving forward. "Greetings, my friends," Juan Carlos said. He waved to them as they approached. Noticing it was only Wax and Dragon he looked puzzled. "Just the two of you?" he asked. Dragon appeared nonchalant. "Sarge is under the weather, he gets sea sick and he's feeling the effects of the Tequila," Dragon said. "Very well then, come aboard and we will set off," Juan Carlos said. He only had two henchmen, which was a slight concern. They climbed aboard the Diablo, as Juan Carlos fired up its huge engines. Its exhaust was through the transom, noisy and powerful as it surged to life.

"Where's your other guy?" Dragon asked, appearing reticent. "Have no fear David; he just didn't fit in to my organization after all. He was as you say 'expendable,'" Juan Carlos replied smoothly. Dragon nodded, gathering that for whatever reason, he was dead now. The remaining men untied them, securing the ropes and jumping aboard as they reversed.

They reclined in the open cockpit, the usual cooler of beer present and bottle of Tequila. They cruised at a wake less pace out of the Marina boundaries, as Juan Carlos chatted about the tides and the annoying sail boaters that didn't know how to get out of the way. Dragon and Wax did their best to keep themselves blocked from prying eyes, not wanting to be seen on the boat as they departed. When they had cleared the land Juan Carlos pressed the throttles down and the Diablo planed out into the open ocean, heading south along the coast. It was a beautiful boat and Dragon had to admit it would be fun to play with its speed.

Sarge had held her, as Dragon and Wax drove off; she hated not being with him and feared for him, knowing what was to come. She clung to Sarge now as he stroked her hair and let her gather herself. "Ok," he said. "Let's go, you're worried about nothing." She grappled with her emotions, forcing them into check and finally stepped back from him. "Come, on, we need to go," he said again. She nodded and they picked up the bags they had prepared and got in the Hummer. Sarge drove and they headed to the Marina. He eyed her from the driver's seat, looking stunning, his long blonde hair a mess in the breeze, sunglasses covering his blue eyes, but his smile taking her away. "Not used to just driving are you?" he teased her. She couldn't help but laugh then, as his efforts to cheer her up had worked. "You just wish Sergeant Willis," she said.

They were aboard the Dream Weaver and Sarge had the engines running, idling quietly, as the Marina Manager approached, asking if everything was satisfactory. Raven ignored him and Sarge just nodded. "Mr. Li is asleep and doesn't want to be disturbed," he lied. "Very well sir," he said.

The dock hands had freed her and secured her lines. Sarge told him they were going south to another small tourist port and would be back by dark. It was roomy enough for him to turn the yacht himself and soon they were sailing free of the Marina's breakwater. They cruised for an hour, radioing the Port Authority there that they were present and would be anchoring for a few hours, which they did. Then they waited. They were to be seen and made a matter of record at this port. It was a scenic place that many boats stopped at to take in the rocky coastal scenery and expansive beaches. There were bars, cafés and restaurants lining the picturesque shoreline. They sipped some Tequila to ease the stress as they waited.

As the Tequila soothed her, Raven reflected on the evening before. They had undressed and held each other and he had finally told her what he intended to do. It was a good plan, some parts of it she didn't like but that seemed to be the nature of this entire mission. The evening had been hard on all of them, testing their nerves, their boundaries and their wits. It had been exhausting, disturbing and overwhelming. She had rubbed his back again for him, smoothing away his stress as best she could, until he relaxed enough to make love to her.

"Hey you," Sarge said. His voice brought her back to the present. "Look, Dragon found out what we were sent to find out, it's time to end this. It will be over soon." She gave Sarge a pouty smile. "I just hate that we are not together, it's not protocol and they are vulnerable," she said. "Dragon and Wax are hardly two guys I would consider vulnerable, in any situation," Sarge said. She thought about that and had to agree.

They had spoken to the General earlier advising him they had plans to go fishing and find out more. But the General had become concerned about the involvement with a Drug Cartel. Juan Carlos was just a pawn in the whole scheme of things and he felt another approach would be safer. Also, now that he thought David Li had a corrupt side he needed to be terminated before he passed the information on to anyone. They were to avoid any further involvement and ordered to eliminate him.

Dragon's plan involved a way to remove Juan Carlos and give them enough time to be gone before his disappearance was discovered for what it was.

Raven and Dragon had spent the earlier part of the day on horseback with Diego. They had ridden a long trail through various terrains and picked their way down to a beach. The horses had been agile and surefooted as it had been steep in some areas, but they made it to their destination. It was a small but perfect beach. The horses walked freely about resting and looking for edible grass. Diego sat on a rock watching over them and trying not to watch Dragon and Raven in the water.

They had made love without it looking like it, she thought. They had at least left their clothes on and the water hid details. She smiled at the thought of it now. She recalled the longing look in Diego's eyes as he absorbed the depth of their feelings for each other and their obvious sexual expression of it. Dragon had talked to him privately for awhile about those things because she had asked him to. She thought Diego needed a male confidant. Later she would ask Dragon how it went. It had been a beautiful day, one she would never forget and she wanted it to stay that way. She went to Sarge and curled up on him.

He held her, shaking his head at her. "You're pathetic," he said. He kissed her forehead and she tried to be mad at him. "Shut up," she said. They could have been 7 again.

Juan Carlos had throttled back, as they had reached his preferred area. One of the goons had manned the helm then, as the Diablo idled, gently moving in the low seas. Dragon eyed Wax, it was time. They had moved to the stern deck, talking about fishing gear. The other goon had gone out onto the front of the foredeck, appearing to be keeping watch for who knew what. Wax had a back pack that he had produced another Tequila bottle from and sunglasses and sunscreen, the kind of harmless things a person would have on a fishing trip.

In a swift motion he tossed Dragon the 357 and pulled out a Desert Eagle. Dragon leveled his gun at Juan Carlos, as Wax hit the helm goon between the eyes killing him instantly and leaning over the side nailed the one on the front through the back of his head. He fell overboard dead before he hit the water. Juan Carlos stood, raising his hands and taking a step back.

He laughed, low and dark. "David Li, who knew," he said. "Please, tell me what this is, before you kill me. I think I have a right to know." Clearly aware he was going to die, he wanted to know why. Wax had made sure there was indeed no-one else on the Diablo with them, taken the remaining dead man's gun and tossed it over board and pulled a roll of duct tape from the bag. "Sit," Dragon said. He motioned for Juan Carlos to sit in a deck chair. He did so and Wax taped his arms to the hand rests and his feet together. They eyed the surrounding waters being sure they were alone.

"What have I done to you David Li?" he asked. "I have friends and I have means, if this is some sort of test I assure you, it is not necessary." Dragon eyed him. "It is what people 'like' you have done to me Mr. Guerrera that's brought you to your present point." Juan Carlos developed a light sweat now but did well at controlling his fear. "While you have me here, please enlighten me," Juan Carlos said. He was impatient now as his nerves had kicked in. Dragon nodded to Wax, who pulled a small leather case from the back pack now. Juan Carlos waited, as Dragon sat down on the padded stern bench, leaning back casually. He tossed the bag in his hand and then sat up, opening it and laying it flat on the bench beside him. Juan Carlos eyed it, getting the picture. Dragon took the items out and proceeded to cook a speedball, slowly and methodically preparing the drug.

"Do you know what it's like Mr. Guerrera?" he asked. His eyes moved from his task to Juan Carlos and back again, casually. "The answer is yes, you do know what it's like and you don't care." "What the fuck are you talking about," Juan Carlos yelled at him now.

Dragon pulled the drug into the syringe and turned on him, leaning into his face. "Shut your fucking mouth, or rather than be nice, I'll beat you death you piece of shit." Dragon exploded at him, now staring into Juan Carlos' eyes, hatred meeting evil. His rage fully upon him he let it spill out, graphic and alive.

"You see Mr. Guerrera, I was one of your 'victims', a child, the ones you sell for profit, the ones whose souls you take, the ones who are expendable!" he said. Rage flowing out of him like it never had, he poured it out, inches from his face now. "You want to know why you're here? I'll fucking tell you why you're here!!" Dragon raged. In sharp detail he relived some specifically horrible incidents, causing Juan Carlos to pale and Wax to feel sick from hearing it.

When he was done he stood back from Juan Carlos and spoke quietly, breathing hard, still a powder keg of anger. "Do you know how many times I was made to do those things? Made to take it? Do you know how many times I was beaten unconscious because I tried to defend myself? It all ran together; minutes into hours, hours into days and days into months until over the years it was all I knew. Do you know how many innocent lives were taken, including mine?"

Dragon was now visibly trying to calm himself. He looked down at Juan Carlos, leaning again right into his face, speaking with the hatred and despite he felt. "I spent my life tied up, exploited, beaten and tortured. I was made to do things that haunt me to this day Juan Carlos Guerrera, that's why you are here!!"

Wax thought his heart was going to stop, he knew some of Dragon's stories but had never heard them directly from him or seen the pain it evoked in him. Dragon turned his back on Juan Carlos, who had gone silent. He picked up the syringe. "So now you are going to mainline a nice speedball, I'll watch you die and for maybe one second I will feel peace," Dragon said.

"I'm not afraid to die, Mr. Li," Juan Carlos said. Dragon nodded, flicking the needle with a knowing grin. "I wanted to die Mr. Guerrera, I prayed for someone to do this to me. Now I am glad it's you and not me. I thought it would be a nice gift to you, you know to go with the Tequila. But really it's a gift to me." And with that he tied Juan Carlos arm and sunk the needle into a vein. "Adios," he said. Looking into his eyes a final time, he released the lethal Cocaine Heroin cocktail into his blood.

He left the needle dangling in the vein and turned away, walking to the side of the boat. He didn't care to watch Juan Carlos die now for some reason. Dragon didn't know how long he had stood there, but he felt Wax's hand on his shoulder. He realized he had been looking but not seeing, breathing but not feeling. With Wax's touch he came back to the moment.

Juan Carlos sat slumped in the chair, foam bubbled from his mouth and his head had fallen back. Dragon nodded to Wax, as he fully returned to the task at hand. They removed the duct tape, cleaning it off the body and the chair. Wax put the scraps of it back in the pack. They moved him to a lounge chair and using a cloth they had brought, Dragon carefully removed his finger prints from the syringe as it hung. He then took Juan Carlos' left fingers and printed them onto it, then placed the hand open in his lap as if it had just come to rest there. They also finger printed the gun Wax had used to kill the others and placed it beside him on the lounge. It was unregistered and untraceable.

They rearranged things, making it seem as though no one but Juan Carlos and his men had been occupants of the boat that day. Taking the beer bottles they had drank from; Wax put them in his pack as well. Getting binoculars now, Wax searched the waters for Dream Weaver. He could see her about a kilometer away. They checked and rechecked things while they waited. The body of the other man had floated up against the side of the boat and they managed to get it to the stern platform and drag it back on board. They surveyed their work, as the Dream Weaver approached now. It should look like for whatever reason; Juan Carlos shot his men then overdosed himself. It may look suspicious but difficult to prove it happened any other way. Wax had wiped everything he knew they had touched.

Sarge had come to an idle about 30 meters away. Dragon had switched off the Diablo's radar beacon and now waited on the stern, shouldering the pack. Wax moved the engines into forward gear and then positioned the yacht westward out to sea. He locked the steering wheel so it wouldn't move unless someone moved it by hand; it was a feature it had to keep it straight in rough water at high speeds. Nodding at Dragon he thrust the throttles forward to full speed. The yacht leapt out of the water, like an angry black demon. As it surged forward Wax was propelled to the back barely keeping his balance and they launched themselves over the stern, diving into its wake as it roared to a plane. It would go until it ran out of fuel and be left drifting in the pacific, hopefully not found ever or for a long time. They bobbed for a moment watching it go, then swam the distance to the Dream Weaver's stern platform.

They climbed the ladder up to the stern deck. Dragon dropped the back pack as Raven ran into his arms. He scooped her up and held her against his wet body. She was so warm and soft and he buried his face in her hair, as she wrapped herself around him letting him soak up her love. Sarge moved them, turning and heading for the Marina again. They pulled their wet clothes off, standing naked now and drying themselves. Raven handed them the dry things she had brought for them to wear and they dressed. She wrapped up their wet clothes and put them in the bag from the dry ones. Dragon summoned Chekov on the laptop as they now sat, cruising slowly back.

"It's done," he said. "Any problems?" Chekov asked. "None. It was almost too easy. We set it up perfectly; the rest is out of our control now. We just have to hope that boat stays lost," Dragon said. Chekov just nodded blankly at Dragon. Dragon paused, thinking. "Chekov, why did we kill him so quickly? Would it not have been better to try and find out how the operation worked, where they get the children, you know?" he asked.

Chekov looked up from one of his other screens, almost absentmindedly. "Not this time. The General doesn't want David Li associated with Cartel. If I'm being honest this mission was somewhat tactically flawed. If Juan Carlos stayed alive any longer he may have told someone about you. It had to be this way. We need another angle inside. Like a plant. I'm working on a new approach, but for now you did the right thing and you did it very well I might add."

Dragon paced thinking about Chekov's words. "Ok, I guess getting rid of him messes them up temporarily but they will continue, someone will replace him, he said. "Yes," Chekov said. "This is definitely not over, but the General wants to take more time to profile it another way. For now, stay for another week, continue the vacation you're supposed to be on, then leave for Los Angeles. Stop at your friend Dusty's for a visit, like you did on the way down there. Have you ever been to New York?"

Dragon eyed Chekov with a pained expression. "Why New York, Chekov?" he asked. "It's a stopover. The General wants you to go to dinner, enjoy yourselves, that kind of thing. It's one night," Chekov said. "Raven, tell your husband it's not a punishment. It's partly work, you need to be seen there, but you should enjoy yourselves at the same time."

Raven smiled at him, making him blush into the screen. "Chekov, I don't 'tell' my husband things, but thank the General please and I will do my best to see that we have a wonderful time," she said. "Yes, good. Keep me posted please," Chekov said. Then the screen went blank as he disconnected.

She turned to Dragon and used her bossiest tone. "This is not a punishment." It broke the tension and they all laughed. He grabbed her then, pulling her across his knees. "I'll give you punishment," he said. He spanked her butt playfully through her shorts, making her yelp. He let her up and she jumped on him pushing him backwards on the padded bench, straddling his waist. He let her pin his arms back, laughing at her now.

"Don't spank me unless you mean it Mr. Li," she said. He grinned up at her and gave her his sexiest smile. "That sounds like an invitation to me," he said. He was laughing at her, letting her hold him down. She let his arms go and fell down on him kissing him softly and eagerly. Then, sitting back up, eyed him sexily. "That was an invitation," she said. He sat up, wrapping his arms around her waist, his face close to hers. "Give me a time and a place and I will be there," he said.

"Well this is neither," Sarge said. "I'm afraid the man is right," Dragon said. "But it is time for Tequila." "I'm on it," Wax said.

He went into the cabin to get a bottle and some glasses. He wondered to himself and decided he would talk to them both about what happened earlier. He was concerned for Dragon, who now seemed to have completely dismissed the nightmare scene he had just been through. They'd have a drink and he'd bring it up before they reached the Marina.

They sat cruising slowly and relaxing. Wax had decided to approach the situation by being honest and direct. "Hey man, what happened back there? I've never seen you angry like that before," he said. Dragon shrugged, but said nothing.

Raven eyed both of them and Wax could see it wasn't going to be easy to get him to talk about it, but he had planted enough of a seed that she would do it for him. "What do you mean 'angry' Waxy?" she asked.

"Don't answer her," Dragon said. With his eyes he warned him, knowing what Wax had just done. "Then you answer me," Wax said. Challenging him, knowing he was pushing him to anger but doing it anyway, he met Dragon's stare. "What Wax, what!" Dragon said, glaring at Wax now. "Baby don't," Raven said. "Wax is obviously concerned about you for some reason." He softened with her words, sighing, giving Wax an understanding look.

She sat beside Dragon on the padded bench and took his hand. Wax looked at Dragon. "I'm really sorry man; I mean I knew things, but hearing it and seeing how it haunts you," Wax said. "If there was ever anything I could do." He felt helpless and frustrated. "You're doing it," Dragon said. "Just keep doing what you're doing, we can't change the past." Wax nodded to him, downing his shot.

Sarge got up and poured him another. "I know, I'm the girl in this relationship," he said, rubbing Wax's shoulder. They all laughed, breaking the tension.

"Come here man," Dragon said. He dragged Wax into a man hug. "You were on it with me today, just like you always are. That's all you need to do for me. I can always count on you and you're my friend and I need you in my life. That's what you do for me, what makes it alright for me now."

They sat down again and Raven went to Wax, taking his chin in her hand and making him look at her. His concerns were fading and she was relieved. "I could give you another lap dance," she said. He grinned at her. "Baby girl you keep that little thing of yours over there with him," he said. He was smiling 'Hollywood' again.

"It's my turn," Sarge said. Raven flashed her eyes at him. "Not a chance, you wouldn't be able to control yourself and you'd come all over me," she said. "Yes I would and you'd like it," he said. She said something in French then, playing their little game. "And what did the little tease say," Sarge said. "She wouldn't fuck you if you were the last guy on earth," Dragon said. "We'll see about that," Sarge said and launched at her.

She dodged him and ran into the cabin. Wax and Dragon watched in amusement as he chased her and finally caught her, tackling her to the sofa. They wrestled, as she cursed him some more, fighting him as he used his size to overpower her. She was laughing now, as he had succeeded in pinning her, laying on her between her legs missionary style, holding her wrists in one hand above her head, knowing if he didn't she would pull his hair until he had to give in. He supported himself on his elbows over her, her wrists in his right hand.

"Now, this is what you've been dreaming about your whole life," he said. "Say it with me." "No," she protested, laughing too much now to have any strength to fight him. He moved himself against her then. "Come on, this is what you want," he teased. "Nooo, get off me you fucking pervert," she said, squirming under him. "Say it with me," he said. She relented and through their laughter she followed his lines with him.

He let her go then, rolling off her, onto his back on the floor. "See it feels good to tell the truth, now doesn't it," he said. She replied in French. "I faked that, like your girlfriends fake their orgasms," Dragon translated. Sarge rolled onto his stomach laughing again and she jumped on his back, straddling him, getting her chance to pull his hair, the traditional thing she did to him that he had hated since childhood. "Fuck, get her off me." He called to Wax and Dragon, who could barely move from laughing at how funny it looked. They came to his rescue, Wax pulling her off him by one arm and handing her to Dragon. He looped his arm around her waist and scooped her out of the air.

Wax pulled Sarge up and he smoothed himself, eyeing her. She grinned at him. "Stupid," she said. "Stupid," he said back to her, mimicking her voice, which he did very well, having had 15 years of practice.

"You two quit this shit or we're going to end up beaching this thing," Dragon said. He carried her out and sat, distracting her away from teasing Sarge any further. Sarge stood there and laughed again to himself, shaking his head. "Ok" he said. "Coming up?" he asked. He ascended the steps to the upper bridge.

They followed him up. "You know what?" Wax said to Dragon. "We should have done a collateral risk assessment on leaving these two alone together." "Don't you get funny with me now Waxy," Raven said. "It's bad enough I have to deal with fucky the clown over there." They laughed at her again. "Hush you," Dragon said. Pulling her onto him, finding her mouth with his to keep her quiet, he kissed her.

"See, that's truly the only way she will ever actually shut-up," Sarge said. She didn't register the remark because Dragon was blasting sexual white noise into her mind that was turning her into a wet mess in his arms.

Back at the Marina, they locked up the Dream Weaver, taking their bags, which looked like things you would take on a picnic or a hike. They were silent, as the empty space next to them reminded them of the day's events again. Not wanting it to kill the happy mood they had all achieved, they simply ignored it and departed up the docks to the Hummer. Dragon made a point of them being seen together, stopping to advise the Marina Manager that they had returned. Dragon drove and they made their way back to the Hacienda.

"Baby, I'm glad we can stay for a bit longer, we just started to get to know these people," she said. She smiled to him as he drove. "What did you tell Diego?" she asked. She was remembering their afternoon at the beach with the horses.

"We talked about relationships, I guess," Dragon said. "Their religion doesn't allow premarital sex." "What the fuck," Wax said. "Did you tell him, fuck that shit?" Sarge asked. "I told him that nothing about expressing yourself physically to someone that you love is bad." Raven thought to herself for a moment. "It must be hard to meet girls, way out there," she said. "Ya, he told me he has never been alone with a girl. There are some at his church or something. I warned him not to marry one simply to have the experience of being with her," Dragon said. "Watching us in the ocean made him long for it I think," Raven said. "He's a teenage boy baby, longing for it is a 24/7 thing," Dragon said. He eyed her sideways. "Remember?" With that, they had arrived at their front door, as the sun had set. It was around 9 pm and they were all starved.

CHAPTER NINETEEN

SENSEI

Raven gasped when they walked into the Hacienda. Standing in the kitchen stirring something on the stove, was Sensei. She ran to him, throwing herself in his arms. "Papa!! What are you doing here?" she said. She buried herself in his embrace. Dragon bear hugged them both, squishing her between them. "Sensei," he said. "Hello," Sensei said. "Boys," he said. He accepted hugs from Wax and Sarge. "You all look well." He was beaming at them.

"We are even better now," Raven said. "Except you should have seen what Sarge did to me Papa, I had to spend the whole day with him and then he made me say the dumbest things," she said. Sensei took her by the shoulders, looking at her in utter amusement. "Do you think I haven't learned anything over the years my dear?" he said. "You have my sympathies, Sergeant Willis." Sarge nodded. "Greatly appreciated Sensei," he said. He eyed her triumphantly.

"Now let's sit and we can eat, Ok?" Sensei said. "Let me help you Papa," Raven said. She happily pulled him back into the kitchen. He had made them a delicious fish soup and some homemade flatbreads. They ate hungrily and entertained Sensei with a recounting of Raven and Sarge's antics on the trip back to shore.

Having filled themselves, they all helped restore the kitchen to its perfect state and retired to the pool area with a Scotch bottle and some Champagne. Candle lit lanterns surrounded them in the warm Mexican night and the lighted pool glowed around them invitingly. After awhile Sarge and Wax stripped off their shirts and dove in, washing away the day in the pristine water. Dragon was stretched out in a lounge chair and Raven sat cross legged between his legs, sipping her Champagne.

"Papa, you can meet Dusty on the way to LA," she said. "Yes my dear, I'm looking forward to us all having some time together on the boat before we get there," he said.

"How are things at home?" Dragon asked. "They are fine son; Kona is overseeing some more construction while I am gone," he said. "Did the General want to see you?" Dragon asked. "Yes, I believe so," Sensei said. Dragon eyed him, raising an eyebrow at him which was his way of saying, 'And'. "I wanted to be here when you had completed your mission, my son," Sensei said. "If you wouldn't mind, I would like to discuss it for a moment." Dragon looked at him passively, feeling suddenly relieved to be able to talk about it to him now.

"It went a lot quicker than we thought it would," he said. "It was difficult for all of us, there were things we said and did that worked the way they were supposed to, but were hard. Nonetheless, he offered up the information we were looking for fairly readily and we were ordered to eliminate him, which you probably know already I'm sure." Sensei looked at Dragon, patiently. "And you know that's not what I'm asking about," Sensei said.

Dragon sighed. "Ok, Wax and I were on the boat. Wax took out the others and we secured him. There was something about his attitude that pissed me off, I don't know," Dragon said. "Maybe it was when I was cooking the speedball. Maybe he reminded me of the way it was, people like him, their evilness. I just wanted him to know what they do to people, children, the lives they take away."

"Yes son, I can understand that, you've listed some good triggers right there," Sensei said. "Any one of them could have pushed you over the edge." "Well, that's what happened I guess," Dragon said. Sensei looked then at Wax, who realized he was supposed to speak. "I've never seen him so angry." He looked at Dragon then. "You wanted to beat him to death instead and I thought you might have. It wouldn't have mattered I guess, but I didn't want to see you get there, it was bad enough already," he said.

Sensei looked at Dragon. "It takes a lot of rage to beat a man to death with your own hands Kai Li. How close were you?" he asked. Dragon shrugged. "It was right there. You already know this don't you?" he said. "You know I do, but the point of this is for you to verbalize it. What I see in my head because we are connected is not what will help you, just because I know it," Sensei said. Dragon sipped is Scotch again. "I wanted to kill him, I wanted to cause him pain, I wanted to put all of my pain onto him and not stop until it was gone," Dragon said. "What surfaced would have allowed me to. I don't remember how I didn't, to be honest now." "What part don't you remember?" Sensei asked. "I was in his face, I think I had the needle, but the next thing I recall is Wax pulling me, something like that," Dragon said.

"Ok," Sensei said. "It's alright, how do you feel about it now?" "I don't feel anything about killing him; it became just another day at the office after that. My feelings now are not for myself but for Wax and all of you. I'm sorry for what this does to you," he said. "You needn't be. Being with people that love you means not having to say you're sorry," Sensei said. He placed his words into Dragon's mind as well. "What hurts us is not your fault, it is our own love for you that causes the hurt and that is a price I and any of us would pay willingly for you. We cannot help it, cannot change it and don't ever want to."

Dragon felt close to his own tears now. Sensei always made everything right and simple. "Can you understand this, my son?" Sensei asked. His love was clear in his mind and on his face. "Yes I guess so. Will I be alright now?" Dragon asked. His fear was a dream happening. Sensei gazed directly into him. "I don't know son, but I am here and you are not alone." Dragon understood it all then. "Yes Kai Li, I am here because you need me. And I like it that way so you must live with it and indulge me because I love you," he said.

Dragon smiled back at him then, feeling much better than he had at the beginning of this. "Ok Papa," he said. Sensei smiled. "Good, now it is late so I am going to retire and I'm sure you are all exhausted as well. Tomorrow is another day and we shall live it as if it is a gift, which it is by the way." He got up and as he was leaving them he turned. "And Dragon, my advice would be to take her to bed and make her forget her name," he said. They all smirked at that, always finding it funny when Sensei was crude. "Papa!" Raven said, scolding him playfully.

They sat for a few more minutes, finishing their drinks. Raven sat up then and looked at Dragon with a sexy smile. "My name is Raven," she said. "Remember it while you still can," he said. He stood up then and pulled her to the bedroom, giving Wax and Sarge his customary back wave and a "Later bros." Shutting the door behind him, holding her hand still he pulled her into him. "I'm going to have a little fun with you tonight. That I can promise you," he said. He kissed her hard then, holding her through her hair.

He then pushed her back on the bed and pulled her clothes off of her. She lay back on the bed naked. "How wet are you?" he asked. He looked at her, sexily removing his shirt. She obediently let her thighs fall open for him to see. He undid his shorts but left them on, making her gasp as he ran his middle finger inside her. He pulled his breath in at the feel of her and removed his finger, wet and slippery with her juices. Grasping her legs behind her knees he pushed them up and back flat against the bed.

"I want to watch you," he said.

He looked from her openness to her face, his hair messy around his shoulders, dark eyes smoldering now. She knew what he liked about this and would give it all to him. His eyes went to hers then and he bit his lower lip. Just watching him watch her was enough to do it for her. She worked herself to it with the thought of him over her, the idea of him inside her making her get there. She watched him as his view of her affected him. That was it for her and she let her head fall back, as her climax built. He trailed his fingers along the inside of her thigh, helping her. Just as the first waves of it hit her, she felt his fingers on her, spreading her open, then his tongue, tasting her as she contracted with it.

He moaned with her then as he pressed his tongue against her, licking her softly as she finished. He lingered, as she lay breathing hard and gently kissed her inner pinkness and let his tongue taste as he searched her everywhere with his lips. "Baby," she whispered. "Did you like that?" she asked. "Yes sweetheart," he said.

She moaned from the feel of his fingers holding her open and the pleasure he got from playing with her this way. He was watching what he was doing, as he gently pressed his finger against the soft spongy inner area of her that he used to give her the mind shattering vaginal orgasms she always had.

"I know baby," he said. She was moving against his finger now. "You're going to come again. Take your time, but you are." He watched, still working on her with the same continual movement. "Oh god baby," she moaned. "It feels so good, you make me so crazy, don't stop," she begged him now. Sliding two fingers into her, he flashed his eyes up to her briefly. "I'm going to get you there now," he said.

He let her have it, making her cry out as he moved his fingers in her. He used his left hand to press down gently on her from the outside, forcing her against the motion of his fingers. She arched her back on the bed, grasping the bedding, letting it push her over the edge.

"Baby, oh god," she cried. Taking in her breath and holding it, she exploded over his hand, letting it out as she gasped through it. "Good girl, let it go for me," he said. He looked at her lovingly as she laid there, eyes closed, breathing hard and moaning.

"You're beautiful sweetheart," he said. He was wet through his shorts from the pre-come that leaked from his almost painful hardness. She eyed him, thinking he was beyond hot like that. "You need it bad baby," she said. Pulling her legs back for him, wanting him to satisfy his needs with her now, she waited for him.

"That's what you do to me," he said. He got rid of his wet shorts and leaned over her on his hands, letting himself press lightly on her openness. She reached down, stroking him, making his eyes close. "Baby you're so hard, my god," she said. "I almost came with you both times," he said. His face was soft, sweet and wanting. "My god I love you," she said. "Come on, fuck me now."

She gasped as his size opened her and he groaned as he felt her around him, warm, wet and tight. It took him about 30 seconds and he exploded. Moving off her, he pulled himself out of her into his left hand and directed his hot come onto her tummy and breasts. He moved his hand over himself as it flooded from him, making him shudder, his abdominal muscles flexing with it.

They lay recovering for a few minutes, letting the day's events completely evaporate from their minds. "Now that I've taken the edge off us, I have some more things to do to you because I still think you can say your name," he said. She trembled for him when she saw what was on his mind. "Be a good girl now," he said.

He tied a bandana around her mouth, letting it slip tightly but gently between her lips. She thought he was going to blindfold her with it. He had almost never gagged her. Sensing her thoughts, he turned his head sideways, looking into her eyes.

"Easy baby, I'll make it good for you, don't worry. But you are going to scream, so this is best," he said.

He turned her onto her tummy then and leaned away for a moment. She was crazy with an animal lust for him now, aware that she was moaning and grinding herself onto the bed. She saw the belt in his hand then, as he held the buckle into his palm and coiled the soft leather around his hand covering the Platinum DLI.

"I know what you need and when you need it. And right now you need a little David Li," he said.

He was careful how he used it with her, timing it, timing his words and timing his gratification. When he had got her to the exact point of need he paused, leaning and whispering to her.

"Maybe I should fuck you," he said. "What do you think?"

He let the belt lace her again across her butt now, hard and fast, stinging her as she cried out again from it. She was nearly there then and he knew how to make it perfect for her. He moved between her legs and placed the head of erection just inside her vagina. She squirmed, trying to get more of him.

"Show me how good this feels," he said.

He drove himself into her. She cried out again, the sound stifled by the gag, breathing hard now, unable to stop her involuntary motions, moving on him. He had approached the fine line point and made his move.

"Ok baby, you need this more than you should but I'll give it to you," he said.

Withdrawing but still in her he brought the belt down on her, one last time, as low as he could get, then drove into her as she screamed through her gag now. She was a hot mess then and moved her hips gratefully into him. She cried literally now as she came with his insistent movement, his talent inside her leaving her with no choice.

He felt her relief and there was nothing more left to do but let himself go inside her. He fell down over her, pulling the gag off for her, moaning deeply as everything he had poured from him, his heat, his love and his passion. It blew his mind and he wanted to stay in her forever.

They lay like that, both face-down with him inside her until they had relaxed completely. He didn't want to move because she was so warm under him but eventually he slid off of her, turning her onto her back and laying over her to kiss her. He gazed down at her, seeing her little face, wet with sweat and tears and her lips puffing slightly from the pressure of the gag. Her green eyes glowed from her sexual release. She was so beautiful it took his breath away.

She just lay looking up at him, catching her breath so she could finally speak. "Baby, when did you come up with that?" she asked. "I was making it up as I went along," he said. "Very nice Mr. Li," she said. "I'd say that might have to go down as one of the top three versions of that game that you've ever given me." He just smiled at her, loving that she was happy and that he had pleased her.

They had slept then and he did not have a dream. Whether it was because Sensei had been there, he didn't know, but he awoke happy. Sensei was sitting quietly as usual at the bottom of the bed, a tray of tea at hand.

Dragon was relieved the mission was over, but even though it had only been a short time, Raven had fallen in love with the horses, with Diego, with Jose and Isabella. They had hoped to be there so much longer.

"I don't know what to tell these people," Dragon said. "Son, they knew you were to be temporary guests, but I know you are not the average person so you will find a way to leave them with something of yourself," he said. Dragon thought about that and sipped his tea.

"I don't know Sensei, I would love it if Diego would come with the horses to Hawaii, but he can't leave here. I know that. I don't know what to offer him. From what I can tell, all he wants is a true love and a simple life," he said. "You can give him that, my son, think with me," Sensei said. Taking Dragon's hand, he gave him the images.

CHAPTER TWENTY

MOVING ON

A while later, they joined the others in the kitchen area. Raven had a lime green bikini with strings to hold it on and a pair of tiny white shorts. Her hair was in a high ponytail which still hung long down her back. Dragon had tied his own hair back, as the humidity made it stick to his neck anyway. Their first order of business was to check in with HQ Munich. Isabella had gone about the morning chores and Jose was watering the gardens outside. They sat in the shade in the courtyard and summoned Chekov. He answered readily and handed them off to the General himself. The General was seated at his desk, dressed in his usual formal suit and tie.

"Hello everyone," he said. "General," Sensei said. "Ah, good, I'm glad you are there Sensei," the General said. "I do look forward to seeing you all soon." Pleasantries aside, the General went straight to business. "Thank you Dragon, for completing your mission so efficiently. I'm sorry you must leave there so soon, but it is best that you be here sooner rather than later. Not only will it benefit Damascus, there is something further for you to do. It will be facilitated much more readily from Munich and can be taken care of before you return to Hawaii," he said. "Yes General," Dragon said.

The General just smiled and sent his eyes around to all of them, acknowledging them. "Chekov can brief you when you are here, in the meantime, enjoy yourselves, you deserve it. The arrangements in New York should be to your liking and I shall see you when you get here," he said. The screen magically changed back to Chekov.

"What's relevant to the upcoming few weeks Chekov?" Sensei asked. "I've downloaded the Marina information regarding Los Angeles. You're reserved and expected about 14 days from now. The DLI jet will be waiting at LAX to take you to New York," he said. "Fine thank you," Sensei said. "I will contact you if there are any questions." They disconnected from Chekov and looked at one another, deciding how to go about the day.

Sarge and Wax went to deal with the items in Wax's pack from yesterday and double check details in case they were searched by authorities. Raven and Dragon took Sensei to the stables to see the horses. Diego was filling the water trough as they approached. He smiled at them with his cute boyish grin. As usual he was shirtless with his hat hanging down his back, dusty jeans and worn boots. "Buenos Dias, Senor Li, Senora Raven," he said. "This is Sensei," Raven said. "I'm going to show him the horses," she said. She took him, leaving Diego with Dragon so they could talk. Diego stopped his work and came closer to Dragon, drying his hands on his pants.

"I'm sorry," Dragon said. "Our plans changed at the last minute and we have to go much sooner than we had hoped." Diego nodded, not seeming to have any words available to him. "Listen," Dragon said. "I realize your home is here with your family and your people." Diego nodded. "My mother and father need me to work. I sometimes wish I could see the world Senor Li, but I can't leave here." Dragon thought for a moment he could easily take care of that, but decided to stick to his plan.

"Diego, there is someone that lives with us that I think you would like. She has no family and she has been with us for many years now, but it is coming up to her time to decide what she wants to do with her life. I think she would like the opportunity to come here and learn about the horses. Sensei spoke to her and she was very excited about it," Dragon said.

He could see Diego realizing what he was suggesting. "A girl wants to come here?" Diego asked. Dragon couldn't help but smile at Diego's sudden alertness. "Yes, a pretty girl Diego," he said. "See, I have her picture."

The girl was Keri, she was Diego's age, a mix of Asian and Caucasian, with long dark hair, olive skin, brown eyes and a beautiful smile. She was tiny like Raven and Sensei had suggested her because she was a soft spoken reflective type that liked gardening and growing things for food. She was ever present in the fields at camp, preferring to work with her hands more than anything. She loved animals the most and was always taking care of the stray cats that came around from time to time. She was a perfect fit for the life that Diego lived.

"She can come here if you would like," Dragon said. "She can stay in a room in the main house and help your mother and you can teach her everything about the horses." Diego looked confused. "Why would she want to come here?" he asked. Dragon couldn't help but laugh at him then. "Please Diego, don't doubt yourself. When she saw your picture, she thought you were um, very handsome," he said. "'Hot' was the word Sensei said she used."

Diego blushed and looked at the ground, but couldn't help a smile. Dragon just continued with what he had planned on saying. "She is interested in other cultures. It would be good for her to see another place, beyond where we live. It is an opportunity that all the children get when they turn a certain age. They can choose a path to take. Some go to school, some stay with us, it is up to them. It's part of the David Li Foundation, which offers a future to orphaned children."

Diego blushed again. He had found her very attractive, from her photo. "If my mother and father agree, then she can come if she wants to I guess," he said. Dragon reached out and put a hand on Diego's shoulder, getting him to look up at him. "I think you'll like her Diego. She is a nice girl that is used to a simple life and working outdoors. She's quiet to be around, easy to get along with and she is very kind on the inside," Dragon said. "When would she get here?" Diego asked. "In a few weeks," Dragon said.

The whole idea of this had come to Sensei as he had talked with Dragon that morning. He knew it would be a good experience for each of them and she could return to Hawaii anytime if she wanted to.

Dragon put his arm around Diego and led him a few steps away, then stood to face him. "This girl has no experience with boys," he said. Diego looked up at him, wanting to hear more. "I want you to know, like I told you the other day, it is not wrong to express yourself physically to another person if they feel the same way of course. You won't go to hell or wherever and bad things won't happen to you or your family. Those are ideas that your religion has brought to you from the middle ages. Back then it controlled people. But you can respect yourself and your religion still by being a good person. And you are. Just follow your heart when it comes to physical matters Diego." Diego nodded. "Yes Senor Li, I don't want to do something 'bad' but yes I do," he said. He smiled shyly at Dragon.

Dragon laughed. "Of course you do, and it's because you are male and that's what males want to do. Raven and I were not supposed to do things, but we did anyway. Every chance I got, I would sneak her away, behind a wall, behind a tree; it didn't matter as long as I got to kiss her. And when we were older and were finally permitted to be together that way, I spent every moment I could, getting her under me every chance we had. We spent more hours of a day making love than doing anything else sometimes. It never stops Diego and that's how it should be. It will make you happy, you will see," Dragon said.

Diego nodded again. "Thank you Senor Li, this is not the way I can talk to my father, we do not discuss things and it makes me feel 'ok' hearing you tell me this." "Good, and here, I have something for you," he said. He handed Diego a cell phone. "It is an extra one we had and I programmed it for you so you can call me or text me, or send me pictures whenever you want. We can talk if you need to, anytime; it's all paid for and will continue to be."

Diego hugged him. "Thank you Senor Li, I would like that very much and I will call you, I know I will." Raven and Sensei had joined them again. "I want to see pictures of Keri and you when she gets here and the horses and everything Ok?" Raven said. He looked genuinely excited then at the thought of the possibilities. "Yes, I will, and you must send me ones of you so I can see you where you are going in the world," Diego said. "That's a deal," Dragon said.

It had turned from a sad goodbye into a happy new friendship for all of them. Raven hugged Diego and then kissed his mouth softly. She could feel his instant reaction, as she stepped back. His eyes flew to Dragon's, who grinned at him.

"Now you know, my friend, I was not wrong about it when I was your age and I am not wrong about it now," Dragon said. Diego grinned back at him then, looking at Raven then back to Dragon. "No you definitely are right about it Senor Li, behind the walls and trees you know," he said, winking at Dragon.

Dragon pulled her to him and kissed her passionately then as Diego looked on, not embarrassed anymore. "Right out in the open works for me too," Dragon said. "I will go one step at a time Senor Li," Diego said. And with that they waved their goodbyes, promising to come and ride tomorrow.

"Once again you amaze me baby," she said. She referred to his ability to talk to kids. "And you turn me on Angel," he said. He eyed her sexily as they walked hand in hand back to the Hacienda with Sensei. "Then you can fuck me senseless later," she said. He hardened with her talk. "I'd like to fuck you senseless right now," Dragon said.

"I'm right here," Sensei said. He eyed them like they were appalling to him.

They were lost in it at that point. "Or we can take that little car for a drive and I can do the next best thing for you," she said. "I'd say it's on par actually and I can't fucking wait. Come on," Dragon said. He pulled her with him, running the rest of the way.

Sensei rolled his eyes, watching them go.

They enjoyed their remaining time in Mexico, seeing everything they could, taking in the history and the beaches and the people. The week had gone by quickly and it had been time to say their goodbyes.

"Thank you for having Keri," Raven said. Isabella and Jose smiled to her. "It will be wonderful to have a new face around here," Isabella said. "I know Diego is lonely." "Not for long," Dragon said. He made knowing eyes at Wax and Sarge that Isabella didn't see.

As they came to their mooring at the Marina, they saw the Mexican Police. They were standing by the empty space left by the still absent Diablo, talking to the Marina Manager. As they approached the yacht, they were eyed by the two policemen. They reached the Dream Weaver and Dragon was immediately approached.

"Senor Li," one said. He used heavily accented English. "May I have a moment of your time?" Dragon knew it was not really a question. "Do I have a choice?" he asked. His dark sunglasses masked his annoyance, but his voice didn't. The officer stepped up to him and looked up as he was a typical short Mexican man. "I understand you were to go fishing with Juan Carlos Guerrera," he said. "I was, but cancelled," he said. "So you did not go anywhere with Mr. Guerrera on his boat?" he asked. "No," Dragon lied. "Have you ever been on Mr. Guerrera's boat, Senor Li?" "Yes," Dragon said. "Do you know the whereabouts of Mr. Guerrera?" he asked. "No I don't," Dragon said, not a lie. He continued to question Dragon as to his whereabouts on the day Juan Carlos Guerrera disappeared. "You can check my log book if you want," Dragon said. "What is this about?" He appeared annoyed by it now.

He ignored Dragon's question and continued. "Why are you leaving town Mr. Li?" Dragon looked exasperated and made a motion to go. "I have business in Los Angeles and New York, which is none of your business," Dragon said. "But some things are my business Mr. Li. We are looking into the disappearance of your neighbor," he said. Dragon just looked indifferent. "My yacht is moored next to his but I'm afraid that's my only connection to him. I can't help you," he said. He turned to go aboard the Dream Weaver. Pausing he looked back at the man. "He's probably gone somewhere and hasn't come back yet," he said.

The officer pretended to smile at Dragon. "It is not that simple Mr. Li, I assure you. He has not attended to his business and people are looking for him. You understand that Mr. Li," he said. "Not really Senor," Dragon said. "I turn my phone off and unplug the laptops and disappear all the time. It's how I stay sane." The officer nodded and smiled slightly at this, knowing of David Li's status as a paparazzi victim. "Have a safe trip Mr. Li," he said.

Dragon climbed aboard and joined in the preparations. Sarge had started the engines and they were idling and warming as diesels needed to do. On the main bridge he was plotting a course to submit to the Coast Guard for their trip to Los Angeles. There were a number of check lists to go through and details to be attended to. Eventually they were backing out of their mooring and beginning the journey north. Dragon radioed the Coast Guard to register the route they had charted and planned to take, as Sarge piloted the huge yacht out of the harbor. It was bittersweet, in that they loved being together on the yacht, especially with Sensei there too, but were leaving Mexico too soon.

As they cleared land and began north, it was a sense of relaxation. It was mid-afternoon and Sarge brought beers. They stripped to their shorts and took in the sun and ocean breeze and life itself. Raven lay face down her top untied and took in the sun. Dragon poured sunscreen on her back.

Rubbing it down her he thought to her, 'thinking of you is making me insane.' 'Stop thinking of me baby,' she replied silently. It made her smile to herself. To tease her he sent her a steaming image of them from the past, making out behind the munitions shed at camp. She felt her thighs contract involuntarily, but answered, 'Bad boy.' 'Yes I am.' he had mentally replied.

They spent a beautiful afternoon moving north. Sensei had prepared dinner and they had enjoyed it with some Sake, which they hadn't done for awhile. He had grilled a white fish of some sort and had put a Hawaiian flare on it that he had learned from Marietta, making Raven slightly homesick for their island life. Sensing her thoughts, Sensei entertained them with stories of the new camp, filling them in on the progress. Raven helped Sensei clean up afterward and they took drinks up to the flying bridge. It was a beautiful warm night and the sun wouldn't be setting for a few more hours.

They would have to share watches that night as it would take until halfway through the next day to reach the Marina Mazatlan where they had chosen to stay. Dragon chose first watch so he could make love to Raven as soon as possible. He had been thinking about it constantly now as the evening drew to a close. He was going to take her to pieces up there as soon as they were alone. His thoughts were driving her crazy and she couldn't keep her hands off him now. Sensei was grinning at them, shaking his head. Dragon had tried to shield his thoughts somewhat but had clearly failed and now he had to contend with hiding his erection which was causing him grief and her to salivate.

Sarge and Wax were going to do the second watch together so they retired early for a game of chess then bed, and Sensei went with them, kissing Raven good night. He touched his fingertips to Dragon's forehead, raising an eyebrow to him.

"Some of those thoughts you have are going to keep me awake tonight son, if you know what I mean," Sensei said. "Oh, well I hope that's a good thing Papa," Dragon said. "Not as good as it will be for you I would imagine," Sensei said.

Raven looked at both of them and shook her head. "Papa, this is where he gets it from, now I know," she said. "At the end of the day we are all males my dear, a feeble excuse I know, but a legitimate one," Sensei said. "Well I suffer too you know, as in right now," she said. She sent a wanting look at Dragon. Sensei smiled and turned to go. "You haven't stood a chance all day my dear and you are exactly the way he wants you right now," Sensei said. He winked at her and left them.

She immediately slid to her knees in front of him and pulled him free of his shorts. He ran his hands into her hair and smoothed it back so he could watch her lips on him. She wanted him inside her everywhere but just had to use her mouth on him, wanting to devour him. It was the images he had given her earlier of them behind the munitions shed that had been driving her crazy all afternoon. He really wanted to touch her now, but she was too good with her mouth and he didn't want her to stop. She was teasing him to pay him back for making her wet all afternoon. She didn't have a cock ring so she gripped him at the base with her thumb and forefinger of her right hand, holding back his orgasm as she pressured his glands with her lips.

It was so exquisite he didn't want her to stop it yet and she brought him to the edge twice more as he worked his hips against her now, straining for his orgasm. She let go then as he begged her for it and worked it through for him with her hand as he exploded onto his belly and chest, gasping, his head back, hair everywhere. Finally he looked forward again and down at her as she knelt between his thighs, licking him up and down still. He laid breathing, relaxed while she spent time on his body.

"Baby, that was so good, and you are so sexy right now," he said. She finished cleaning him up with her tongue. "I need you now," she said. "Show me baby," he said.

She stood then and removed her top as he watched. She cupped her breasts, squeezing them and making her nipples hard as he eyed her. She then undid the strings at the sides of her bikini bottoms and let them fall away. She turned and knelt on the padded bench on her hands and knees beside him so he could see her wetness and her sexy butt. She gasped as he touched her gently, parting her with his forefingers.

He knelt down then and turned her so he could use his tongue on her from behind. She tilted her hips to give him a good angle and moaned as his tongue hit her nerve endings. He held her open, teasing her with his tongue, licking her wetness from on her and inside her. He exposed her most sensitive parts and worked on them with his tongue until she cried out for him, coming sweetly for him. She lay her face down on the seat padding now, still on her knees and spread open for him. He licked her everywhere, spreading her inner pinkness and making sure she was relaxed and open because in a second he was going to let her feel him.

"Stay like that baby, I like you in this position," he said. He stood up and let his already open shorts fall to the deck. He put his hands on her butt, squeezing gently and opened her with his thumbs. She could feel his erection pressing against her, sliding inside her. They moaned together at the feel of it.

"I'm going to let you feel me," he said. This was his way of letting her know he planned to get rough. "Give it to me," she said.

She looked wild now, her hair in her face, all around her, as she had braced herself on her elbows. He was all the way inside her warmth then and she had relaxed around him. He groaned with the pleasure of it, driving himself into her hard, again and again. He paused at a certain point, to control his orgasm, her orgasm and to give her a break as he repositioned her.

He turned her onto her back laying her on the top of the back of the helm chair. It was padded and about a foot wide and long enough for her body, leaving her exposed to him at exactly the right height for him to stand and be inside her.

"Baby we're going to come this way Ok, I'm just going to get us there," he said.

She reached behind her knees pulling them even farther apart for him. He leaned over her, putting his hands on the railing of the bridge for leverage and gave it to her with a punishing rhythm. He was close and she was almost there, moaning and working herself against him. As her orgasm hit her he let go finally, coming with her hotly. Even the droning engines couldn't cover their noise, but they didn't care.

"Oh my god baby, I've needed to do that all afternoon," he said.

He pulled her up, still inside her, holding her on him as he sat back on the padded bench with her on top of him. She lay in his arms as they both caught their breath. She cuddled into his chest.

"Are you sore sweetheart?" he asked. She nodded. "I think so," she said. He laughed, kissing her hair. "You think so?" She laughed then too. "I don't know baby, you will fix it if I am so I don't care," she said. "Yes I will baby, but I just want to hold you like this for awhile OK?" he said. She cuddled into his warmth feeling him soften inside her gradually.

She moved her hips on him, their wetness mingling. "Baby," he moaned. "Be careful or I'm going to need it again." He was worried about her soreness. "Baby, take me again," she said. She softly kissed his chest and let him know what she wanted with an image. "Sweetheart, you naughty little thing," he said. "I want you in me everywhere baby," she said. It made him harden again. He leaned her back on the padding beside him then. "I'll give you whatever you want Angel," he said.

He used the slipperiness he had already left inside her to lubricate himself, then her. He pressed her legs apart and back and positioned himself to enter her anally. He eyed her to be sure she was ready.

"Breathe in baby, and breathe out," he said.

As she did he held himself and slowly eased inside her. She gasped and tried to breathe through it, taking him, adjusting to his size where she wasn't used to it. Dragon knew how it could hurt and he was careful to let her relax enough for it before going any further. He moved slowly, watching what he was doing and watching her face. She was wincing but moaning at the same time.

He moved inside her then, taking in the erotic look and feel of it. It wasn't something they did all the time but included when she asked for it or it was part of a game they were playing. Dragon knew how to be gentle and careful, to make it pleasurable for her.

Using his voice to coax her and his expert touch on her he got her to climax first then finished himself in a steady easy motion inside her.

A light sweat shone on his skin in the lamp-lit night. He pulled out of her gently, having left himself everywhere inside her now. His hair had fallen around his face and shoulders and the lust in his eyes and on his lips was mesmerizingly sexy. He looked at her then, taking his eyes from between her thighs to her face.

She eyed him back, feeling hazy. He moved to lay over her then, between her legs, supporting his weight with his elbows as he gently savored her mouth with his. He kissed her neck and then moved lower to her nipples, tantalizing her softly in a French kiss with each one of them. When he was satisfied he had tasted her everywhere, been in her everywhere and calmed their sexual energy for the time being, he rested over her, his hair falling around their faces.

"I love you," he said. "And I love you," she said. She caressed his face above hers. They held each other then, listening to the sounds of the night around them.

"Baby," he finally said. "I need to clean you up; I'm everywhere in you and on you now." She smiled. "You better find Sensei's cream too," she said.

She was now feeling her soreness everywhere. He sat up then and reached for a soft towel from a drawer under the bench. He gently dried his come that was dripping from her in every place it could. He directed the lamp light so he could see her as he gently wiped it from her, making sure she was Ok after what he had just done to her. Noting that she was sore to his touch, he considered where the cream would be.

"If I have to ask Sensei for it, he'll give me shit," Dragon said. He grinned at the thought of Sensei being pissed with him.

"You don't have to ask son," Sensei said. They looked to see him standing there. He held it out for Dragon to take. He had been unable to tune them out completely, their energy overwhelming him. "Thank you Papa," Raven said. She wasn't the least concerned that she lay that way in front of him.

Dragon took it from his hand and proceeded to apply it to her, gently opening her and coating it on her outer skin first then smoothing it onto her vagina. "Inside her as well," Sensei said. Dragon laughed. "Do you want to do it?" Sensei frowned at them. "Neither of us would need to be doing anything if you could manage your libido more effectively," he said. "Hai Sensei," Dragon smiled. He coated his middle finger and giving her a warning glance, pushed gently inside her, smoothing it into her inner walls to ease the bruising effects he had left her with. Satisfied, he closed her thighs. "Come here baby." He kissed her, pulling her to curl up against him.

"If you can't sleep Papa, you can keep watch with us," Raven said. "Is that what you were doing?" he asked. "Papa, Dragon was keeping a very close watch on what he was doing," she said, naughtily. "I am aware," Sensei said. He handed them a blanket he had brought. "Thank you Papa," she said. She took it from him and wrapped them in it. Sensei sat across from them, crossing his legs on the bench.

They sat and talked more about camp and about HQ Munich. "Why are we going there again?" Raven asked. "So Dragon can see Damascus, mainly," Sensei said. "The General wants to see you as well, he alluded to another mission," Sensei said. "I wonder what it is?" Raven asked.

"It's probably something in Asia that it is closer to do from Munich than Hawaii," Dragon said. "You are likely correct," Sensei said. "Tomorrow son, you should read the information Chekov sent you regarding the David Li Foundation and David Li Industries. It's quite interesting," Sensei said. "I plan to," Dragon said. "I have to admit I'm curious." "Its' things you should know about as you move forward," Sensei said. Dragon nodded.

The hours passed and he put Raven to sleep eventually, letting her lay against him under the blanket as Sensei kept him company. At three am, Sarge and Wax appeared, looking disheveled from just crawling out of bed.

Sarge eyed the Bikini which was still lying where she had dropped it. "I'm not going to slip in anything am I?" "You might," Dragon said. "Is there any place on this boat you haven't fucked her?" Sarge said. "Your bed," Dragon said. "Be my guest; just be careful you don't slip in anything yourself when you're in there," Sarge said. He made a jerk off motion with his hand. "Thanks for the visual," Dragon said. He looked like he wanted to puke.

Sarge laughed. "My pleasure." "Apparently it was," Sensei said. "Are we seriously having this conversation?" Wax said. "I'm not having a conversation," Dragon said. "Especially about Sarge's masturbation habits."

"You're the one with the habit," Sarge said. He glanced at the discarded clothing. Dragon just grinned at him, and shrugged. "You got me there."

The next day they reached Mazatlan Marina about mid afternoon. They had needed to anchor as the Dream Weaver was too large to fit into any of the available spots. It was part of the Marina service that they could get a ride ashore if they wanted. They had decided to eat dinner at one of the local spots that Wax had looked up on the internet. It was waterfront and casual and specialized in locally caught fish.

Dragon pulled the back zipper up on a tiny red sundress for Raven that tied at the neck in a halter style neck line, was fitted under her breasts and hung straight from there. She looked sexy as usual but appropriate at the same time. He pulled the top section of her hair back and braided it together behind her head, and brushed the rest down her back. Her tanned skin looked smooth and sexy and he wondered if would be able to manage himself for the whole night. They had taken it easy that day so she could recover from the previous night.

He forgot to put panties on her but remembered at the last minute. "Here Angel, I forgot," he said. Holding up a tiny red lace thong that he knew he would probably destroy later, he smiled to himself at the thought of it. "You better stop that," she said. She ran her fingers over the outline of him through his shorts. "I don't want every waitress in this place checking you out." "That's not helping," he said. He moved himself away from her touch. "Keep their eyes from the waist up please Mr. Li," she said. They went out of their cabin then, joining the others. "I can't help where they look," Dragon said. "If you don't, I will," she said. She warned him playfully. "A girl fight," he said. She laughed. "Now you sound like Sarge."

"I'd enjoy a good girl fight," Sarge said. "So would I," Wax agreed. Dragon shrugged to her, and she glanced at Sensei for help. "Do I have to say it my dear," he said. She rolled her eyes at all of them. "I know; it's a guy thing. Oh my god," she said.

They had gone into the small tourist town and had dinner. Having enjoyed the food, the view and the weather, Dragon, Raven and Sensei left Sarge and Wax to find their conquests. The three of them wandered the beach, carrying their flip flops, letting the surf catch their feet. They had walked for an hour and when they returned, Sarge and Wax were at various stages of accomplishment.

They approached Wax at a table, lip locking with a girl. He saw them and broke it off. "Hey man," he said. Dragon smiled at him as the girl sat gawking. "Are you David Li?" she asked. Dragon eyed Wax as if to say 'really??' but faked a smile at her and nodded. "Wax get a ride whenever, we're going now." "Sure, see you later," Wax said. He smiled to himself as he could see it dawning on the girl who they were.

Sensei and had interrupted Sarge from his reverie into a blonde with large breasts that had her hand in his pants under the table. Raven had kept silent, eyeing Sarge with a look, as Sensei advised him they were leaving and to get a ride on his own with Wax later. Sarge had thanked them, but wanted them to go away, which they all laughed about. They walked slowly back down the streets, as the nightlife of the town continued to develop. Drunken tourists lined the streets now, the bars had gotten loud and the smell of tobacco and weed was everywhere. They were relieved to finally climb aboard the Dream Weaver where they were free of it and back in their own world.

"Papa, will Wax and Sarge be OK?" Raven asked. She was sleepily leaning on Dragon. "Yes child, I have no reason to feel otherwise," he said. Nothing in his psychic mind caused him worry. "Ok Papa. Baby, take me to bed," she said to Dragon. "Goodnight Sensei," Dragon said. They nodded and went to their cabins. "Baby you are so tired," he said. "Am I drunk or something?" she asked. He smiled at her, taking her face in his hands. "No baby. I wouldn't let that happen. Do you want a bath? Or should you just sleep?" "Can you just hold me baby and make me sleep?" she said. He loved her with his kiss then. "Yes baby." He undressed her and let her fall into his arms. He removed the tiny red thong thinking what he would have done, but she was exhausted now and would no doubt fuck his brains out when she woke up. He loved to hold her and she curled up into the safety of him. "Sleep baby," he said as he kissed her, letting them both fall into the warm light of it.

CHAPTER TWENTY ONE

LA, NEW YORK, MUNICH

Sensei arrived with tea in the morning, waking Dragon in the usual way. "Did Wax and Sarge make it back?" Dragon asked. "Yes," he said. He rolled his eyes, giving Dragon an image of Sarge falling face first onto his bed, where Wax had dumped him. Dragon laughed. "Are you going to be pissed if he doesn't make it to Yoga?" "He'll make it, but I'm going to make him puke," Sensei said.

They discussed the next part of their trip across the Sea of Cortez, which they would begin as soon as they were done Yoga.

"Shall I wake her now?" Dragon said, eyeing Raven. "After I leave," Sensei said. "I would imagine she is going to need something from you so I'm out of here." He smiled and closed the door behind him.

Dragon turned on his side toward her, kissing her softly, getting her to respond to him. She awoke, her eyes moving to his instantly as he left her lips. She looked at him questioningly. "Did I fall asleep?" "Yes but on purpose Angel, we were tired. Remember?" he said. He kissed her, smoothing her hair from her eyes. "But baby, did you want me?" she asked. She gave him eyes like she was going to cry. "Of course I wanted you, but you didn't deny me, you just needed to sleep more than I needed to give you this," he said. He pushed his erection against her hip. "Mmmm baby, you need me now, don't you?" she said. He kissed her neck and pushed her hand onto him.

An hour later he pulled her to the shower having lost track of how many times they made each other lose it. They were sweaty and messy with each others' juices. They soaped one another and he did his best to remove as much of himself from inside her as he could. He needed her clean and sweet for something he had planned for later. He handed her a toothbrush and after a kissing inspection of her mouth, they made it to the galley with ten minutes to spare before Yoga. Sarge and Wax were sitting. Wax was having some food but Sarge was managing only water so far and probably Tylenol.

"Is everything Ok Sarge?" Raven said. Referring to his obvious hang over, she was concerned for him. He eyed her, not taking offense. "Here, let me fix you," she said. He had showered but hadn't tied his hair back for Yoga yet. "Do you have a hair tie?" she asked. He passed her one from the pocket of his shorts. She rubbed his temples, easing the headache she knew he had and then pulled her fingers through his hair making him close his eyes and relax as she tidied it into a pony tail for him.

"Didn't you have a good time last night after we left?" she said. "I don't know it was weird," he said. She pulled him up. "Well tell me later, maybe Yoga will help you. I hope it helps me, I was so fucking horny this morning I could have come ten more times," she said. In spite of his hangover he laughed at her crudeness. Sensei cleared his throat, "Young lady." "Sorry Papa," she said. She grinned at Sarge, reminding him of the old days when she would get into trouble from Sensei for her Tomboy ways.

Sarge gave Dragon's shoulder a squeeze as he passed by him. "Got anything left for Yoga?" he asked. "I hope so," Dragon said. He pulled Raven against him. "And then you can have your ten more times."

Yoga completed and final preparations made, they headed out with the tide increasing speed to 20 knots. But as they moved farther offshore to the open sea, they encountered some bad water. The winds were stronger than before, coming from the north down the Baja and they were getting rollers from the side. Sarge took the speed back to 10 knots and angled them somewhat off course so they wouldn't roll as much. He had already been sick twice from it.

They had moved to the main bridge, where the motion was less. Raven held a bucket for Sarge to puke into and brought him a cool wet cloth for his forehead. Eventually he had simply had to lie down and puke for the duration. She and Sensei tried to keep him hydrated. He dutifully drank the water and then dutifully vomited it up again.

They were in no danger, just discomfort. The seas were 6 to 10 feet, enough to disturb their journey, but not to threaten their safety. Dragon and Wax took turns watching the ocean for any unexpected rogue waves that they needed to react to. It made for a long day.

As they worked their way through it they eventually rounded the tip of the Baja, a little farther off the coast than originally planned, due to having to angle further west. Dragon calculated they were 2 hours off course now and would arrive in the cove later, but before dark still. Raven and Sensei made food, it was early for dinner but they had not eaten anything since fruit that morning, it having been impossible to use the galley in the rolling sea. Sensei decided to make a Miso soup with fish, noodles and bamboo shoots. It was something traditional to him, that he thought would help Sarge and rejuvenate them.

Raven woke Sarge and they all sat at the table in the cabin. Wax and Dragon looked exhausted and gratefully ate. "Here, Sarge," Sensei said. "Eat this, and keep it down, or you're going to be in trouble." He managed barely because he was shaking and it was hard to eat soup when your hands were shaking. He was badly dehydrated and Sensei wished he had a saline IV for him. He helped him, taking it and feeding it to him. Sarge managed its salty warmth and he seemed to recover somewhat. His color improved and his eyes became less dull. Dragon pulled Raven down beside him, as she had been caring for Sarge all day and needed to eat as well. He had concern in his eyes now. He held a piece of fish for her with chopsticks for her to take and then made her drink the broth after he had fed her all the other pieces in the bowl. Between them they consumed the entire pot and decided to take some Sake to the flying bridge.

The seas were calm again and it was a beautiful sunny early evening then. The sun felt wonderful as they had been inside all day and the Sake eased the remaining tension. Sensei's soup had done its job and they all felt ten times better. Sarge had managed to keep it down and was recovering as he rehydrated. He stuck to water, leaving the alcohol to the others for that night anyway. They made it to the shelter of the cove, finding a spot among the other sailboats and yachts and set their anchor. The sun was getting ready to set and they were tired from a long day.

Dragon had wanted to take Raven to bed and eyed her as the sun slipped off the horizon. She got up and pulled him to his feet, taking in his shirtless body.

"Ok Mr. Li, show me what you got," she said. She motioned for him to follow her to their cabin. "You know what I have, I gave it to you over and over again this morning," he said. "I know you have something in mind." she said. He closed the door and pulled her to him kissing her wetly, as she rubbed him through his shorts.

It was a string of beads and she watched as he began knotting them at one end. Sensei had given them to him that morning and explained what to do. She had seen Sensei purchase them from a street vendor the day before in Mazatlan and hadn't thought much of it.

Dragon completed two knots together at one end, leaving about an eight inch piece. He took some lubricant and dripped it onto them as she watched. She started to moan as she realized what he was going to do. When they were good and slippery he eyed her. She pulled her bikini off and lay back for him.

Using his thumb and forefinger he parted her and pressed the knotted end inside her. She closed her eyes and moaned at the feel of them as he pressed them against the front spongy wall of her vagina, keeping his finger inside her, holding them where he wanted them and massaging them against her.

They moved against her in their knots. They were smooth and hard but with the perfect pressure of his finger against them, it was driving her off the map. She was building and he could feel it as he kept the pressure up with his finger. She was moaning now, reaching a point of no return. He took the long left over piece looping his left fingers in it and massaged the slippery round beads against her nerve endings gently. She cried out at the feel of it, arching her back and gasping at the pleasure they gave her as he worked her forward into what he knew would be a monumental orgasm for her.

He was dying of it himself now, sliding a second finger inside her, pressing the beads harder against her, rolling them insistently into the sensitive area he used to make her come. He pressed the other end against her nerve endings simultaneously.

She exploded into his hand, trying to quiet her cries as it hit her.

"Come on baby, let me do it for you," he said.

She arched her back, spiraling into it, digging her fingers into the bedding, letting the waves of it take her with an intensity she hadn't expected.

"Good girl, good girl" he said.

She lay breathing hard, unable to find words for it as the feeling of it left her in an advanced state of arousal. Dragon knew what was next as Sensei had explained to him.

"You're not done," he said.

He dripped lubricant onto his fingers, then looked up at her letting her know what was next. She closed her eyes and he pressed them into her anally. She gasped as the beads moved against her again from his pressure inside her that way. He moved his fingers in her, to prepare her, then taking the loose end he gently withdrew the beads, again causing her to arch into him as they teased the opening of her vagina. "Baby, you're driving me crazy," she breathed. "I know angel, that's the idea," he said. Turning her over onto her knees, face down, he applied his slippery fingers again to be sure she was ready. "Now you're going to feel it fully." He pressed the beads back into her vagina positioning them where he wanted them. "Oh god baby I'm going to come again," she said. "Yes you are," he said.

He knelt behind her. Coating himself with the lubricant, he instructed her to breathe in then out, the way they always did it and entered her carefully. As he moved into her, the beads pressed against her with each stroke he made. The feeling made her scream, as he moved hard into her. She was crazy with it and he brought them off together as she had an off the map orgasm for him, making him lose his own composure and flood her with himself, groaning with her cries as they both came in long exquisite waves.

He gently withdrew himself from her, then the beads and fell back on the bed pulling her to lay on him on her back, as they caught their breath. She lay back on his body relaxing into his arms as he gently caressed her breasts.

"Baby, the things you do to me," she said. "I can't help it baby," he said. "I just want to do things to you that make it good for you." "Baby everything you do to me is good for me, because it's you doing it and you are so good at it. You make me come and it feels so good I think it was like nothing I've ever felt and then you do it again," she said. "You can thank Papa for the beads," Dragon said. "He has a naughty side," she said, giggling then. Dragon laughed lightly. "I think you are right."

Let's shower baby," he said. "My come is all over you." He led her to the shower, turning it on, kissing her sexily while they waited for it to steam warm. They washed each other's bodies for the second time that day, not speaking just touching. She poured soap into her hand and washed his now semi erectness and he smiled down at her.

"Be careful baby or we won't make it out of here clean," he said. "That's Ok with me," she said.

Feeling her warm hand over him, he lost it. Picking her up, he pressed her thighs apart and drove into her, nailing her against the shower wall as she wrapped her legs around his waist. She clung to him, letting him hammer himself into her, digging her nails into his back as he fucked them off the radar.

The next morning, they joined the others in the early morning sunshine on the stern deck. Sensei had left them alone and had tea with Sarge and Wax, for a change. She eyed him coyly and leaned to kiss his face.

"Thank you Papa," she said. She gave him a sweet smile. "No need to thank me child, I heard how much you liked that last night," he said.

"We all heard how much you liked whatever it was," Sarge said. She looked at Dragon, who shrugged.

"Your windows are open," Sensei said. "The entire cove probably heard how much you liked it."

"I don't know what it was but I wanted some," Wax said. "I'll tell you later," she said. "Please do," he said.

They had tea and ate breakfast and before long were heading north again, looking forward to reaching Dusty's by the evening. Sensei led them in Yoga and they were able to work out afterward. They passed the day, reaching Dusty's just before sunset. Dusty had no idea they were coming and Dragon hoped he'd be there.

Sarge spotted him on the deck of his bar and waved and in a few moments they saw the Boston Whaler heading to pick them up. He pulled alongside the stern platform and Sarge held him off of them in the gently moving water, as they boarded. Dragon introduced Sensei and Dusty nodded a greeting. They congregated at the same table as before and a waitress dropped off beers and a bottle of 1942 with shot glasses. Dusty poured for them.

"Cheers," Dragon said. "We're all addicted to this shit now." "It's not an addiction, it's a love affair," Dusty said. "So what are you doing here?" "Nothing," Dragon said. Dusty actually laughed then. "Well, here's to fucking nothing," he said. They drank again. The bar was quieter that night than it had been before. Raven asked Dusty about Anne Marie and he said she and her band were playing gigs up in Northern California on a road trip.

Dusty looked at Dragon remembering something. "Hey, some of my regular bikers were in a few days ago and were saying some shit about a missing Cartel player, from Puerto Vallarta," Dusty said. "Went out in his boat and never came back. He was out of that same Marina you were heading to." Dragon nodded and appeared to recall things. "There were some police at the Marina looking for a guy," Dragon said. "We saw them when we were leaving. Who is he?" He hoped he wouldn't hear something he didn't already know, sorry he had to be misleading with Dusty.

"Just some piece of shit; like all of them," Dusty said. "Drugs, guns and the sex trade. The bikers are the bottom of the totem pole, selling the drugs on the street, and the guns, and the girls for that matter. I guess their shit got disrupted from what I could tell. I don't ask questions."

Dragon nodded, then shrugged, and changed the subject. They joked about Sarge and Wax getting laid the last time they were there. "It was good for business," Dusty said. "Chicks were coming in here for days after, hoping for a little 'some of what she got', but only getting the usual." He laughed nodding at the scattered regulars. "My beer sales doubled." "Well, sorry we missed it," Wax said. "I'll say one thing," Sarge said. "That girl liked to fuck." They laughed at that, remembering Sarge's condition the following day.

Dusty turned to Sensei. "So how do you fit into this? I don't think we met last time." Sensei gave Dusty his warm friendly smile. "We didn't, and I basically have no reason for being here other than I missed them," Sensei said.

"Sensei raised us Dusty," Raven said. "Remember? We grew up together?" Dusty had a bad memory, mostly due to alcohol but also because he paid little attention to what people said most of the time. "Right, right," he said. His foggy mind put the relationship together then.

"We've been together for a long time," Sensei said. "I join them whenever I can. It keeps them grounded." Dusty eyed him, throwing back a shot. "This keeps me grounded," he said.

Sensei smiled at him, 'seeing' the same Dusty that Dragon had. Sensei was good at curing addictions and could have put a thought in Dusty's head that would have subliminally caused him to dislike alcohol, but he didn't. Dusty was living the life he wanted.

"So, where you headed," Dusty asked. "Not that I give a shit." Dragon laughed. "LA, New York, and Munich," he said. "Oh yea, I forgot," Dusty said. "You're that David Li guy. The world won't turn if you don't show up in it?" Dragon nodded. "Yes, something like that," he said. "For some reason there are people out there that will buy a magazine if our pictures are in it. It's fucked up shit to me." Dusty nodded, doing another shot. "I get that man, but I mean my bar made more money because some girls wanted a piece of the boys here. It's how it works," he said.

They talked into the night until Sensei nodded to Dragon. They had enough Tequila and if Dusty had any more he might not make it back to his dock safely. They made their way to Dusty's boat then and he guided them through the surf and onto the stern platform of the Dream Weaver.

"Stay safe kids," Dusty said. He waved and wheeled away, his Marijuana joint leaving a smoke cloud in the air after him. "Interesting man," Sensei said. They went up the stairs to the main cabin.

Dragon gave them all a wave as he pulled Raven to their room. Inside, he shut the door. He crossed his arms in front of him and eyed her for a moment. She looked back at him shyly wondering what he was going to do to her. After a moment, he raised an eyebrow at her, letting his sexy half smile melt her, then walked to the window, and slid it closed.

"Now you can make as much noise as you want," he said. In seconds she was naked and he pushed her back on the bed and devoured her.

The following day they reached the waters off the coast of Los Angeles. Gathering their things, including their weapons, laptops and all the cash from the safe, they prepared to leave the Dream Weaver in the care of the California Yacht Marina. She was to be refueled, a maintenance profile done and cleaned while they were gone. The Marina Manager assured them she would be safe and well taken care of in their absence. Sarge locked the cabin doors and they left to go to the Marina office and then the waiting Limo.

They enjoyed a glass of Champagne on the way to the airport. Sitting waiting was the DLI jet, sleek and sexy. They climbed up the steps, greeting the ever formal Simon.

"Mr. Li, welcome aboard, we are ready when you are," Simon said. "Thank you Simon. This is your plane so do what you do," Dragon said. "This is your plane, Mr. Li. It is simply my honor to fly it for you," Simon said. Dragon eyed Sensei, asking 'since when' silently. "Thank you Simon. In any case, take us to New York please," Dragon said.

"Another gift from the General," Sensei said. Dragon regarded Sensei and shook his head. "He is one for giving expensive transportation," Dragon said. "I now have a private jet, a yacht, a helicopter and numerous fast cars, not to mention priceless horses." Sensei just looked at Dragon, proud of him as ever. "It's what he likes to do I guess," Sensei said. "You deserve it son and whether or not you realize it is beside the point."

Dragon shrugged, as it still boggled his mind sometimes. Money was something he had never cared about, material possessions of no value to him and the General's gratitude not a motivating factor.

Catching his thoughts Sensei smiled at him. "The General is very grateful Dragon. He knows a person like you, the things you do and the way you have chosen to live your life doesn't come along every day. His mandate and his mission in life would not be fulfilled if it were not for you, all of you. He wants you to know that."

Raven eyed Dragon adoringly, knowing Sensei was right and willed him to know it to. As the flight went on they enjoyed some drinks, laughing together about some of their past adventures. With about an hour and a half left in the flight, Chekov joined them, on Sensei's laptop. He seemed busy and stuck to business.

"There will be a car waiting of course, it will take you to The Plaza, they are expecting you. Have a late dinner somewhere there I would suggest and enjoy the city for the next day. Take a car to LaGuardia for 7pm and I'll see you here the following morning I believe it will be," he said. "Are there any questions?"

They all looked at each other and then to Sensei, who nodded to Chekov that they understood and that was all.

Chekov was looking at screens and glancing around but finally eyed them one last time. "Well I have to go, but there's one last thing," he said. "You know the pictures of you from Sarge's camera? Someone got a hold of them and they are everywhere, the news, websites, all over the internet. We don't know how yet, likely a breach of security by a marina staff member, who got paid good money for them I would imagine. That kind of thing is huge. Sorry. Get ready for the media fall out Dragon, I'm already overloaded on DavidLi.com with requests for photo shoots of you and Raven, all of you. Magazines, tabloids, TV shows and Fashion designers, endorsement advertising, it hasn't stopped," Chekov said.

Dragon ran a hand through his hair, recalling the photos of them in the waterfall, on the horses. "Everything?" he asked. "Yes" Chekov said. "Jesus fuck. We've only been gone hours," Dragon said. "I'm looking into it," Chekov said. "Is this going to cause any strategic problems Chekov?" Sensei asked. "Not immediately but we are doing a profile now on existential effects. I should have a report in a few hours, but you will likely be accosted in New York when you arrive, regardless. You were already a popular target; it's just going to get worse now. I will let you know what the profile findings are and how the General wants to handle it. I ripped the Marina Manager a new one and he is getting back to me on who is responsible. I know nothing more right now. What's done is done. I've hired a private security company to cover the Yacht 24/7. Everyone is scrambling here right now, I have to go." And with that the screen went dark.

None of them spoke, thinking. "The camera was in a drawer in my cabin; maybe a cleaning person found it and downloaded them," Sarge said. "It's not your fault Sarge," Sensei said. Sarge downed the rest of his Scotch. Dragon walked past him to the bar, picking up his glass, and putting a hand on his shoulder. "Never mind buddy. Hope you didn't have any dick pics on there," he said. "I wish I did," Sarge said. "Me too," Raven giggled. "Alright, I'm glad you aren't concerned son, but it could make things annoying for you for awhile," Sensei said. He did not reveal what he was truly concerned about. He would talk to Dragon about it at tea.

CHAPTER TWENTY TWO

NEW YORK

Dragon wished he could have had a little longer with Raven before putting her dress on her, as she stood now in tiny black silk and lace panties that had very little to them. They had the privacy of the back cabin and he had just made love to her for a few hours before they had to get ready and land in New York. Dragon pulled a tight black V-neck T-shirt on and black dress pants. He matched her dress, which was black satin with an off white choker collar. It had a keyhole neckline that showed off her cleavage and was fitted perfectly to her figure. She stepped into a pair of Louboutin heels and they joined the others. Sarge was desperately handsome in a white dress shirt, highlighting his tan and blonde hair, with dark grey dress pants, and Wax looked sexy and smoldering in black everywhere. Sensei eyed them as he pulled a dark navy jacket over a light silver shirt and black pants. Raven helped him with it, fixing a strand of his hair that had decided not to stay with the others.

They taxied to a distant tarmac away from the lights of LaGuardia's main terminal. When they had come to a halt, they waited, all quiet now, as Simon went about shutting the plane down and opening the doors to lower the stairs. They all rose, and guiding Raven first they descended to the waiting Phantom Rolls Royce, the signature car used by The Plaza Hotel. It had darkly tinted windows which they were grateful for as Paparazzi lined the ten foot high chain link security fencing. Cameras flashed in the distance, but telephoto lenses captured it close up.

They arrived in front of The Plaza, a beautiful historic building dating back to the beginning of the 1900's. It was chaos as photographers and news reporters, entertainment reporters and onlookers lined the red velvet ropes that were the only thing allowing them to pass safely between the car and the hotel doors. Dragon eyed it and they all looked at each other. When the car door opened for them it began. They stood as a group for a moment.

Dragon held Raven's hand and they looked around at the throng. Cameras flashed and questions were shouted.

It ranged from the basic "What brings you here?" "How long are you here?" Then a new one, "Where's the waterfall Mr. Li?" "Show us the love Mr. Li." They all eyed each other. Dragon smiled now, his usual sexy half grin, as Raven looked up at him, thinking he was beyond beautiful in the flashing lights.

Then a woman at the edge of the rope addressed her. "Raven! What's it like being married to David Li?" Raven looked to her and smiled her beautiful glowing sweet smile. "You've seen the pictures. What does it look like?" she said. She transferred her gaze to Dragon, her green eyes shining at him.

"Actually it looks like this," Dragon said. He gently tilted her face to his and kissed her, sexily, wetly and deeply, taking his time, running his other hand through her hair at the back of her head. She reached up, placing her hands on his chest and kissed him back.

Cameras went crazy and the hungry wolves that they were, nearly shredded each other trying to get to the front. Dragon softly let her go after thoroughly kissing her, looking into her eyes, as he had somehow managed to forget what he was doing for a moment, lost in her even then. "I love you." He mouthed to her silently and she looked up at him, beautiful, soft and completely in love with him.

He took her then and they went forward into the hotel. Some female reporter had grabbed Wax's arm and wanted a 'private' interview. He took her card, smiling at her like only he could. And as usual Sarge was propositioned at least three times in as many steps. And Sensei didn't escape unscathed as two girls made him have a selfie on one of their phones as they sandwiched him between them. The hotel doors were pulled back for them, the Paparazzi not allowed in and they made it gratefully inside the tranquil, sophisticated and extremely elegant Plaza.

They were quickly seen to by an Executive Manager, who personally escorted them to their Suite. He was well informed as to who they were and was used to dealing with the rich, the famous, the A list, rock stars, athletes, and anyone really that crossed the threshold of the famous Hotel, wanting to be treated like one. They moved into a large elevator, and using an electronic key, he made it take them to the penthouse suite.

They looked around them now. The Royal Plaza Suite was a stunning mix of old and new, very traditional, as in traditional wealth. It had three bedrooms a large living space with a grand piano, and huge table that seated 12, and a private gym. It was elegantly furnished, over looked Fifth Avenue and was private.

"Nice," Wax said. "Let's get Chekov," Dragon said. Sensei found his laptop and hooked them up to the Wi-Fi. Chekov appeared after a minute or so.

"Anything new?" Dragon asked. "Only the latest pictures of you kissing your wife on the hotel doorstep in front of hundreds of people," Chekov said. "Already? What the hell that was only like five minutes ago," Dragon said. He was stunned by it. Raven giggled, as Chekov flashed the images onto 50 percent of their screen while he stayed on the other half. "I think this one is my favorite," Chekov said. He revealed a photo of them mid-kiss, as Dragon had run his hand behind her head in her hair, his fingers on her chin tipping her up to him and her hands on his chest. Their eyes were closed and their lips perfectly on each others.

"This is fucking ridiculous," Dragon said. "Well you did the right thing playing along with them," Chekov said. "May as well give them what they want to see." "I guess so, but fuck," Dragon said.

"It's Ok baby, you kiss me in public all the time. I don't get what the big deal is," Raven said. "Ok, I need a drink," Dragon said. Raven moved to the kitchen area. "I'll find you something babe."

After a quick search she managed to come up with a bottle of Patron. She poured them all shots. "Here's to New York," she said. They toasted together and hit them back. "Does anybody want to eat?" Sensei asked. "We could I guess," Dragon said. "But I don't want to go anywhere and put up with that shit all over again."

"I can see what's in the Hotel," Wax said. He looked at the guest services book that lay on the table. It was late but New York had no time limits and most places were just beginning to get started.

"Hey, there's a food hall, they call it," Wax said. He showed them the pictures. It looked like fun, casual but sophisticated and everything there. "Ok, let's do it," Sarge said.

"Ok, give us five minutes," Dragon said. They all got up then and getting their things went to get settled.

"Baby, you want out of that dress?" Dragon asked. "I like you in it but I like you out of it too." He took her in his arms and held her to him. "Well baby I would love to be a bit more comfortable right now and later let you undress me for good and show me some New York David Li, right there on that bed over there," she said.

"I like that idea a lot," he said. He kissed her and pushed himself against the black satin. "Maybe just the shoes," he said. "Whatever you want baby, but please, I'm already hours beyond wet and you can't now, so get me out of this before Sensei gets pissed that we are taking too long," she said. She turned so he could unzip her. "Damn this shit," he said. She stood there, little panties and the shoes and they looked at each other, her hands beginning to tremble. "Fuck," he said. "Talk about orgasm denial." He let his head fall back, running his hand through his hair. "Ok, we are going to pick this up right where we're leaving it off as soon as we get back here."

In a few minutes they appeared to a waiting Sensei, Sarge and Wax. She had on a tight pair of jeans, black leather boots with a wedge heel and a white loose fitting silk top, covered by a tiny cropped black leather jacket, her hair in a pony tail. Dragon concealed his hard-on with his jacket. Using the electronic key they made their way by the speedy elevator to the food hall level. They found their way to it and immersed themselves in the overwhelming sights and sounds. It was touristy yet local, and people were everywhere. There were so many things to choose from, eventually they let Sensei's focusing abilities lead them to Sushi. They found a Sushi bar with enough room for the five of them and sat, relieved and dying to eat now.

A Sushi Chef had recognized them and came to serve them exclusively and prepared them the most wonderful things they had ever eaten. They enjoyed their food and repartee with the Chef, Sensei especially, reclaiming his Japanese roots, speaking the language and translating for the rest of them. It was entertaining and rejuvenating.

But always aware of what was going on around them, as they had been conditioned to be, it became apparent that it was time for them to go. The restaurant had become overly busy and girls were beginning to approach Wax and Sarge. They paid their bill and made an attempt to depart, through the now crowded area. But it was inevitable they had to stop, talk to people, take photos with people and sign things for people. Dragon kept his arm around Raven, holding her to him, dying now to get her back to the room, as they slowly made their way being as polite and decent as they could be. Sarge and Wax were accosted by girls, inviting them, touching them and overwhelming them.

"That was fun until that shit went down," Sarge said. "I had like 20 propositions in five minutes," Wax said. "Somehow I suddenly don't want to get laid that much." "Ya I know what you mean," Sarge said. "I might need a shower."

They all laughed at that. "Well I'm surprised; you animals may have just turned a corner," Raven said. Sensei eyed them smiling. "Come now, let's get back to being us and tomorrow we can see some things, then we are back to work. Remember, every moment is a gift."

Finally inside their suite, Sensei pulled Raven to him, hugging her. "Embrace every moment, OK," he said. Kissing her forehead he released her to Dragon. "All of you," he said. His Buddhist beliefs guiding him always, made him stop sometimes and appreciate all that had become of them. Dragon nodded. "Thanks Papa," he said.

He picked Raven up, so she could wrap her legs around his waist and turned and headed for their room. He understood Sensei's words but he also understood his needs. She kissed his neck as he held her.

"Good night," he said. He smiled back to them over his shoulder. "Some-one's going to get reminded of what it's like to be married to David Li." He kicked the door closed behind them.

Finally able to have her, he let his self control slip, pulling her clothes from her. They hadn't made love since he couldn't remember, even though it had only been a few hours ago on the plane. They stripped each other, she couldn't wait to get her hands on the Platinum belt buckle and he couldn't wait to get his hands on all of her. She pulled his shirt over his head, and he pushed her back on the bed, pulling off her boots and dragging her jeans off of her, not stopping until they were naked and he lay over her.

He reached and softly touched her to be sure she was very wet because he was going to lose control. He gasped as he felt her soaking, soft and open. She moaned at his touch, dying for him. They were both trembling now and he brought his arm up again bracing on his elbows, his face against hers.

"I'm going to love you baby," he said.

She cried out with relief as he began a rhythm in her. They held their kiss, their lips pressed together, not being able to get enough of each others' tongues. He began to moan into her and fucking her harder, he knew it was close for him. She let her head fall back and sideways and he pushed into her three or four more hard thrusts taking her there with him.

Wanting to stay completely connected, he lay deep inside her, their bodies touching everywhere, their lips on one another, fingertips feeling soft skin and their passionate desire for each other washing over them like surf on sand. They made love, making each other come, making each other crazy, until they fell soft against each other, their sweat mingling, their saliva everywhere and their juices coating each other. It got like that for them sometimes when they just couldn't get enough and would fall into each other. It always left them wet everywhere, breathing hard and physically exhausted. They slept in their wetness.

In the morning, Sensei woke Dragon for tea. Dragon opened his eyes to see Sensei eyeing him. "What?" he said. He didn't realize but he was a mess, mainly his hair, the ends of it were crisp with someone's come, likely his own, maybe hers, possibly both. His neck had a classic hickey on the side where she had sucked on him slightly too hard.

"Oh, we fell asleep, I don't know, but I'm going to run a bath for her when we're done tea," he said. Sensei sat then, passing him tea, and smiled. "You're going to need to cover your neck," he said. Dragon touched his neck recalling. "We were both a little off the charts I guess, it seemed like days since the last time and I had to wait, while we went for dinner and she'd been crazy since we got off the plane, I don't know Papa," Dragon said.

"I need to discuss something with you," Sensei said. "The pictures, they show the dragon." Dragon thought about it for a moment, so he could understand where Sensei was going with this. "You are worried about the tattoo being recognized?" he asked. "We eliminated everyone in the place that day and every connection we knew about at the time. Chekov has a program that routinely scans for images on the internet. So far there have never been any of you. VHS copies of any content regarding you have never surfaced, if there even still are any. Nowadays if a person posted anything of that nature anywhere online they would be arrested. The risk lays in the possibility that there is still someone who knew you, that wasn't there that day."

"Well, they wouldn't be able to admit it if they did, because they would be guilty by association. You can't just point a finger and say; 'Yup' I paid to fuck that guy a long time ago," Dragon said. "Dragon the threat is not of public exposure for you, but of someone seeking to eliminate you," Sensei said.

"Have you heard this from Chekov?" Dragon asked. "Yes, earlier. Their analysis indicates the risk is low but it does exist. Remember what I said about when I found you? They were trying to eliminate you then, because of our raid," Sensei said.

Dragon had no recollection of those moments as he was deep in the misery of withdrawal at the time. He sat thinking. "Well, as you are always saying, 'Life is a Gift'." Sensei smiled at him then. "Yes son, you are on the path you are on."

Dragon listened to the familiar speech Sensei often used to remind them of what was important, what was not, and what choices could be made and what ones couldn't. "Here's to your excellent timing," Dragon said, drinking his tea. "It had nothing to do with me," Sensei said. Dragon laughed then. "You are funny this morning Sensei."

Dragon understood Sensei's belief that actions were just reactions to other things. "Well, I'm glad you are amused. I will leave you and you can wake her and take care of the mess you're in," Sensei said. "You know we will just be making a new mess," Dragon said. "I assumed as much, just show up clean for breakfast and Yoga." And with that he stepped out, pulling the door closed

Dragon and Raven joined the others awhile later and found they were hungry. Sensei had ordered them the things they routinely ate for breakfast and they sat with Wax and Sarge.

"Did you two have fun sharing a bed?" Raven asked Wax. "It was all good until Sarge tried to give me his morning hard-on," Wax said. "You wanted it," Sarge said. "You were fucking spooning me with it," Wax said. Sarge laughed and winked at Wax. "Just like old times," he said. Wax shook his head. "Sorry brother, it's never going to happen."

Raven was giggling at them now, remembering how they used to share a tiny bed, not wanting to sleep apart even when they could have. They decided to work out for the morning, go for Sushi again at lunch and afterward, Sensei, Sarge and Wax were going to hit a museum, while Dragon and Raven took a carriage ride in Central Park. They would meet back at the room after and get ready to catch their flight to Munich. Things had gone mostly according to plan. Splitting up had been a good idea as it was more difficult for the Paparazzi to keep track of both groups of them. They had endured a few photographs but had declined to stop and speak to any of the insistent microphones.

Dragon and Raven had returned from their carriage ride and were alone, as Sensei, Wax and Sarge were still in the Museum. Dragon had done just about everything he could think of to her on the piano and the kitchen island and finally in the shower.

"What do you want to wear?" he asked. He eyed her laying in a huge towel on the bed now. "Nothing really baby," she said. He smiled at her. "When we get home, I'll make love to you for all day and night if you want sweetheart, but we have to go and we need clothes for that." "Baby I wish we could do that right now," she said. She let the towel fall open with her legs, touching herself, knowing he would have a difficult time saying 'No'.

His breath caught at the sight of her and he went and sat between her legs, eyeing her gently rubbing herself for him to watch. "Go ahead." He smiled to her, teasing her. "No, not without you," she moaned. She sat up and curled herself up on his lap. He stroked her hair. "Poor baby, but I just fucked you shameless, amongst other things," he said. "But I have an idea. Come here." He pulled her with him to the closet. "Wear this and I can fuck you on the plane," he said. He held up a black leather miniskirt. She smiled. "I like your style Mr. Li, and you're dirty mind," she said. "My dirty mind?" he said, feigning astonishment.

Kissing her forehead, he held the skirt for her to take. She stepped into it and he zipped it up for her at the back. He found a deep pink silky top with small ruffles down the neckline, along the buttons and he put that on her. The color made her eyes glow. It was sleeveless, revealing her tanned arms, but he handed her a jacket to cover up with because it would be cooler when they arrived in Munich. The jacket was a slightly off white; jean jacket style made of a shiny silk and cotton, and had a black leather stand up collar and black leather trim on the sleeves. She put on black leather ankle boots with spikier heels and an open toe.

He eyed her. "Might not make it to the plane," he said. He turned away to find himself some clothes before he came all over her, thinking of her wearing nothing under her skirt. As a second thought he handed her a black satin thong. "That skirt's pretty short and I am just as horny thinking of you in this as I am without it," he said. She smiled at him and sexily pulled it over her heels, drawing it slowly up her thighs, eyeing him watching her. "You're literally trying to kill me I think," he said. She laughed at him playfully. "I'm sorry baby, this place has made me crazy for you since we got here," she said. "Come on, put your clothes on and I will try and keep myself from ripping them off you." "Well thank you, Mrs. Li, I need to get rid of this hard on before I pass out," he said.

He finally pulled her with him out of the room. He looked gorgeous in dark fitted jeans that hung just right on his hips, clung to his thighs and his butt and made her doubt her efforts to keep her hands off him. He eyed the DLI belt buckle as he had fastened it and sent her an image of her undoing it on her knees. He had pulled on a button down dress shirt so the collar would hide the mark she had left on his neck. It was black which he always looked smoking hot in and he had tied his hair back. He had brushed hers long and pinned just the front pieces smoothly back on the top of her head, keeping it out of her face. She carried a black leather jacket for him, soft with little detail, but beautiful lines that fit him exactly. Another thing she would make him leave on sometime, he knew.

A Limo brought them back to the waiting plane. They had endured more photos on the way out of the hotel, once again not responding to questions. Dragon had made a vague comment about them leaving New York and allowed them to take some pictures. Again they wanted a demonstration which he did not indulge, but simply kept his arm around Raven's waist possessively as he led her to the waiting car. They were glad to be back aboard the plane and free of it. In Munich they would be transported from the plane by helicopter and not encounter anything and no one knew where they were going anyway this time.

CHAPTER TWENTY THREE

MUNICH

The General had a new Sikorsky helicopter that he had sent to pick them up at Munich International Airport, piloted by none other than Tom-Tom, whom they hadn't seen since leaving the jungle. They had walked from the plane to the sleek black helicopter, one word lettered on the side in crisp silver, 'STRAUSS'. They had stepped into the comfortable interior through the waiting open door and saw Tom-Tom, greeting them in his usual way.

"Boys." He waved back to them, recognizable just from his smile, as he was covered in a flight helmet and large Aviators. They all greeted him, high fives and handshakes. "Welcome to Munich," he said. "Get us the fuck out of here," Dragon said. He used his usual remark to Tom-Tom. "Fucking right," he said. He turned back to his controls and shortly lifted them off. It was a quick flight to the helipad at the top of the DLI building. When they had landed they all reunited with Tom-Tom, man hugs and girl kisses that made him blush. "You guys look great," Tom-Tom said. "Good to see you. Let's catch up for sure while you're here."

They made plans to have a drink and then departed for the elevators as it was cold on the top of the building. Tom-Tom had somewhere else to be and went back to his new ride. Dragon placed his hand on the glass panel and so it began. Wendy the elevator voice responded accordingly, welcoming them and taking them somehow to the destination they were meant to arrive at. There were no other controls in the elevator. Chekov had control over where all the elevators went, who was on them and when and programmed it to accept or deny its occupants, typical Chekov and classic HQ Munich.

Seeing Tom-Tom had been a reminder of how much they had missed camp and some of the things from their old lives and some of the people. Dragon held Raven's hand as they followed Sensei through the corridors to the main control area to find Chekov and the General. So much had changed, from how they had usually arrived there in the past. They were older now, well dressed, sophisticated looking and accomplished. Dragon recalled arriving there dirty, disheveled, bleeding, exhausted and brooding. That was Damascus's role now he thought as they made their way. Had all this really happened, it seemed like a dream. He snapped out of his thoughts as they approached Chekov, who had stood to greet them. It had been a long time.

"Welcome." Chekov nodded to them all. He had changed somewhat, looking different in real life he looked almost normal Raven thought. He actually almost smiled and Raven figured out he must have a woman. Dragon caught her thought and tried not to laugh.

"The General is anxious to see you all, so let's not keep him waiting any longer," Chekov said. In his usual crisp manner he led them to the office. Wendy admitted them into another elevator and no-one spoke as they all silently recalled their last adventure with Chekov on the very same elevator.

"I know what you're thinking about Dragon," Chekov said. Dragon just eyed him and appeared to consider it. "That if you were not all here my wife would be up against the wall right about now?" he said. Chekov's eyes flashed to Dragon, always shocked by his deliberate crudeness. Before he could respond Wendy did. "That would be unsafe."

They all burst out laughing then except Chekov, who shook his head reminding himself not to engage in it and risk a similar outcome as last time. Sensei eventually cleared his throat, cuing them to regain their composure, as the elevator halted.

"Entertaining as always Dragon," Chekov said. He smiled to himself, feeling he had for once got the last word.

They stepped out into the austere glow of the General's office, seeing him immediately as he stood twenty paces off, hands clasped in front of him, waiting for them. He wore his usual crisp gray suit, white shirt and black silk tie. His hair was all white now and he looked older. It tugged at Sensei's heart to see him again. They stopped in front of him and Sensei made a traditional Japanese half bow in a show of respect, which the General returned slightly less so, and then he held out his arms for Sensei to hug him.

"It's good to see you old friend," the General said. "And you," Sensei said. They released their embrace and smiled at one another, their mutual respect and friendship was obvious and it was clear they had missed each other.

"Dragon," the General said. "Come here young man." He pulled Dragon into a hug. It was hard for Dragon to even man hug him because he was so much smaller in stature. "General Strauss, how have you been?" he asked. "Excellent, excellent, and even better now, I'm so glad you are here, it's been too long," the General said. He released him but clasped his hand in his two hands, not wanting to let go. "You are as handsome as ever if I may say so and we have many things to discuss, but first I can wait no longer." His glance turned to Raven.

"My dear," he said He looked upon her with happiness in his eyes. "How is it you could be even lovelier than ever?" She took both his hands in hers and leaned up to kiss his cheek. "General please, how is it I can hold my own with these boys yet you make me blush like a school girl?" she said. It charmed him out of his socks. "Oh my dear, you are beautiful and as usual make my day," he said. He smiled at her with adoring eyes. "I do hope your husband here is being good to you," he said playfully. "Every minute of everyday General," she said. She leaned into Dragon and circled his waist in her arms, as his arm involuntarily went around her shoulder pulling her into him. "Aah I can see it is as always, and it's delightful," the General said.

He always loved to see them together, their special connection making up for a loss of his own, just as it somehow did for Sensei. He turned then to Sarge, pulling him into a hug.

"Sergeant Willis, you are all grown up now, and I don't know why you haven't found a wife," he said. Good naturedly he eyed Sarge's good looks, still boyish but nearly 25 years old now. "It's probably because I'm not really all grown up General," Sarge said.

"I can vouch for that," Raven said. "I see nothing has changed," the General said. He eyed them laughing, amused as ever by them. "Well Sergeant Willis, you take all the time you need."

He moved on to Wax then, hugging him and actually staring at him momentarily. "And you young man, you don't have a wife because there are too many fish in the sea I am guessing," he said. He had hit the nail on the head when it came to Wax. "You would be right about that General," Wax said. "Don't have to choose, so I don't." He smiled his 'Hollywood' smile and shrugged in his carefree Wax way. The General grinned at him. "If I looked like you and were your age I would be saying the same thing I would think." "It's all good General," Wax said. He put a hand on the General's shoulder. "If I ever meet the lady that can do to me what she does to him..." he said.

Their eyes turned to Dragon, but Sarge interrupted. "Then shoot you??" he asked.

"Sergeant Willis!!" Raven flared at him.

Dragon put his hand over her mouth, pulling her into him from behind as she had advanced on Sarge. Her eyes flashed and Sarge grinned at her, knowing she couldn't attack him now. The General was still laughing, enjoying their banter. It was such a contrast to the sterile lives they led there.

Sensei interjected. "Alright then you two," he said. "I could blame it on jet lag General, but as you know I have been listening to it for over 15 years now." The General just beamed at him, thinking he couldn't remember the last time he had laughed this much. "Then you are a lucky man my friend," the General replied.

Sensei thought he knew not of what he spoke but agreed with him anyway. Dragon uncovered her mouth and brushed her face with the back of his hand which was his way of warning her he was going to spank her.

Chekov had been watching silently, trying not to, but also finding them amusing.

"Well, Dragon what would you like to do first?" the General asked. "See Damascus," Dragon said. "Of course, Chekov will take you. And one other thing," the General said. They all eyed him waiting. "I would be honored if you would all join me for dinner tonight at my home." "Of course General, thank you," Raven said.

"Good, General," Dragon said. "I would like the opportunity to formally thank you for your generous wedding gifts and well really, everything," he said. "Well Dragon if you attend dinner tonight that will be thanks enough. It's charming that you don't seem to see that the shoe is on the other foot," the General said. Dragon smiled at him genuinely, and shook his head in a 'no I don't get it' way.

"Everything you need will be in your rooms, and I shall see you at eight," the General said. Chekov led them back to the elevator.

They found Damascus and his remaining team members at a table in a corner of the large sterile grey walled room that was HQ Munich's Common area. As they approached him, he stood, as did his team. He was slightly taller than Dragon remembered him to be and he had filled out. He was slighter in stature than Dragon but he had chiseled muscled arms, broad shoulders and muscular thighs.

He could have passed as Dragon's younger brother now. He wore his black hair long and in layers, a long spiky one covered down around his ears, spiking around his cheek bones and the rest spiked around the back of his neck, framing his jaw line. His almond black eyes were shadowed by a strong brow like Dragon's and as he saw them a bright smile crossed his now handsome face, his perfect white teeth taking Raven back in time.

Dragon grinned at him and pulled him into a big man hug. "Hey man," Dragon said. "Dragon," Damascus said. They released each other and Raven couldn't help herself and jumped into his arms. He lifted her off her feet, his arms almost making it twice around her. "Damascus," she said. She hugged him, breathing in his scent of leather, gunshot residue and body-wash.

He set her down on her heels and looked at her, starting with her toes and moving to her leather skirt then finally her eyes. He looked back to Dragon, with a crooked grin and then immediately launched into hugs and playful shoving with Wax and Sarge. Sensei took his hand in both of his.

"Son, it's good to see you looking so well," he said.

Dragon and Raven greeted all the others and finally they sat. Damascus turned a chair around straddling it backwards and rested his arms, crossed on the chair back, and Dragon sat half on the table.

"How are you? Clearly you got yourself out of Schultz's grasp," Dragon said. He referred to the strange doctor at HQ that they all disliked, including Sensei, rumored to be conducting cloning experiments on humans. "Didn't take long," Damascus said. "I got out of there before he cloned me I think." They all shared a knowing laugh. Damascus eyed Raven again, liking her new look, not being able to resist the temptation.

Dragon picked it up instantly. "I see you haven't changed much," he said. He was noting Damascus's line of sight. "No girls here?" Damascus just smirked at him. "Too many actually, I never get any sleep," he said. "But you know me. I've always wanted what I can't have." Raven blushed, now knowing Damascus had a lustful crush on her just like they had told her.

"You look good," Dragon said. Damascus eyed him back and pointed a finger at Dragon's leather jacket. "You've gone all 'David Li' on me I see," Damascus said. Dragon shrugged. "I wear what Chekov puts in the closet." Damascus eyed Raven's miniskirt again, "Well that explains a lot," he said. Dragon laughed, "Ya I guess it does."

They talked together some more, catching up on gossip and happenings from both of their worlds. Sensei eventually nodded to Dragon and mentally cued that they should try and get some rest before they had to leave for the General's dinner. They could get a few hours of sleep before they would need to get ready. Dragon agreed, and stood then.

"Well, we should go, Sensei's telling me I have jet lag so I'm going to use it as an excuse to be alone," he said. Damascus stood then and he touched the leather on Dragon's shoulder, looking questioningly. "Maybe I should get one of these," he said. He eyed Raven and smiled at Dragon. Dragon smiled back at him. The disarming smile, that made people stare or look away. "You're not a big enough asshole yet," he said. Damascus stepped aside so they could pass. "You don't know me anymore," he replied. His ever cocky personality surfaced making Dragon wonder if he was indeed right. Dragon shook his head, grinning as they left.

Wendy took them to their usual floor and they found their ways to their rooms. They paused together at Dragon's door. "We need to meet here at 7 pm," Sensei said. "Are you going to Erika's room Sarge?" Raven asked. She was not able to resist bringing up the subject. "No but I think Wax is," Sarge said. "Fuck off Sarge," Wax said.

"Excuse me," Sensei said. "7 pm? No swearing and no fucking the staff."

Wax and Sarge walked off and Raven giggled as she heard Wax saying to Sarge. "You're such an asshole I think you're made of leather jackets."

Wendy slid the door closed behind them and Raven turned to face him. He pulled her against him then. "Should I spank you for your impulsive behavior in the General's office earlier?" he asked. He was kissing her face everywhere between words. She smoothed her hand over his erection through the denim now, dying at the sight of him hard against it.

"Baby, you want that?" he asked.

She had nodded, so he let her stand waiting for him as he undressed completely, slowly taunting her. She watched him, biting her lip and meeting him at his game.

"This I adore," she said. She touched the leather jacket, smelling it, loving the combination of him and it together. "Put it on," he said. She smiled sexily at him getting an idea. "I will put it on, but first…" she said.

She got up and stood away from him as he sat on the edge of the bed, watching what she was up to. She eyed him as she pulled the dark pink top over her head, letting him see her breasts. She let it drop to the floor and brushed her hands over them, squeezing them together and teasing her nipples between her fingertips, her face showing her reaction to the stimulation. He swallowed hard as he realized what she was doing.

She then ran her fingers down her middle, flat and muscular, letting them draw to the center of her lower belly, before moving to the back and slowly unzipping the leather that had taunted him all day. She held it and lowered it, gradually revealing herself to him.

He was falling into her sexual realm then, his heart now beating hard in his chest, his eyes never leaving her and glazing over with the building passion.

She stepped out of the skirt and it dangled from one finger, as she turned and walked a few steps to lay it on a chair back, letting him see her perfect sexy butt, with all she had left on. The sexy black spiky heel ankle boots and his leather jacket, as she pulled it onto her.

She stood in front of him, and took a step in to him, letting him touch her. He found her nipple with his lips.

She was blowing his mind now, covered in his jacket, revealing herself beneath it. He was moaning with his want for her and trying to stop himself from throwing her down and smashing himself into her. Instead his fingertips softly touched her everywhere under the leather.

She looked sexily at him, her green eyes on fire, her lips parted and wet. She was successfully making him insane.

"Baby, I'm losing it," he said. His hands were trembling for her now. "You're going to kill me here. Again," he said. She knew her effect on him and let it go only a bit longer, dying for him herself. "Do you want something now baby?" she asked. She was kissing down his neck driving him closer. "Oh god baby," he moaned.

In one quick movement he laid her back on the bed, the leather jacket all around her, her sexy body within it and he consumed her. He felt he was seconds from coming and had been since she'd undressed, had been since earlier that day and had been since he met her.

He had left himself on his knees for her sexy game at least three times and afterward lay over her breathing hard, a light sweat on his skin and his hair everywhere. He waited while his head cleared. She lay beneath him, her eyes beginning to focus again, as she breathed for air, sweat sticking her hair to her face, her lips wet from his kiss on her. The leather still surrounded her and her ankles were interlocked around his waist holding him inside her as he had rocked her through her last orgasm.

They were literally in each others' minds and he kissed her to sleep.

Sensei had come to wake them at 6pm so they could be ready for 7, after about a four hour sleep. He stood shaking his head as he had arrived to find Dragon sleeping half on top of her. The duvet covered his lower body and she laid apart half under him. All Sensei could see of her was half her leg in a spiky black heel and something leather and hair. The dragon tattoo eyed him as he approached, and he avoided eye contact with it, smiling to himself at his strange superstition when it came to the inked image. He touched Dragon's shoulder, pulling him back to the world.

Dragon woke and remembered, seeing her under him. "Shit, Sensei," he said. He moved off of her warmth, brushing her hair off her face as she lay lost in the leather, once again covered in their sexual cocktail. "You will need a whole hour as I thought," Sensei said. He was eyeing the situation, amused as always by them. "You'd better get started son." He smiled at Dragon, and turned to go. He paused by the doorway. "Leather jacket, Hmmm, I never had one. Who knew?" he said. "You can borrow mine," Dragon said. Sensei slipped through the door as it hit the wall beside where his head would have been.

He smiled to Raven as he wakened her from their sleep. She regained herself in the moment and he pulled her with him into the hot shower. They washed each other with an amazing smelling wash that made them want each other more, but later. Dragon wrapped her in a big towel and tied one around his waist. He was wondering what to do next just as Wendy announced the presence of Erika.

"Let her in," Dragon said.

Erika was the wardrobe and extras person at HQ Munich. She took care of their fake personas and equipped them to look like the people they wanted to look like. She was good at her job but had an attraction for younger men, really any men.

"Hello babies," she said. "I see my timing is perfect." She was eyeing Dragon up and down. "What are you doing here Erika," Dragon said.

He was not amused by her fucking him with her eyes. Raven was brushing her hair out ignoring her. Raven had never really disliked anyone before but somehow was experiencing it for the first time.

"I have your wardrobe for this evening, it would have been here for you but Chekov kept changing his mind and there were alterations," she replied. She again eyed Dragon's upper body. He glared at her then. "Give it up Erika, I know you fuck every operative you can get your hands on but you should know by now I will never be one of them." He flashed his impatience with her and she never even flinched, just shrugged nonchalantly. "I was actually thinking both of you together, but whatever."

She turned her attention to Raven then. "Raven, I can help you with your hair, maybe smooth it out, long and shiny. This dress is backless and will show it off?" Raven looked at Dragon, and he nodded, they were getting short on time so he let her help.

Erika took the brush from her and began smoothing out her hair. "Damascus?" Raven asked. Erika was good at her job and continued, molding Raven's hair as she spoke happily about her love life. "No he turned me down, much in the same manner as your husband just did. I don't know what's with it," she said. Erika shrugged and kept working. Raven giggled. "You should try Sarge. He's always game."

Dragon dressed himself in what appeared to be 'black tie'. He somehow remembered how to tie a bow tie and finished it squarely thinking he would strangle to death in the thing. He fastened cufflinks to his sleeves, again platinum DLI's with a single half carat diamond inside the letter D. He wondered who thought of this shit. Were they either more gifts from the General or Chekov's gay alter-ego? His hair had dried and he eyed it. It naturally went back off his forehead in an almost cowlick. It was even longer now than it had ever been and he would ask Raven to cut some off soon. He decided to leave it down, feeling already formal enough. He pulled the black jacket on as Wendy announced Sergeant Willis.

Sarge entered, dressed exactly like Dragon and they laughed when they saw each other. "Fuck this, how do I tie this fucking thing?" Sarge asked. His tie was hanging loose around his neck. "Here," Dragon said. He positioned him in front of a mirror and did it for him.

Becoming aware of voices Sarge looked around. "Who's here?" he asked. He looked and realized Raven was in the bathroom with someone. Dragon grinned at him. "Take a guess," he said. Sarge leaned so he could see the back of Erika. "Fuck, hide me; she's going to make me fuck her," Sarge said. He looked panicked, making Dragon laugh. "You didn't seem to mind before," Dragon said. Sarge looked wide eyed at Dragon. "Well yeah, I was a virgin and dying for it. But now she's not my kind of ride, it's like you're in the passenger seat or something," he said. Dragon laughed at the idea of Erika being in control of her sex partners.

"It's Ok the first time when you don't know what you're doing anyway," Sarge said. "I knew what I was doing the first time," Dragon said, looking puzzled. "Of course you did," Sarge said. Sarcastically he rolled his eyes. "All you had to do was stand there and little miss, 'just put your big dick in me baby and I'm good, ya fuck me Dragon,' made you an instant rock star," Sarge said. Using his imitation of Raven's voice they were both laughing as they turned and realized Raven herself was standing there now.

"Very amusing Sergeant Willis," she said. She was grinning at him and he swallowed, knowing he was fucked now. "There's someone here you've been waiting to see, what a coincidence," Raven said.

Erika followed Raven into the room and walked straight up to Sarge. "Missed me did you Sergeant Willis?" she said. She was eyeing him like a starving wolf would eye a deer carcass, which is what Sarge would have rather been at that moment. "Erika," he said. He tried to back away from her without looking like it. "You have changed Sergeant Willis, all grown up, handsomer than ever and very sexy with a suntan," she said.

She seemed to be growling now. Sarge wondered why people kept saying he was all grown up and had to force his mind to focus so he could hopefully have enough wits about him to deal with the 'Cougar'.

Raven turned the screws. "Sarge has been hoping to see you while we are here, right Sarge?" He wanted to strangle her. Erika slid toward him like a python about to coil him up. "Well Sergeant Willis I can hardly wait. Call me, ASAP," she said. She slithered around him to the door, letting her hand cup him as she passed. He shuddered and moved out of her reach. Raven turned away stifling her laughter. "My work is done here, Dragon, take a look at your gorgeous wife," Erika said. Mercifully for Sarge she exited.

He did, and she was. All he could manage was to stand staring at her. She walked to him in beautiful gold leather strappy sandals with a four inch heel that showed off her tanned legs. The dress was a stunning color on her, deep red like a fine Cabernet. It was essentially a sheath covered in sheer chiffon that somehow had sparkled gold flecks throughout it. It clung perfectly to her figure and Dragon had to close his mouth and remember to breathe. Her hair was smooth, like he had never seen it done before. It was so thick and wild most of the time, which was how he liked it, but it was beautiful this way and had the right effect considering the dress. It shone like gold down her naked back, longer even from the straightness, and it moved like silk. Erika had smoothed it with one of Sensei's oils and a flatiron, and then pulled the top layer back from her face, holding it in a gold hair clip at the back. Her lips shone with something that Dragon couldn't wait to taste. She had 2 carat diamond studs set in gold in her ears, something from the jewelry the General had given her.

Sarge gawked at her, forgetting he was going to strangle her moments ago. He spoke first. "You look amazing." She looked at him smiling, also forgetting she was pissed at him for imitating her. "Thanks Sarge, and look at you. Very sexy," she said. She tugged a blonde curl. He let her pull his hair when she was being sweet to him. "And you Mr. Li," she said, turning again to Dragon. "I don't have words, really, but later I can show you how I feel about you in that black tie," she said. "Come here baby," he said.

He didn't want to mess her up but he had to taste her. He kissed her lips parting them with his tongue, holding her chin, tasting her. He released her after a blissful soft moment, looking in her eyes.

"I have no words either babe so I hope you could read my lips," he said. She had and it made her wet. Black silk panties concealed her desire for the time being.

Wendy announced Sensei then and it was time to go. Dragon held her coat for her, it was an elegant black wool shrug edged in golden brown fur trim from some unfortunate animal no doubt. She didn't think it could get any better, but it did. As they made their way to the elevator, Damascus approached them from the opposite direction, tying his bow tie as he walked. Raven watched him, thinking he looked very sexy. He looked at her and blushed, not prepared for her to stun his senses so definitively. They all boarded Wendy's conveyance, and were on their way to wherever she was taking them.

"Here let me do that," Raven said. She took over, finishing a perfectly knotted bow for him. Damascus looked at Dragon then, and explained.

"The General asked me to join you tonight," he said. "I see that," Dragon said. Damascus squirmed in the shirt collar. "I told him he would only get me to wear this thing on one condition." "Really," Dragon said. He looked at Damascus and raised an eyebrow prompting him to continue. "24 hour leave. No holds barred, for my team and some of the other guys, all the beer they can drink and all the girls from HQ, when they are off duty of course," he said. Dragon laughed out loud then, as did the others. "Nice one kid, and did he agree to this?" Dragon said. "Of course he did, I'm here aren't I," Damascus said.

"You wouldn't get away with that shit with me," Sensei said. "Of course not Sensei," Damascus said. "That attitude would have gotten you two nights trekking in the jungle," Wax said.

Raven looked at them all and smiled. "Well I'm glad you're joining us Damascus so we can all spend as much time together as we can," she said. She squeezed Damascus's hand, making him look at her then look away, his shyness back where it belonged on his face.

Wendy let them out below ground in the parking garage, bidding them a goodnight. A Limo sat waiting, the driver standing with the door ajar. "Good evening," he said, politely. Dragon handed Raven inside, and when they had all sat, the door closed. "Do you know where the General lives Papa?" Raven asked. "No child, I have never been to any of his homes here. I didn't even know he lived anywhere but HQ," Sensei said.

"Hey Damascus, what's with Erika, these days, is she still the um same?" Sarge asked. Raven giggled into Dragons' arm. Damascus grinned at Sarge. "You're asking the wrong guy Sarge, she didn't get anywhere with me." "Really?" Sarge asked. "Really!!" Damascus replied. He copied his surprised look, mimicking him.

He then continued with his Erika story. "I mean I like her style. You know, stuff from pages 422 to 450ish, Dominant Submissive stuff," Damascus said. "But just not with her. It was like she was trying to recruit me into her little army of Submissive boys, so I said no."

It was silent for a moment while they all considered it. "I like those pages," Raven said. She whispered under her breath, taking the conversation to another level.

Wax was pondering it and was next to offer his opinion. "It's Ok if I feel like that kind of thing," he said. "But I know what you mean about her. If I want to be with her it has to be like that, nothing else. Only she plays the Submissive with me. It's like she seeks me out if she wants to feel the whip, with some orgasm denial on the side."

Sarge and Damascus kind of gaped at Wax and Raven dug her nails into Dragon's arm.

"Change the subject boys or Cinderella's not going to make it to the ball," Dragon said. They looked at him then and he raised his eyebrows at them.

Damascus had blushed then, getting what Dragon meant. He had yearned to know what it would be like to possess her in every way, the way Dragon did. It had kept him awake, many nights. As he had gotten older he had looked for her in the girls he had, always disappointed in the end. Picturing her as his partner made him hard and he had to work to conceal his thoughts as he knew Dragon would 'see' them if he didn't.

Sensei saw them though, and felt for Damascus. He had long been aware that Damascus was in love with Raven and he knew he needed to do something to help him.

"Wax eyed her and gave her his best 'Hollywood,' eyes. "Easy baby girl, I'm sure when you get back tonight Chippendale there will handle all of your little fantasies." Dragon looked at him, eyes wide. "Who??" he asked. "The Chippendales," Wax said. "Some hot male strippers wearing bow ties and not much else."

They all laughed and Wax Googled it, showing them a picture of the Las Vegas act making them all fall apart laughing.

"Wax stop it, I'm going to be laughing all night at the General's thinking of all you guys like that," Raven said. "Go for it baby girl. You'll get your private dance later," Wax said. He winked at Dragon.

"That's not going to happen," Dragon said. Raven giggled even more now, seeing Dragon cringe at the thought of doing a strip dance for her. "Don't worry baby, you know what I want later. It will involve some ties but not the kind you're wearing," she said.

CHAPTER TWENTY FOUR
THE GENERAL

Nearing the General's home soon Sensei turned their attention to their whereabouts. It looked as though they were in the country somewhere, as it had become rural. In a short time the car slowed and the entered through some old stone pillars with a large wrought iron gate that bore a coat of arms in the centre of each gate, and opened automatically for the car to pass. They travelled along what was a very winding, treed drive until they emerged in front of what could only be described as a castle.

The car stopped finally in front of a massive flight of stone stairs. It was just beginning to get dark and lanterns lit up the front of the Castle and the stairs. It was cool with no wind as they departed the Limo and followed Sensei up the ten or so hand laid stone stairs, ancient and timeless, arriving on a huge expansive stone entry way. The doorway was set into a large stone archway which framed two massive oak carved doors. On one of the pillars supporting the archway was a stone carved plaque with the name Strauss and a coat of arms beneath it. It was dated 1752.

The structure itself stretched off in both directions and upward. They didn't know where to look first it was so stunning and overwhelming. It reminded Raven of a cross between a boarding school and a medieval castle from a story book. She held Dragon's hand tighter, as her senses were bombarded with visions of the past, of royalty and grandeur, ladies in beautiful gowns, men in military finery and horse and carriages lining the drive, her clairvoyance sometimes stronger than others. Sensei was having the same visions, as the many ghosts of the past touched his extra sensory perception. Dragon shut them out, his instincts to survey his surroundings taking precedent.

They approached the massive door and it seemed to magically open with a loud clanking of the latch, and the hinges pierced the evening with the task of supporting the massive door. A butler stood to greet them and admit them to the General's home.

"Good evening," he said. "Please come in, the General will be with you shortly."

He was a very formal looking older black man, with grey curls on his head, dressed in a tuxedo with tails, white crisp shirt and ascot, and the shiniest shoes Raven had ever seen. She fought an urge to giggle, eyeing Dragon for help. He looked down at her, his eyes soft. Behave angel, he told her with his mind. The butler led them across the marble foyer. It was like something from an architectural magazine, with a towering ceiling plastered in ornate designs, chandeliers of unimaginable value and art to match.

They followed along to what was a salon or sitting room, used for receiving guests from era's past. It was beyond huge, meant to accommodate hundreds of people. The ambiance explained the formal black tie attire and Raven's elegance. They stood, looking around, uncertain, as the Butler offered them Champagne.

They all gratefully accepted delicate crystal flutes of the perfectly chilled bubbling wine from him. They could have sat in any of the available comfortable antique chairs and settees, but chose to stand. There was so much to look at. Raven wandered out of Dragon's hand for a moment, moving to one of the six huge windows, lead paned and deep set, adorned with priceless brocade in greens and gold's. They stood on Persian rugs, handmade, hundreds of years old.

They all turned as the butler announced the presence of General Strauss. "Thank you Cedric, that will be all for now," the General said. He addressed his butler politely, who nodded and retreated into a wall it seemed. "Welcome," the General said. He moved toward them with a casual grace. He too was dressed for the occasion in white tie attire. "Thank you General," Sensei said. He tried to pay attention, finally remembering his manners. He was busy sorting the past from the present in his mind as the visions kept interfering with his concentration. "I'm so glad we have the opportunity to meet like this," the General said. "I rarely entertain here and I'm pleased to have you. Even I enjoy time away from HQ, when I can get it."

He stepped to the huge buffet table that the butler had prepared with the Champagne chilling, along with three more bottles, and an array of sparkling glassware, linen napkins, and other dishware. He graciously filled more glasses and Raven figured out they were supposed to use a new glass with every drink.

"Please, I decided to be informal tonight, let us serve ourselves, shall we," the General said. He invited them to help themselves to another drink. "Thank you General, it's an honor," Dragon said. He passed Sensei a new glass and then Raven. "The honor is all mine Dragon," the General said. His grey blue eyes were sparkling and he looked happier than anyone had ever seen him.

Just then, the butler appeared leading Chekov. "Mr. Chekov," he said. "Hello everyone," Chekov said. "General. Forgive my lateness, I had an issue. It's been dealt with." "Never mind Vladimir, we will not discuss work tonight, I want you to try and enjoy yourself for a change," the General said. "Yes General," Chekov said. He took a glass of Champagne and eyed the others. He was dressed as they were but an off white silk scarf hung around his collar and down the front. He looked elegant, perfectly groomed and had on a different pair of almost invisible framed glasses. Raven eyed him, sipping from her glass to stifle herself.

"Well, now that we are all here, I must let you in on a little secret," the General said. "This is not just a simple dinner party. It is a celebration of sorts."

They all waited, wondering. He stood before them as they all listened, not sure what event had brought them into his personal life. The General raised his glass and looked at them all, sad but proud.

"I've invited you all here because it is a very special birthday today. My daughter Kathryn would be turning 40. I would like to celebrate for her in her absence. So if you would be so kind; to my darling daughter," he said.

They toasted her and drank. It was unexpected and emotional. They all knew of her but the General had never mentioned it once over the years. They felt privileged but sad, triumphant yet failing. There were no words, except from Dragon, who as always could pull himself together.

"General," he said. "It's been my privilege to serve you on her behalf, a duty that has become my life; that I owe my life to. It has fulfilled me beyond my understanding. I only hope that I can continue doing so and give due respect to the circumstances that have led us all here."

The General was overwhelmed and he let a tear fall from his eyes as he regarded Dragon. "Young man, thank you," he said. For a few moments he was lost for words. Gathering himself he continued. "Thank you for everything, for surviving your past, for being who you are and for being in my life."

"Cheers," Sensei said quietly.

They clinked glasses together as they all felt the emotion and the truth of it and the sadness of it, along with the happiness that they were all together in it. The General took a deep breath then, sighing and moving on as he always did.

"Alright then, I did say party and so it shall be one, such as it is in this old antique monstrosity. Please now, breathe some life into it for me."

Breathing life into things was Wax's specialty and he was quick to prove it. He eyed the General. "First of all; something stronger, and then some music," he said. "By all means Wax," the General said. "Over here."

He led Wax to a wall panel behind the buffet table and pressed it so it opened, revealing a huge stocked bar. "General Strauss," Wax said. "You dog." Sensei turned three shades whiter at Wax's informal words, but relaxed as the General replied. "I may look a certain way son, but I assure you, in my day, there was no bottom of a bottle I couldn't conquer and no ladies that were safe." Wax laughed, as did they all, even Chekov, who actually almost choked on his champagne. "No doubt General, no doubt," Wax said. "Let's see if you still have it going on." He challenged the General. "Name your poison." The General eyed the liquor supply and chose a single malt Scotch, likely hundred year old stuff.

"I've had my eye on this but never wanted to open it for only myself, so now seems like a good time wouldn't you say?" he said. He eyed Wax playfully. Wax gave him his perfect 'Hollywood' grin, and nodded. "Hell yeah," he said.

Sensei cleared his throat at Wax's swear word, knowing the General prohibited the use of profanity. "It's Ok Sensei, this is my home and we can fucking swear here if we want to," the General said.

They all burst out laughing, shocked. And Chekov did finally choke on his Champagne. Raven patted his back for him until he recovered. He had never seen the General drink, never heard him swear, never seen an emotion from him and he thought he must have slid through a warp in reality to another life or something.

"Don't fret Chekov," the General said. "There are no camera's here, no recording devices and I intend on indulging myself with the only people I care about on this troubled planet, and you should do the same." "Come on Chekov, I'll get you some more," Raven said. She pulled him over to the buffet table. "Here," she said. Handing him another glass, she smiled at him. "Let your hair down, come on, I know you have one hair that you can let get out of place for one evening," she said. He smiled, and touched his hair wondering if she meant he had one out of place. She laughed at him, and he had to give in, so he downed his Champagne in one gulp.

"There, is that what you mean?" he said. "Now you got it," she said. "Have a few Scotch's too and you will find out what a good dancer you think you are. Sarge does it all the time," she joked. "I get better looking too," Sarge said. "Smarter, and sometimes I'm even a good guitar player." Raven was giggling uncontrollably at him now.

"Sergeant Willis, you will have to show me how it's done later," the General said. He was happy that they were attempting to draw the ever serious Chekov into their world. "General really, you have no idea how annoying Sarge is, ordinarily I mean, but when he's drunk it goes to a whole other level," Raven said. The General laughed, eyeing them both, well aware of their sibling-like relationship. Sarge changed his mind about his decision earlier not to torment her. He approached Raven and whispered in her ear.

"Is big Daddy there going to let the cat fall on your little pink self later?" he asked. He nodded over in Dragon's direction. She flashed her eyes at him, realizing his game. "If you fuck with me tonight, I'm going to take that tie you don't know how to tie and knot it around your dick so tight you'll have orgasm denial for a year." She hissed back in his ear.

He laughed out loud then, but he was never sure to what lengths she would go to get back at him and he cringed at the visual. "If you want to put your hands on my dick that bad, be my guest." He taunted her anyway. They both eyed Dragon as he now stood there looking at them.

"I'm not even going to ask," he said. He turned his direct look onto Sarge. "But I suggest you behave before Sensei 'cuts' your dick off." He then directed it toward Raven. "And, I decide to forget how use a cat whip."

"Yes baby," she said. She pretended to pout at the thought of him denying her. "Yes baby," Sarge said. He risked imitating her and ignoring Dragon's warning. Dragon just smirked at him, shaking his head. "Be a good shithead and get us some Scotch," he said. "Coming right up man, that's just the kind of shithead friend that I am," Sarge said. He went to pour them some.

Sensei, Wax and the General had already done a shot of it, and were admiring its smoothness. "Ah Sergeant Willis, join us," the General said. "And where's Damascus?" They looked around and Raven spied him at the far side of the room, looking out one of the large windows. "I'll get him," she said. She went toward him, as Dragon joined the others for some Scotch.

She went to his side and looped her arm through his, taking his hand in hers. She smiled up at him, looking in his eyes. "Hey, what are you doing over here all by yourself? I need you to help me deal with Sarge," she said. He shrugged, unable to speak in her presence all of a sudden.

He masked his thoughts from her, but it was too late because she had snuck up on him as he had been letting his fantasy of holding her in his arms run through his mind just then. She flushed as she caught it. He blushed, his eyes wanting to look at her but not wanting too.

"Damascus," she whispered. It was dawning on her and she realized Dragon had been right about him. "I'm sorry Raven," he said. "I've really missed you, I mean all of you and a lot has happened. Sometimes I wish I could turn back the clock, I don't know." "Come here," she said. She pulled him into her arms. "Just hold me for a minute Ok, I've missed you too."

He put his arms around her and she sank against his chest. Involuntarily he tightened around her, holding her as he had in his mind moments before. He couldn't resist touching her long silky mane at her back.

She was purposely letting him have his fantasy for the moment. She could feel his heart pounding in his chest as he held his arms around her. She let him take her in, the smell of her hair, her warmth, her firmness in his hold, and she could feel his hardness, his want of her as she lay against him. She could sense his every feeling now, as he was no longer able to hide from her, which was what she hoped would happen. She could 'see' what he didn't want anyone to see. She looked up at him again then, as he released her only because he knew he had to. She brushed an errant spike that had caught in his long eyelashes. She knew him then, better than she ever had. It only took a few moments of his guard down for her to know.

He loved her, in every way a man could love a woman, he was lonely at HQ, he was scarred deeply by his team member's deaths and he hid everything from everyone. He was hiding a growing darkness that worried her.

"Damascus, I will ask Sensei to ask the General if you and your team could be stationed in Hawaii, back in our camp. There's a lot you could help do around there when you're not away," she said. "You can't be unhappy Damascus; it hurts me to know that you are."

He looked her in the eye and she could tell he thought he was truly unhappy because he couldn't have her.

Deciding to address it she told him. "I can see you really have been lonely and are missing things in your life. We can fix that, but some things I can't make the way you dream of," she said. She looked down, shy now. "I'm not capable of loving anyone but Dragon. It's always been that simple for me." Damascus nodded and she knew he had no words now. "We have to join the others now," she said.

She had felt Sensei pulling her and she knew Dragon had also been connecting to her thoughts as she talked with Damascus.

He nodded again. "I won't leave you alone with this anymore, Ok?" she said. He let her pull him by the hand.

"There you are young man," the General said. He was feeling the effects of his third scotch then. "Do you know the bargain I had to concede to in order for him to grace us with his presence?"

Raven noted Damascus had his mask back in place.

"Just a simple deal," Damascus said. "What do you mean a simple deal? Every operative I have is probably drunker than the Irish on St. Patrick's Day and the girls, well I won't say," the General said. He was pretending to be appalled. "They needed some down time," Damascus said. "You get down time, this is debauchery," the General said. "Debauchery it is then," Damascus laughed. "Well, I admire you young man for looking out for the well being of others, while you suffer my whims," the General said. "I am not suffering General, I'm honored and would much rather be here than anywhere, and besides, it's 24 hours so that will leave me plenty of time for some debauchery of my own later anyway," Damascus said.

Dragon looked at Damascus, taking in that he was indeed a man now. "As I said before, nice move," he said. He smiled at him and handed him a Scotch. "Here, you need to get started on your debauchery."

Damascus accepted the drink, and he downed it, eyeing Raven as he did so. His thoughts were guarded now and he planned to drink her off his mind. They followed through to another room, clearly the hugest dining room any of them had ever seen. They sat and Cedric was joined by a team of servers, whom he bossed around quietly and fastidiously. Two pretty girls and two young men did his bidding. Sarge flirted shamelessly with one girl making her blush crimson and nearly spill soup all over him. Sensei eyed him, and Raven looked across the table at him and made a motion on her neck of adjusting a bow tie, reminding him of her earlier warning. They both laughed quietly between them, and proceeded to enjoy the dinner and listen to the General's story of how his family had come to acquire the castle.

Many generations ago it was built and then lived in it generationally since. Miraculously it had survived the wars, having never been bombed or occupied. As he was the legal heir, he and his sister had been living there since the death of his mother, who survived his father for long enough to raise them. Educated and supported by his family's immense wealth, he was an astute business man and had gone into business himself, adding to and maintaining his inheritance. He could remember his father's words at times, emphasizing that it was important above all else to always be financially stable so as not to ever be at another's mercy.

The General had been helpless only once in his life, when Kathryn had been taken and he had lived in the hell of that feeling every day since. It drove him to where he was now, everything he did, everything the ones present at his table did, everyday. They listened, fascinated by his stories and enjoyed some fine wines, which Raven loved and Dragon forced himself to drink with their food.

Wax and Sarge entertained them with their competitive bantering about who shot what from farthest away, who kicked whose butt more often in hand to hand, and who had the best looking girl when they were at Dusty's. They finished dinner and toasted Kathryn again, and retired to another room, filled with comfortable furniture, more liquor and more large windows.

The General had switched them to Cognac. "Dragon let us discuss something," he said. "Of course," Dragon said. "I want you to kill Sheik Abdul Saadad Abdwhali." "Who, the ff... I mean who??" Dragon choked. "He's the son of one of my business acquaintances, Sheik Mohammed Sindur Abdwhali. I will be sorry for his loss, being a father myself, but his son, number one, offended me and number two, is a homosexual pedophile. I met him in Abudabi when I purchased your Arabians. He insinuated I was racist against Jews. I am the farthest thing. He keeps a harem of young boys, sex slaves, purchased for his use. I'm not aware if his father knows but I suspect he does. They have wealth beyond mine and yours put together and it must be handled carefully. The father may stop at nothing to find out who killed his son." "No problem General," Dragon said. He looked at Chekov. "Profile?" It was supposed to wait until tomorrow but Chekov laid it out.

"Best plan according to current data indicates an intrusion," Chekov said. "Indicators show that you and Damascus undercover will yield the best result." "What the fuck are you talking about Chekov?" Dragon said. "You go and take Damascus with you and one other of his team. The details will follow, but essentially you will appear to share the same like for boys as the Sheik. You will meet him as a friend of the General's on a pretense of buying horses and then have the chance to kill him," Chekov said. Dragon looked at the General. "Are you suggesting I use Damascus as a boy toy? Why bother, I can just meet him and kill him," he said.

"It will be very difficult to get him alone, he is heavily guarded, almost to the point of ridiculousness," the General said. "It's an ego thing with them, the more guards you have the more important you are. You will need extra leverage to get him alone. There is an annual horse auction that he attends every year, I have arranged for you to attend it with him on my behalf. You will have only that one chance to lure him into privacy; otherwise after the auction is over he will be out of your reach." Dragon sat thinking. "How many guards?" he asked. "At least 6," Chekov said. "You will need all of your team and Damascus to take them out. I suggest Jacob as well, he's boy toy material and very capable with weapons."

"I can't just shoot 6 people in my hotel room," Dragon said, thinking out loud. Chekov addressed them again. "The auction takes place in Dubai, he stays at an apartment there which he owns and you will be a guest there as well," he said. "Why don't we just ambush him?" Dragon said. "It's too public, you won't get a chance," Chekov said. Dragon thought for a moment. "I'll figure out a way to get into his place, attack them and make it look like a religious or terrorist thing. Someone must hate them, find out who Chekov," Dragon said. His mind was working now. "We need the weapons they would use, preferably large caliber, military issue Israeli made, they need to die violently and pointedly.

The General smiled. "Very good, that is excellent Dragon. And he's right Chekov, find an enemy for them." Chekov had been busy on his phone and responded. "The Taliban," he said. "They get blamed for everything anyway and according to this, they have been in a dispute over oil with the Saudi's including one Sheik Mohammed Sindur Abdwhali. It's perfect; I'll request the appropriate weapons. You leave tomorrow night."

"Damascus, be sure to see Erika for wardrobe," the General said. "If you are going to be a boy toy you will have to look the part." This made the rest of them laugh. "Be careful or she'll make you 'her' boy toy," Sarge said. "Sorry," Chekov said. He genuinely commiserated with them when it came to Erika. He rose to leave.

"General I have to go, I need to re-profile this for Dragon and finalize quite a few things." "Of course Chekov, have Cedric show you out and thank you for coming," the General said. They all rose, shaking Chekov's hand. "Later man," Dragon said. "Don't sweat it, just get me the right guns and keep us covered." Chekov nodded.

He was unfamiliar with Dragon being civil to him. Raven kissed his cheek, making him blush, and he fled the way he had come in.

After Chekov had left they were finishing their drinks and thinking about going as well. Sensei had been pacing and wondering. He calculated his move and made it.

"We should also retire. It has gotten late and by the sounds of it we have a busy day tomorrow," he said.

The General nodded, realizing it was time to call it a night. They never allowed themselves social time and this had made them all know that an early morning would appear.

General Strauss organized himself in a sophisticated manor. "Very well," he agreed. "When you have completed this mission Dragon, please return to HQ as I would like to see you all again before you disappear on me for another two years."

Sensei had been waiting and he approached the General when all had been completed for the night.

"I have a few things I would like to discuss for a moment General. Dragon, would you mind waiting for me in the car?" Sensei said. "Good night General and thank you so much for allowing us to make this special day enjoyable for you," Dragon said. Raven kissed the General on his cheek, and they all expressed their thanks and proceeded to the entry way where Cedric handed Dragon Raven's jacket.

Sensei joined them in the car after a few minutes and finding a quiet group he eyed them, sending Dragon a questioning look. "What?" Dragon said. "We're just waiting for you, so we can go. Damascus still has 8 hours left to get drunk and fucked."

"Better believe it," Damascus said.

He wanted to drink Raven off his mind at the General's but it didn't work. Sitting next to her at dinner and then again in the Limo, he couldn't stop letting his eye wander up her thigh as she sat leaning on Dragon. His plan was to get back to HQ, down a few beers and fuck the living hell out of this red head that wouldn't leave him alone. It was the only way he was going to get rid of his hard on. He didn't give a shit about her but was going to take his frustrations out on her big time, he thought to himself. He knew he was not fair to a lot of the girls he used for sex but it was the best he could do and all they were going to get. He guarded his thoughts from them not realizing he could not keep them from Sensei who was now concerned having just caught his latest one about what he planned to do after.

Damascus liked to get rough sometimes, especially when he was frustrated as he had been a lot lately. He had taken to placing his hands around their necks in the guise of 'auto erotic asphyxia' but actually was taking pleasure in nearly strangling them to death as he fucked them.

They were always too smitten with him to question it or deny him. The ride back was quiet, as Sarge fell asleep against Wax's shoulder, and Raven waited for what Dragon had promised her later. Damascus sat fantasizing about it, knowing it was how he was going to achieve his orgasm later, using the red heads body he would imagine taking a cat of nine tails to Raven after he had tied her mercilessly to his bed. It wouldn't be the first time either. Seeing her and holding her earlier was taking him there and that's how it would have to be for him tonight.

Wendy admitted them to the elevator and they exited on their floor. As they stepped out, a figure lay against the wall in the hallway, a drunken member of Damascus's team that didn't quite make it to his room. "Shit," Damascus said. "Give me a hand with this failure," he said. Dragon helped pull the unconscious boy to his feet and they dragged him to his room where they tossed him on a bunk. Sleeping in the opposite one was Jacob, and from what they could tell a blonde. Dragon and Damascus looked at each other and laughed. "Hope you haven't missed all the fun," Dragon said. "I have some plans for someone myself, I just have to find her," Damascus replied. "Good luck with that," Dragon said. "Goodnight Damascus," Raven said. She brushed his cheek with a kiss, leaving him trembling slightly.

"Damascus," Sensei said. They were finally alone. "Yes Sensei," he said. He looked young and vulnerable again, like he had years ago. "Let's talk please, in your room if we may," Sensei said. "Sure," Damascus said. They went further down the hallway to another door and entered his room which he did not have to share with anyone because of his rank.

"I'll give you the opportunity to tell me, everything, and you will tell me," Sensei said. His expression warned Damascus. "You need me right now son and I am here so start talking."

Damascus knew, as did they all, that it was useless to lie to Sensei, or try to keep anything from him. He realized Sensei had probably seen things now and was giving him the chance to tell him, rather than be confronted with it. He sighed and sat down on the bed and Sensei sat beside him waiting.

"I'm in love with her, I always have been and sometimes I can't stand it. The girls here, I use them, sometimes I hurt them, they keep coming back for more and I don't get it, but in the end I dislike the person I see in the mirror after," he said. "It's confusing because I know I can't have her, but I keep using it like a drug to keep me going. Sometimes I can't even have sex unless I fantasize about her being the one under me, the one I'm pleasing and the one that wants me. When I see that it's not her sometimes that's when I want to strangle them. They think I'm playing a game with them but I'm not," Damascus said.

"I've asked the General to transfer your team to Hawaii; I think he will if tactically you can work from there," Sensei replied. Damascus nodded his approval, relief showing on his handsome face. "Thank you. This um problem has gotten worse since I've been here because I miss seeing her, I miss my old life and I miss you Sensei. I still need you in my life," he said. Sensei could see his sadness coming to the surface and knew Damascus needed to let it go.

He touched Damascus's face, brushing a spike out of his eye. "Raven loves you Damascus, but as you know it will never be as you want and you also know that it is not what you really want anyway. Right?" Sensei said. "It isn't?" Damascus asked. "Then why is this happening to me?" He begged for answers now.

Sensei smiled to him, trying to reassure him with his eyes. "You were a lonely frightened little boy when you came to camp and you developed very strong attachments to us all. I'm sorry I didn't recognize that you needed to stay with us," Sensei said. "Coming to live here may have triggered that again, made you lonely and scared again. You think you love Raven like Dragon loves her because you have transferred your loneliness here into a fantasy to help you cope. If you see her under you, see her with you, need her physically, then you don't feel so alone. Am I right?" he asked. "Yes, it's like that," Damascus said.

He was realizing what he had been doing in his mind. "And I get angry with the girls here because they want me and they aren't her, and it reminds me of it. I don't want to hurt them, I want to feel what it feels like to enjoy sex with them, not hate them, then myself. And all the while I hide it, and it gets worse," he said.

Looking now at Sensei, tears had begun to line his beautiful face. He was desperate to feel normal for a change. Sensei hugged him then and Damascus let his tears fall, crying for his broken heart over his lost team members, his love of Raven that he thought he needed, his sadness from all the months of missing them and still doing his job, his dislike for himself over the girls whose feelings he had hurt. Sensei held him until he was quiet again. Then letting him rest in his hold he told him some things he needed to know.

"Where you have gone a bit astray is that you have allowed yourself to believe in your fantasy, to want your fantasy to be real. And when of course it is not, you create frustration and then anger within yourself." Sensei paused for him to think about it. "I'm just so lonely here Sensei," he said. "Thinking about her made it bearable at night." Sensei nodded his understanding. "I knew you had a crush on her but everyone does, she's irresistible. But you've hidden yourself away in it, in order to cope with your life," Sensei said. "But she's not your answer Damascus. Your happiness is within your heart, within the love you deserve to have for yourself and need to feel from all of us." Damascus sighed then, feeling drained but clearer than he had in over a year. He looked at Sensei then, sitting back, his face wet and his eyes still brimming.

"Take me home Sensei, please," he begged. "I will son," he said. He let his own tears fall then, his heart breaking for his young son that he had let fall emotionally through the cracks. "I'm so sorry Damascus that I didn't read this sooner," Sensei said. "How could you have, I'm half a world away," Damascus said. "Not anymore," Sensei said. He took his face and kissed his forehead. "There's one more thing; until you have truly sorted out your feelings, you should avoid sexual relations with anyone. Just satisfy yourself the way you used to, enjoy your fantasies for what they are in a healthy way, that you're in control of. When you are ready you can start over," Sensei said. "I understand that Sensei, it's a relief actually." He sighed falling back on his bed then.

Sensei smiled at him then, feeling he had accomplished what he set out to with him. He thought about the upcoming Dubai mission. "You better be comfortable with your sexuality because by the sounds of it you're about to become Dragon's boy toy," Sensei said. Damascus grinned at him then. He sat up, a genuine smile on his face. "I will try to make it entertaining for you Sensei," he said. "I'm sure we will be sharing a few laughs on this mission," Sensei said. "Now get yourself out of that tie and go to bed, I'm going to stay right here with you." Damascus obeyed him and undressed and climbed naked into his bed.

"Hey, Sensei," Damascus said, closing his eyes already, "thanks." "You're welcome my son," Sensei said.

He sat back on the bed beside the now sleeping boy, crossed his legs and let himself drift to his own peace. There would be no red head tonight. Damascus slept then, slept soundly for the first night in a long time as Sensei guarded over him, the way he had done for Dragon so many times. It was his reward that his boys needed him, and that he could help them. It was what made his life worth living.

Later the following day they boarded the actual War Horse and flew to the Munich International Airport. The memories flooded back to Dragon as Tom-Tom took them forward with their lives but back in time together. His mind fell back into the memories of the War Horse, its sound and smell, the blood they had shed on its floor, the way he had loved it for saving them so many times, grateful for their lives as they'd risen above the mayhem. He wanted to go home soon, all of them together.

CHAPTER TWENTY FIVE

DUBAI

They boarded the DLI jet, a now familiar Simon greeting them. Dragon didn't know how long a flight it was to Dubai and didn't care; he planned on relaxing, discussing their game plan, indulging his sexual appetite and having a few Scotch's. As they reached their cruising altitude and were free to move around, Wax passed the Scotch's out, as per usual. Damascus enjoyed one but Jacob paled at the thought of more liquor, having finally emerged from his hangover.

"According to Chekov's profile, we are expected at the Sheik's apartment building and then I am to attend this horse auction with him," Dragon said. "If it works out I plan on inviting him to see my other interests, besides expensive horses."

"We are your other interests, I'm assuming," Damascus said. Sarge and Wax laughed. "This I got to see," Sarge said. He eyed Damascus who had just almost thrown up in his mouth. "Don't worry Damascus, Dragon's a good kisser," Raven said. "Jesus fuck." It was all Damascus could manage. Jacob pulled a hand over his face, the nauseous feelings of his hangover returning.

Getting guns into Dubai was not easy and it had taken every bit of the General's leverage to have it so they were not searched. They had cases containing six Israeli made automatics, all high caliber and completely illegal anywhere, plus everything else they usually carried. Dubai was a strange guarded place and only someone of David Li's reputation and wealth would possibly be allowed to pass uninspected. They jumped through the hoops according to the customs of the country and were finally in a palace like dwelling, high above Dubai's gleaming impossible wealth.

Dragon really wanted to get it over with. "Ok, listen up, especially you boys," Dragon said. "With any luck, I'm going to bring this shithead here to check you out. Play the part like you've wanted it all your life. If I can sell you to him, we can get in and finish them off." Dragon had figured out a plan and needed it to work perfectly.

Damascus and Jacob nodded, prepared now for anything, as they had all absorbed the seriousness of what they were doing. "I will get him here after the horse thing, Raven you will be hidden of course but help Sensei make them look like something the Sheik would want to fuck, and I will sell them to him. When we deliver them, it will go down, it will be our way in," he said. He was pacing and thinking out loud. In half an hour they had devised a plan.

"We should retire," Sensei said. "Dragon I will wake you. The horse auction begins early, there will be a car waiting." He was eyeing Chekov's profile on his laptop. "I will confirm things with Chekov again now before bed and see you in the morning. Damascus, come with me, you too Jacob," Sensei said.

They followed him to the bedroom they were going to share. Jacob fell asleep immediately and Sensei sat with Damascus. He smoothed the long spiky layer of black hair away from his eyes and looked into the dark brown mirrors to his heart.

Damascus looked up at him with a peaceful eye. "Are you staying?" he asked. "Yes son. You can sleep now and I will be right here."

Damascus nodded and removed his clothes. He walked naked to the bathroom and turned on the shower. It had been a long day and he had struggled briefly with his lust for Raven, but overall he had felt more normal than he had in awhile. On the plane it had been fun, but when Dragon had taken her to the back cabin, he had been unable to stop himself from picturing what he was doing to her behind the closed door. It was those thoughts now that he took with him into the hot shower. Sensei had told him it would be normal to engage in fantasies for the purpose of relieving oneself and he needed to then.

He hadn't touched himself that way in quite some time. He leaned his forehead against the wall of the shower as the water washed over his back, hot and soothing and his come washed over his belly, hot and soothing. It hadn't taken him long as he had pictured her mouth on him, soft lips on his hardness and finally her beneath him, taking him to the end of it.

He soaped himself clean, feeling relaxed and oddly free of it then. He thought maybe Sensei was right, he had simply satisfied himself to some pleasant thoughts and now he was relaxed and tired. He dried himself and returned to the bedroom, finding Sensei sitting on one side of the bed, cross legged as usual, against the pillows. He crawled in the other side.

Morning arrived and the mission was at hand. Having showered and dressed, Dragon inspected her. Raven had just wanted to wear one of his T shirts, so he let her; she had to stay inside for most of the day with Sensei so it didn't matter. And if he had a chance he could just get at her underneath it, which he liked the idea of. She had spanked his butt for his thoughts, which he had also liked. He tied his hair back as they left the room to join the others.

"What are we going to do while they are gone Papa?" she said. "Figure out how to make you look like a delivery person with access to this building. According to Chekov, a woman would not normally have access to the Sheik," Sensei said. "Also it says here he is to be addressed as 'Your Royal Highness'." They all looked at each other then burst into laughter. "Are you kidding me?" Dragon asked. "No absolutely not," Sensei said. "And you can't touch him. Don't shake hands or put a hand on him in anyway." Dragon ran a hand through his hair. "No problem with that one," he said.

He brought them back to the issue at hand, which was getting Raven to deliver flowers to the Sheik as a way inside his apartment later. "Dress her in one of those things that covers her everywhere and have Chekov mess with their systems to make her appear legit," Dragon said. "Just make it happen. And I'll do what I can to set it up when I leave." He would have a word with the security desk on his way out.

It was time to go and get it done. He held her body in his big T shirt and kissed her goodbye. "I have to go now, so be good and wish me luck with this creep," Dragon said. "Mmmm Baby he's going to love you," Raven said. She was pressing against the front of him with her body during his goodbye kisses. "Honestly child," Sensei said. He pulled her off him so he could go.

When they reached the lobby Dragon approached the security desk, manned by two guards. "Good morning gentlemen," he said. "Good morning Mr. Li they both replied, standing and trying to look official, having been given strict orders to treat him with the utmost respect. "I have instructed my staff to order flowers as a gift for 'Your Royal Highness'," Dragon said. "Someone will be here later. Allow them to proceed but do a security check on them of course," he said. This placated them for a moment but one finally found the nerve to speak. "Of course Mr. Li; however it is not generally permitted. The Sheik allows no-one." Dragon glared at them, his brow darkening his eyes. He took a step closer to them. "People don't say no to me, permit it or I'll see to it you're shoveling camel shit for a living by the end of the day!"

He didn't wait for their response and turned to leave. Wax and Sarge hesitated for effect, eyeing them with intimidating looks, as if they should do what he asked unless they were extremely stupid. A car waited and they climbed in to the relief of its coolness. Even a few moments in the 50 something Celsius heat was stifling.

Dragon assumed the driver knew where they were going and they sat in silence as they were unable to scan the car for wires. Sarge easily discovered one but they left it in tact and didn't speak. Dragon pressed a button on his phone and quickly re-read Chekov's profile, memorizing the details. He sent an untraceable signal to Chekov that they were on their way.

"What do we do next Papa?" Raven said. "Damascus, you and Jacob load the weapons, check them thoroughly, and leave them ready with the safeties on," he said. Damascus nodded and they went to Dragon and Raven's room to do it. Sensei pulled her with him and they followed them. He sat down on the bed and she curled up on Dragon's side of the bed, smelling his scent and wanting him, remembering him over her only an hour ago.

Being impossibly curious, she asked about the boys life at HQ. "Jacob, do you have a girlfriend at HQ?" He eyed her, and blushed. "Um kind of," he said.

Jacob was a quiet reserved type, who reminded her a bit of Sarge when he was younger, only likely smarter than Sarge. He had wanted to study medicine and was still considering it as a sideline. He was Chinese like Damascus and shorter, but well built as they all were and cuter than anything, Raven thought. He wore his hair longer, like a lot of them, but his was one length to his shoulders, straight and cow licked back off his forehead like Damascus's did, and Dragon's. He looked up at her through it, as he sat on the floor. He had grown up and was adorable Raven decided and perfect for what Dragon had planned today.

"So who is this lucky girl?" she asked. "Well she's a technical analyst, and um, I don't know," he faltered. He was shy of Raven as all the boys were. Damascus helped him out then. "Raven," he said. "The girl's at HQ are kind of 'different'." He chose his words carefully. "They either want you for one thing or they want you to be serious, like marriage material or something," he said. "Jacob's 'girlfriend' was getting too clingy."

The blonde Jacob had been with only a few nights before wasn't his girlfriend and had been in Damascus's bed many times as well.

"Ya, it's like that I guess," Jacob said. "I don't have time to be serious and don't want to be." Raven looked puzzled about something. "Papa, why are they allowed to have sex all over the place? I thought the General was strict about that stuff."

He smiled at her. "Too many questions little one," he said. "I think Damascus should answer. Why do you boys seem to be having sex all over the place? I know you are 21 years old and it happens but I thought there were rules at HQ?" He was offering it to Damascus on purpose. Damascus grinned and eyed Jacob.

"We aren't supposed to but the General doesn't seem to notice, or if he does he doesn't let on," he said. "It's the girls, they find a way to come to our rooms," Jacob said. "All you have to do is look around at lunch in the common. One will catch your eye and then you know that later she will be at the door, usually after curfew. They are good at sneaking around."

Raven looked at Sensei. "What is the matter with these girls Papa? Why do they give themselves to be used as sexual objects?" She couldn't understand such a thing. "Raven, it's not all their faults," Damascus confessed now. "I am guilty of letting them believe what they want about me, just to use them. They don't know what's up until they see me with someone else." He looked down, not proud of the way he had behaved. "I didn't care how they felt, I could have said no to the ones who were simply needy and would do anything for attention. I could have been truthful with the ones that wanted more. I could have been more honest with myself about how I was feeling," he said. Jacob looked at the ground now, knowing he had also been guilty of some of the same things, that he had followed Damascus's example.

Raven looked at Damascus, seeing into him. He was kneeling on the floor and she climbed off the bed. Her tears had already begun to fall and she knelt in front of him and pulled him into her, against her. He wrapped his arms around her, holding her to him. She felt his warmth against her and felt him reacting to her. She let him take her face in his hands then as he looked at her. She wanted him to enjoy the moment of her; touching her face, gently brushing her wet cheeks, entranced by just being able to touch her. She could see in his mind about his kind of love for her, his passion for her, how he wanted to love her, the dreams he had.

It had made her slip into visions of her and Dragon and she went with him into it. He never left her eyes, leaning in and touching his lips to hers. She let him have what he had wanted for so long to feel, his soft lips on hers, the taste and the feel. He kissed her then and she let him, she felt his lips soft against hers as he touched her with his tongue. His breath catching with it, he held her face gently on an angle to his. She let him kiss her fully, sweetly, and for as long as he needed. She felt his passion, and could see him as a lover in his mind, sweet, insistent, talented and sexual. She kissed him back gently, letting him feel for the first time what it was like to share passion with someone you loved. Maybe for those moments he would feel what it was like, to feel how Dragon felt when their lips met.

She opened her eyes, not realizing she had closed them because she felt she had been looking at him. He had let her lips go, staying just an inch away as they trembled from it.

"Thank you," he whispered.

She heard his words to her as his eyes took in her lips so close to his, still parted from his kiss. She knew he didn't want for one second to be away from it, the places he wanted to go with her. She reached up and touched her fingers to him, brushing her thumb along his wet lower lip.

"You're welcome," she said.

She looked softly to him, blinking as she returned completely from where she had been. He released her face from his touch and pulled her against his shoulder, stroking her hair, just holding her then. Jacob had been staring at the ground and Sensei had waited silently on the bed. After a few moments, Raven sat up still kneeling and took his hands in hers. She pulled the strand of black spike that liked to get stuck in his eyelashes.

"No more of that HQ stuff for you Ok," she said. "The next time you kiss, it better be like that, make you feel like that and make her feel how you made me feel." "I've never felt like that before," he said.

He let her know he still wanted to lay her down and use his tongue to find out about what was under her shirt and to show her what was aching in his pants right now. She smiled at him thinking he was super sexy right then and she no longer wondered why those girls did whatever he wanted.

Just then, they heard Sensei's laptop, Chekov was summoning them. "Shit," Raven said. "Where did the time go?" "It's Ok; we're done with the guns," Damascus said. "Ok go get me the stuff Erika gave you that you are supposed to wear," Raven said. They packed the guns away again, back in a closet and went off to their room, while Raven followed Sensei to the laptop.

Chekov looked up at them, going back and forth to his screens. "You have twenty minutes; he set the hook and is reeling him in as we speak. I have to say, Dragon has an uncanny ability to read people and manipulate them," Chekov said. He felt safe saying it, seeing as Dragon was not able to hear the compliment. "Ok Chekov," Sensei said. "Are you staying with us?" "Yes, I will disable your screen so I am unseen of course," Chekov said. "Ok we need to get the boys ready," Sensei said.

The morning had gone surprisingly smoothly for Dragon. He found the Sheikh polite, formal and well spoken. His guards were present but not thugs, like Juan Carlos Guerrera's were. The hard part for Dragon had been to feign knowledge of Arabian horses of which he had very little, really relying on what he had learned from Diego. He worked it with the Sheikh, allowing him to be the far more knowledgeable one, pretending to be hanging on his every word when it came to the intricacies of the lineages and origins of the ancient breed.

They walked about, looking at horses and then sat and watched some auctioning, the Sheik nodding or shaking his head in approval or disapproval of the prices. Dragon had been looking for an opportunity to raise a different subject. He took the chance when he noticed the presence of some young stable boys who were handling the waiting horses, making a point of eyeing them.

He attracted the Sheiks attention when he didn't respond to conversation because he was staring at a particular boy. He apologized and alluded to the fact that it reminded him of another type of auction he would like to be at, nodding in the direction of the stable boy he had been eyeing. It piqued the Sheikh's interest. He had caught that the Sheikh had been intrigued and also that he had sexual thoughts towards Dragon himself. It was all working out to be even easier than he figured it would be.

The Sheikh was very interested in Dragon's invitation to see what he had referred to as 'other expensive, exclusive purchases' that he had invested in and had been very costly to acquire. His Royal Highness had waved a hand at his men and stepped away with Dragon to speak privately.

"Mr. Li, just what exactly do you want me to see?" Dragon half smiled and postured himself in a sexual way, meant to disarm the Sheik. "If you're not interested in purchasing anything here today I may have something more to your liking. I purchased them in Bangkok, and they're quite unique. I don't want to reveal too much as it would ruin the surprise," Dragon said. He let his eye move to a young attractive boy, holding a grey stallion. "Maybe you could imagine a perfect cross between the two of them," he said. It was a crude analogy and Dragon had risked it. The Sheikh had let a slight smile cross his face. "You are a very interesting young man Mr. Li," he said.

Dragon then received a clear idea that it was he who the Sheikh had decided he wanted. He had begun to unravel that it had been he who the Sheikh wanted all along. It was the only reason the Sheikh had agreed to his father's request, as a favor to General Strauss, who he disliked. When he had heard it was David Li, he had readily agreed to it.

Dragon put on his sexiest smile and the Sheikh was hardly able to contain himself. Not only was David Li the best looking male he had ever seen, but he shared his passion for the same things. He had readily accepted the invitation then.

"This has been an interesting morning, 'Your Royal Highness,'" Dragon said. "I have learned a lot." The Sheikh eyed Dragon, letting a smile curl to his lips. "Indeed it has Mr. Li, more than interesting. I too have learned a lot."

He let his eyes run down Dragon's body, stopping at the front of his pants then travelling back up to his eyes. Dragon nodded a very sexy smoky eye back at him.

"Soon," he said.

It was quiet and almost imperceptible, so only the Sheikh could hear. It caused the other man to let his jaw drop and turn away, really unable to look at Dragon any longer without losing composure. The rest of the morning played out until it was time to go. Nothing more was said but plans were made to meet in Dragon's suite.

They had travelled back to the apartment in their separate cars, once again Dragon and Wax and Sarge not speaking except about the horses. The cars arrived together at the apartment building. It was perfect because the security guards could see firsthand that David Li was tight with the Sheikh. There was no further discussion but Dragon knew to expect the Sheik shortly, as the curiosity had been building in him all morning.

In the apartment, he found Damascus and Jacob. "Fuck look at you sexy boys," Dragon said. "He's going to be here any second to check you out. I need to make it look real so respond to me like you mean it, I'm expecting a lot. I had to have this guy's eyes all over me already. He's mentally sucked me off three times, so don't feel sorry for yourselves." "We're good Dragon, bring it on," Damascus said. Dragon raised his eyebrows at them as he heard the door chimes. They moved out of sight then.

Wax admitted the Sheikh and the same two of his guards that were with him earlier. Dragon stood by the huge expanse of windows overlooking the ocean. He postured himself for effect and had opened all the buttons on his shirt with it hanging loose on his body and let his hair down. He had an act to put on and was about to do it. He prepared his mind for it and turned to greet his guest.

He walked slowly toward him, letting him take in his relaxed appearance. The Sheikh said nothing but eyed him like a ravenous dog, nearly drooling, eyes staring.

Wax and Sarge stood silently watching Dragon and even they were amazed at his ability to possess such a cool demeanor and convincing appearance. He looked like he did when he had Raven in his sights, the way he moved, his eyes, the way he tilted his head and his half smile that curled up at the corner. They had seen this look many times.

Dragon stood close in front of the Sheikh, who was now breathing hard. "Your Royal Highness," he said. "I promised you something, and you don't seem like a man that likes to waste time."

He stepped closely around the Sheikh who followed his path, turning to watch. Damascus and Jacob appeared into the room and stopped, standing together, looking down at the floor. Raven had put eye makeup on them, eyeliner specifically and some gloss on their lips. It was designed to mask how old they might be. The Sheik preferred boys under a certain age.

They were dressed in their black nylon pants and their usual boots, but no shirts. They had dog collars around their necks, black leather, studded with rings dangling on both sides. The collar matched leather studded cuffs they wore that had clasps that could either hook to each other to restrain the wrists, or hook to the collar on either side of it, or hook to any other device.

"Come here, someone wants to look at you," Dragon said.

They moved and stood in front of him, Damascus slightly ahead of Jacob. They were gorgeous, muscled, sexy but boyish and the Sheikh had begun to salivate. Dragon took his fingertips and raised Damascus's chin, smiling a sexy, devious facade. Damascus looked at him then, giving him a soft, vulnerable and in love look, that was perfect. Dragon smiled at him like a lover and then eyed the Sheikh.

"Do you know what I mean now?" he said.

He let his eyes fall back to Damascus and leaned in and kissed him, softly, sexually. Dragon knew about faking it in front of a camera and this was very much like it. He transported himself to somewhere else and did what he had to do.

Damascus kissed him back, wetly, eagerly, as if he was dying for his attention. Dragon broke it off, touching a finger to Damascus' lips, resting his forehead on Damascus's.

"So wanting, aren't you? You're a good boy," Dragon said. "Yes sir," Damascus said. He answered, as if he had fallen under Dragon's spell.

Dragon moved around him now, standing behind him, letting his hands trail around his waist and up his chest caressing his muscled body. He moved his hair aside and gently bit his neck above the collar, behind his ear, eyeing the Sheik as he did it, sexily drawing him in.

"Damascus likes it rough. Don't you?" Dragon said. He was holding him while he pressed himself against him from behind, for emphasis. "Yes sir," Damascus said. "You can never get enough, can you?" Dragon asked.

He curved his body into Damascus', holding him back against him, moving his lips down his neck. The Sheikh stood watching, a slight sheen of sweat forming on his skin, even though it was well air conditioned in the room.

"Well, you might have to wait until I see your friend here," Dragon said. "Yes sir," Damascus said.

Dragon turned to Jacob then, pretending to have to drag himself away from Damascus. Tilting his head to one side he eyed him, with a longing, loving look.

"This one is Jacob," he said.

He reached to brush the long strand of hair back that had fallen forward at the side of his face as he looked at the ground.

"Let me see you boy," Dragon said.

Jacob raised his face slightly upward because of Dragon's height compared to his. He kept his eyes averted though. He looked sexy and vulnerable, like he was anxiously waiting to please Dragon in whatever way he could.

"Jacob has some very nice skills. Don't you?" He put two fingers on Jacob's lips. "Yes sir," Jacob said.

He licked Dragon's fingers, sexily putting his lips on them. Dragon just let his eyes go to the Sheik, as Jacob sucked his fingers. He could see it was making the Sheik light headed. He moved behind Jacob then and pulled his arms back behind him, somewhat roughly clasping them together behind his back. Jacob did his best to appear sexually entranced in it and it worked.

The Sheikh could barely contain himself now and Dragon was about to seal the deal. He pushed Jacob to his knees.

"Show the man what you want Jacob," he said. He moved around to face him, pulling his head back by his hair. "Tell me Jacob, look at me and tell me," he said. "You, I want you," Jacob said. He licked his lips and flashed his eyes up at Dragon, looking, begging him. "All of me Jacob?" Dragon asked. He pressed Jacob's face sideways against the front of his pants, rubbing himself along Jacobs' cheek. "All of this?" he asked. He was still holding him by his hair. Jacob closed his eyes and kissed Dragon through the fabric of his pants. "Yes, all of it," he said.

Dragon let his own head fall back, pretending to enjoy the moment, but thinking what he would have to do next, when it happened.

"Enough. How much?" the Sheikh asked.

Dragon had his mark, at last, he let Jacob's head go like he meant nothing to him, and moved to Damascus, binding his wrists together and roughly forcing him down beside Jacob, appearing finished with them.

"How much do you want to pay for the best my friend? They are untraceable by the way. They don't exist anywhere," Dragon said.

He walked away, and the Sheikh turned and walked away as well. Dragon waited for him, his instincts and his inner eye giving him the guidance he needed. The Sheikh really wanted him, but sensed that was not the deal on the table and decided to take the offering.

"One million US," he said.

Dragon turned and eyed him smiling. And like a cat about to finish off his prey, he walked to the Sheikh. "Expertly trained in everything you would ever want. Every fantasy you've ever had. They've been worth every penny I paid for them," Dragon said. "One million each and we have a deal."

He tilted his head at the Sheikh, like he wanted to think about it over a long slow kiss. The Sheikh wanted to faint, so he agreed to buy Damascus and Jacob for one million dollars each. Carefully Dragon raised his hand to touch the Sheikh's face, knowing Sensei had said not to touch him. At the last second he withdrew it, leaving the man faint.

"As you wish, 'Your Royal Highness'. They will be delivered shortly, along with my bank account numbers," Dragon said. He turned and went back to look out the window now, dismissing him basically.

The Sheikh did not look back. Money was of no concern and at this moment he was frustrated that David Li would not be his. He planned to make a nice mess of the boys he had purchased. A shame, he thought, because they were exquisite and under other circumstances he would have enjoyed them immensely. He was jealous of David Li and he would exact his usual price for his feeling inadequate next to other men.

Dragon had almost for a second taken pity on him, thinking he couldn't kill someone simply because they were homosexual and liked younger men. But when he had truly seen the man at that moment, he knew what he had to do. Any young unfortunate boy, as he had been, would be terrorized in this psycho's hands.

As the Sheik had felt defeated even though he had allegedly acquired something he wanted, Dragon had glimpsed his darkness. He was cruel and liked to dominate. Visions from him hit his inner eye not unlike things he had lived through himself as a child.

After the door had shut, the Sheikh departed, the room fell silent. They waited. Dragon let out a huge sigh. He pulled Damascus and Jacob to their feet and headed for the bedroom needing her in his arms. Sarge and Wax let their hands free. They were all silent, as it had been a lot. Wax nodded at them, giving them the respect that they deserved. It had taken a lot out of all of them to go through that. Wax and Sarge had to watch Dragon push himself through scenarios from his painful past, and be strong enough to do it.

Chekov was at the helm now. Dragon and Wax and Sarge had changed into their HQ standard issue clothes, and looked like old times, as had Damascus and Jacob. They were armed and ready. They all boarded the elevator, to meet Raven in the hallway. After the Sheik had left, she had gone with Sensei to get the flowers and enter the building as planned. They lay flat against the walls, as Chekov blurred the security cameras. No one spoke as it unfolded.

Damascus and Jacob stood behind her, as she knocked on the door to the Sheikh's apartment, looking submissive in their leather shirts. A bodyguard looked through the eye piece in the door and saw them standing there, and a female, covered in a Burkha, holding a large container of flowers. He asked who was there. Raven answered. "A gift from Mr. Li." She spoke it in perfect Arabic, something she had just learned.

In a moment, the door opened. She entered, eyeing the whereabouts of the occupants of the room immediately. Damascus and Jacob followed her, hands behind their backs. The Sheikh had risen from the sofa and turned to greet his new acquisitions with a look of pure animal lust. Raven took in his look and wanted her first knife to be through his forehead, but that was not her job. She placed the large pot on a console table and let it begin.

They were completely unaware as she pulled the knife from the soil. In a quiet undetectable motion she turned and hit the closest guard through the neck. Turning again, not waiting to see if it hit or not, because she knew it would, she already had the other knife spinning in the air. It hit the next closest one between the eyes. They burst through the door then, tossing Damascus and Jacob Uzi's.

It was over in seconds, there was no time for more than a slight surprised look on the Sheikh's face. They unloaded on them, over killing them. Raven retrieved her knives from her victims, while Sarge obliterated any trace of the knife wound in a gruesome blast of close range gunfire, which they both avoided looking at. It wasn't their best work, or the way they usually did things, but it needed to look personal. It was ugly and bloody.

When their guns fell silent, they checked all the rooms and found no one. The smoke and the smell of gun powder permeated the air. It looked like a war zone. They had blown the hell out of the people and the room they were in.

They had left on the DLI jet, departing Dubai as scheduled. It would appear they attended the horse auction then left. As Chekov had scrambled the cameras there was no record of them doing anything except going legitimately in and out. They would be away before anything was discovered and hopefully not connected to it in anyway.

With the removal of the Sheik it was hoped that exposure and awareness would be drawn to the kind of activity he was involved in and also free his victims. It was a personal issue for the General as well but all in all another vile entity had been removed.

Dragon wanted to discuss nothing for the moment, pulling Raven into the back bedroom area, as soon as he was able to. Their needs now overruled the day. For now there was nothing but them. He looked into her eyes, stopping briefly from his lips tasting her shoulder. He smiled his sexy half smile, the one he had for her and only for her.

In the cabin of the jet it had been quiet. Wax got up and found a bottle of Scotch. He didn't need to ask, handing Sarge a triple and Sensei the same. Damascus nodded as Wax eyed him, as did Jacob. They enjoyed a drink, as they fled through the sky, away from the mystical place that had been Dubai. It was a surreal feeling and almost left them floating with a sense that maybe they had all been dreaming it.

"I'm not the same person I was three days ago," Damascus said. "Dragon sold you for a million dollars," Sarge said. "Now you're a 'million dollar' fuck up. That's something." Sarge nodded at them and gulped his drink down. Damascus and Jacob looked at each other and laughed at Sarge. They had missed his arrogant taunts.

"That was some crazy fucking shit," Damascus said. "Thank god it wasn't for real," Jacob said. "That guy was about as creepy as they get." "Don't worry, he's very dead. I pretty much cut him in half," Wax said. "Your Royal Halfness," Sarge said. There was nothing left to do but laugh then.

Back at HQ finally, Wendy delivered them to what they thought would be the control centre and Chekov but turned out to be the infirmary and Dr. Shultz. They all eyed each other, wondering what the cloner wanted with them. Dr. Schultz eyed Sensei, aware of their mutual dislike for one another.

"What do you want?" Sensei asked. Schultz turned away, ignoring the question. He behaved indifferently to them, disrespectfully. He thought he was superior. "Dragon," he said. "How are you?" Dragon flared at him. "Don't forget your rank Schultz. Sensei asked you a question. What do you want with us?" Dragon said.

Schultz turned to them, holding a large caliber needle, his fingers looped through two surgical steel rings, his thumb on the plunger. It appeared to contain a small shiny capsule shaped object, also surgical steel.

"Who's first?" he asked. Dragon eyed the doctor then. "Don't fuck with my last nerve you freak. Do what you have to do and keep your mouth shut while you do it." He glared in his face, ordering him.

He just looked at Dragon, his usual strange expression on his face. They had all wondered if he was on a personal drug cocktail at times. Dragon allowed him to push the sleeve of his shirt up revealing his shoulder muscle. Schultz had a gleam in his eye now as he jabbed it deep into the muscle. It stung, and he knew it did. Dragon tuned it out, as he pressed the plunger, setting the device deeply into the centre of the muscle.

"Next," Schultz said blandly. He unloaded on all of them and as they left Sensei couldn't help a quiet remark. "You disgust me and I'm going to have the General get rid of you."

They were transported to the control centre then, their arms sore from the subdural tracking device Shultz had implanted in them all.

"What's the matter with that fucking guy?" Sarge asked, rubbing his arm. They followed the corridor to Chekov's lair, where the General waited for them.

"Ah, welcome back," he said. "General," Dragon nodded to him. "Once again I thank you Dragon, all of you. Well done. "It was a good call General," Dragon said. "Yes, I'm glad you agree," the General said. "Now, I hope your implanting procedure went smoothly."

"I must discuss that with you General, before I leave," Sensei said. "Of course," the General said.

"Damascus, Jacob, we will miss you here, but Sensei has advised it is best that you operate out of their Hawaii camp. I hope we will get to see you on occasion," the General said. "Yes General, and I'm sorry," Damascus said. "Don't be son, it is most important to me that you are able to give me your best service and if it requires you to live elsewhere, then so it shall be," the General said. He was truly concerned for his welfare, as an operative and as a person. "Now, I must see to other business. Chekov has a profile for you."

"What?" Dragon said. He thought they would be on leave after Dubai, as they all did.

"Ho Chi Minh City, Vietnam," Chekov said. "The War Horse leaves at 7 am, so be on it. I will upload the profile for you Dragon." He looked from one to the other and then sighed as he could see their dismay. "Exploited children. Human trafficking. Drugs, brothels? Remember?" he said, sarcastically. "It's an infiltration and rescue, which I know you don't do anymore Dragon but it involves Raven and Damascus, which is why you all must go, including all your team Damascus. Read the profile and it will make sense. After, you are on scheduled leave for a month," Chekov said.

"Damascus, get your team and meet me in conference room three," Dragon ordered. He was anxious now to see what about this involved Raven. "It's free, thank you for asking," Chekov said, dryly. Dragon eyed him, snapping slightly more with each second. He stepped up, close to Chekov's face. "Chekov, in your little miss-wired fucked up world, you may have failed to notice something, so let me fill you in. In the past 24 hours, I mind fucked with a pervert. I sexually assaulted my own operatives and ripped six people to death with close range machine gun fire. I spent 6 hours on a plane to then face that asshole Schultz. So if I don't give a god damned fuck whether someone's using the conference room, excuse the fuck me!" Chekov paled, and looked away. "Come on baby," Raven said.

She gently brushed his hand with her fingertips. Wax put a hand on his shoulder blade guiding him to turn away from Chekov and they all moved toward the corridor. Damascus was on his phone summoning his remaining teammates to the conference room as they proceeded there.

They sat, all accounted for, and Dragon pulled the profile up on the laptop in the conference room. The details appeared for them all to see on an overhead 52 inch screen. When they had all studied it silently, Dragon dropped his head into his hands and ran them through his hair.

"This is the stupidest fucking thing I've ever seen. Sensei you can't expect me to send them, send her, unarmed and alone into one of those places," he said. "It breaks most of the protocols, plus the collateral risk percentage is far beyond anything we've operated within before."

CHAPTER TWENTY SIX

DREAM WEAVER

The Dream Weaver had been peacefully waiting for them in Los Angeles and they all were never so happy to see her. Dragon sat in the helm chair of the flying bridge, watching to the east as the sun had begun to rise. It was the final hour or so of his turn at night watch. They had been sailing for just a day now, heading west and home at last. The night breeze had chilled down and he wore a sweat shirt over his T shirt, and was warmer still as Raven lay against him sleeping soundly now. She had stayed awake with him for the whole time and he had just put her to sleep with his kiss, so she could get some rest. She slept against him and he let his fingertips touch the fading scars on her back. Sensei said they would go away completely with time and hopefully her emotional ones would fade with them. A tear had begun to creep to the corners of his eyes as he remembered the painful times of the previous weeks.

As Dream Weaver cruised through the flat surf Dragon had let his mind drift back to the horrors of the last mission. After Ho Chi Minh, they had eventually left HQ Munich, making a stopover in New York again, before continuing to LA. It had been nearly 8 weeks since they had left Mexico. Right after the Dubai mission had been Vietnam.

The mission had consisted of Raven and Damascus posing as village children, purposely being taken and thus uncovering the eventual whereabouts of the operation. It was a common problem in that area of poverty ridden villages. Children were allegedly supposed to obtain work in the city, to send money back to their families. They would willingly go or be sent either way by unsuspecting fathers and mothers, only to never return and never send money. They would then enter the world of prostitution, or slavery of some kind. They were being dispersed to many places in the world and it was HQ's goal to find out where it all started and cut it off.

Dragon recalled how they had waited at the edge of the village in the jungle until the caravan had arrived to take them. Raven and Damascus had left them then. He and Wax and Sensei had sat silently watching them go un-noticed, into the line forming to board the canvas tented truck. They were dressed as village youngsters. Large hats, typical hair styles and clothing made them blend in with the other children. Dragon hadn't slept since learning of the profile, knowing it was flawed. Sensei and Wax had pried his arms off her as Damascus pulled her away. She had been reassuring him the whole time that she would be fine and see him in less than a day.

As Wax and Sensei pulled him to return to the waiting Blackhawk, 10 kilometers away, where Sarge waited for them, he had fallen to his knees vomiting uncontrollably on the jungle floor. They had dragged him up and he recovered, wanting nothing more than to get her back. His sickness was foreshadowing but it was too late to turn back.

Chekov was tracking Damascus and Raven, which was the point of it. They did not know the destination of the caravan, where they took the children, where it all started. When it reached its destination Chekov would send them to retrieve the two of them and the children, eliminating the perpetrators and exposing them. It had seemed simple enough but Dragon never liked the idea of them being separated, unarmed and vulnerable. It was against protocol for a reason. They were supposed to be safe, if they just kept quiet and waited for them to come. It didn't happen that way.

Wax, Dragon and Sensei had made it back to the Blackhawk and Sarge had flown them back to Ho Chi Minh City and they had waited anxiously. A seedy hotel housed them while they waited for orders. They had disguised themselves as common Vietnamese, except Sarge who just hid his hair and wore dark glasses. The Blackhawk was hidden in the jungle and they had an old covered truck to transport them to the city. Chekov watched and they waited.

Chekov had the destination that the tracking devices had provided and was about to order phase two, directing them to move in, when he detected Damascus moving away from the target on foot. He gathered he was carrying Raven because they did not show as two separate signals to him. He made an instant decision ordering Dragon's team to Damascus' location and Damascus's team to the target to continue with the elimination segment.

Damascus and Raven had followed through and sat quietly, waiting. It was tactical not to let their true ages become evident so they kept their faces down for the most part. They had not been given any water, and it had been 14 hours in the heat. They had been held in a back room of a dirty store that sold cigarettes, news papers and pornographic material, their hands tied behind their backs since they arrived.

The room was guarded by one man with a bamboo cane. Now frightened, children wept, and Raven had tried to comfort them, but couldn't do much as Damascus had silently begged her not to attract attention to them. They would be rescued soon enough. That was supposed to be the plan.

It fell apart when another man had come and tried to take one of the youngest girls. Raven had not been able to stop herself and had intervened, wanting to be taken instead. It nearly cost her life. The child was pulled from the room in spite of her protests and Raven had then endured several cutting blows from the bamboo cane. It was a painful destructive instrument, lashing the skin into welts that bruised into the muscle, and caused bubbling painful blistering and eventual loss of all the layers of skin. It was painful to receive and even more so later. He had hit her across her arms and back before Damascus could stop it.

He fell on top of her begging the man to stop and hit him instead. And he did, beating Damascus mercilessly, ripping him to shreds in his anger, realizing they were not children, calling them spies. There was nothing Raven could do then and she lay crushed under Damascus' weight with her hands tied. She cried and begged for Dragon to find them then. Children's cries and screams echoed around her, completing the scene from a horror movie.

Damascus was losing consciousness in the end. He forced himself to keep aware, not sure if it was the end, as his blurred vision took in Raven being dragged by her bound wrists out of the room.

His head lolled but he tried to force his mind to think when he could hear her screams from somewhere. He knew he had to free himself. He curled up and managed to slip himself through his arms so his hands were in front of him. He had used his teeth to free the knot. He had nothing but adrenalin left in him then, as he heard her screaming, following the sound. He had found her in the next room and the man with the cane was in the process of brutally raping her with something far too large, punishing her, trying to make her tell him who she was, who she worked for. Damascus had taken the ropes from his wrists and choked him to death from behind, interrupting his cruel endeavor.

Blood had poured from her, to his unending horror. His wits and his body were failing and he knew he didn't have much left to give. He took his tattered bloody shirt off and shrugged her into it, untying her hands, desperately trying to give her back some dignity. With what he had left, not knowing where it was coming from, he picked her up. He was staggering then but pushed them both out a window, into the dirty street. He knew Chekov would find them so he ran.

He went as far away as he could, through the back alleys, dirty sewage lined garbage strewn paths behind shops. Loose roaming dogs barked at him, chickens scattered and stray eyes saw him, but no one helped. He ran then staggered for as long he could, until his legs began to give out.

His muscles were tying up from the beating. He was too dehydrated to see straight anymore and the pain finally overwhelmed him. He had fallen to his knees behind the garbage and hid them. It was as far as he could go and he hoped it was far enough. He was leaning on a wall, holding her to him like a mother would hold a baby.

Dragon had lost his mind when they had finally gotten to them. They were in a dirty alley, used for garbage collection, where Damascus had hidden them. She was catatonic and he lay near death, never letting her go.

When Dragon had gotten to them Damascus was unconscious, breathing faintly and it was uncertain whose blood covered who. Raven's eyes were open but she was not there when he pulled her into his arms. Sensei and Wax lifted Damascus into the back of the covered truck they had been supplied with and Wax floored it, taking them through the crowded streets and away to their remote hotel they had been using while they waited.

Dragon sat with her in the back, huddled in a corner as Sensei worked on Damascus. He initially held his head and poured water from one of their bottles slowly into his mouth, using every ounce of his willpower to bring Damascus back enough to drink it. Tears streamed down Sensei's face as he feared they were too late.

Raven had become aware on some level and had started crying into Dragon's chest, clinging to him and choking as he tried to get her to drink some water. He had held her so she could speak to Damascus then. She had coaxed him into her light with her words, begging him not to leave them. Gradually his eyes had fluttered in response and Sensei had seen him swallow the water.

They had stayed at HQ Munich for two weeks while Damascus and Raven had recovered enough to travel. Damascus had spent a week of it laying face down while his welts blistered, leaking fluid in open long red flesh lines. Sensei had kept him as pain free as he could with morphine while the wounds lay open and raw. Damascus had suffered terribly from it and it had broken Sensei's heart. He had kept at it diligently applying his creams until they had begun to heal. Damascus had struggled with his doubts and his regrets, feeling he had not done enough to protect her and it was his fault for what had ultimately happened to her.

Sensei's further challenge had been when he had discovered it. She had been bleeding vaginally and he questioned Damascus to understand what happened. Damascus had broken down as he recalled to Sensei what he had seen when he had entered the room, how she had been screaming, what he feared had happened.

Sensei had calmed Damascus and turned his attention to her, forcing Dragon to put her down on the table. She had panicked as he had set her down and he had to lay with her on the table so she would be calm enough for Sensei to examine her torn body. In the end Sensei had needed to put her under as she had refused to let him see her, falling back into a state of panic when he tried to put his hands on her.

Damascus' fears were real and Sensei had learned to his horror that her uterus had been irreparably ruptured from the assault and he would have no choice but to remove it, leaving her forever unable to carry her own child. He knew they had decided against it anyway but always thought they would have a change of heart. Now it was not an option.

Dragon waited for Sensei to tell him what he knew would devastate him in some way and saw utter blackness when he heard the ultimate outcome. Sensei had scrambled to get Wax and Sarge from the other room, as Dragon slipped from the realm of sanity. Wax had stepped in the way of Dragon's fist before it hit the cement wall, three of his ribs breaking with the impact, as Sarge and Sensei struggled to overpower him. It had taken all three of them. They pinned him against the wall while Sensei knocked him out with a sedative.

Dragon felt the breeze from the bridge of the Dream Weaver, letting the final hour of his watch tick away. The rest of the details after that moment at HQ he didn't recall clearly. She had recovered quickly from the simple unobtrusive way Sensei had done the operation. He had lived without her body for the first time in a long time as she was unable to make love to him. He wasn't even sure if she would want to when she was able. The assault had marked her and he didn't know how deeply.

After though, she had needed him badly and had used his body unrelentingly, never getting enough, in a way he recognized, sadly from his own past. She couldn't get enough of trying to cleanse or erase the feeling, the unclean memory and the feelings of somehow letting herself down and more than anything letting him down. He knew she was looking for some kind of control of it. He knew she felt that she had done a bad thing and it disgusted her. He knew exactly how she felt. He had known what to do for her and it had been another hurdle in a series of many.

He had allowed her to soothe herself with him at first, but eventually when she had approached him for what he knew would again consist of him trying to fuck her pain away, he had said 'No'. He knew she was strong enough to hear it then. She had fallen apart not knowing what to do and tried to seduce him into it. He had held her hands off him, denying her.

He knew she needed to fight it out and she had, taking it out on him, her frustrations surfacing, her anger boiling over, her rage filling her, brimming over the top, and finally her pain. She had fought him, and he let her symbolize him, easily stopping her from hurting him as it all flowed out of her like lava from a volcano, violent at first then slowing to a steaming glow.

She had weakened finally from trying to hit him, struggling with him until she slumped into a ball on the floor, crying like a baby into her knees as she hid from him. He knelt and waited for her.

He knew all too well how it felt to have something taken when it wasn't given. How it felt to have it not be your choice. What violence meant and what pain meant. And he knew what it felt like afterward.

Watching her then he waited, sadly knowing the pain but knowing he could help her. "You need to tell me," he said.

She had nodded, still hiding from him. She had finally crumbled and was ready to climb out of the blackness she had been living in.

He spoke to her his mind, getting her to unblock the things she had kept hidden from that day, getting her to let it play out, let her fears surface, her terror that she was alone and couldn't stop it. She let the details become clear to him as she sobbed uncontrollably, still curled in a ball. It threatened to shatter him but he waited, trying to keep strong, trying to accept it as it hit him.

When she had let him see the entire thing she had quieted, having nothing left to do then. He stroked her hair, fighting his own hatred and anger, sharing it with her, absorbing it from her.

When he felt they were able, he took her arm. "Come here. I just want you back," he said. He pulled her apart from herself then. She allowed him to force her to look at him. "I'm sorry I couldn't protect you from this. It's not your fault and nothing matters to me except that I need you back in my life, so badly," he said. He had used his sight and spoken to her from his mind, brushing her hair gently away from her wet face.

She had crawled against him then and she kissed him like she hadn't been able to. He gave to her then with a need that scared him and a passion that drove him. His tears fell as he took her into his arms and made love to her on the floor, bringing her back to him again.

Listening to the comforting drone of the Dream Weaver's diesels now, he pulled her over him and wrapped her in his arms, wanting her then but having to wait until they had slept. He smiled to himself thinking of her earlier, teasing him into the cabin before dinner, wanting his tongue until she couldn't see straight. He couldn't wait to get home and pull her into the ocean with him, lay her on the fur rug in front of the fire, make the water splash over the side of the hot tub, ruin the seats in the Lamborghini and leave hand prints on the hood of the Ferrari.

Now Dragon looked to see Sensei and Damascus arriving on the flying bridge to relieve him. Since everything had happened, Damascus practically never let Sensei out of his sight. Dragon wiped his eyes, hoping they didn't notice. Sensei put a hand on his shoulder, obviously never missing a thing.

"Go to bed son," he said quietly. Dragon got up, carrying her. "Take it easy, I'll see you later," Damascus said.

He had taken them to bed around 6 am and let them sleep until noon, so they could join everyone for lunch. They emerged from the main cabin to find everyone on the stern deck. Wax and Sensei were about to bring the lunch to them and they were starved. Raven wore Dragon's favorite navy blue bikini with the white Hawaiian flowers on it and he had just shorts, it was so hot and sunny. It made them feel good to have the sun and it's warmth on their skin again. Dragon put his sunglasses on, still hanging from the thin rubber cord around his neck.

She loved how he looked in them and had tried not to think about the front of his shorts, as they sat with everyone. He had already left her breathless and trembling, wet and satisfied, a half hour ago. The plan was to have lunch together and then Yoga, so they could all join in.

Sensei had toned the routine down because they weren't in the same shape they had been in before and Damascus and Raven needed to use their muscles carefully still for the time being and Wax's broken ribs were also an issue. Dragon and Sarge were able to extend themselves into some of the more advanced moves and did so.

They would spend the afternoon on the foredeck of the yacht, taking in the sun and maybe a Marguerite or so. Damascus lay on his stomach on a lounge chair, letting his back get some sun. Sensei told Raven to put sunscreen on him, his new skin sensitive to burning. It had been hard for her sometimes to see what had become of his back. Sensei would remove as much of the scars as possible but he would forever have lines of scar tissue in uneven stripes marking him.

He closed his eyes enjoying the feeling of her gentle hands on him. She was careful not to press to hard on the scars, but to cover them thoroughly. She was connected to him now in a special way, one of love, mutual respect, and trust. She had begun to feel about him the way she felt about Sarge and Wax. He was a part of her world, like they were. Dragon had crossed that threshold as well, knowing Damascus would have given his own life for her that day and very nearly had.

He had told Damascus how he felt when they were still at HQ, as Damascus had lain face down, suffering the aftermath. He wanted him to know that he was proud of him and would be ever grateful for his bravery and selflessness. He had encouraged him to fight to get well so they could finally take him home.

Wax still had taping around his broken ribs and would for another few weeks at least. He had taken Dragon's hit instinctively, seeing that had his hand hit the cement wall, it would have shattered every bone, potentially ruining his bow hand permanently. His ribs would heal and he would do it again the same way if he had to. He cared nothing for himself at this point, knowing Raven's loss, Dragon's loss, and the gravity of Damascus' health. It had been more than they had ever gone through.

Sarge had been unable to cope with any of it and still had to fight off his tears when he thought of anyone hurting her, especially that way. He wanted to talk to her alone at some point but wasn't strong enough himself to do it yet. He wanted to comfort her but if he didn't get his shit together, she would be comforting him instead. He was just glad they were going home and wanted nothing more than to spend a blissful five days aboard the Dream Weaver with all the people in his life that mattered to him sitting around him.

When Raven had finished with Damascus she had lay down on her back next to Dragon. She had needed to be near him more than ever since it had happened, still feeling shaken at times and needing his reassurance. Sensei said it was normal. She wasn't familiar with anxiety, but had been experiencing it lately. Dragon was patient and understanding and knew when to indulge her and when to gently set her straight. Sometimes she would just need him to hold her and help drive the memories out of her mind, until one day they didn't come back. That's what Sensei had promised her. And she felt an even deeper respect for Dragon because she now knew how terrifying it could be, if memories came unbidden, or haunted your dreams.

Now, sitting in the sun, finally heading home, Dragon felt his world was returning to him, returning to normal. Raven had healed her body and her heart for him, give or take a moment here and there, which he was more than happy to help her through. His plan was to take her home, love her as much as he could and occupy them with life in camp, something they had been missing. He had plans for Damascus and his team and was looking forward to them all being together again. There were younger boys to bring along, and little ones to nurture. She caught him thinking his thoughts, and rolled on top of him, smiling and kissing his neck.

"Are you happy baby?" she asked. "You know I am sweetheart," he said. He felt her hair and involuntarily moved his hips to press himself against her. Her warm smooth skin against his was causing him problems south of the border.

"You need a Marguerite," she said. "If you're mixing, I'm drinking," he said. "Otherwise I'm going to drag you below and inspect your tan lines with my tongue." She liked the sound of that. "Baby will you? Before dinner?" He smiled, enjoying that she was as insatiable as ever.

She climbed off him and playfully tossed a towel over his obvious erection, making Damascus laugh at him.

"Sarge! Get over here and help me make us Marguerites," she bossed. He jumped up and in two strides had scooped her up, pretending to throw her over the side. She squealed clutching her arms around his neck. "Don't you dare," she said.

She laughed, hugging him and he set her down. She pulled him by his hand down to the galley. They had been closer than ever since everything had happened. He had been inconsolable. He was angry and frustrated and concerned. And being 'Sarge' he couldn't express it very well so he just loved her and was there for her. In the end she had consoled him. She made him understand that she was fine with everything and would live happily ever after no matter what.

"What are you going to do first when we get home?" Sarge said. He passed her the Tequila from a shelf she couldn't reach. She eyed him coyly. "What do you think I'm going to do?" she said. He smiled at her, looking gorgeous with his tan and blue eyes, blonde hair everywhere. "Besides that!" he said, rolling his eyes. "I don't know whatever Sensei wants us to do I guess, see the kids, drink champagne, and go for a ride. Oh, well, that would be like doing what I already said I was going to do, again." She giggled.

"Those cars are like an aphrodisiac for you aren't they?" he said. He crushed some ice for her with his fist. "Well you would be the same way. You can't tell me it wouldn't cross your mind if you were on a deserted road with someone you love, with her in a mini skirt and no panties," she said. He grinned, thinking about it. She handed him a glass. "Here taste this." He downed it. "Perfect," he said.

"It's probably never going to happen." He shrugged and was looking adorably boyish like he used to. "Come here you," she said. She brushed his crazy hair out of his eyes, holding him around the waist. "You are going to find the perfect person for you, I know it and when you do I am going to tease you about it endlessly like you've done to me for the last 8 years." He kissed her on her forehead, smiling down at her. "You go right ahead if it makes you happy." "I want 'you' to be happy Sarge. And hurry up about it because I have to find

Damascus someone and I can't handle all of you now, all by myself," she said. He pushed her off of him and picked up the heavy jug. "But I have nothing to offer a girl; I don't even know what to say half the time. I've only ever had one night stands." She listened to him as they made their way to the foredeck.

"Sarge, don't talk like that. It's not about what you have to offer. When I met Dragon do you think I was wondering what he had to offer?" she asked. "Well you probably were wondering what he had to offer in his pants," Sarge said. She giggled. "I was not, and I was 13!!" "Bullshit," Sarge said. Dragon eyed them wondering what they were going to go on about today.

"Baby, Sarge thinks all I was interested in when we met was what was in your pants," she said. Dragon let his head fall back, smiling. "Well I was pretty interested in showing you, not going to lie," he said. Sarge and Wax laughed. "Now someone's being honest at least," Sarge said.

She responded by shoving a piece of ice down the front of Dragons shorts, while his eyes were closed against the sun. "Fuck," he gasped. Reaching it out, he tossed it at her. She caught it in her hands and with her mind let him picture her licking it. "Jesus," he said. And Sensei smirked.

They drank Marguerites all afternoon, until Sensei and Wax had gone to start dinner. It was their day to cook.

Dragon had pulled her to their cabin to give her what she wanted before dinner, with regard to her tan lines. He kissed her, using his tongue to tease her with his thoughts. He knew what she was waiting for and he eyed her then. Taking his lips from hers he whispered to her 'make me'. He had simply wanted to dive on her, but held back the urge, wanting to play a game.

She stepped back from him, and reaching behind her she undid the string of her top. She held the strings taught, releasing her breasts but not exposing them all the way to him. She then turned away and removed it, looking over her shoulder at him as he waited. His sexy half smile trembled slightly as he took in her seductive pose. She pulled the strings on the sides of the bottoms and pulled them from her, so he could see her sexy butt.

"Are you going to lose control Mr. Li?" she asked. She looked over her shoulder again, flashing her eyes at him. "I think you are." He swallowed and let his breath out now, knowing she was very right about that. She walked to the bed and lay back, slowly opening her thighs and let her hands run down the insides. She touched herself then, exposing herself to his eyes as he focused on her, her fingers gently caressing, her wetness coating them.

He looked desperately sexy as he took a step towards her, his shirtless body gleaming, his erection straining his shorts and his eyes deep with desire for her.

"Can't help it now Mr. Li?" she asked. He fell to his knees. "No," he said.

He pulled her fingers from inside her and sucked on them, the taste of her and the sight of her driving him insane.

"Oh my god, come here," he said.

He pulled her against his mouth, spreading her apart and losing all of his mind at once. She arched into him, her hands in his hair as he drove her wild.

He made love to her after, sinking into her wetness slowly and passionately. He could have kept her there for the rest of the night, but it would have to wait. Instead he pulled her to the shower and shortly they appeared to join the others for dinner. Wax and Sensei were almost finished preparing it and Raven went to help them with Sake. Sarge had been put in charge of treating Damascus's wounds and was applying Sensei's cream to his back.

"Ouch, fuck." Damascus complained as Sarge was too rough on some of the still sore spots. "Stop being a little bitch," Sarge said. "Sergeant Willis, take some care please," Sensei said. "Hai Sensei," Sarge said. He deliberately began massaging Damascus like he was a lover. "There baby is that better?" he said. "Get off me you fucking shithead," Damascus said. He squirmed out from under his touch. Sarge feigned desperation and confusion. "Wait, I was just about to come," he said.

They all laughed then. Sensei shook his head, thinking it ridiculous that none of them seemed to be able to do anything without making it a joke or crude in some way.

CHAPTER TWENTY SEVEN

HOME

They watched the sun set that night together on the flying bridge. They witnessed five more sunsets before they lay eyes on the islands finally that they had missed so much. It was a relief to finally put their feet in the sand, feel the warm ocean and smell the wonderful scents in the air. Dragon had wanted to pull her into the surf right then and promised her in his mind it wouldn't be long.

Damascus stood in awe, loving it instantly. He thought of Jacob and his remaining two team members and how much they were all going to love being here. They made their way off the beach and up the stone path through the manicured lawn to the house. Climbing the expansive steps to the patio, Marietta waited for them by the open air doors. Raven hugged her as did Sensei and she had smiled kindly to Damascus, welcoming him.

They had barely had a moment to take in their surroundings, when the front door flew open. They all turned their attention, as a frantic, exasperated and beaming Lily ran through it, dragging Paulo like a teddy bear along with her. "Sensei!!" She ran to him and jumped into his arms, leaving Paulo to look shyly at them all. Dragon picked him up. "Lily," Sensei said. She kissed his face everywhere. "Child, please, say hello to everyone now." He set her down and she ran to Raven, hugging her tightly. "Raven, I missed you so much, it's been terrible, Monique is too strict and wouldn't let me have the golf cart when Sensei was gone and Paulo cried so much, he kept me awake."

Dragon looked at Paulo who now sat perched on his hip. He brushed the boys black curls off his forehead. "No more of that now little man, OK? We brought you Damascus to help with all these girls," he said.

Raven laughed at Lily's outburst, as Sensei shook his head. "Well my sweetheart, Papa is here now so I'm guessing you will be allowed to have your way again very soon." She remembered what a soft heart Sensei had when it came to the whims of little girls.

"Hey kiddo," Wax said. He picked her up and tossed her above his head. She was 8 years old now but still a tiny thing, weighing nothing to Wax. She laughed as he caught her, pretending to drop her. "Waxy, what happened to you?" she asked. She frowned at his bandaged ribs. "Nothing for you to worry your pretty little head about, I will be good as knew before you know it," Wax said.

To distract her, Damascus tugged her hair from behind. "Hey, what about me?" he said. She turned to him, wrapping her arms around him, her face only coming up to his abs. He ruffled her hair. "That's better," he said. "Are you here to stay Damascus?" she said, looking up at him. "You bet, and Jacob will be here, and Sonny and Mishka," he said. He hadn't seen her in so long and she was still as cute as he remembered.

Sarge picked her up then and she pulled his hair, like Raven had shown her to. "Sarge, did you miss me," she said. "I sure did," he said. "Raven nearly drove me insane the whole time we were gone. Now I can look forward to you bugging me for a change." He was trying to wrench his hair out of her clutch. She giggled. "Oh Sergeant Willis," she said. She tried to tease him the way Raven had taught her to.

Dragon sat down then, on one of the chaise lounges, with the little boy on his thigh. "So Paulo, tell me what you've been up to while we were gone," he said. Dragon liked taking the time to engage him as his past traumas had left him introverted and easily frightened. Paulo smiled at Dragon, trusting him and relaxing enough to tell Dragon he had been learning to read books and print letters.

"Lily taught me how to," he said. "She's bossy and I have to do what she says," he added. Dragon nodded, looking serious. "I know, that's how it is with girls Paulo." "Well I like learning words so it's Ok," he said. "That's good, now what else. Did you have fun doing anything?" Dragon asked. "Lily and I took the golf cart once and went to the pineapple field and ran through the sprinklers," he said proudly. Dragon grinned at him and it went quiet as Sensei turned an eye on Lily.

"Paulo!" Lily snapped. "I told you that was a secret!" She reddened, eyeing Sensei.

Dragon tried not to laugh. Sensei walked to her and took his familiar stance where he waited for you to speak. The wheels were turning in her head and quickly she flashed her almond eyes up to him. "Papa! It was so hot and Monique was mean to me that day and I was lonely and Paulo was being a baby and I just wanted to do um, something! Check on the pineapples!" She had come up with every excuse she could think of on the spot. Sensei nodded, barely holding back his amused grin. "I see. And why was Monique being mean to you?" he asked. "She made me wash all the dishes from everyone that whole day, instead of having play time," she said. She was avoiding his question, thinking he would feel sorry for her.

Before Sensei could respond, Paulo whispered to Dragon, audibly enough for them all to hear. "It was because Lily made me put a big ugly spider in her bed the night before." Lily's mouth dropped open and she gave him the evilest eye she could. "I see," Sensei said. "Well my dear, I am glad to be back then, so we will have no more of this. If you are annoyed with someone, it is better to discuss it with them, rather than play tricks." "Ok Papa," she said. "But I did it mostly because I thought it was funny." Everyone smirked and didn't know where to look.

Then Paulo laughed, his little boy laughter warming Dragon's heart. "It was." He whispered to Dragon, nodding his head and grinning.

Sarge shook his head, eyeing Raven. "This can't be happening." He feigned a look of alarm at Sensei.

"Well, Miss Lily," Sensei said. "We will discuss this all in good time. Finding something funny does not always make it a good choice of action." Raven wanted to say 'Yes it does,' but kept it in her head for only Sensei to hear. "I have huge problems, I can see here," he said. He turned away so they couldn't see his smile.

It was decided that they would show Damascus around then. Damascus would share Sensei's room with him but they showed him around the whole house, Lily dragging him everywhere and explaining things as they went. Kona had a glint in his eye and suggested they go to the garage as well. Being guys they wanted to show Damascus the cars and they readily agreed.

Damascus didn't know what the big deal about the garage could be but he followed along. They all went out the still open front door. The white Lamborghini and the red Ferrari sat waiting, but there was something new. A shiny black Porsche Carrera convertible was beside the Ferrari. There was a large red bow on the windshield and a card. Kona grinned. Dragon stepped over and pulled the card off the bow, realizing what was going on. He handed it to Damascus.

"What the ffu..." Damascus stopped himself before he fully swore in front of Lily.

He took the card from Dragon and turned away as he opened it and read it. It was of course from the General, an apology for what he had gone through. He ran a hand thru his spikes and turned back to them. He raised his eyebrows at them then, a grin spreading across his handsome face.

Damascus spun the tires out of the driveway, heading through the gates and onto the road, Lily's arms waving in the air from the passenger seat as they drove off.

"Look out Lanai," Wax said.

"That's so exciting for him," Raven said. "Very," Dragon said. He smiled down at her and with his mind he showed her what would be exciting for him later on.

They went back to the house, as Damascus's tour was over for the moment. Marietta was planning their lunch. They decided on beers, even though it was early and went out to the pool. Paulo sat quietly on Dragon's lap, leaning against him, playing with his glasses that hung on the rubber cord. Raven sat at the foot of the lounge chair, watching him amuse the little boy. As they finished their beers, the front door opened and Damascus came in dodging as Lily ran past him coming to Raven.

"Look what Damascus did to my hair!!" she cried. Her little black mane hung wildly on her now. "Get me a brush and I'll fix it for you sweetheart," Raven said. She ran off to find one as Damascus came out to the pool, eyeing them all.

"How was that?" Dragon asked. "Like getting with something so fine you don't know where to start," Damascus said. "It happens to me all the time," Dragon said. He stroked Raven's cheek.

Sarge had moved to stand close to Damascus then. "And for sure as close as you'll ever get to it," Sarge said. He used his superior size and shoved Damascus into the pool before he had a chance to react.

Lily had returned then and grinned at him now soaked in the pool. "You deserve that Damascus because you don't even know how to drive a car. He nearly crashed into a pineapple truck!" she said. "I did not," Damascus said. "Someone gave him the middle finger, Papa," she said. She looked smugly at Damascus as Raven put the finishing touches on her hair.

Sensei shook his head at both of them then. He repressed a grin at her naughtiness, as she once again reminded him so much of Raven. Damascus had climbed out of the pool and peeled off his wet shirt as Wax tossed him a towel from a nearby pile.

"What happened to your back Damascus?" Lily gasped when she saw his scars. He knelt down so he could look in her face. "It was a monster, and it got me," he said. He made scary eyes at her with a spooky tone in his voice, trying to get her imagination working. "Did you beat it up?" she asked. Getting caught up in his story she looked at him eagerly. "Yes I did, and I got away," he said. "What's that?" she asked. She touched the now fading scar from his gunshot wound. Damascus fought not to lose his composure as he remembered what it really was. "Something else bad happened, but it's ok now," he said. He was not able to make light of it. "Did someone hurt you Damascus?" she asked. "It didn't hurt sweetie, but yes, kind of," he said. Sensei bailed him out then. "Lily, tell us about your art work."

Dragon had been thinking about one thing and one thing only and he couldn't wait any longer to pull her to their bedroom. He caught Sensei's nod telling him to go and have fun until lunch.

Behind the bedroom door now, the possibilities were endless. Now that they were home he had access to all their favorite toys. He found some leather cuffs and secured each of her elbows to her knees and blindfolded her just to start. In the end he lay with her in their bed, holding her in his arms. They were sweaty and wet everywhere.

"Thank you baby," she said. She was kissing his chest as he stroked her hair off her forehead. "My pleasure baby," he said. "Did you get enough?" he asked. "Yes baby, you always give me enough and more," she said. He smiled, knowing she'd want more that night.

They joined the others for lunch and made plans to spend the afternoon on the beach and the evening at Bobby's. It was a beautiful first day and night back home. So much had happened and they all needed each other more than ever. The security of their home, the tranquility, peacefulness and beauty would comfort them now.

In the morning Sensei had brought tea for he and Dragon and they had discussed Raven while she still slept. Sensei had been ever concerned for her welfare and mental state since the incident. He knew Dragon didn't care for the subject but needed to address it anyway.

"You know son, it is possible to have your own biological child," Sensei said. "It would simply have to be carried and delivered by someone else. It's not uncommon."

Dragon eyed him, not wanting to be having the conversation at all. Sensei left it alone and they discussed the plans for the day and some future issues until he left them with an hour to use up before Yoga. Dragon woke her and it only took her three seconds to pull him into a sexual dream world.

Wax, Sarge and Damascus were sitting at the table when they emerged about an hour later, showered and fresh and ready for Yoga. Sensei wanted to get them back in shape. Wax's ribs were nearly healed and he could move fully again, so Sensei led them with the most strenuous routine he knew.

They worked out for the rest of the morning, finishing with a run down the beach. The water sparkled in shades of turquoise; the sand was soft and the waves easy. Palm trees and beautiful fragrant flowers were everywhere and the weather was always perfect. Later in the day they were to take the Sikorsky to Honolulu to pick up Damascus' team when they arrived from Munich. But first after lunch they were going to practice shooting and then had a meeting with Chekov. They hadn't heard much from him since leaving Munich as he had promised them down time.

Returning from the shooting range later, they gathered by the laptop desk, while Sensei summoned Chekov. After a few moments he appeared for them.

"Hello, hope you are all well," Chekov said. "Jacob, Sonny and Mishka will arrive in Honolulu at 5:35 pm, for you to pick up Dragon," he said. "Raven, I hope you are well." She hugged in to Dragon and smiled at Chekov. "I'm fine Chekov, don't worry about me," she said. "What did you want to discuss with us Chekov?" Dragon said.

"I know you are on leave," Chekov said. "However there is a mission if you are interested. I will download the profile and you can look at it if you don't mind and let me know. You are not being ordered to take it of course." They all eyed each other. They were happy to be home and did not want to go anywhere again for awhile. "I'll look at it," Dragon said.

"It may interest you actually," Chekov said. "It's Hong Kong, a business venture if you will and a little of our business on the side. You will have the opportunity to invest in an African gold mine, through David Li Industries, with Lee Tran of Hong Kong, Tran International. He is raising Capital and has a share offering available and he has contacted us asking to see you personally. It will make you even wealthier, FYI. We need to answer him soon."

"Is he legit? What has he got to do with our real cause?" Dragon asked. "We believe he is affiliated with a cover for child prostitution and trafficking, but you would have to find that out. We aren't sure, but if it is indicated then you would eliminate him, after you obtain shares in his company of course," Chekov said. "I've invested in it myself and market indicators show that if DLI were to invest, it would boost the share prices, making me richer," he said. He cracked a grin then.

Dragon shook his head. "Whatever Chekov, what makes you think he's involved in the trade?" "From what we can tell, he is a married man, but gay and transmissions have been intercepted indicating he has an interest in young boys. Also, his father in law is a very wealthy man who may be connected as well. It requires you to get to know them, you know, the usual," he said.

"When?" Dragon asked. "It's in the profile, but soon. If I respond to him that you will meet him to negotiate the purchase of the shares, you could stipulate when. You could delay it, or get it over with, whichever," Chekov said. "Tell him I'll meet him," Dragon said. "I will talk to Sensei, read the profile and let you know when." "Excellent," Chekov said. "I know this guy's bad news, we just can't prove it. He's Hong Kong elite and there's no one on the inside. All I have is from hacking him, which shows he is into some nasty things, but we need to know more." "Ok," Dragon said.

He considered the matter closed until he could read the profile and go over it with Sensei. They signed off and looked at each other silently. Dragon shrugged and ran a hand through his hair. He knew they didn't want to go anywhere just then, but work was work.

"Sensei, can we take a look at it?" Dragon asked. "Later tonight, of course, but now you need to relax for the rest of the afternoon until it's time to go to Honolulu," Sensei said.

They all couldn't go because there weren't enough seats in the Sikorsky once they picked up Jacob and Sonny and Mishka, so just Dragon, Sarge and Damascus went. Sensei had wanted some time alone with Raven anyway and this would give them a few hours together. Dragon had passionately kissed her goodbye, as Sensei pulled her away so they could leave.

Sensei and Raven and Wax had gone to see Monique and the children. It was a good distraction to pass the time. After they had a visit it was time for them to go and make dinner, but Raven had only one thing on her mind. She didn't like being away from Dragon ever since Vietnam. Sensei made dinner and Wax tried to distract her, getting her to help, having fun like the old days. In the end, waiting for them to come back had been too much, she couldn't eat anything without him there and knowing Sensei and Wax were worried about her had made her cry. Taking her in his arms Sensei finally had made her sleep. Wax had cuddled her into his big arms laying her against his chest, trying to comfort her as best he could.

The flight had been uneventful and they made it back, somewhat later than planned. It was an exuberant greeting as it was obvious the boys were happy to be back together and to be where they were. The jungle had been a secluded happy place to grow up but this was paradise. Damascus was happy to have his now small group back together and it seemed one last piece of the puzzle he needed to feel normal again.

Dragon found Raven lying across Wax, asleep, and looked at Sensei wondering.

"She wouldn't eat and came apart a little bit so I made her sleep," Sensei explained. "She has separation anxiety now." Dragon nodded. "Thanks man," he said to Wax. Wax released her to him as he picked her up. "No worries. Just look after her," Wax said.

Jacob, Sonny and Mishka looked around, awed by where they were and quickly dispersed to stow their gear and go swimming.

Dragon carried Raven to their bedroom, tired from his flight but knowing she needed him. He could have left her asleep but decided to wake her because that was what she would have wanted. He held her against him, like a sleeping child. Kissing her softly, she responded from her sleep, seeing him there for her.

All of her awareness was focused on her desire for him and her relief to feel his arms around her, his smell, and his warmth. It was pushing the memories away for her, the feeling of fear and vulnerability she had come to know since the rape. She needed him near her or she didn't feel safe.

He made love to her, keeping her under him until she was calm again, consoling her, making her safe again in his arms.

"Did you have a hard time baby?" he asked. She answered him softly. "I can't be away from you I guess." "I know angel, I just wanted to get back," he said. "It's Ok now," she said. She curled into him. "Yes it is," he agreed. He held her for a little longer until he could feel Sensei's pull.

"We should go back out there and see what those boys are doing," he said. "But I don't want to put my clothes back on," Raven said. "Here," Dragon said. He handed her one of his shirts. She took it from him and it was warm and smelled like him and she pulled it on. "We just have to visit with Damascus' boys and I need to look at that profile with Sensei," Dragon said. "And then I will bring you back here and finish what we started." "Ok baby," she said. She took his hand and let him pull her from the room.

Damascus and Jacob were having a poolside battle, which Jacob lost, getting shoved in. They had gone through a few beers and were having a good time. Sarge and Wax were sipping some scotch with Sensei, offering Dragon one, which he took. Dragon sat in a chaise and Raven curled up on his lap, not needing anything but him at the moment.

Sensei went and got a laptop and opened Chekov's latest profile. There were pictures of Lee Tran and a complete run down of the business affairs of Tran International. It was indicated Lee Tran only did business in person. He owned 25% of the shares in a division of his company; Tran Mining Inc. and the rest were divided into smaller public holdings, leaving him the major share holder.

They studied the info Chekov had accumulated regarding Trans interest in homosexual undertakings, seeing he was indeed interested in child pornography involving young boys. There was not a lot of history on his father-in-law's past, only that he was now a wealthy real estate investor in Hong Kong's expensive housing market, owning high rises and hotels through a company registered as New West Development Corp.

"I'll go in for 25% then," Dragon said. "Just to piss him off for making me go there. If he needs to see me so badly he can be partners with me." "It's interesting that Tran has attempted to contact you," Sensei said. "Usually we approach subjects we are suspicious of. It's like we are being invited to walk right into a situation." Dragon eyed him. "Do you suspect something?" "Yes, but I always do," Sensei said. "I will think on it. At this point it just raises my suspicions because it seems too easy." "Get Chekov to go over things again, examine everything again and try to be sure it's just random," Dragon said. "And even if

Tran is trying to make contact with me for reasons other than a share offering, we should proceed and find out why. We can defend ourselves if we have to."

The rest of the profile dealt with details of the mining venture. It did look lucrative and would be a good investment no matter how things turned out otherwise, especially if Tran accepted Dragon's offer of 25%.

"Well, let's discuss this with Chekov tomorrow and decide when to do it," Dragon said. They all nodded, except Raven who was lost in Dragon's embrace, happily lying against him as he held her. "After Chekov responds to Tran that I will meet him, maybe we could leave it for a month or something, and then go. That would give us a decent amount of time to relax and for Wax to heal completely." "We will check with him in the morning and see what he says then," Sensei said. They sipped their drinks and paused, thinking.

"Whatever, anything works for me," Wax said. "Me too," Raven said. It was the first time she had spoken since they had come out of their room.

Dragon smoothed her hair absentmindedly, feeling her relaxed mood as she lay warm against him. He loved the way she never questioned anything and was happy all the time, just to be together. They sat finishing their drinks with Sensei, feeling the peace of the night, looking at the stars. He hardened under her as she traced her fingers over his bare chest, telling him anytime he wanted her she would lay back for him, giving him a mental image of her on the bed, which made him harder as they sat there.

Sarge and Wax eyed each other. "Typical," Sarge said. "Shut up Sarge," she said. "How many times have you done it today, considering we were gone for half of it?" Sarge asked. "The usual ten?"

"Likely," Sensei said. He was preparing to give them his psychological analysis. "I'm out of here," Dragon said. He tossed his drink back and pulled Raven to the bedroom.

"Sensei, you can tell us all you want that there's a psychological reason for how they are but the fact is they just like to fuck each other, end of story. She's sexy as hell and he can't help himself and Dragon's Dragon. If I was a woman I'd want to fuck him all day too. It's that simple if you ask me," Sarge said. Wax laughed then. "Ok, moving on," Sensei said.

He eyed Damascus and the others. They had been listening to the profile and waiting now for Sensei to tell them what to do. Damascus had been sleeping in Sensei's room with him. There had been room made for the boys in the common building and they were ready to turn in as their travel had been lengthy that day and a few beers and a little fun had worn them out. They all made plans for Yoga the next morning, and a work out. Maybe they would have some fun in the afternoon Sensei had promised. Maybe take the Dream Weaver to the waterfall with everyone, and have a sunset dinner on board.

They ended a peaceful night and Sensei retired, sitting in his meditative pose at the bottom of his bed which held a sleeping Damascus, peaceful and serene. Wax was sound asleep and dreamless in his bed, his heart free and clear and his mind sound. Sarge was dreaming about a girl somewhere. Dragon lay on top of Raven taking them somewhere into the Stratosphere with everything he had left to give her that night.

In the morning, they all had breakfast together. Damascus would be there soon as he had gone to the common to show his guys where to eat and take care of things, and introduce them to everyone.

Sensei greeted them when they arrived. They were all fit, however had not done Yoga likely since leaving the jungle, so he knew he needed to take it somewhat easy on them, which would surely earn them crap from everyone else. They would have to get used to it, being around here now.

"I hope you ladies remember how it's done," Dragon said.

Damascus just laughed, because what they didn't know was that he had kept up with it while they were at HQ and had convened them each morning just as they had always done.

"Go ahead Sensei, we're ready," he said. "Being proper ladies, we're ready to kick some ass."

So Sensei took them all through to the entire, most difficult level, just as they had always done together and sure enough all of them completed every pose as if they had never missed a day.

Marietta never tired of watching them. It made her morning kitchen duties quite enjoyable. Not only were they fabulous to look at from a female eye, they were skilled and impressive. She never understood what yoga was other than an exercise form, but was stunned by the physical difficulty of some of the moves and poses, respecting the years it would have taken to achieve them.

They all sat in their final sitting position, relaxing and letting their breathing return to normal, minds clear and energy balanced. Sensei finally spoke, letting them know he was done with them.

Sarge let himself fall backward from his sitting position so his head lay between Damascus and Jacob. Looking up at them as they still held the final position, he grinned as they eyed him.

"One of you can spot me on the press and I'll show you how that's done," he said. "Maybe you'd like to suck my dick," Damascus said. Sarge laughed. "Just because Dragon sucked it for you in Dubai doesn't mean I'm going to."

"Fuck off Sarge," Dragon said. "Or I'll make you suck mine right now."

"All of you!" Sensei said. "End this conversation now or instead of an afternoon at the waterfall you'll be picking pineapples." "Hai Sensei," they mumbled.

They got themselves together to head to the workout room. Dragon and Sarge ended up face to face on the now crowded patio and burst out laughing, their posturing returning to its usual good natured humor. "I'd like to see you try," Sarge whispered. They both laughed at the mental image of it. "Stop it you two," Raven cautioned. "Sensei was serious. He has to manage this entire testosterone frat house shit, so stop pissing him off!"

"She's right." Sensei seemed to appear from nowhere. He had clearly heard them. "Maybe just you two would like to spend a week away in the pineapple fields. I hear its lovely work, and Dragon; you could try and make Sarge suck your dick all you want in the privacy of your camp tent."

It was all Damascus could do to keep himself and his boys from laughing out loud. He turned and eyed them quickly and they took off down the hallway to the gym and laughed once they were behind the closed door. Wax had turned away, with Raven, also stifling their laughter, trying to look busy piling up the towels. They also retreated to the gym, but not before they caught Dragon's response, and then Sensei's, which made them laugh even more.

"Um, no thank you Sensei," Dragon said. He had replied politely and with a respectful apologetic tone. Sensei just stood feigning ignorance. "Really? Well your behavior and that of Sergeant Willis is telling me otherwise. Are you sure? I'm confused now," Sensei said.

"I was only kidding when I said I would like to see him try," Sarge said. Sensei nodded. "Oh I see now, the two of you think it's funny," he said. He was trapping them now. "Yes, um I mean No," Sarge said.

"No, Sensei," Dragon said. Sensei stood, waiting for the rest. "Time and a place, please excuse us Sensei," Dragon said. He knew what he wanted to hear.

"Listen you two, I expect a higher level of behavior in the presence of the younger boys and you know that, so don't forget it again," Sensei snapped. "Observe my boundaries on that or I will make an example of you to earn back the respect you seem to have selective disregard for."

Dragon simply nodded to him then, and Sarge looked at the ground. Sensei rarely took this tone with them, and when he did they took him seriously.

"Join the others, and start with basics. I am going to speak with Chekov and I will be there afterward," Sensei said.

Dragon and Sarge eyed each other and Sarge followed him as Dragon headed for the workout room. When they got to the closed door Sarge caught Dragon's arm. "Wait, Damascus started all this shit," he said. Dragon just shook his head. "Sensei doesn't care, you heard him. We need to tone it down sometimes," he said. "But I always set a bad example, everyone knows that," Sarge complained. "Time and a place Sarge, and you know how he is about Yoga. We were fucking around. It was disrespectful and it allowed Damascus to be disrespectful. Do you get that?" Dragon said. He went to push the door open. "Kick some ass in here. You'll feel better."

When the door opened, the room went silent. "Where's Papa?" Raven asked. "He'll be here in a minute, he's talking to Chekov," Dragon said. Sarge snaked himself up to Damascus, who was eyeing him with a mischievous grin. "I'm going to kick your ass," Sarge said.

Damascus just smirked at him and knowing not to start anything at the moment he said nothing. They all proceeded to warm up and take themselves through their basic routines until Sensei finally arrived.

"My dear, come and we can use the ball," he said to Raven. He paused then in front of Dragon. "Dragon, take Damascus and Jacob through squats please."

He sent Dragon a mental note to pass his message from earlier on to Damascus in whatever way he saw fit. Sarge went with Wax to the bench press and as he stepped away from Damascus he smirked back at him.

"You're fucked now," he whispered.

Damascus didn't react but knew he was right. He and Jacob followed Dragon to the machine to accept their fates. "I'm going to make this as unpleasant as possible for you," Dragon said. He was smiling, not taking his eyes off of them. "Jacob didn't say anything, it was me," Damascus said. "Guilty by association then," Dragon said. "Jacob likes to follow your example Damascus, so why don't you set one for him?"

He then proceeded to torture them both. In the end they were grateful as it pushed them beyond what they thought they could endure and Dragon had not gotten the better of them but had bettered them in their own opinion and in his.

CHAPTER TWENTY EIGHT

FUN AND GAMES

Marietta was in the kitchen and appeared to be nearly ready with their lunch. They all came into the main room, shiny, hot and bulging muscle everywhere, dying to jump in the pool. After lunch, they sat outside settling, while Damascus and the boys went swimming. They discussed their plans with Sensei for the rest of the day. Kona and Marietta would join them, and mind the yacht while they all went to the waterfall, then they would sail back slowly, and have a moonlight dinner.

They were ready to go and had taken what they needed for the trip over to the yacht already. Raven had on a bright pink string bikini with white Hawaiian flowers on it and all of them just had board shorts, it was such a hot day. They piled into the Zodiac and headed for the Dream Weaver. Jacob, Sonny and Mishka had never seen anything like it and were amazed. Hawaii itself was such a beautiful place and as they headed out along the shore in the blue pristine waters, it was like a little piece of heaven for all of them.

Raven grabbed Sarge and dragged him into the galley to make Mai Tai's. Marietta was stowing things and organizing. She was going to make them a wonderful dinner. Sarge and Raven amused her with their comedic bantering while they made the drinks. They emerged to the stern deck a short time later and set the pitcher with some glasses on the serving table so the guys could help themselves. Dragon was on the flying bridge explaining some boat stuff to Jacob and Sonny, while Damascus and Mishka had gone to the foredeck and were watching the blue water disappear beneath them as they cruised along.

It was just Wax and Sensei and Raven and Sarge for the moment and they toasted themselves.

She relaxed against Sarge, while she waited for Dragon.

"That was hot earlier," Sarge said. "That was lovely my dear," Sensei agreed.

She had performed a handstand on the exercise ball, letting her legs fall to the sides in a perfect right angle to her body, while Sensei spotted her.

"I was just trying to distract you Sarge so you'd drop the bench on yourself," she said. "Figures," he said.

He wrapped his arms around her and tipped his icy Mai Tai so it dripped freezing liquid down her cleavage. She squealed from it in his grasp, cursing him in French. Dragon had just climbed down the ladder from the bridge but declined to translate it considering Sensei's earlier admonishing remarks.

Instead, he pulled her from Sarge's hold, sitting next to them on the bench. Holding her in front of him he sexily licked the cold sweet liquid from her cleavage. Tasting her skin, kissing her breast, he wanted to take her top off. Sensei cleared his throat, as Sonny and Jacob eyed them.

Dragon ceased his assault on her but he had drawn her into his sensual thoughts making her need him. She leaned against him, standing between his legs and put her arms around his neck. 'Take me inside for a minute please,' she thought to him. He stood then, letting her body hide his erection from the others. Before Sensei could scold him he shoved Raven ahead of him into the cabin.

He pushed her face down on the bed. "You're going to get me in trouble," he said. "It's your fault for licking me," she said. He nearly tore her bikini bottom off her, pulling open his shorts at the same time. "You need it? Well you're going to get it," he said.

Holding her hips he slammed himself into her. She cried out at the feel of it. He knew she would be wet enough for him to take that approach with her and he needed to make it quick. He stood at the edge of the bed and buried himself in her over and over again. Driving into her one last time, pushing her over the edge into her orgasm, he waited until she had fully come on him then pulled out of her, squirting white thick mess onto her back, groaning as it exploded from him hot and wet all over her.

He cleaned himself off her back with a wet cloth while she still lay panting. "We have to go back out there sweetheart," he said. She rolled over, letting her thighs fall open, looking up at him. "You have to wait," he said. "Since when do you care what anyone thinks baby," she said. "Sensei ripped me a new one earlier, we have to behave in front of the boys," he said. She wasn't sure she liked this; he had never denied her before, never been able to deny her. "Ok," she said.

She found her bikini bottom and put it on and reached for the door. She turned the handle and pulled it open, not understanding what had just happened between them. Lost in her strange thoughts, she was shocked into awareness when he reached out and pushed the door shut again and stepped in front of it as she took a step back. She looked into his eyes and his mind then, completely confused.

"What Dragon? Did you just fuck me because you had to?" she asked. "You turned me on like you always do. I thought you wanted to. Did I do something wrong?" She was nearly in tears then. "Am I supposed to feel ashamed because I want you?"

She was trembling now, wanting him to hold her, afraid he was angry with her, even though he had never been angry with her. Her mind slipped and she began to doubt. Fear was creeping in, scaring her that things would not be the same between them because of the rape.

He was angry at himself then. He knew he had hurt her feelings and confused her. He felt her pain, seeing her fears and her doubts in her mind and cursed himself for being insensitive. He needed to fix this for her. He looked down into her anxious eyes. It broke his heart because they used to be always happy, where now there was pain and doubt.

"Do you still want me?" he asked. His half smile was on his lips and he was smoldering for her now. He took a step toward her. "Yes," she whispered. He took another step. "Are you ashamed of that?" he asked. "No!" With conviction she flashed her eyes at him. "Good," he said. "And for the record, I don't give one single fuck what anyone thinks, except you. And I want nothing more than to take you to pieces right now." Holding her to him then he kissed her softly. "But I'm going to ask you to wait."

He had let her 'see' what Sensei had said to him and Sarge, so she could understand his behavior.

She looked up at him and nodded. "Ok baby, I'm sorry, you're right," she said. "Sometimes I don't remember that there are other people in the world besides you and me." He smiled at her cuteness and kissed her forehead. "And I love that world sweetheart and later we can pretend exactly that, all night if you want." "I love you," she said. "Good," he said.

Sarge pulled the yacht around to where they were the last time they were there and they set the anchor. Because of the surf they had to paddle to the beach from about 75 meters off shore. They all decided to just swim because the surf was cresting on the beach and they would just have to swim through it. They made it there and the waves pulled at them as they fought their way free of the ocean.

It was all a wonderful adventure and they couldn't wait to move forward. They made their way along the narrow sandy trail, upward along the edge of the runoff stream. And as before they came to the part where it got steeper and it became a rock climb. Again Raven led them as she was the most agile, showing them the foot holds and the way to go. They followed, climbing until they were all there standing on the black sand.

Sensei felt it, when their feet touched it. There were welcoming spirits surrounding them, pulling them into the waters and to the waterfall to feel its happiness and peace. It was what had drawn Dragon forward before and was drawing them all now. Sensei knew what was there because he could 'see' it. He moved them forward and they all followed into the pool of beautiful green water. No one spoke as there were no words for its beauty and the feelings they were having.

For Sensei, lights danced, energy weaved through the air, surrounding them.

They had each found a spot and seemed to be individually focused on some aspect of the waterfall's beauty.

Damascus sat crossed legged and was examining the lava rock in front of him with his fingertips, fascinated by its color and formation. Sarge and Wax had sat where they had before on an outcrop, with their legs hanging freely over the side. They were watching upward as the water fell from above, it's endless motion fascinating and if you stayed looking at it, somehow it seemed to not be moving at all.

Dragon and Raven had gone to the outcrop behind the falling water and sat against the wall, he was cross legged and she sat on him, also cross legged, leaning back against him as he folded her in his arms. He was not going to make love to her there this time but the overwhelming love they had felt before was there and he held her, feeling their heart beats as just one, shared between them. Their minds blended as images of them together moved about in their heads.

Jacob and Sonny stayed on the lower rocks with their feet in the water, feeling its smoothness and softness. The glassy reflections of the surrounding rocks and trees played a visual trick on their minds as they stared. The water was so soft to the touch it almost magically disappeared as Jacob ran his fingers through it.

For Mishka, things had been intense. He sat by himself on a rock, the mists of the waterfall around him. He hugged his knees into his body and let the feel of the mist cover him. It was like a warm coating, cleansing him of some things. He had somehow received clarity all of a sudden and he felt free now.

Many things had travelled through Sensei's mind as he had meditated into the world around him. He saw futures, he saw pasts, he saw the present, and he learned things. Most notably, he had a vision. Looking at the scars on Damascus's back, they had disappeared before his eyes. Then he had seen a plant, native to the island, growing freely that he could obtain and make a substance to heal the scars off his body with. He had seen clearly how to do it, like he had known it all along.

He had seen a possible future for Dragon and Raven, seen Mishka accept an alter ego he had been denying and he had seen things about all of them which had brought him a peace and contentment. They all sat for awhile longer, mesmerized by the surroundings. Then when Sensei stood and walked to a different spot to admire some of the foliage, the boys felt safe to explore and be playful.

Damascus found them a place to get higher up where they could dive from. They entertained Sarge and Wax with their antics, holding a mock Olympic competition which Sarge and Wax judged harshly. It was very amusing, making Raven giggle at their remarks. Dragon and she had joined Sarge and Wax on the ledge watching the boys take turns diving into the water. They wanted Damascus and his team to have a fun day because tomorrow Sensei was putting them to work.

Dragon had been leaning against the rock face next to Sarge and Wax and Raven was against him, her head on his chest. They had shared a long wet passionate kiss and had lost track of how long they had been caught up in it. It had to end when Dragon could feel Sensei intruding politely as it was time to go. They had all been unaware that over two hours had passed and they still had nearly an hour trek back.

They all followed him obediently away from the magical place. They had just enough energy left to make it through the surf and back to the stern platform. They didn't need towels; as it was so hot from the sun they would be dry soon. They lifted anchor and began their sail back to their beach and dinner.

Damascus and his boys had tired themselves out and lay around on the stern deck napping in the sun. Dragon and Raven went to the flying bridge with Sarge and Wax and Sensei, so Sarge could pilot and the breeze would keep them cool enough under the late afternoon sun.

Kona and Marietta had been in the galley finishing off the dinner. Marietta had prepared them a traditional Hawaiian menu. They were still cruising home while they ate. Kona manned the helm for Sarge while they enjoyed dinner. Sensei had complimented Marietta on everyone's behalf. He was familiar with most of the Hawaiian dishes she had prepared and was mastering them himself. Hawaii lent itself nicely to their style of eating having many species of fish right at hand, that weren't found in any other waters. They were finishing up with the food, just as the sun had dropped down in the west behind the island as they pulled up to their mooring in front of their beach.

It was still very warm as the evening dimmed and they sat relaxing together on the stern deck, drinking Mai Tai's and talking. Sensei summoned Mishka to the fore deck, away from the others. Damascus and Jacob and Sonny eyed each other, pretty sure they knew what it was about.

Mishka was the same age as the others, 21 or so. He was 5' 11', same as Damascus, and had a muscular build. He was mostly Russian in descent and was a favorite of the girls at HQ, just like they all had been. He was a stunning combination; creamy even skin, dark nearly black hair, with deep navy blue eyes and a strong jaw line. Girls liked him and so did men. He had a similar past to Dragon's.

Growing up, Mishka had been kept, sold as a child to a wealthy Russian aristocrat. Homosexuality was against the law more or less in Soviet Russia, so he and others were kept a secret, living in a remote village, visited regularly by their benefactor. Different from Dragon's past, he was treated well, never beaten and allowed freedoms.

He was however severely sexually abused before he was recovered by one of HQ's teams. His owner was attempting to sell him because he had gotten past the age he desired. He was found during a raid on a Black Market trafficking ring.

His past left him uncertain of his sexuality. He had read the Kama Sutra as they all did and Sensei had been long working with him to sort out his sexual definition. He was heterosexual but had developed an ability to be bisexual to seek the affections of his male captor, out of loneliness, desperation and misguided role modeling. In a misrepresentation of love, Mishka had loved his captor.

He was however, sexually attracted to females and had very much enjoyed his time at HQ with many of the willing girls there. He didn't understand why he also had the capacity to find males attractive as well.

"Mishka, I know you know now," Sensei said. "Yes Sensei, something at that waterfall happened in my head," Mishka said. "You are simply bisexual son and need to accept that about yourself. Are you able to understand now, what I have been telling you?" Sensei asked. "Yes, I'm attracted to what I'm attracted to. Gender isn't really a deciding factor," Mishka said. "Yes son, a very common developmental issue for children who grew up such as you did. It's not a flaw or something to be afraid of," Sensei said. "Dragon had no sexuality whatsoever, he hated any form of it, hated it about himself and hated that it existed," Sensei said. "What?" Mishka said. He found that unbelievable. "Yes, and look at him now," Sensei grinned. "Seriously," Mishka said.

"Well, on that note, I will caution you as I did Damascus. You boys had quite the time of it at HQ, and as you all are still working through issues, whether they be sexual or emotional, or both, it is best to abstain from any further meaningless ventures for the time being," Sensei said.

Mishka smiled and nodded. "It's Ok Sensei; I'd prefer to stay focused on the things we need to do here and just do our jobs. HQ was Ok but it was lonely and we missed everyone and we missed having stuff to do besides practicing shooting and practicing fucking," he said. Sensei smiled at his reference. "Have you kept up with your studies and your craft?" he asked.

Mishka had an I.Q. well into the genius levels and was a math wizard, chess master and computer program designer. He also had a hobby. He could pick locks, any kind of locks and he could also design the software necessary to do it.

"Yes Sensei, I think I'm close to finishing a program for the best anti-security device I've thought of yet," Mishka said. "Chekov and I were working on it." Sensei put his arm around him. "I will look forward to seeing that. Now come here," he said.

He pulled Mishka into an embrace, transmitting his warm supportive thoughts to the boy, pleased he was relieved of his sense of confusion today. He hoped he could accept himself and allow himself to move forward in life without questions anymore.

They rejoined the others, who were into their second or third Mai Tai and visibly becoming more animated. Marietta and Kona had taken the Zodiac and headed in for the evening. Wax was providing tunes from his iPod and things were showing every sign of heading south.

Sensei eyed the situation and raised an eyebrow at Dragon. Dragon knew he was expected to set an example and he never did get drunk, but couldn't say the same for Sarge and sometimes Wax. He told them all to finish it up for the night, giving Sarge a knowing look.

He wanted to take Raven to bed soon anyway. She looked so sexy, curled up softly next to him, her hair loose and everywhere. She looked up to him in the lamplight, her tanned face glowing, her sweet lips innocent and begging him to kiss them.

"Mmm baby," he said. He took her face in his hands, feeling her smooth skin on her cheeks with his thumbs. "Come here," he whispered. He kissed her softly and wetly. Holding his mouth to hers he pulled her to sit astride him and hide his erection which he gently pushed against her. "I need to take you to bed," he said.

They all decided to swim ashore. It was refreshing and a good idea after all. The boys were wrestling in the outdoor shower, entertaining Wax and Sarge. Sensei just shook his head, telling Damascus he would see him at the house. Dragon had wrapped Raven around him and was heading for their bathroom shower, with one thing on his mind.

He hit the shower on and she was dying for him now, biting his neck, moving her hips against him as he held her. He pulled their things off them and moved them into the warm streaming water. Leaning back on the wall, he slid himself inside her warm body as he held her, moaning at the feel of finally having her around him again. He began sexily kissing her mouth and her neck as the water streamed over her pulling her hair off her face. She was so sexy, wet and shiny hard against him; her nipples aroused brushing his chest muscles, driving him crazy.

The water washed over them, taking away the oceans salty residue. She clung to him, dying for him to give her enough motion to make her come. He turned around so her back was against the shower wall and pinning her he gave it to her, driving into her until she was there and he could feel her wetness around him, her contractions squeezing him, her nails digging into his back. He waited for her to finish then pulled out of her letting her down to her knees in front of him, tipping her head back and ejaculating in hard spurts. He held himself so most of it made it over her lips and tongue for her to lick up. The shower rinsed the rest away.

He pulled her to her feet and into his arms, kissing her. He shut the water off, wrapping a towel around them as he carried her to the bed. He laid her back on the bed, in the towel, making her moan with desire for him. He gave her his sexy half smile, knowing he was driving her crazy.

Her eyes flashed to him, begging him to do it to her. The feel of his tongue on her made her wild. The way he did it, the sensation of it and the erotic vision of it in her mind drove her over the edge every time. She couldn't open herself enough to him, pulling her knees back even farther, exposing her sensitive parts to his persistent tongue even more. She squirmed against him so much he held her down with his hands on her thighs so he could finish it for her.

She ran her fingers into his hair as he softly licked her everywhere, letting her settle; her libido resting for a moment. He moved up her body, pausing at her nipples, then letting her lick her taste from his lips, wanting to hold her before he finished them both for the night.

They didn't need to speak verbally, they just lay together thinking their thoughts into each other's minds. All she needed now was for him to make love to her and put her to sleep. She had been softly running her hand up down his erection, gently getting him ready to be in her. He was already fully hard anyway, but she pressured him in just the right spots, making him need it from her. He kissed her more urgently now as she stroked him harder. His lips trembled slightly. "Careful baby you'll make me come," he said. He breathed the words between kisses. "Fuck me then baby," she said.

She lay back, taking him and pressing him inside her as he rolled on top of her. He moaned into her hair, moving against her, holding her tightly to him, her soft body enveloped by him, as he loved her with everything he had. They had lay in each other's arms, warm and wet until Dragon had put them to sleep for the night.

Sensei arrived an hour earlier than usual, waking Dragon for tea. They discussed the plans for the day which consisted of yoga and the usual things, beginning with hand to hand combat practice. Then they had surfing plans after they helped Damascus locate a site for a Flags course.

"It should all work out fine," Sensei said. "Raven can come with me to look for the plants I need." "Have you heard from Chekov about Tran?" Dragon asked. "Yes, Tran is pleased you wish to meet him, and it has been set up three weeks from now, if that is alright with you," Sensei said. "You can't make it direct to Hong Kong from Honolulu, so it will take forever to get there. He will have an itinerary for you in a few days." Dragon shrugged, not wanting to think about it.

Sensei had left and he had made love to her as usual. They emerged later to join the others for a quick breakfast then Yoga. Damascus and Sonny were in a heated but animated confrontation over who could kick whose ass in mixed martial arts. Sarge wagered Sonny could kick Damascus' ass just to piss Damascus off. Wax was staying out of it, until he saw Dragon.

"Now here's the man whose getting his ass kicked today," Wax said.

Dragon and Wax loved to spar, in any of the disciplines. They were relatively evenly matched in size and skills and it often came down to who got a lucky break to decide a victor. Dragon eyed him back and shrugged offhandedly at him.

"It's a nice day, maybe you'll get lucky," he said. Wax just grinned at him. Raven gave Wax a kiss on the cheek. "You feeling like a fight today Waxy?" she asked. "You didn't wear him out already did you baby girl? You left me something I hope," he said. She smiled at him, playing back his sexiness. "We ran out of time, or I would have," she said. Sensei cleared his throat, as he noticed Marietta was listening to them.

Raven flashed her eyes at Wax, just to amuse him, not saying anything further, minding Sensei's warning. Damascus and Sonny had toned it down as well and they finished eating with no further antics. They would save it for the practice. They concentrated on their Yoga for the next hour, getting their bodies to yield to their requests and relaxing their minds, preparing to take on the tasks of the day.

Hand to hand combat practice varied in degrees, depending on how far Sensei thought they should go, what they needed to work on and who was in what mood. They had basics to go through, then specifics, then free for all, for whoever wanted to go that far.

They always warmed up with a series of basic Shotokan Karate Katas, which they all knew and followed as Sensei led them through the ancient art form of Samurai combat. Having completed them, they went on to attacks and defenses in pairs, orchestrated moves back and forth, non contact. Dragon and Wax attacked each other aggressively, pushing each other, cutting it close, cutting no corners and cutting no slack. They were impressive to watch and as close as it came to the real thing, should any of them ever need to fight for real. The whole lesson showed the necessity for quickness, agility, strength and awareness.

They practiced things for awhile longer until it was Wax and Dragon's turn to let loose. The others watched as they prepared for a full on mixed martial arts, grappling free for all, no holds barred fight. Raven liked to watch Dragon fight; it was something he needed to do. For some reason Wax had it in him as well and they went for it on occasion and under certain circumstances. Sensei would let them, as long as it stayed under control. It was full contact; there would be black eyes, bruises, cuts and ice packs when it was over.

They went at it, using martial arts initially, looking for a way to get the other to the ground. Wax was fast and a quick starter, getting aggressive right out of the gate. He had gone with a number of fast jabs which Dragon deflected but had spun with a fast hard round house. Dragon saw it coming and blocked and avoided it, but in doing so left a hole in his upper guard which Wax filled with a right hook. It caught Dragon high on the left brow, as he ducked but not enough, splitting the skin of his brow. Wax was on fire and didn't stop, taking a huge offensive run at him, causing Dragon to be in the defensive more than he liked.

He knew he better change things fast or Wax would connect with one that would take him down. Wax had gotten another on him, using a series of hits that he couldn't defend all together, causing another split across his nose, between his eyes. He was going to have to take him down soon. Seeing an opportunity after letting Wax nail him in the ribs, he stepped away in a spinning momentum and caught Wax behind the leg, hard in the hamstring muscle, with a backward round house. It made him stagger.

In that split second that Wax was off balance Dragon was on him, taking him fully to the ground in a grappling hold. He twisted his arm back and up behind his back and elbowed him hard, hitting him squarely in the temple to stun him and it worked. Wax fell flat and stop resisting, wavering half conscious, allowing Dragon to flatten him and pin him, pulling his arm back in a submissive tap out hold.

Dragon was bleeding profusely from two face wounds and Sensei decreed a tie, as Wax had more points for hits even though Dragon had technically won the fight, nearly knocking Wax out cold. They were both a mess and Sensei then wondered how he was going to explain it to Marietta if she saw them.

"Ok, nice work boys, but come, Dragon you need stitches and Wax an ice bag, both of you." He fussed, worried about them now. Dragon pulled Wax to his feet and they fell into a golf cart with Raven and went to the house. Damascus and Jacob discussed it over and over again with Sonny and Mishka, reliving what they would have done and how awesome this was and totally cool that was, as they walked back to the house with Sarge.

"Now that's another level," Sarge said. "Ya no kidding," Damascus said. "I would love to actually go for it, but they'd kick my ass. They're both huge." "Why don't you and Jacob go at it or Mishka?" Sarge asked. Damascus looked at Sarge, pissed off. "Why don't you and Dragon go at it or Wax?" Damascus said. "Oh yes, because they'd kick your ass for you."

Sarge stopped walking and shoved Damascus. "Why don't you fuck off?" he said. "Why don't you try not being such a huge fucking dick?" Damascus said. "Maybe I am one because maybe I have one," Sarge said. It was getting even more juvenile by the second. "There's a fine line between reality and delusion," Damascus said. He shoved Sarge back, getting him off him.

Sarge's temper flared out of control then like a flash fire. "I'm going to kick your ass right now," he said. "You have it coming you fucking prick, you got us in shit earlier and I'm sick of you annoying the hell out of me." Angry now, Damascus yelled back in Sarge's face. "Bring it on, you fucked up asshole!"

They launched into their own free for all then. Sarge was sick of Damascus' smart mouth and wanted to shut it for him and Sarge's antics had pissed Damascus off for years and he was more than ready to exact vengeance. Sarge was bigger, older and more experienced but Damascus didn't care, he would go down trying. Jacob, Sonny and Mishka didn't interfere, knowing the two Alpha personalities needed to sort it out on their own.

They fought it out, hitting each other repeatedly, before falling to the ground and grappling it out. It was hard for Sarge to pin him even though he outweighed him, because Damascus had learned well from Sensei about using his smaller size to make it harder to get him. He was fast and tough and it was only Sarge's undying commitment and resilience to pain that got him through.

It was dirty and ugly but Sarge did it in the end. He had pinned Damascus eventually but they both had bloody noses, broken lips, black eyes and bruised knuckles. They looked worse than Dragon and Wax, as their fight was a fight, with intention to hurt each other. It had resembled a bar fight rather than a skilled execution of techniques.

Sensei was just finishing stitching Dragons eyebrow with three stitches when they came in, looking worried but needing his attention. Wax was slumped on the sofa, Raven holding an ice bag to the side of his face, when he looked up and saw them.

"What the fuck did you two do?" he said. Raven looked shocked at the sight of them. "Sarge for fuck sakes," she said. Sensei turned and eyed them. He finished Dragon's last stitch, holding gauze to it to clean the last of the dripping blood. "Ice now son," he said. He released him to Raven's care, turning his focus on Sarge and Damascus. "One of you explain this immediately," he snapped.

"My bad Sensei, I pissed Damascus off into a fight," Sarge said. "No he didn't, I pushed him over the edge," Damascus said. He was not about to let Sarge take credit for their follies. Sensei eyed them, his mind searching for the truth and deciding he had received it more or less. "Why don't you have a fight over who started the fight? Clean each other up then, if you're so fond of putting your hands on one another."

He inspected their wounds, deciding no stitches were needed, no broken bones, mostly bruises and dirt, and swelling. "Clean the cuts and use ice packs," he said. Dragon and Wax had eyed them with amusement. "Idiots," Wax said.

Sarge had heard and gave him the middle finger where Sensei couldn't see it. The bridge of his nose was swelling, he had an abrasion on his right cheek bone and half of his right eye had turned red from broken blood vessels and was turning purple underneath. Damascus was no better; sporting similar afflictions, one of his eyes would be closed in half an hour as broken capillaries filled his eye lid and under eye tissue with blood. Sensei moved to inspect it more closely, wondering if it needed to be drained.

They had all sat then, resting and drinking water, holding ice packs to their various areas. Wax nursed a blossoming headache that concerned Sensei, prompting him to suggest Wax not go surfing, wanting to keep an eye on him. Marietta arrived to get lunch, stopping cold staring at them.

"Don't worry my dear," Sensei said. "The boys enjoy a little Mixed Martial Arts, as part of their fitness routine. It's all in good fun." "Oh my," she said. She was thinking that they were an odd bunch.

"Ok, you boys get showered before lunch, put on some clothes and try to behave," he said. He wanted them out of Marietta's sight until they were looking more like gentlemen than unruly animal cage fighters.

They dispersed, quietly, Raven pulling Dragon by the hand to their room as he still held the ice pack to his forehead. She sat him on the bed and took the pack from him gently, eyeing the damage to the bridge of his nose. "Baby we can't let that swell or Sensei's stitches will pull and you'll have a scar. Why'd you let Waxy hit you so many times?" she said. "He was just fast, I don't know. He wanted it to go down that way so that's how it went. He wasn't going to open the door and wait for me to walk in," Dragon said. "I'm glad I got him down when I did though, or he would have had me eventually if he kept it up." "Ya baby, but I don't know, he has a bad headache. Maybe you guys shouldn't fight for real like that, you could really hurt one another," she said. It worried her then.

"Come here sweetheart," he said. He pulled her into his embrace as he sat on the bed. He kissed her. "Just let me love you in the shower OK? Then I'll be good as new."

She smiled a sexy smile at him, giving him a picture of what she would save for him, for their car ride to the beach after. He let his head fall back, moaning at the thought of it, fully hard in his shorts now.

"Baby undress me now, I'm going to explode just thinking about that," he said.

They made it quick, he took her once on the bed when they got naked and then again in the shower, up against the wall. They soaped each other after with wonderful smelling body wash Marietta had put there and emerged shiny and clean for lunch, even before Sarge and Wax.

Damascus was sitting waiting, his spikes drying over his now completely swollen shut eye and the rest of his hair lay wetly down the back of his neck. His knuckles were swelling and turning a blue red. Jacob, Sonny and Mishka walked in moments later, as Marietta laid the lunch out for them. Sensei had been at the laptop at the desk emailing Chekov, as it was not appropriate for them to speak in person at the moment.

Sarge appeared next, and Raven summoned him so she could apply the cream to the abrasion on his cheek bone. He complied, his one eye almost all red now and dark purple underneath it. She shook her head at him, but said nothing, not wanting to start anything with him. He obviously had his regrets, clearly showing on his face.

Wax had come back as well and Sensei went to him, laying a hand on his forehead. "You aren't going anywhere son, that's a mild concussion now, don't try and hide it," he said. Wax nodded, his head was hurting beyond comfort now. Dragon went and sat beside him. "Sorry man, it was me or you," he said. Wax smiled at him, eyeing his stitched brow and nose. "Fair enough," Wax said.

Dragon gave him a gentle shove. "No surfing lessons for you, so I guess I'll have to look stupid by myself this afternoon," he said. "Sarge will help you with that I'm sure. And take rain checks for the ladies I'm going to disappoint today," Wax said. Raven giggled, "Waxy, I'll take care of it for you and make wonderful promises to them for next time." "They'll just have to wait," Wax said.

Good natured as always, he smiled through his headache. Wax and Sarge were both popular with the girl's at Bobby's. She brushed a wet dread back from his face, noting his eye swelling shut on the side Dragon had elbowed him on.

"Poor baby," she said. It took a lot to knock Wax and he was clearly not himself. "Don't worry baby girl, I'm going to help Damascus build a 'Flags' course that caters to your Daddy's weaknesses, so we can kick his ass at something," Wax said. He winked at her and his comment got a sly knowing grin from Damascus and his one functional eye.

CHAPTER TENTY NINE

SURFING

They were heading to Bobby's that afternoon. You could get lessons right there on the beach out front. Raven had a white bikini with green Hawaiian flowers this time and a pair of little white matching board shorts over top. Dragon wore his usual navy blue board shorts with the white stripe that Raven thought made his butt look even sexier and a white T shirt, made of SPF 30 fabric. Her hair was loose, but she had a tie to put it up later for surfing. She pushed her sunglasses back on her head to hold it out of her face. Dragon couldn't wear his because of the cut on the bridge of his nose, which pissed him off in the bright afternoon sun.

He sat on the door of the Lamborghini and Raven stood between his knees and they kissed passionately. She was dying to get her hands on him in the car. Dragon looked over at Sarge, telling him to lead the way and not look back. Sarge was talking to himself about Dragon being an asshole as he hit the gas, pulling out of the garage ahead of them, a little faster than he needed to. The Ferrari's revs could be heard, letting Dragon know his thoughts.

Dragon let Sarge get ahead. He eyed her and she looked so sexy to him. She turned her pretty face towards him, smiling slightly, her eyes innocent, her lips soft and wanting, her mane of hair everywhere. Her breasts were so sweet in her little bikini top he wanted to devour her.

"My god baby, you turn me on," he said.

She licked her lips, her perfect white teeth just visible between them, as she pulled him out of his shorts. She said nothing, but let her eyes flash up to him as she leaned down and proceeded to mess him up. It was all he could do to keep his eyes on the road, as she drove him off the deep end.

"Oh fuck baby," he moaned. She was working on him and had him very close. "Don't stop," he gasped.

She brought him into it as she had promised him and made it very sweet for him. He exploded down her throat, trying not to close his eyes, trying to keep the wheel straight as it rolled over him, all the way up his thighs and into his belly, rocking his world like only she could do for him.

"Take your shorts off," he said. He managed it between breaths. "Take it all off."

He wanted her naked from the waist down. He pulled over, there was no one around and he jumped over the driver door, went around to her side of the car and pulled the door open. He knelt on the ground and pulled her thighs apart.

"You're going to get it now sweetheart," he said. He laid his tongue on her, making her cry out and grab him into her. She lay back over the console, draped her left foot on the dash board and held her right leg back for him. He devoured her, as she moved her hips into his skilled tongue. It took him less than a minute to make her leave the reality of it all over the car seat.

He kissed her sweetly when she was done, vaguely remembering where they were, as a pick-up truck of young surfer guys drove by, honking, yelling something at them. Raven burst out laughing, trying to sit up. He pulled her thighs together and sat back on his heels until they were out of sight. He was laughing then too.

"Shit they'll probably be at the beach," he said. Getting to his feet he moved back to the driver's seat of the idling car. "Oh well, fuck it," he said.

He hit the gas and sent gravel everywhere as he moved them back onto the road. She let her hand fall onto his thigh; leaning back in the seat, looking especially fucked then, her hair everywhere and that glassy look in her eyes.

"Baby, you're a bad boy," she said. "I am what I am but you deserved that after what you just gave me," he said.

She just smiled at him, and rubbed his thigh. They would be in town in a minute and Sarge was probably wondering what happened to them although he would likely guess. At the last minute she remembered to put her bottoms back on and her shorts, fastening them closed just as they pulled up to Bobby's beside the Ferrari.

Sarge was waiting so they headed into Bobby's together. It was all good until a voice was heard from across the bar as they entered. 'Yeah dude, way to rock the roadway.' Indeed the surfers that had caught them in the act were there. Dragon eyed them, smiling a megawatt grin at them and shrugging. Raven blushed slightly. He just waved a hand to the bartender as they passed by and a familiar waitress arrived at the table shortly after with Long Board beers.

They were vaguely aware of cameras and people now taking note of them. It sucked but not really because nothing sucked in Hawaii. They drank their beers then went out to the beach to meet for their surfing lessons. A girl named Stephanie took Sarge. They were well acquainted.

"Billy's waiting for you," Stephanie said. "Ok thanks," Raven said. "Have fun Sarge." She gave him a teasing eye. "Come on babe, let's do this," she said. She pulled Dragon to the waiting Billy.

"Hey dude," Billy said. "Raven, how's it going?" He was trying not to stare at her perfect body and failing. "Hey Billy," Dragon said. "Dude there's cameras and shit," Billy said. He handed them boards. "Ya I don't know," Dragon said. "That's seriously lame," Billy said. "Well anyway I don't give a fuck. Show me how to surf," Dragon said. "We'll rock some shit for sure dude," Billy said. "What happened to your face?" "MMA," Dragon said. "Awesome," Billy said.

It seemed like he was smiling and nodding at the same time as he dove into the oncoming wave. They paddled out beyond the break and turned waiting for the waves. They would worry later about what pictures of them wiping out would appear where, but for now it was time for some fun.

They spent the better part of the next three hours surfing. They had definitely gotten the hang of it and were now fully enjoying the whole experience. When they finally came ashore for good, Dragon told Billy to hook them up with boards, deliver them to the house, have a beer with them, whatever, and Billy had been happy to oblige.

"Sweet," Billy said. "Later man." He had jumped into a worn out Jeep with Marijuana leaf stickers on its' bumper and a peace sign dangling from the rear view mirror. Sarge and Stephanie had lingered back and were now kissing passionately on the sand. "My guess is we should just go baby," Raven said. "I think we've seen the last of Sarge for the night."

Dragon grinned at her and put his arm around her, walking to the car. The photographers had gotten their fill and dispersed awhile ago, likely to rush off and make deadline with whatever photos they were able to get. Tourists were roaming along slowly, taking in the shops, the surfers were hanging in Bobby's, discussing their "Sick" rides, and Sarge was going to make it happen with Stephanie as soon as he could get her back to her apartment.

All Dragon cared about was getting his hands on Raven as soon as he could, hitting the gas and speeding out of town. He had his hand between her legs the minute he got the chance, and she moaned at the sight of it. He had big hands and the sight of him covering her little parts made her crazy before he even started anything.

He screeched the tires up the driveway, whipping the little car into its parking spot. They were crazy for each other now and hoped no one except Sensei and Wax would see them, preferably no one, as they headed for the house. Dragon tossed the door open, dragging her behind him by her wrist. He didn't even look to see who was around and headed straight for their bedroom, picking her up and shoving them both through the door, kicking it shut behind him.

Sensei and Wax were out by the pool, having a Scotch. They looked at each other, and broke out laughing. Sensei just shook his head, knowing there was nothing to say.

Wax had worked hard all afternoon with Damascus and the boys building the 'Flags' course, his headache subsiding after awhile thanks to Sensei's ministering. Dragon was very right handed and had to work at doing anything to the left, so they had designed the course to handicap him. Damascus had passed out asleep for a few hours and the boys had gone back to the common, likely doing the same.

They all ate a light dinner together after, minus Sarge and Dragon and Raven. Sensei left them to their lovemaking, thinking it best after how they were when they came through the door earlier.

Sarge spent the night doing the Kama Sutra proud and making one beautiful Hawaiian girl fall madly in love with him. He made it to Yoga with maybe an hour of sleep, had managed a shower but hadn't combed his hair and eyed Raven for help.

Her night hadn't been much different except they had slept for about 6 hours. Dragon had been insane for her and used half a bottle of lubricant showing her how much he appreciated her sexy butt, amongst other things. He had a hickey on his lower belly which was hidden by his shorts and some now fading scratch marks on his back.

In the midst of Yoga she tried to push thoughts of it out of her mind as Sensei pushed them into a grueling hold of a difficult position. After when Sensei was satisfied that they were all of sound body and mind, more or less, Raven gave Sarge some loving, fixing his hair for him.

"What are you saying this morning Sergeant Willis?" she asked. "Seeexxxxxx, no more seeexxxx," he said.

"Sergeant Willis," Sensei said. "That young lady has responsibilities and so do you." "I think she can still walk," Sarge said. "Well if you spent all night and she can still walk then you're not doing it right," Sensei said. "Hai Sensei," Sarge said.

They were all laughing now. Sarge's eyes were still closed but a huge grin he couldn't suppress crossed his face. Sensei was funny when he wanted to be and Sarge couldn't resist laughing with them, even if he was the object of the joke.

Sensei took a glance around to be sure Marietta or Kona weren't nearby and then spoke. "Listen, as we are all here, on a serious note, we have the Hong Kong mission in two and a half weeks. We need to practice skills we may need, such as shooting, which we will do shortly. Dragon please read the profile and decide on the tactics, as soon as possible. HQ wants to know what you want at your disposal, what airports you want, and Blackhawks etcetera." "I thought that was Chekov's domain," Dragon said. "It is but he wants you to tell him what you want, um in light of the last missions' flaws, you are now required to stipulate how you want things done, in accordance with your experience and your comfort zone. It is one of the new mandates they've instituted, I hope you will agree it's a positive step," Sensei said. "You can speak to Chekov about this and he can fill you in on all the details, new procedures and changes."

After lunch, Dragon studied Chekov's profile regarding his upcoming meeting with Tran. "I think this can play out like the Mexico and Dubai thing. We will be in Hong Kong for business to meet Tran, do the stock purchase and find out what else he's in to. I'm not sure exactly how yet, until I meet him and find an 'in' somehow," Dragon said. "We'll need the usual basic weapons, guns only I think, one Blackhawk and we can get from the airport to the hotel in it and back. Damascus and the boys can keep in the background, just in case it gets ugly and we need them. Better safe than sorry as we are all well aware of now. Can you think of anything else Sensei?" he asked.

"Not for the moment other than I have always had suspicions regarding Tran's insistence on meeting you personally. You need to be really careful, that's all I know right now," Sensei said. Dragon eyed him, looking for something in him. "I'm always really careful." Sensei just looked back at him. "Yes I know, just let your sight tell you things, be aware, that kind of thing." He was not really sure himself.

The rest of the afternoon was spent leisurely. Sensei had given Damascus and the boys the afternoon off and they had gone to Bobby's and the beach to surf. They had taken Damascus's car and the Ferrari, which Dragon had lent them, wanting them to have a good time. Sarge had gone to bed and Wax was taking it easy still, listening to Dragon and Sensei plan the mission as Raven played with his dreads, separating them and conditioning them for him. She had remained quiet, absorbed in her task of grooming him, not really listening to the plans. She would do what was asked of her, same as always.

"It's a long fucking flight," Dragon said, checking a map, and calculating it. "Over 11 hours, we will have to stop at least once, actually twice, once in Los Angeles and then I think we should make it Paris, then Hong Kong. We can stop in Munich on the way back for a visit if you'd like to Sensei, but I don't know what Chekov was saying about it being a shorter flight from here. He was probably being an asshole," Dragon said. "Well, we're taking an overnighter in the city of lights and he can go fuck himself."

"Ya baby, Paris is nice," Raven said. "Well that's why we are stopping there," Dragon said. He was sending her an image of what he recalled doing to her in the elevator last time. "Really?" Sensei said.

He glared at Dragon for forgetting he also would get the message. It made Raven blush and giggle. She whispered to Wax what it was, and he eyed her approvingly. Dragon gave Sensei his fabulous smile, "Sorry, my bad."

CHAPTER THIRTY

PARIS

The Hotel Ritz Paris looked exactly as they remembered it. Dragon got out of the Limo, turning to take Raven's hand and helping her out. They were all dressed formally, suits and ties. Raven wore an off white jacket and skirt that matched Dragon's tie that he had wanted to hang himself with.

The questions began instantly and Dragon answered them briefly in perfect French, thrilling the reporters and onlookers. He advised he was on his way to Hong Kong on business but had to stop in the wonderful city that they had honeymooned in. As he curtailed the questioning, he embraced Raven and then gave them his most gorgeous smile, saying good day. He then proceeded inside with everyone.

As usual he was greeted by a waiting Manager who attended to seeing that they got to their suites with every possible thing they could ever want. The boys shared a suite, Wax and Sarge another, and he and Raven and Sensei their own. They had all agreed to meet in half an hour. They were tired from their travels and needed to unwind.

Damascus and the boys were overwhelmed and never thought they would be participating in the David Li missions. For the past years at HQ Munich they had toiled in jungles, dirty cities, cramped helicopters, slept in the back of trucks, or not at all and gone without showers for days. This was beyond what they thought possible.

Dragon had untied his tie and unbuttoned his shirt, shed his jacket and was drinking a Scotch with Sensei when Sarge and Wax knocked. Raven had a glass of champagne and sat like a lady on the lovely Louis IV sofa, her Louboutin heels sexily showing off her tanned legs. Dragon had pulled the top section of her hair back and made a perfect braid with it, the rest hung down her back. The waiting photographers always had a field day with her, noting the designers she wore, her hair styles, her poise and her beautiful smile.

Damascus knocked moments later and Wax moved to let them in. Sarge was scanning the room for bugs and Wax motioned Damascus to not speak for a moment until he was done. Dragon had set up his laptop and Sensei was summoning Chekov. When Sarge nodded it was clear he pressed a final key and Chekov's image appeared. It was 4:30 pm Paris time.

"Gentlemen, nice to see you have arrived safely. Images of you are already streaming on the news Reuters, very nice Dragon; your French charmed them, almost as much as your wife's beauty," Chekov said. "Thank you, Chekov. My wife's beauty is extremely charming, in any country, in any language." Raven blushed into her Champagne glass. "Stop please," she said. She rolled her eyes at Sarge who had come to sit beside her. He eyed her legs and the gorgeous shoes. "Very charming," he teased.

Looking at Sarge she got an idea. "Sarge, there's a shop in the lobby I saw, it has…" She leaned over to whisper in his ear, telling him of the exclusive lingerie boutique she'd seen. "Let's go there and you can help me find something Dragon will like. After all we are in the city of love." He eyed her, sipping his Scotch. "I like your thinking. What about him?" Sarge nodded at Dragon who was still busy with Chekov. "I don't know. I can ask Sensei to distract him. That would be the only way I could go anywhere without him. I'll say you want help buying something for Stephanie. He would rather die than go shopping so he will let me go with you alone," she said. "Ok it's a plan," Sarge said.

Dragon appeared beside her and sat. "What's a plan?" he said, eyeing them. Forcing the truth out of her mind she smiled at him and thought sexy thoughts of him from the plane earlier to distract him. "I want Raven to help me pick out something for Stephanie from that jewelry store down in the lobby," Sarge said. He lied perfectly. "Ok," Dragon said. Raven was completely in his head, distracting him from seeing Sarge's blatant lie and as she predicted he wasn't the least bit interested.

"So what are we doing for dinner?" Wax said. "Chekov made reservations at this famous place downstairs I guess, for 8 pm," Dragon said. Damascus stood, as they finished their drinks. "We are going to check out the Eiffel Tower if that's Ok and we'll meet you back here at 7:45?" "Sure," Sensei said. "That's a good idea. We only have this evening and half a day tomorrow so go see as much as you can and be back for dinner. Don't get lost." "I know how to get there and back," Sonny said.

Sonny was a perfectionist and once he learned something he never forgot it. He had an Eidetic memory. It came in handy and he was usually used tactically for things on their missions. He could remember maps, layouts, floor plans, numbers, codes, combinations, anything he looked at or heard, including faces and names. He was Korean and Caucasian, something like Dragon, light skinned, black hair that he wore like Jacob's, long but in the front only he had an inch or so wide piece of it that he bleached blonde. It was his artistic side. He was handsome like they all were and also popular with the women at HQ and on the beach at home. He had come to camp with a shipment of children from North Korea that had been intercepted. His mother had been poor and relied on the sex trade; she had gotten pregnant and had him, then traded him for money when he was only six.

They piled out the door to go and change and hit the city.

"Baby, maybe Sarge and I should go and shop now quick and then be back, is that ok?" Raven said. "I guess so, do you want me to come with you?" he asked. "No baby, stay here with Sensei and be sure Wax doesn't drink all the Scotch." She winked at Sensei and shoved Sarge out the door. "We'll be right back," she said. Dragon stood looking at Sensei, wondering what they were up to.

Sensei shrugged, wanting to keep her cover for her. "Sarge is in that phase, you know," he said. "He thinks he likes that surfer girl." Dragon and Wax laughed. "Ya he's fucked," Wax said. "I didn't even know he was seeing her, you know, for more than a night here and there," Dragon said. "It's gone a bit beyond that, I don't know," Wax said. "Put it this way, he's had sex with her more than one time. So for Sarge...he's hovering on marriage." Dragon and Wax then laughed about that for another half an hour while Sarge and Raven were gone.

Sarge and Raven hurried to the elevator, and pushed the button, suddenly eyeing each other and laughing. They had not actually been alone together in ages, since they couldn't remember when. The elevator opened and they shoved each other, trying to fit through the door at the same time.

"Stop it you asshole," Raven said. "You're a pushy little bitch," Sarge said.

Finally getting them both inside he pushed the L for Lobby button. The door closed and Sarge leaned against the back wall looking at her, smiling. He had a look on his face she wasn't sure of and suddenly felt a shyness coming over her. Sarge was very sexy by anyone's standards and he looked that way to her now for some reason.

"Come here," he said. He pulled her against him. "I miss you," he said. He looked both sad but happy at the same time and stunningly handsome. She looked up at him and picked an errant strand of blonde away from his eyes. "I know," she said.

He took her chin, held her gently and kissed her. He had kissed her and she had kissed him many times before, playfully, but this was different. He kissed with his heart in it and she could feel him building. There was a passion within it that had never been there before. It didn't make sense to her now.

He held her into him and turned so she was against the wall, still kissing her, soft and wet and sensuous. He was breathless and trembling now, but stopped himself, resting his forehead against hers, his eyes on her lips, his hands in her hair. He was hard and hot against her. He reached back and hit the stop button on the elevator.

"Sarge, this isn't us," she whispered. Her eyes searched his for an explanation. "I don't understand this," he said. "Ever since Vietnam I haven't known how to tell you how sorry I am. And I'm so angry. I just want you to know I love you and if I could have done something..." She took in his completely desperate confused face. "Come here," she said. She held him, kissing his cheek. She looked down at what he had been pressing against her. "Sarge, this can't be for me." He smiled, seeing where she was looking. "I'm sorry, but there's no way I could kiss you in an elevator and not be like this," he said. She pushed the button for the elevator to resume its descent and eventually the door opened. She took his hand and led him out of it, barely noticing anyone and pulled him to a private bench.

"Sarge thank you but I'm fine now. Please don't feel bad for me," she said. She was very confused now herself. "Ok," he said. "I just needed to talk to you about things, I don't know." Clarity had come back into his eyes and she recognized his expression again. She nodded to him. He looked down at himself then back at her and smiled with his blue eyes. "Sorry about that," he said. "I've seen you hard before Sarge," she said. "And you liked it? You did, I know you did," he teased. "Very nice Sergeant Willis and you know it. But you are not the one I care to make hard, so if you don't mind, I want you to tell me what will do the job for my sexy husband."

He stood and pulled her to her feet, thinking Dragon got hard over nothing when it came to her. He took her arm like a gentleman and they proceeded to the shop. They entered the plush pink and sexy environment. Beautiful things were everywhere and they didn't know where to look first. The shop girl approached them, addressing them in French, which Raven responded to, but asked if she spoke English so Sarge could understand what she was saying. She directed them to a change room area, and proceeded to provide Raven with numerous super sexy things for her to model for Sarge, thinking Sarge was her husband.

Their final decision was made based on Sarge's opinion of what Dragon would lose his mind the most over, considering he lost his mind over her with nothing on at all. It was a white corset with pink laces running up the front; the bodice was sheer white lace. The cups were push up and made her breasts look delicious. It had stockings and garters with pink bows and a tiny thong that did up at the sides so it could be removed without removing the garters. It showed off her beyond sexy butt that Dragon never got over looking at. The ever gorgeous Sergeant Willis was on his best game, getting his hard-on back thinking she looked off the charts in it.

They charged it to the rooms of David Li, but Raven stipulated that it be taken to their suite after 8 pm and left in its pretty box on their bed, for Dragon to find. It was in a lovely soft pink box tied with a beautiful silk pink bow. The sales girl looked somewhat confused at the instructions but didn't ask any questions realizing who they were when they had authorized the room charge. Raven Li was shopping for Lingerie with one of David Lis' body guards. This was Paris and anything went. She texted her roommate as soon as they had left the store, gushing about Sarge's good looks, Ravens figure and beauty, what she bought and that she had modeled it for the body guard. Front page gossip. It would not get that far though as she would be fired if she ever revealed anything about the guests of the hotel to the public.

They went back to the elevators and this time Sarge kept his hands to himself. When the elevator finally arrived at the top floor she stopped and turned around to him and kissed his lips, surprising him.

"What was that for?" he asked. He wondered that she would risk it after he had been all over her. "It's for being a friend, and helping me in that store. I'm not good at shopping." "Well you looked really good in what you were shopping for," he said. "Daddy's going to come unglued." "He's going to come unglued if we don't get in there, Come on," she said. She pulled him by his hand down the hall, back to being their usual playful selves.

Dragon was standing by the ornate French doors that exited to the terrace, looking out over the city. His shirt hung all the way open and was gently blowing in the summer breeze and when he heard them come in the door he turned to find her, setting his Scotch glass on a ledge as she came to him. He looked like something out of a romantic movie; dark, sexy and waiting. She ran her hands around his bare waist under his shirt and it instantly sent electricity through him, her scent, her touch, her green eyes and her smile all at once surrounded him and he considered how he could miss her in only an hour.

She was putting kisses on his chest and lower neck, further intoxicating him. He held her then and looked lovingly at her.

"Will you come to bed with me for awhile?" he asked.

To answer him she pulled his hips into her and ran her hands up his chest to his shoulders, pulling his shirt off them, biting him gently by his nipple. He let his smile curl up in the corner of his mouth, pleased at her response. He didn't address anyone, just pulled her into the bedroom and shut the door.

Sensei eyed Sarge, wondering if he should bring things up but decided against it and offered him a Scotch instead. "No, I think I might go chill and even shut my eyes for a bit before dinner." He was actually feeling drained and wanted to be alone. "Wax?" Sensei said. Wax eyed his empty glass but declined as well. "I'm going to go with Sarge I think. If I have to endure one of Chekov's dinners I'm going to need a nap first." "Ok boys; see you at 7:45 with Damascus then," Sensei said. He went out to the terrace to sit cross legged and meditate.

Sarge and Wax headed to their suite and Wax could tell something was clearly bothering Sarge. "What's the matter?" he asked. "I don't know," Sarge said. "I just had a fucking moment where I fucking wanted her." He was now angry at himself. Voicing it to Wax after the fact made it sound bad to him. "Whoa, really?" Wax said. "I don't know what it was about," Sarge said. "I've wanted to give her something ever since Vietnam. You know, after what happened to her and everything."

"We're guys," Wax said. "You wanted to express yourself to her but of course it comes out below the waist. You should have stopped at the heart man," Wax said. "You need better brakes." Sarge looked at him, understanding finally. He pointed at his forehead. "Ya, it went from here," he said. "To here." He grabbed himself through his pants, making Wax laugh at him.

"How bad did it get? Is Dragon going to knock you into tomorrow? You know she will tell him, or show him, or whatever they do," Wax said. Sarge shook his head. "Nothing we haven't done before or she hasn't seen before, it was more the fact that she knew it was different, I wasn't kidding around, I fucking wanted her," he said. "What did you want; to fuck her? Well, you were in an elevator," Wax said. He shrugged like it was all explained as simple as that.

Behind their bedroom door, Dragon stood her in front of him, unbuttoning her jacket and removing it. She didn't speak, waiting for him, knowing he had questions for her, as well as a physical need for her. He silently removed everything from her except her white satin panties and her shoes and finally he let her hair down. It cascaded out of the braid around her face and made him inhale sharply at her beauty. She eyed him now as he stepped back, looking at her. She smiled shyly, as he sat down on the edge of the bed and removed his shirt which still hung sexily off him. He undid his own hair and let it fall.

"Tell me what you and Sarge were up to, tell me or show me," Dragon said. "I can see it's bothering you sweetheart." "She knew it was literally impossible to keep anything from him, she just hadn't been sure if he would want to make love to her first. She moved to him, and stood between his thighs, placing her hands on his chest and looked into his eyes. He took her hands in his. She let the whole thing play out from her memory and he saw it all exactly as it happened, as if he were there. Dragon looked away when she was finished, but still held her hands. He sighed and looked back to her.

"Sarge isn't good with words. He reacted physically, that's all. He loves you and he's angry like we all are. He just couldn't use words so, well he, you know..." Dragon said. "I thought you might be mad at him, or me. I don't know." She couldn't find words and he pulled her in to him, stroking her hair. "It's Ok baby, I would never be angry at you. Sarge is just confused and you've dealt with him before with a hard-on. When doesn't he have one?" He grinned at her then, picturing it and thinking it kind of funny. He kissed her again and looked innocently at her. "And you know what? I've been hard for over an hour now."

She loved him more than anything right then. She thought she was going to have the explaining to do but in reality he had explained it to her. She stepped back and looked at him. He raised his eyebrows at her, bringing his slow sexy smile to his lips and began to undo his belt. She smiled back at him and took over the task for him, pushing him back on the bed. She made him relive a day back in camp in the shower. He then made love to her for another hour before they needed to dress for dinner.

Wax and Sarge were waiting with Sensei in the suite when Dragon held the bedroom door for her. He hadn't tied his tie yet, but looked fabulous as they all did, especially Raven. She had on a long dress, bright red, sleeveless, with a plunging draped neckline, showing her tanned cleavage. It had a long slit up the side to her hip showing off her sexy legs in gold sandals with an ankle strap. Dragon had attached a beautiful gold necklace with a beautiful diamond dragon pendant on it, courtesy of Chekov, and the 2 carat diamond studs in a gold setting in her ears. Her hair was long, pinned off her forehead on top. Dragon had left his loose. He looked at the time on his phone, it was 7:30, and suggested a quick drink.

"Damascus and the boys will not be joining us," Sensei said. "They are enthralled in Paris and wish to experience it on the level of people their age." "They're not going to fuck up are they?" Wax said. "I have warned them and they are simply seeing the museums and taking in some Cafés. They will meet us after dinner," Sensei said.

Dragon could tell Sarge was holding something in, and confronted it. "Sarge, outside!" he said.

He turned and walked out onto the terrace. Outside, the air was warm and the daylight was beginning to fade, bringing the sunset in an hour or so. The city rolled by beneath them as they took positions leaning on the railing overlooking its beauty. Dragon eyed his friend and wished Sarge could 'see' what was in his heart. It would be hard to put into words.

"I'm sorry about the elevator," Sarge said. Dragon turned to face him then. "Look at me Sarge," he said. He waited while Sarge managed to face him with the blue eyes. "I don't want to kick your ass. You love her and it shows sometimes in a way you may not want. There's nothing any of us can do to fix what happened to her. I know that first hand. So let yourself off the hook. It happened and we have to move on. If you want to express your love for her, just be there for her the way you always are. That's how she needs you; it's what you can do for her," Dragon said. Sarge just looked at him and nodded. "Thanks, for understanding; I mean I nearly forced myself on your wife in an elevator," Sarge said. He ran a hand through his hair not wanting to remember it. Dragon gave him a knowing smile. "Can't blame you for that," he said. "I mean it was an elevator. Those things have magic powers. We all lose our minds as soon as the doors close."

They both laughed at the idea of it and Dragon put his arm around Sarge's shoulders, in a reassuring embrace. When they came back through the terrace doors, Wax was standing, just downing a last sip of Scotch, Sensei was gathering himself to go, eyeing the surroundings one last time. Raven stood and looked from Dragon to Sarge. Sarge looked at her, and took a deep breath. His face showed the love he had for her, the gratitude of just having her in his life. She could read his mind and went to him, brushing his hair away as he looked down at her.

"Thank you for loving me and I hope you will still get a hard-on for me," she said. She tugged his hair playfully. He laughed then and held her away from him, wanting to throw her down and spank her but stopping because he couldn't mess her up then. Instead he eyed Dragon. "Did you hear that?" he said. Dragon just shook his head and it was back to normal just like that.

They were all in a nice mood then, relieved and relaxed and ready for what Chekov had done to them yet again. They took the elevator to the lobby and they all burst out laughing in it, the whole thing amusing now. They found their way to the Restaurant, somewhat composed by the time they entered its stately traditional doors. It resembled the theme of the rest of the hotel. French traditional, privileged and elegant, it created a feeling of floating back in time. The Hotel was known for its discretion and people stayed there that didn't want to be seen or gossiped about, so they made their way leisurely and found it pleasant. Sensei paused and spent a few moments with the Maitre 'D', learning that Chekov had pre-ordered for them.

The food was unbelievable and they had a wonderful time enjoying it and one another, although it was far more formal than what they preferred. None the less they were in Paris and their formal dress, formal dinner and formal surroundings made sense.

They discussed going out afterwards with Damascus and the boys for some fun, maybe a club or bar. Dragon was skeptical after San Diego, but said he'd consider it. Raven looked so amazing he didn't know if he may just take her straight to bed when they were done with the dinner. They decided to return to the room when dinner was completed and see if Chekov had provided any appropriate wardrobe for a night on the town. That would be a deciding factor.

Back in their suite Damascus and the boys waited. They were excited as they had met some girls, travelling Europe for the summer and made plans to meet them at a club if Sensei allowed them. Sensei asked Damascus if he could have a word in private and took him out to the terrace.

"What are you telling me son?" Sensei asked. "If I get a chance to be with someone, I want to," Damascus said. "Could I? I need it now." Sensei thought about it for a moment, knowing Damascus had pretty much returned to normal. When Sensei intruded on his private thoughts they were typical now, non obsessive and normal for someone his age. Maybe some casual sex with a consenting person he would never see again would be fine for him. He trusted Damascus when he said he was ready.

Sensei realized he was going to have to deal with them all. They were off the island and had a chance to meet some females. It was actually perfect. There would be no consequences as they were leaving tomorrow. Wax and Sarge would definitely be availing themselves and there would be no logical reason to deny the boys. He made his decision.

Sensei led him back to the others and picked up the desk phone and summoned the manager. Speaking in French, he requested five additional rooms be made available to them for that evening. The manager was more than happy to comply and shortly had five keys delivered to the suite.

It was all very amusing to Dragon, but he resisted the urge to tease them, knowing they were young and wanted to have fun, but he made up his mind he wasn't going. Wax could take care of them for tonight.

Sensei eyed the boys. "You may take a key. Don't reveal anything about why you're here or who you're with, don't speak to the media, don't get drunk, stay together and do what Wax tells you. Got it?" They all nodded and they were looking respectful but eyeing each other with knowing eyes. They planned on having a very good night and had hoped Sensei would let them out.

Wax eyed Sarge. "Come on Romeo, I need my wing man." "Present and accounted for," Sarge said.

Having a night cap, Raven sipped her second glass of Champagne, and was feeling relaxed. Sensei and Dragon had a second Scotch on the go and they relaxed out on the terrace then, having put the nights' follies to rest. Raven then remembered what lay waiting in their room and crossed her legs, quivering slightly.

Always aware of her, Dragon eyed her then. 'Need something little angel?' he asked her silently. Then realizing Sensei was in the loop, apologized. Raven giggled.

"Never mind, I am going to retire after this drink," Sensei said. "Well not really because I will be keeping an eye on Damascus as best I can until they are safely back here." Raven looked puzzled. "Papa, if Damascus takes a girl to a room can you 'see' what they are doing?" she asked. "Not really. If I tune in to Damascus I can sense him, some of his thoughts, whether he is good or bad let's say, for simplicity. But I can't watch, so to speak, like I can with you two." She laughed playfully and made eyes at Sensei. "Papa, you don't want to see the things he does to me." Sensei grinned back at her with his wisest expression. "It's far too late for that my dear. And it is 'your' naughtiness that is the most shocking."

She decided to dish it back, knowing he was just teasing her. "Well then Papa if you tune in tonight it will make you need a cold shower." She had a sultry look and stood, eyeing Dragon. "Ready?" she asked. Dragon downed the last of his Scotch just like that, never taking his eyes off her. "Always," he said. He got to his feet and she pulled him with her. "Goodnight Sensei, I'll try and make this worth your time," Dragon said.

Sensei smiled to himself, finishing his own drink. He would be blocking them actually, as he wanted to focus his mind on what was going on with the others more importantly.

Dragon let her pull him into the room then turned and closed the door. She waited, looking at him, beginning to tremble now at the sight of him. He turned back to her and leaned against the door eyeing her with the love and want he always had. She looked at the box on the bed and he followed her gaze. Seeing it, he raised an eyebrow to her and she desperately tried to hide in her mind what was in it. He walked around her then, very close so she could smell him. She resisted touching him as he passed her slowly, moving around to the bottom of the bed to pick up the box. She turned and watched him, trying to hold her hands still in front of her, uncertain why she was so nervous suddenly.

He picked it up and took a few steps back to stand in front of her, seeing she was trembling.

"What has you like this baby?" He gently brushed her cheek, wanting to calm her. "Maybe if I see what's in here? Will that help?"

He was smiling his absolute sexiest smile at her, unintentionally. She nodded, and was almost unable to look at him he was making her so crazy now. She thought she was going to lose it, her knees felt weak he looked so gorgeous, his shirt open, the way he was standing, his expression, everything.

He pulled the pink ribbon away, and put the lid of the box on the bed. He eyed the beautiful white lace, pink ribbons and satin garters, folded provocatively, surrounded in pink tissue and scented somehow with a heady sexual scent. He looked from it to her, once he had control over his line of sight again. His eyes had nearly rolled back in his head as it dawned on him what this was all about. He looked deeply into her, wondering how she could still throw him off his game, even now.

"Put this on," he said.

She took the box from him, with no words, only her eyes obeying him and went to the en-suite, closing the door but leaving it ajar, just enough so he couldn't watch her. He sat down on the bottom of the bed and waited, realizing what she and Sarge had been up to all along and adoring her for it.

Raven eyed herself in the mirror when she was done. She had slipped back into the gold spiky sandals and fastened the ankle strap over her ankle, now covered in the sexy white silk stockings with a three inch lace elastic top that she had attached the garters to. The tiny white lace thong just covered her front and was only elastic string otherwise. The corset was perfectly fitted to her waist and the pink crisscrossing ribbon travelling up the front of it to between her breasts was adorable, matching the ribbons on the garters. The little padded cups of the corset pushed her breasts up and together and they glowed with her tanned skin in the soft light.

She brushed her hair around her and decided she should not keep him waiting any longer. She took the clip out of the top of her hair and watched it fall sexily around her face. She hoped he would like her in it. She took a deep breath and tried not to shake, as she pulled the door open.

Sitting at the bottom of the bed, he watched her as she walked slowly towards him. He nearly gasped at the sight of her, knowing he was going to lose it and not knowing where he was even going to start with her. He moaned then and ran both his hands through his hair, looking at the ceiling then back to her as she now stood inches from him. She smelled like something beautiful and looked like heaven to him.

"Oh god baby," he breathed.

She reached out; her fingertips touching his face lovingly, then his lips. His hands went to her fingers and he kissed them, closing his eyes and letting his breath out, about to come apart.

"You are so beautiful, wrapped up like a lacy pink gift that I just need to get my hands on. Come here." He pulled her into him, kissing her, feeling her body through the lace, running his fingertips over the swell of her breasts and around to the soft smooth skin of her butt.

"Baby let me feel you and taste you everywhere in this," he whispered. Moving her hair away he began kissing her neck, his hands roaming down her body and back up, touching her breasts, and kissing them. "So sexy," he breathed. She ran her hands through his hair as he moved down her body.

He slid to his knees then and let his hands move down to her butt, squeezing her, gently kissing the pink lace ribbon down the front of her. He found her thighs with his fingers and gently, slowly, ran them under the sexy satin garters, before finally making it to the front of her, kissing her through the silk of the tiny thong. He traced his fingers up the inside of her thigh, the smooth silk stockings leading him upwards, just barely touching her, feeling her wetness. He undid the delicate Velcro elastic and pulled it from her, exposing her to his kiss. She started to shake.

He stood then and she ran her hands up his chest muscles and back down, kissing his neck where she could reach in her heels, wanting him, wanting him to take her. She couldn't get her hands off his erection through his pants now. He was hard and wetness from him had coated the inside of his pants as she undid them, pulling them from him. She wanted to get on her knees at the sight of him, but he wanted her on the bed and put her there. He lay beside her, letting his naked thigh rest over her as he leaned against her, over her.

He slowed them down then, taking her in, smiling softly to her, brushing her hair softly back from her face.

"You're so beautiful," he said. He trailed his hand down her body feeling the lace gently while he looked into her eyes. "Thank you for this."

He was overwhelmed with the emotion and feelings that he had then. She looked up at him, her green eyes soft with desire for him, and he had no words as he moved over her, sliding himself inside her. They clung to each other, pressing their lips hard against one another as he made them come.

Dragon spent the rest of the night undoing her piece by piece until she lay naked and quivering, wet and flushed, glassy eyed and vulnerable. Wanting the touch of her body never to leave his, he kissed her and drew them both into sleep together. It was a beautiful night for them and Dragon had left them blissful as they finally drifted off into his light.

The boys were all also blissful. Morning came quickly for them, and via text messages they had agreed to meet in their suite at 7 am. They all fumbled their ways there as agreed, having sent hung-over girls off in cabs, before the rest of the world was really awake. Wax had used a room and Sarge had gone to their suite with someone. He had been uncertain, but couldn't resist a spunky English speaking French girl, with a smoking tiny hard body, black spiky hair, wild eye makeup and a tongue piercing. It had sealed the deal when they had been dancing and she had pulled him behind a pillar. In the throng of dancers, darkness and pounding music she had pushed him against it and taken him with her mouth, giving him the expertise of her tongue with its little pleasurable accompaniment.

His current mindset made him have to have more, and more he got. She wore him out and took him everywhere he had wanted to go lately. She made him come like he only had in his dreams, laying him down, doing it to him, destroying him more than once. She had craved him and he had obliged, giving back to her until she was good. He woke at 6am with the alarm and she was gone. She left her black silk panties by his pillow with a note. 'Thanks for the awesome fuck, call me next time.' And her number was there. He never knew her name and she never knew his.

Wax rolled in right then as Sarge was sitting naked on the couch shaking his head, wondering what the fuck he had done.

"You got it good, didn't you," Wax said. He went to the fridge for water, amused by the look of Sarge. "Yup" was all Sarge could come up with. He took water from Wax and then gathered his thoughts. "You go first. Where, who and what?" Wax sat, drinking his water. "I was here. A blonde and mostly standard things. I'm assuming you were somewhat beyond?" Wax said. "Yes," Sarge said. He recounted to Wax the public oral sex and the later not so public sex including anal sex. "So you got done!" Wax said. "I got done," Sarge nodded. Then they both looked at each other remembering. "Shit, call Damascus now!" Sarge said.

He tossed Wax a cell phone from the side table. Damascus and Jacob had two girls and it had looked like a little group effort was going to take place. They were worried the boys would not make Sensei's morning curfew.

Damascus answered right away. "Whaattt?" he asked. He made an effort to sound bored and affected. Wax became patronizing because of his tone. "Where the fuck are you, Valentino? Times up and play time is over," he said. Damascus postured even more by not answering immediately because he was drinking some juice. "Sorry. What? We're here in our suite. All of us, so relax you're fucking dread head." Wax rolled his eyes at Sarge and then looked annoyed. It was too early for Damascus' smart mouth. "You don't need to get cute with me just because you had a little group fuck-a-thon. I invented that shit," Wax said. "If you say so, Waximus," Damascus said. Wax tried not to laugh, holding the phone aside. Damascus was so cocky it was funny. "Well, you're a disappointment. I was looking forward to you fucking up and catching huge shit from Sensei. Now I have to go cuz I'm just not giving a fuck." Sarge eyed him, as Wax hung up the phone and let his head fall back on the couch. "That kid is so fucking cocky it's ridiculous. 7 a.m. and I can hardly outwit him. What the fuck!" He was exhausted from it already. "Did he tag team some girls? Shit, Sensei will probably freak. I feel like we're getting shit, I don't know," Sarge said.

"Ok just get your fucking naked ass self in the shower please, before I develop morning sickness at the sight of you," Wax said. Sarge laughed, eyeing himself. "Ok but you should know, your shirt is on inside out and some of your dreads are stuck together, just saying."

He headed for the shower before Wax decided to kick his ass. As Sarge stepped into the shower, Wax answered the door and let Sensei into their suite, having quickly reversed his shirt.

"Good morning Wax," Sensei said. He looked fresh like it didn't matter what time of day it was he always looked the same. "Sensei, everything ok?" Wax asked. "I came to ask you just that," Sensei replied. "Ya the boys are all back." Sensei raised an eyebrow. "Where is Sarge?" "Showering, why don't you go jerk the boy's chains and come back in 15 and he'll be done," Wax said.

Damascus let him in, wearing a towel around his waist, his spikes wet and everywhere. Jacob lay face down on the sofa, also in a towel and Mishka was just emerging from a bedroom, naked and toweling his hair. Sensei could hear a shower running and assumed that would be Sonny.

"Boys," he said. He was standing and waiting. Mishka finished with his hair and wrapped the towel around his waist, hiding the red marks on his butt left by some very red nails. "Sensei," Damascus said. He walked casually to the bar fridge for some water. "As you can see we are all present and accounted for and no one is here but us. We had no trouble at the club, used the rooms, remained as anonymous as we could and came in the back way with no photographers. No one's hung-over, just 'tired' if you want it politely. Have I covered everything?"

Sensei nodded and walked slowly through the room, eyeing the comatose Jacob and arrived in front of Damascus who sipped his water and met his gaze. Damascus spoke quietly then. "I'm fine Sensei, just a physical release, nice healthy sex with nice healthy girls, I enjoyed it, and I'm good. Ask Jacob, he was there the whole time, kind of a group thing. This city has some very nice uninhibited girls it seems."

Sensei studied his eyes for any hint of dishonesty or misleading words, consciously or subconsciously, but sensed Damascus was being clear and truthful. He smiled at him and touched his shoulder.

"Very well son," Sensei said. "Take a few hours and sleep or whatever; we aren't getting picked up until noon. I'm leaving Dragon asleep for awhile, order food from room service, don't go anywhere and come to his suite ready to go at 11:30 am." "Got it Sensei," Damascus said. "And thank you, from all of us, Ok?" His boyish grin looked young again to Sensei. "You're welcome," Sensei said. He let himself out.

Sensei's last stop was the foot of the bed where Dragon lay sleeping with a very messy Raven laying across him. Evidence of their night lay everywhere in the room and Sensei decided to leave him asleep a little longer. He crossed his legs and drifted off himself. He mentally revived himself 2 hours later and woke Dragon then, as time persisted in moving forward. He brought tea that had been delivered to the room.

Dragon ran a hand through his unruly hair, glancing around the room.

"Shit, sorry about the mess." "I doubt you are son," Sensei said. He gave him a playful eye. "Did you catch any of that, last night I mean?" Dragon asked. Sensei gave a light laugh. "No son, I tuned you out. I had to keep my mind open for what was happening with the others." Dragon looked relieved. "We haven't gotten like that in awhile. She was wearing this fucking sexy thing." He held up the corset that lay on the bed still. "Very nice," Sensei said. "I can only imagine what that must have done to you." "Look around," Dragon said, eyeing the room.

"How did the boys do, did they have fun?" Dragon said. He changed the subject before Sensei had a chance to give him shit for having made such a mess of her. Sensei smirked. "Oh I think so, Damascus and Jacob had a foursome, and Wax a blonde, Sonny and Mishka did I don't know what with I don't know who, and Sarge, well..." "Let me guess, he got his dick sucked," Dragon said crudely. "To say the least," Sensei said. "Don't elaborate please," Dragon said. "Apparently French girls are a new favorite with everyone," Sensei said, leaving it at that.

Dragon looked at Raven then. "Well, she's not French but something got her feeling it." He brushed her hair off her face and kissed her forehead. "You get her feeling it son, nothing more. She wanted to show you, to give you something special," Sensei said. "That she did, I literally was unglued, she looked so sexy and the whole idea of it made me go out of my mind. She was so shy to wear that for me, she was shaking," Dragon said.

Sensei nodded, thinking of her love for him. "It's a wonder to me that after all this time and how much you mean to each other that she could even wonder in the least if you would be pleased," Sensei said. "It was like she was showing herself to me for the first time, it made me crazy," Dragon said. "Well son I hope you showed her that," Sensei said. "Of course I did, over and over again until we couldn't anymore," Dragon said.

"Well, wake her and remind her again, then clean yourselves up, OK? There's food, and the rest will be here at 11:30, we leave at noon," Sensei said.

After Sensei had gone he kissed her awake and she cuddled into him, warm and soft, making him hot and hard. She was wet but he did it slow and gentle, until they made it. They lay attached and kissed softly and held each other, until there was no more time and they needed to shower.

They met at 11:30 am, looking all business, and ready to work. Hong Kong was next and Dragon had a dinner meeting that evening with Lee Tran. The fun was over and the mission had begun. They made their way to the waiting limo, using the back exit, and headed to the airport. They boarded the jet and were off, a 6 or so hour flight ahead of them and more to come before they would sleep. The flight was quiet, as most of them were using the time to sleep.

Dragon read and re-read Chekov's profile, and discussed quietly with Sensei some questions he still had. Raven lay on the seats beside him with her head in his lap, sleeping softly. He covered her with his jacket, as she had on a short dress for summer, her hair smoothed back in a pony tail.

CHAPTER THIRTY ONE

HONG KONG

Dragon wanted to know who Tran's father in-law was. Sensei glanced through the information and also couldn't see anything. He emailed Chekov. The response was the same as the profile, only adding that his name was Richard Ng. His Chinese name was not documented anywhere that Chekov could find. He didn't have a picture of him either.

The plan was to meet Tran in a private dining room of the hotel they were staying at. The customary way of proceeding with a business transaction of this nature was to take as long as possible to get around to discussing it. Dragon didn't want to make Wax and Sarge stand around waiting forever for him, as they would not be included in the dinner arrangements, so he decided to go alone. He would, as always have an earpiece so they could hear everything. Also he wanted to appear trusting and confident.

According to the profile, they were located in the centre of Hong Kong's cosmopolitan district. Damascus and his team needed to be invisible as their presence could not be explained. They were to blend into the landscape after they arrived at the airport. They could hide in plain sight, being Asian, except for Mishka but he was dark haired and had dark glasses that hid his vibrant blue eyes. Once there, they would wait. Raven and Sensei were to go shopping the next day and take in the city, appearing to pass the time while her husband was there on business.

They touched down about 6:30 pm Hong Kong time and taxied to a private jet way. Dragon nodded to Damascus, as he departed with his team in a waiting Limo. They would be meeting later.

Dragon headed to the waiting Blackhawk. It had been painted black, adorned with the gold lined lettering DLI, disguising it as a missionary transport vehicle for the various peacekeeping missions carried out by the David Li Foundation. It was piloted by Tom-Tom, who would be at their disposal for as long as they needed him. Hopefully no one would question its' guns. This particular Blackhawk was equipped with various missiles, rockets and machine guns. They all noted its' hardware as they climbed aboard. They greeted Tom-Tom and Dragon's first question to him was what was with the heavy heat it was carrying.

Tom-Tom shrugged. "Orders from the General," he said. He went back to his instruments, readying for lift off while they all strapped in.

The Kowloon Shangri La Hotel was a beautiful landmark amidst the many gleaming towers of the pulsing city. They landed on the roof, in the dimming evening light. The Manager and Executive Assistant Manager awaited them. Once clear of the helicopter, they were greeted with professionalism and escorted into the elevator.

Dragon could hear the rotors of the Blackhawk, signaling Tom-Tom's departure. Tom-Tom would wait for them, only a ten minute flight from start to finish if they needed him.

It was the usual business with the hotel formalities; the welcoming, the explanation of amenities and the offer of undying service. Dragon was polite but preoccupied with getting to his dinner meeting in two hours. He had a lot to prepare himself for.

They were all sharing a massive suite, Wax and Sarge had assumed their roles, silently going about preparing themselves. Sensei went about his usual ritual of establishing communications with Chekov, once Sarge had completed the bug scan. Damascus and his team arrived as Chekov's image appeared.

"Dragon," he said. "You are to meet him in a private dining room."

He produced a floor plan. It showed the main entrance and two exits, one through the kitchen and another led to a stairwell. There were six surveillance cameras, all functional. It appeared safe for him to be there alone; it was a legitimate place to meet and carry on business and was done all the time. None the less, they would all be listening in and Chekov would be watching.

Dragon nodded affirmation. "Is there anything else Chekov? Anything that you feel is different or even slightly off?" Chekov looked blankly back at him. "I don't deal in feelings Dragon, or with things that are 'slightly off' as you put it. If it adds up statistically and tactically, meets protocol standards and collateral risk assessment percentages then I am good with it," he said.

Dragon moved on, ignoring Chekov's arrogance, eyeing Sensei with the same question. Sensei simply nodded, letting Dragon know he would discuss it with him once the communications with Chekov were completed.

Dragon turned away, very much done with it. Pulling Raven with him, he wrapped his arm around her and they went to the master bedroom of the suite.

She looked around, took in the view and came back to him as he stood waiting for her. She saw the expression on his face and felt his heat hit her. She didn't think he would need her then, maybe after, but he wanted her now. She went to him and stood.

He pulled his jacket off and tossed it on the bed. She turned and he unzipped the little white dress she wore, letting it fall, leaving her naked after running the little silk pink panties she wore down her legs, kissing her between her thighs from behind. Standing again, he pulled the tie from her hair, unleashing her pony tail, letting her mane fall around her shoulders and back.

"On the bed sweetheart, face down please," he said.

He kissed the side of her neck and she moved to position herself for him. She spread her knees apart and arched her back, tilting herself to be as open as she could be to him. She felt his hands on her, his touch gentle and inquisitive. She moaned as he teased her with his soft touch on her sensitive spots.

She heard the sound of him undoing his belt and the front of his pants and then felt him pressing against her, slowly until she had taken him fully inside her. Closing her eyes to his soft familiar groan, she let him do what he wanted, now dying for it.

He held her by her hips and made her feel him.

After, she lay flat, still face down and he was beside her, gently tracing his fingers up and down her back, enjoying the feeling of her soft skin. He was relaxed now and ready for what he needed to do.

Time had run out and he needed to get dressed. He still wore his pants, undone and half off, the DLI platinum belt buckle lying open. He eyed it and taking a hold of it he pulled it from around him, grasping it in his palm and wrapping the soft leather around his hand. His gentle thoughts teased her as he traced the soft leather across her back. It made her shiver as he drew it down and across her butt and along the back of her thighs.

"You laying here like this makes me have some thoughts for later," he said. He traced the leather back up her thighs, across her butt and up her back. "I'd like to tie you here and leave you until I get back, then maybe you'd be ready for it," he whispered. She turned to face him, wanting him. "Baby, why do you do this to me?" she said.

Her voice was pleading, as she moved against him, pulling him into her, finding his lips. He kissed her hard and wet, but then released her, holding her face with the hand that held the belt. He just smiled his ever sexy half smile at her.

"Just wait Angel; just wait for when I get back."

She watched him dress. She had sat up and held her knees, resting her chin on them, her green moist pools following him as he moved. Her hair fell around her and she looked like an exotic animal. He eyed her with a smoldering gaze, as he threaded the belt through the loops of the black Armani pants.

"I'll be thinking about this while I'm out and what you are going to look like when I get back," he said. She tipped her face into her knees, showing him only her eyes, vulnerable and wanting. His breath caught, and he ran a hand through his hair. "I need to stop this or I'm not getting out of here," he said. He finally conceded, as her sexuality was threatening to undo him. He took a deep breath. "Come, I need a shirt," he said. He held his hand for her to take and help him with Chekov's selections.

The Armani suit was obvious, but there were several shirts of different colors. He didn't want to look too intimidating; it wasn't that time in the game yet. It was summer and the colors were pale light tones and she decided on a warm very soft light blue. She always loved him in that color and it gave off a pleasant look that suited the situation the way he wanted it. It was paired with a tie of the same tone of blue but three shades deeper, textured and shiny. His brown eyes were warm and soft against the blue. He tied it and did up the Platinum DLI cuff links and handed her the hairbrush so she could brush his hair back in the perfect way she had of doing it so it was smooth, but wavy, to hide the ear piece. He sat on the bed and she knelt behind him, brushing his hair away from his forehead. She kissed his brow in the corner by his temple when she was done.

"Very handsome Mr. Li," she said. She thought he was stunning. He stood then, smiling at her. "Baby, put something on before we go out there. You can't be naked." She seemed to suddenly realize that about herself, and smiled. "Oh, Ok." She looked around, not knowing where the clothes even were. "In the drawer," he said.

He found her adorable and watched with amusement. She took some bright pink and white lace satin panties and pulled them on. They had white lace only in the back and were only half there and hot pink satin covered her in the front, white lace edged the waistband. They had a matching camisole top that clung to her body, pink satin with white lace trim, lacy straps and lace around her breasts.

He stood eyeing her when she was done. She looked up at him. "Ok, there baby, is this OK?" Usually he handed her what to put on. "Are you seriously trying to fuck with me?" he asked.

He was holding back his laughter, she was so cute. She looked at him questioningly, then down to herself, then across to the mirror. She giggled then, getting him.

"No baby, but if you like this you can play with me in it later." She naughtily went to him. He held her and shook his head at her. "You know what I'm going to do to you later and by all means be wearing that." He put kisses on her face. "But let's go now, or I'll be late; Horny and late." He was now mentally arguing with his hard-on. He took her hand and opened the bedroom door to go.

Wax and Sarge were just attaching their ear pieces, dressed in open dress shirts and black dress pants. Sarge had pulled his hair back smooth and Wax had tied his dreads down tightly and they both looked professional. They pulled jackets on over their guns, and Dragon slid into his, buttoning one button.

"Ok, Sensei, hook me up to Chekov," Dragon said. Sensei eyed him from the desk, waiting. In seconds Chekov appeared, as Dragon fastened the essentially invisible communication device to his ear, perfectly hidden by his hair. "Got you," Chekov said. "Ok," Dragon said. He then eyed Sarge and Wax. "Ready?" he asked. "Yup," Wax said. "Damascus?" Dragon said. He turned to him. He had been waiting quietly, trying not to stare at Raven. "Yes," he said.

He was dressed casually, like a boy his age would look and was to wait in the lobby bar, pretending to be having a drink but watching for any suspicious new comers through the doors. Jacob would join him, when Damascus cued him and they would look like two friends meeting for a drink.

Dragon turned to Raven then and she curled in to him, smelling his scent through the soft blue fabric. He kissed her gently then and mentally spoke to her, telling her to be waiting for him. She smiled up at him, saying no words out loud but 'I love you' in her mind which he kissed her for, then nodded at Wax and Sarge to follow him.

He went out the door then and headed to meet Mr. Tran, whom he would likely be killing in fairly short order. They didn't speak the entire time in the elevator, leery of listening devices. Although Chekov scanned for them, it was not 100 percent and there were always new things being developed that may avoid current detection methods, especially in the Asian countries where technology was a constant changing animal.

The plan was for Sarge and Wax to escort him to the dining room, making their presence known. But as a matter of showing trust and politeness Dragon would dismiss them. They would return to the room but listen to the conversation.

Chekov's analysis indicated there was little likelihood of anything transpiring other than business, during this dinner arrangement. It was to be Dragon's job to infiltrate Trans' personal world somehow, in order to venture into the real reason for their interest in him.

Dragon didn't like to plan conversations ahead of time. He preferred they unfold randomly. Being able to think on his feet was one of his fortes. Also, his ability to see the thoughts of others, guided him accordingly. As he was assimilating everything in his head, they arrived at the restaurant and were immediately addressed.

They were greeted professionally by a hostess and escorted to their meeting. They followed her through the elegant room, adorned in modern serene finishes, with water features here and there, fountains and exotic tropical fish tanks. Shortly they came to an entranceway of sorts, an opening surrounded by palms, with two huge tropical fish tanks on either side of the entrance that shielded the room from the rest of the restaurant. Lee Tran stood waiting, accompanied by three other men.

Dragon eyed him, and waited. 'Mr. Li,' the hostess announced, and then retreated. Lee Tran smiled and stepped forward, his hands clasped in front of him. It was not the custom to touch one another in handshakes, but simply to nod acknowledgement. He nodded at Tran as he approached.

"Mr. Li," Tran said. "Thank you for coming. Please join me."

Dragon smiled, and then half nodded sideways at Wax, who then simultaneously turned with Sarge and left him. Wax had taken in the two obvious guards and the third man, who he could tell was not armed.

Tran raised an eyebrow at their departure. "Do you not wish your 'friends' to stay Mr. Li?" he asked. "No," Dragon said. "Were they armed Mr. Li?" Tran asked. Dragon found the question curious, but answered readily. "Of course," he said. "And you Mr. Li?" Dragon smiled at him again. "I am not carrying any weapons and my wife is not with me Mr. Tran, which leaves me quite unarmed," Dragon said.

Tran smiled back at him then, his teeth having the look of someone who smoked heavily. "You're wife is a very beautiful woman, I hope to meet her," he said. "She is very beautiful and I am missing her already," Dragon said.

Tran kept smiling and Dragon detected a slight annoyance. Tran did not find women beautiful and found Dragon's affection for her a disappointment. He would have preferred to have had all of Dragon's attention to himself. It made Dragon smile inwardly.

"Well, let us have a drink Mr. Li," Tran said. He was eyeing a well stocked bar. "Scotch," Dragon said. Tran very slightly eyed the other man who went to pour the drinks. "Come, Mr. Li," he said.

He moved toward a large window, floor to ceiling which looked out over the Hong Kong shoreline and into Victoria Harbor. They stood taking in the view of the darkening city, its' lights alive like an entity in and of itself. Dragon picked up Tran's thoughts then, his love of it, his powerful use of its offerings and a feeling of familiar comfort from looking out over it.

"This is your city Mr. Tran?" Dragon asked. Tran turned to him, pleased he had been so perceptive. "I feel that way Mr. Li. It has been good to me."

Their drinks were presented momentarily by the other man. "Thank you," Dragon said. "If I may Mr. Li, this is Chang, my Assistant," Tran said. He introduced the man, who Dragon instantly saw was Tran's lover.

A lot of things were coming into Dragon's mind at once, as they all relaxed somewhat. He had sensed eager nervousness in Tran and anxiety in Chang. But as it eased, more things became known to him.

They were both intimidated by his size difference. Tran and Chang were typical Chinese, small in stature and not over 5'7" in height, leaving Dragon seven or more inches taller than them and bigger than both of them put together. Dragon could see they were also struck by his appearance. Their individual thoughts on that had appeared to him in his mind as he opened it to get as much of their inner conversations as he could.

Chang had blatant homosexual images involving Dragon. Tran was more subdued, curious that someone could look as he did, finding it alarmingly attractive but careful to not let it show or overwhelm him in any way. He had a guard up, but nothing unusual to Dragon, considering they were doing business and one had to have a guard up. Tran was simply curious about him, about everything, his wife, his businesses and his past.

Dragon yawned in his mind thinking they would have to go through all of this before they would do business because that's how it was done. Getting a target in his sights made him want to eliminate it and sometimes the tediousness of getting there could be a challenge.

He would wait for the questions as it was not his style to become chatty. He wouldn't be telling Tran anything about himself anyway and he would toy with him, cleverly avoiding them. He really wanted to get down to business, but it would be impolite to rush him. He waited. They drank their Scotch and discussed the latest Hong Kong current events. Chekov was feeding Dragon information on subjects Tran was bringing up and he was impressing Tran with his knowledge and opinions. It was all very amusing to him.

Tran had pre-ordered and food arrived in stages. He had been aware that David Li ate only fish and vegetables and seafood. Dragon would eat anything and gathered he was consuming Octopus and Squid. Not knowing what any of it really was, he ate it, along with more familiar things he recognized as types of fish. None the less, strange or not, it wasn't bad. While they ate, Tran asked questions and brought up subjects, feigning interest, making it appear conversational.

What Dragon really heard was that he was trying to find out about his past, where he came from, where he got started and where he had been in the business world prior to recent years.

Tran inquired about the David Li Foundation, pretending to be interested in David Li's philanthropic quests. Dragon was careful, sensing it was a lure of some sort. His senses were setting off alarm bells. He had feelings that Tran was seeking information about his past on behalf of someone else and couldn't quite 'see' the whole picture.

He had a choice to either be talkative about it, or to be vague. He instantly decided to be vague as saying as little as possible had always worked for him and perhaps in frustrating Tran he would force him to be more direct.

He formed his response. He provided him with a basic Google resume, not telling Tran anything that he likely didn't already know. Tran smiled a knowing smile at him then, recognizing what he was doing, but falling into the trap anyway.

"Mr. Li, you are reluctant to discuss your past I see. Where you were born, where you grew up, how you came to be who you are now? Am I right?" Tran asked.

Dragon was very amused by the direct question. Tran had just obviously stated what he really wanted to know. Or what he had been sent to find out.

"Mr. Tran, it is well known that I never discuss my personal life or my past life with anyone, so let's not waste anymore of each other's time. You asked to see me to make a stock purchase. We should get down to business. Otherwise I will thank you for the enjoyable evening and be on my way. My wife is waiting for me if you know what I mean," Dragon said.

He made a point of ending the questioning, knowing then that Tran was trying to get information on behalf of his father in law. It had come through in Trans' thoughts when Dragon had indeed become frustrating to him. He would report it to Chekov and Sensei as soon as he could.

"Very well Mr. Li, I know you have come a long way, so we may proceed if you wish," Tran said.

He switched completely to business and began discussing the mining project. Dragon was well versed but allowed Tran to pitch it to him anyway. Finally Tran stated that he in fact did own the majority 25 percent.

Dragon sat eyeing him, ready to put it out on the table. "Mr. Tran, see me 25 percent and we have a deal," he said. His eyes never left Trans' as he waited for his reaction.

Tran was solid. He didn't even flinch, not physically anyway. Mentally he cursed David Li, but kept smiling on the outside.

"Nice Mr. Li, but you can't be serious. That would make us partners," Tran said evenly. "I don't engage in partnerships." Dragon kept his expression unchanged. "Neither do I Mr. Tran. It's an unfortunate side effect in this case. If it is that unappealing to you then I could simply make it a take-over. I'm trying to do you a favor and let you keep half your company. You have your choice," he said.

He hoped his very aggressive counter offer would corner Tran into finally cutting a deal. DLI was so powerful it could easily swallow up Tran International. He could see that Lee Tran didn't really want to be sitting before him. Something was forcing him into this position and Dragon guessed it wasn't business.

Trans' face was straight, unemotional and blank. "Very funny Mr. Li," Tran said. "25 it is, tell your lawyer to contact me." Dragon grinned slightly at him and Tran grinned back then. "Done," Dragon said. They nodded to each other and both stood up from the table. Tran crossed his hands in front of him and looked at Dragon curiously. "There's something I don't understand Mr. Li," he said. "You won't tell me where you were yesterday, but you will give me 30 million dollars of your money after a brief conversation." Dragon just nodded and laughed. "My personal life is more valuable to me than my money Mr. Tran," Dragon said. Tran nodded as he thought about it. "An interesting concept Mr. Li," Tran said.

Dragon then caught Lee Tran thinking that a life with David Li would be far more valuable than money. It was the first openly homosexual thought he had gotten from him.

They walked together to the fish tank doorway and paused. "Do you like boats Mr. Li?" Tran asked. Dragon sensed this was Plan B. "What have you got in mind Mr. Tran?" Dragon asked. "My father-in-law would like to meet you while you are here. He is interested in discussing real estate development with you, if you wouldn't mind indulging him. He has a formidable yacht and has requested that you and your wife and any members of your party, be his dinner guests," Tran said.

Dragon had to accept, as a means of gaining further ground and developing a relationship with Tran. He knew Tran liked to bargain. "On one condition Mr. Tran," Dragon said. Tran grinned at him. "I hope this is not going to be another of your partnerships Mr. Li," he said. Dragon gave him a megawatt grin then, disarming him sexually. "This is far less complicated Mr. Tran. My wife likes to dance. I know you own a club here and she would be most appreciative if you would show us the night life your city is known for," Dragon said. Tran looked up at him and smiled back. "It would be my pleasure, as long as it doesn't cost me half of everything I own," he said. Dragon just grinned and shook his head. "No, just as long as my wife enjoys herself is all I'm asking and I will accept your father-in-laws' invitation."

Tran clasped his hands in front of himself again, looking pleased, almost as if he were shaking his own hand. "Thank you Mr. Li, I will arrange it with him. Is tomorrow evening suitable to meet at my club?" he asked. "Yes that would be fine," Dragon said. "I will send a car; it's not far from the hotel. Your friends may like it as well, although no weapons please," he said. Dragon just nodded. "Good evening Mr. Tran. I will see you then."

He left and headed back. As he waited for the elevator Damascus came up beside him but they appeared to not know each other. They stepped into the elevator with another older Chinese couple. They selected their floor, Damascus pushed the floor below Dragon's and Dragon pressed the button for his. The elevator commenced its ascent and nobody spoke.

The woman was eyeing Dragon, and he could tell from her quite visible thoughts that she recognized him from recent media. She was trying not to stare. Damascus looked away from her and pretended to be interested in his phone, just in case he was recognized from media pictures in Paris. Dragon noted that her husband was paying no attention as his mind was focusing on an illegal poker game he was planning on attending later that night.

They reached their floor and departed. Dragon and Damascus eyed each other then but said nothing. Damascus would take the stairs from the lower floor and meet him in the suite. Jacob had departed ahead of them and had exited the hotel and re-entered via the staff entrance. Hundreds of Chinese worked in the hotel and he blended perfectly.

Dragon entered the suite, removing the earpiece and undoing his jacket. Damascus and Jacob were just moments behind him. Sensei eyed that they were all now there and turned to his laptop. Chekov appeared on the screen.

"Well done as usual Dragon," Chekov said. "What did you get that we didn't hear?" Dragon thought back on it and voiced his concerns. "Chang's his lover, first of all. Secondly, Tran's personal questions were on behalf of his father-in-law, I'm pretty sure. Otherwise, like you all heard, he was fairly straight forward, no deception that I could pick up on and simple to do business with," Dragon said.

Dragon paced, running a hand back through his hair. "There is one other thing that doesn't sit right with me. I could tell he didn't want to be in the position he was in. DLI could easily take over his company. Why invite me to potentially do so? It wasn't a good risk for him, offering me shares I mean. Chekov did you think about it from that stand point? Why would he let me own half his company when he was doing fine on his own? Capital for a mining project? I need answers to these questions Chekov," Dragon said.

Chekov was burning up his keyboard and eyed Sensei for his reactions, while he reconfirmed that the Tran Mining Project was legitimate.

Sensei paced then as well. "I couldn't get much more than what Dragon got but I agree that Tran was told to find out where you came from by Richard Ng. I caught a slight concern that he would disappoint Ng having not learned anything, but he had success at having you agree to meet the man. It's puzzling; I need to concentrate on it later. But I think Dragon is correct thinking that the share offer was simply a means to an end. Richard Ng wants to meet you and we don't know why," Sensei said. He was very concerned about Richard Ng. It could be simply business, but he wasn't sure.

Dragon shared a look with Sensei then focused again. "Chekov, find out about the yacht, where it is, details," Dragon said. "Of course," Chekov said. "Also, I am looking at a copy of Tran International's Mining Proposal to the Nigerian Government, dated two years ago, for which they did receive a license and Land Rights Grant. It's a legit project, and he definitely could use capital."

Dragon felt satisfied, wanting to put an end to it for the moment. "Chekov, you're my pretend lawyer so follow through and make me richer, I know you love that shit," Dragon said. "I'm already on it and pretty soon you will have made me richer, so thank you for that," he said. Dragon eyed him through the screen.

"Does money get you hard Chekov? Like pictures of my wife?" Dragon asked. Chekov eyed him briefly then went back to his screens. "Both work very well, thank you for asking," Chekov said.

He was happy with his comeback, not allowing himself to be baited, until Raven had moved beside Dragon making him gape at her.

"Got to go my friend," Dragon said. He grinned at him and turned her so her sexy butt in the revealing lace appeared to the camera, nearly choking Chekov. "Yes I see that," Chekov said. "Um, er, don't let me keep you."

He flushed, swallowing, adjusting his glasses and forcing himself to look away at Sensei instead, pissed off that Dragon had somehow managed to unravel him yet again.

"Good night Chekov," Sensei said.

Dragon vaguely heard Sensei, as he pulled Raven into a sweet kiss, having missed her. "What were you up to all evening baby?" he asked. "Nothing, I sat with Sensei and waited for you. Sarge and Wax were boring, listening; I couldn't even pry into Sarge's private life or anything because he was busy," she said.

Sarge shook his head at her. "Scotch?" he asked Dragon then. "Sure, a quick one," he said. Sarge seemed to just notice Raven then, having been absorbed in things up until then.

"What the fuck are you wearing?" he asked. She shrugged and coiled closer into Dragon's body, pulling him down to the sofa with her. "He told me not to be naked, so this was in the drawer," she said.

"You should wear that stuff more often," Wax said. He eyed her approvingly and downed his Scotch, making ready to retire for the night. "Goodnight people," he said.

"Thanks Wax, you too Sarge, Damascus, guys. Tomorrow we'll move forward," Dragon said.

Everyone called it a night and he stood then, in front of her, so the platinum DLI was about her eye level from the sofa. It taunted her and her eyes glazed slightly. She held her hand out for him to take.

"I just had dinner, but I've got an appetite still," Dragon said. Pulling her into him he hardened.

"Good night Papa," Raven managed over her shoulder as Dragon pulled her to the bedroom.

He closed the door, still holding her firmly by the hand and she sensed his game had begun, trying not to let it weaken her too soon.

He eyed her, assessing her. "As sexy as you look in that you need to be naked right now," he said. She ran her hands over it but looked for his approval as she obediently removed the camisole then the lace panties.

When she stood naked before him he melted her with his look. "Now undress me," he said.

She felt almost faint getting close enough to smell him. She pulled the jacket down his arms, its light wool feeling soft and sexy to her against his hard muscles. She laid it neatly on the back of a chair. She then reached up and loosened the necktie and slid it off from under the collar of the light blue shirt.

The sight of him watching her do this was making her want to pull him down on her, but she kept going. She put the tie with the jacket and continued undressing him, unbuttoning his shirt, forcing herself not to simply rip it off. She removed the cuff links last and as she undid them from his wrists, his hands looked so sexy to her she couldn't help but kiss the inside of his palms.

Her lips on him made him strain the front of his pants even more and he couldn't resist touching them, watching as she sucked his middle finger. Her lips were soft and her silky tongue made him need it.

Remembering her task, trying to focus, she pulled the shirt off him and draped it over the jacket. Moving back to him, she ran her fingertips over his chest muscles, teasing his nipples. She leaned up to lick them but he stopped her.

His upper lip trembled slightly as she affected him but he controlled himself and moved her hands back down to his next piece of clothing.

She eyed the belt. It would have to be next. Using both hands she undid the DLI buckle and loosened the belt, then undid the top button of his pants. That was when he stopped her, taking both her wrists, a calculated sexy look in his eyes, offering her the inevitable.

She looked at his open pants, exposing the wonderful area below his belly button but above his erection. She ran her fingers over it, taught and smooth. She loved to kiss him there and pleaded with her eyes to do so. He caught her thoughts as she looked up at him.

"You want to put your mouth on me?" Before she could answer, with his left hand he grasped her by the hair. "That's what you're going to do," he said. He looked wild now, holding her by her hair and pushing her to her knees. "Is this what you want?" he said.

He took himself free of his pants. She looked up at him with her eyes and parted her lips, begging to touch him with her pink tongue. In response he let his head fall back and pulled her against him.

She kissed his skin from his belly button down, gently licking and biting him. She held him by his hips and took her time getting to the part where he needed it the most. He couldn't wait to feel her soft tongue on his aching hard-on and pushed himself deep into the back of her throat, holding her there, gasping at the feel of it.

He was watching her lips on him, working on him. He had a dark wet animal glow in his eyes, lost in their sexy game. He withdrew, letting her breathe. She was glassy eyed, lips dripping saliva, kissing his length from the base to the tip then starting on him again.

He pulled the belt from around him and she could see it wrapping around his right hand. She paused, holding him, looking up at him. She pressed the tip of him to her sexy pout, tempting him to lose it.

"What do you want?" she asked. "This?" She kissed his most sensitive area, teasing with her tongue and watching him watch her.

It made his lower abs clench and he had to stop his orgasm. He smiled down at her and pulled her hair away. "You'd like to ruin me right now, wouldn't you?" he said. "And you could. It's a nice talent you have."

He took himself and holding her hair again he rubbed the head of his erection across her lips. She knelt at his feet, panting, wanting, her thighs begging for him now, wetness dripping from her.

He pulled her up and clasped her wrists behind her back. Now on fire, he was alive in her mind.

"You make me crazy. Do you like doing that to me?" he asked. She knew she would feel the belt with her answer. "Do you?"

He let it fall quick and sharp across her tummy as he twisted her by her arms to meet its' bite. She was a gasping mess now, his exact use of roughness, pain and sexuality was going to make her come without him even touching her.

Sensing her need he let his smile curl up at the corner. He pushed her to a round console table, laying her roughly on her back on its hard surface, moving between her legs as she willingly let them fall open for him. Using his fingers, his hand still wrapped with the belt, he pressed them into her wet openness. It felt like maybe only seconds to her as she squirmed wetly on his hand, moaning and soaking his fingers with her come.

"Good girl," he said. "But this is what happens when you make me crazy."

Before she could recover he withdrew his fingers and turned her over on the table, easily positioning her as she lay weak from her climax. Taking the blue tie, he tied her wrists to one of the table legs, stretching her over it so she could still stand on her toes. Eyeing his work he let his fingertips caress down her back and over her butt.

"Now," he said. "Do you think I like doing this to you? I have to because you need it."

He let the belt snap across her butt cheeks, the leather biting her, making her cry out. She buried her face between her forearms, her hair hiding her, a light sweat forming over her body now.

"You need to be reminded not to tease me," he said.

He spread her legs and knelt down putting kisses up her inner thighs. He kissed the hot red line forming across her butt and he kissed her wet sex. She was trembling everywhere from it now, from the sensations, from him, his touch, his aura and his power over her. He licked her from behind, tasting her readiness.

"Maybe I should tease you now," he said.

She moaned no, but he made her cry out, tapping her nerve endings quickly and repeatedly with the end of the belt. Stopping short of her orgasm, denying her, he stepped back and looked at her.

He knew she needed one more feel of the belt for it to be perfect for her and it all lay in the timing of it. He removed his pants all the way, toying with her, letting the belt draw across the small of her back.

"Looking at you now, a wet mess like this, what do you think that does to me?" he said.

He pushed against her wetness making her gasp. He brought the belt down hard across her butt. She cried out then and he slammed himself all the way inside her, making her lose it. Letting the belt unwrap from his hand he held her hips and gave it to her. He smacked her butt hard twice with his hand, stinging her until she came all over him.

He held off his orgasm for the moment, even though he was dying for it. When she had finished, he slid gently out of her, making her whimper into her hair. He knelt to untie her hands, releasing her. He turned her and pulled her into his hold carrying her to the bed as she moaned for him.

"I know baby, take me now," he said. She was lost completely in his sexual vibration, pulling him down on her mouth. He moved all the way over her, sliding hard inside her. Not releasing their kiss, he kept his mouth hard on hers and moved himself inside her until he exploded, only letting her mouth go then because he was gasping for breath, groaning as the waves hit him. His wetness flooded into her and she held him, letting him come.

"Baby," he kissed into her neck. "I love you."

She brushed his hair away from his brow, kissing his face softly beside hers, loving the feel of him on her, against her, inside her. He lay down on her warmly then eventually beside her tightly.

They wanted more but exhaustion took over and he sweetly put them to sleep, wanting to wake up to her and love her again then.

It had come to him like it always did but it was a different dream. Still the frightening images, the pain and fear and hatred, but the difference was that he awoke from it on his own, while she still slept. It was the usual horror but it had ended when he had finally won.

CHAPTER THIRTY TWO

RICHARD NG

The next day passed slowly as they waited to meet with Lee Tran at his night club. Sensei and Raven had ventured out into the city, only for appearance sake, to shop and sight-see. Dragon and the rest of them were stuck inside, pretending to be carrying on business, Damascus and his team basically hiding out. They were all stir-crazy waiting for the evening to begin. Chekov had busied Damascus for awhile with a profile for Thailand that his team was to undertake straight after Hong Kong.

Finally they all gathered to discuss the evening's events. Sensei, Damascus and his team would wait in the suite and listen to the evening unfold and be available if they were needed, which they likely wouldn't be. Wax and Sarge would accompany Dragon and Raven, unarmed. A car was coming at 10 pm. They were all restless and wanting to move on with things. It would be a boring night for the boys but they were used to spending time in each others' company. Sensei would entertain them with some stories while they waited out the night. He had promised them that the next day, depending on the future arrangements with their target, they could get lost in the city for awhile.

They had all gone to the Hotel gym and spa earlier and then Dragon had made love to Raven for the rest of the time until dinner. He had wanted it slow and soft and she had adored it. They now held each other, sharing a kiss before dressing for their evening. He found a deep purple almost plum colored dress. It was perfect, clinging to her body. The neckline was a deep V that showed off her cleavage and it was backless, but had long sleeves made of a see-through nylon of the same color purple, the label said Dior. Dragon eyed her in it and thought she looked stunning. It was quite short and he found some black silk and lace panties for her to wear under it. He slid them onto her, making her quiver as he adjusted them on her hips. He looked at the selection of shoes and boots and decided she should show off her legs, choosing a short ankle boot in black leather with a nice spiky heel.

He attached the gold diamond encrusted Dragon around her neck and the gold set diamond studs. He pulled her hair into a thick higher set pony tail, smoothed back from her face but thick and curling and long, flowing down from the thick gold covered elastic that held it. "Beautiful babe," he said.

He pulled on some dark wash denim jeans that fit his butt perfectly and hugged his muscled thighs, sitting perfectly on his hips, buttoned up a black cotton dress shirt, leaving it open at the top and grabbed a black jacket. He pulled the DLI belt on, eyeing her, remembering the feel of it in his hand from the night before. She eyed him and standing just that much taller in her heels, kissed his collar bone and snuck an extra button undone on his shirt, so she could see his chest definition. He raised an eyebrow at her, as she kissed inside the shirt, softly on his chest muscle.

"Are you going to be able to make it out of this room angel?" he asked. "Lead the way baby," she said. Her eyes sparkled and her lips shined a dark pink at him that he just had to taste again. "Stop baby," she said. The touch of his tongue sent contractions down her tummy. "I have to last until we get back here." He smiled at her. His lips were wet from hers. "I'll be thinking about you 'lasting'," he said.

They went out then to join the others, ready to get on with it. Wax and Sarge were dressed similarly to Dragon. Damascus and the boys were in partial states of the HQ uniform, pants with no tops, tops hanging undone, hair loose, half ready for anything. Sensei seemed oddly distant for some reason. It was as if he was partially in one of his meditative states, not quite with them on the same level.

"Sensei?" Dragon said. He was suddenly concerned. "Son," Sensei said.

He became alert then, not wanting to disarm Dragon of any of his natural confidence and demeanor by worrying him. Dragon tilted his head at Sensei, using his mind and intuition. Sensei met his eye.

"I will let you know if there is anything to worry about, but I will say, you must keep your eyes open, I feel that you are going to see something that you will not like," Sensei said.

He hoped to reassure him and provide him with the only advantage he could 'see' for the moment. Dragon nodded, definitely taking it to heart but refocusing as it was time to go. The bellman had called to say a car was waiting. At the last second before they all disappeared out the door, Sensei called out, seemingly not of his own volition.

"Sergeant Willis, you must look behind you," he said. Sarge paused, not understanding what he meant, but taking it in none the less. "Ok Sensei, I will," he said. He turned out the door ran for the elevator.

They were gone and Sensei had an overwhelming need to meditate, he needed to understand. It was important now and he needed to hurry. Why, he was not sure.

"Damascus, summon Chekov and stay on it, I need a few moments," he said. Damascus responded instantly, attaching the earpiece and lighting up Chekov.

They rode in silence the few blocks to their destination. The car pulled up outside a gleaming high rise with the name TRAN in bright red, across the entry. They looked at each other and Wax was the one to speak.

"There's nothing to it, but to do it," he said.

They nodded to each other and the driver opened the door for them to exit the car and another of Tran's people appeared, prepared to escort them to Tran's night club.

Chekov had a swirling image of the building's floor plan on one of his many screens and was analyzing it as they went in. It was located on one of the upper floors of the building. How it passed fire codes and capacity codes he didn't know.

The minion sent to escort them was burly looking, with close cut hair and such squinting eyes it was hard to tell how or if he could actually see out of them. Still they said nothing between them and followed him. The elevator let them out into what appeared to be a plush office like setting. They followed a short hallway, red plush carpet with gold lines running the perimeter. They stopped by a large mahogany door with an enormous brass handle. Using the handle he opened it and allowed them to pass through. Inside was another world.

They were in fact on the 37th floor of a 40 story building. Dragon glanced about him, noticing instantly Lee Tran approaching them. "Mr. Li, welcome, gentlemen," Tran said. He spoke smooth, slightly accented English. He nodded to Wax and Sarge. "Excuse me Mr. Li, if my men may search your men?" he said. Dragon just nodded and stepped aside as two business suit clad, short, slight, Asian men patted Wax and Sarge down. They looked appropriately aggravated by it. "My apologies," Tran said. A slight note of sarcasm gave away that he did not mean it. "You said no weapons Mr. Tran," Dragon said. "Thank you for obliging Mr. Li," he said.

He smiled then. "Ah, this is your stunning wife, Raven." Tran moved on, giving Raven what she flashed to Dragon as a "Creepy" smile. She nodded to him, saying nothing, as Dragon would answer for her. "Yes, Raven, Mr. Tran."

Chang had slid closer then, eyeing Wax and Sarge. Dragon again caught his sexual thoughts, especially about Wax whom he found fascinatingly gorgeous. Dragon made a quick note to tease Wax about it later as Wax was oblivious to Chang's thoughts. Dragon introduced them and they nodded and gave Tran obligatory fake smiles. Chang couldn't resist the opportunity and moving closer to Wax asked if they would like drinks. "Bring us a bottle of Scotch, if you don't mind," Wax said.

They broke off slightly and observed their surroundings. They took note of any cameras or listening devices. Also, who was in the room, where the exits were, the fire alarms and items that could be potentially used as weapons.

"Mr. Li, a drink?" Tran asked. "What are you having?" Dragon said. He feigned flattery but actually wanted to drink out of the same bottle as Tran, a precaution against tainted or drugged alcohol.

"I was waiting for your selection Mr. Li," Tran said. He batted his narrow eyes at Dragon, returning the superficial flattery, coming across almost flirtatiously. "1942 Tequila," Dragon said. "Nice Mr. Li," Tran said. He nodded to one of the suits, who moved off to the bar to get it.

They were in a large observation room, it appeared. Protected from the sound of the music by thick glass, it over-looked the throng of people in the club, dancing and mingling. Dragon moved to the large panoramic window and looked down into the club. It was dark with blue fluorescent lights lining the aisles and dance floor, white and pink and purple neon lines everywhere on the walls. Through the glass they could slightly catch the pounding music. The other wall was windows, out onto the city.

Tran was watching Dragon and wanted his approval but then remembered his manners. "Mr. Li would your wife care for something?" he asked. His disdain for females was very apparent. "She's partial to Champagne," Dragon said. He put his arm around her then, protectively, showing Tran his obvious emotion towards her. "Ah very good, I have the best, Mrs. Li," he said.

He faked graciousness, nodding once again to the suit to bring a bottle of Champagne as well. Raven looked at him innocently and nodded, giving him a half smile.

Tran eyed her then, seeing what it was all about when it came to the two of them. She was a fine specimen, for a female, he conceded to himself. David Li on the other hand was something else all together. A shame he played for the wrong team, he thought, which came through loud and clear to Dragon.

Dragon found Tran much less guarded than he had been during their business meeting so he gave him a sexy half smile, testing to see how easy he would be to charm. Chang nearly fainted, he noticed out of the corner of his eye and Tran had to clear his throat, flashing his eyes at Chang then. Dragon and Raven could see that the two of them had been in a lover's quarrel earlier about Dragon. Tran had berated him for what he considered to be 'Drooling over the man,' during their business meeting the day before and had warned him to control himself during their upcoming evening.

Dragon suspected Tran was an insecure domineering type, the one with the money, the one who wore the pants. Chang had secret animosity for him but stayed because of the life style. Dragon and Raven eyed each other and she mentally suggested he remove his jacket to see what else would come to the minds of the men before them. Dragon slid the jacket off his shoulders, and Raven obediently took it.

He flexed his biceps and adjusted his shoulders, giving Tran another disarming smile. "Shall we sit, Mr. Tran?" Dragon said. The suit was coming with the Tequila bottle, glasses, and the Champagne. Tran stumbled verbally then, seeing Dragon's shoulders, his chest and then the front of his pants, the path of his eyes obvious. Dragon looked down into his face.

"Mr. Tran?" Tran twitched slightly and forced his eyes to Dragon's. "Oh, uh, yes of course Mr. Li," he said. "Please over here." He motioned to a table overlooking the city.

Raven eyed Dragon, trying not to lose it and start laughing out loud. He scolded her mentally and she behaved, but wished she could sit with Sarge and Wax and maybe have some fun at least. They were leaning on a granite bar overlooking the dancing. Chang was pouring them drinks and was now 'drooling' over Wax, much to her amusement.

Behind the bar was a huge 6' by 8' mirror. It was a two way mirror, commonly found in clubs. There was a small office behind it. Tran's father-in-law watched.

Dragon had sat Raven, then himself, opposite Tran, and they had drinks poured for them. Trans' phone made a sound and he eyed it.

"Excuse me Mr. Li, one moment," he said.

He rose from the table and went behind the bar and through a door, into the back office area. Dragon heard Chekov in his earpiece then.

"He's behind the bar wall, talking to another man. There's no one else in there just the two of them," he said.

Tran eyed his father-in-law nervously. "What?" he said. He faced the older man, feeling inadequate as always. "He said he would come to the Yacht tomorrow. I did what you asked. It's all going as planned." Richard Ng stood and took Lee Trans' face in his hands. He kissed him on the lips then smiled to him. "You did good little boy so don't be scared. I have a change of plans though. Don't let him leave. Any of them," Richard Ng said. Tran blanched and he was scared. "Why? I did what you asked. How am I supposed to do that? Have you seen the size of them all?" Tran said.

Richard Ng produced a tiny plastic bag no bigger than a coin, containing a white substance. He handed it to Tran, taking his hand as if in a hand shake and depositing it into his palm. Tran understood then.

"Ok, I'll do my best, but he's a careful man," he said. "Yes I realize that," Ng said. "I'll wait."

He sat back down at the desk, dismissing Tran. Richard Ng had been waiting a long time and was quite happy to wait a little longer. Lee Tran didn't understand but would do what he was told. He knew not to ask questions.

To Chekov's eyes it looked as though they had embraced then shaken hands. It appeared odd but harmless so he did not report anything. It bothered him that he could not hear what had been said and a bad feeling began to creep over him as he instantly perceived the flaw in the profile. He reacted with his instincts then.

"Dragon, I have no explanation but you need to abort," he said.

Tran returned to the table then, his mind on just how he was supposed to accomplish his new task. He had thought it was enough that he had lured David Li to Hong Kong, and then drawn him into a dinner on the yacht, but now this.

Dragon heard Chekov's order as did Sarge and Wax, Damascus, all of them. Immediately he sensed some kind of problem, some kind of warning, and he eyed Raven. He wished he could talk to Sensei and excusing himself from the table for a moment he pulled Raven with him. Holding her he pretended to be looking at the city lights and having a moment with his wife. He reached out in his mind to Sensei then, hoping he could connect, while he figured out a way to end the evening. Raven agreed. She had a distinct feeling that none of this was real. That something else was going on.

Sensei had been in his own mind, away from Chekov and the live world for some time and felt Dragon reaching out to him. He knew he should advise him to leave there immediately. He didn't know why, but he needed to come back to the safety of the hotel until they did know why. He went out of his room to the laptop where Damascus held vigil.

"Chekov what's happening," he asked. Chekov filled him in. "Dragon needs to leave there, now, they all do. I've ordered them to abort, there's a flaw in the profile," he said.

Sensei mentally went to Dragon in his mind, giving him a clear message to go and go as soon as he could. He felt panicked suddenly. He was distracted by Damascus, prompting him to listen to Chekov.

"I found a picture of Richard Ng on his yacht," Chekov said. Sensei froze then, his premonitions were coming true. "Send it to Dragon, immediately!!" Sensei said. He was nearly raising his voice. "Done," Chekov said. They waited.

Dragon got Sensei's message loud and clear and pulled Raven back to the table, eyeing Sarge and Wax, alerting them to a change of plans. He sat again with Raven, deciding to finish their drinks and then pretend to get a business call that would end the evening. He sent her a mental image of his plans and she eyed agreement, having also heard Sensei. She picked up her glass to finish her Champagne.

Dragon's phone vibrated in his pocket as he downed the rest of his Tequila. Assuming it was Chekov giving him an 'out', he pulled it free and eyed it, vaguely aware of Tran chatting about how much he had invested in the club. The message from Chekov read, 'Richard Ng picture'.

Dragon was hit all at once by a mega lode of horror. Sensei's warning came back to him, about using his eyes, that he would see something. He looked at the photo, sure instantly of who it was. He sent his thoughts to Sensei and Raven choked on her last sip of Champagne. Alive and well on Dragon's phone was his past, his nightmare, his hate that was Richard Ng. The very man, who had kept him, tortured him, ruined him and nearly killed him. It was Sensei's fear that someone wasn't there that day; that someone would see the tattoo, someone would find him.

"We have to leave," Dragon said, and that was the last thing he knew.

"Chekov, Richard Ng is from Dragon's past!!" Sensei now shouted. "Get Tom-Tom on that roof, we're going on foot."

Damascus and the rest scrambled to get themselves and their weapons together. Sensei attached an ear piece, threw Wax's gun and every weapon they had into Sarge's pack and they were out the door and running.

"Where are they Chekov?" Sensei said. "Keep talking to me son, get us there." He was panicked now, feeling as if he would rip into shreds if he didn't get to them immediately.

"Upstairs it looks like now, empty space above the bar, the top floors. It looks like Sarge and Wax are in a room, a small room, they're sitting, guarded. There was no gunfire; I heard nothing, just the last thing Dragon said about them having to leave. Then I heard 'bring them', I think it was Trans' voice. He must have managed to drug them," Chekov said.

"Just get Tom-Tom on that roof and get us to the club, to those floors," Sensei said.

A million things were running through his mind, as they plowed their way out of the hotel and onto the street, not caring who saw them. They could see the Tran building four or so blocks away and ran.

Chekov was on fire, running screen after screen of the building, keeping a constant watch on where Dragon and Raven were. He didn't tell Sensei what he was seeing, wanting to keep him focused on retrieving them.

"Sensei, you can't get to them through the club. It's too public, they'll stop you and you can't kill everyone. I can get you in the elevator they used that can take you to the floor they were on and then direct you to them from there. Get to the south side of the building, there's a door. Attach Mishka's decoder and I'll run access codes. It takes a minute or two but it's the only way," Chekov said. He looked at his screens and it chilled him.

Sarge and Wax had been taken to a room at gunpoint by four of them. They were outnumbered and unable to react to anything as they were unarmed and it would have been fatal. Chekov could see they had no choice but to comply. They were locked up and guarded.

Raven was carried and two had dragged Dragon upstairs, above the club, to a vast empty space. He cringed as he could see someone had hit her and she had slumped to the floor at their feet. He was scared for them, but he kept working. He would have the access code for the door any second. Chekov's hands shook as he keyed the code in, finally, the door buzzing for Sensei, who ripped it open. "You're in," he said. Chekov breathed with relief. "Elevator; it only goes to that floor." He realized he was out of breath from holding it.

Dragon had come out of the drug quickly, having not had enough of it for someone his size to be out for long. He took in the situation, trying to control his panic that he could not see Raven. He fought the drug haze, listening to approaching footsteps, trying to understand he wasn't in a dream.

He was chained, hands above his head, thick leather cuffs around each wrist and a large caliber chain, strung over a girder in the unfinished ceiling. He nearly hung, just able to balance carefully on the toes of his feet. The buttons on his shirt had been ripped off, likely in their efforts to drag him, and it hung open.

He heard the voice and turned to see a face from his nightmares. "Ah, Dragon, here we are. I hope you are comfortable, I wanted to make you feel at ease, familiar if you will. Sorry about the drug but I know only too well how it is with you," Ng said.

Dragon had many things go through his mind at that moment but he focused on his survival, like he always had.

He eyed Ng. "Ricky," Dragon said. He recalled the name, so many years ago now.

"How sweet of you to remember," Ng said.

He had a sickly tone in his voice as he came closer so Dragon could look at him. They faced each other for the first time in nearly ten years. Ng's eyes feasted on him and Dragon's burned into him with hatred unequivocal to anything earthly.

Ng just smirked, familiar with Dragon's loathing of him. "You hate me Dragon. Yes, I know that all too well. But you were always my favorite. It always saddened me that I could never reach you. No one has ever come close to meaning anything to me like you did. And look at you now. So impressive, I must say."

He drifted slightly as his eyes roamed over Dragon's body, making up for the ten years.

"And to think it was that lovely Dragon on your back that brought you back to me," he said. He eyed Dragon with adoration. "I was so pleased; you see I thought you were dead, but clearly you are far from it."

He reached inside Dragon's open shirt and caressed his chest. He seemed adrift in his sick mind, gazing inwardly. When Dragon jerked away from his touch it brought him back. Becoming aware again he pulled his hand away and looked at Dragon with anger and hurt.

"The world loves you and your pretty wife, but little do they know. It's you, isn't it Dragon, striking back at all the wrongs that were done to you. It was easy for me to see, when I put all the pieces together." He turned away then, lost in thought. "I got away that day, when your people came. But it was a wakeup call." He turned back to Dragon, looking up at him, bewildered and demented, defeated somehow. "I tried to escape it, the life, but I don't know Dragon, beautiful David Li. I don't think I did as well as you have." His eyes were wet. "Some things in life aren't right. I tried to teach you that."

Dragon looked at him, finding it unbelievable, but not, all at the same time. He had been shocked into silence letting Ng reminisce. But he needed to gather his wits.

"It's not some things in life that aren't right Ricky, it's you," Dragon said. His disgust was clear in his voice. "You and everyone like you."

"Ah yes!" Ng said. He seemed to become more animated all of a sudden. "You were always so difficult to get along with, fighting it. I liked that about you, many of us did. But we had to deal with that didn't we? I'm sorry I had to hurt you so much. It was better when we found the drug." He smiled at Dragon then, fondly like he was remembering wonderful times.

Dragon could see his insanity then. "Where's my wife Ricky? She's going to want to watch me kill you," Dragon said. He looked around, twisting to see other parts of the floor.

Ng smirked at this but snapped his fingers and from a dark corner behind Dragon, Tran and Chang shoved her in front of them. Dragon had to steel his emotions as he could see her cheek red and swelling and blood in the corner of her mouth. Tran brought her to Ng and he grabbed her by her hair and held her toward Dragon.

"She's like you, beautiful, strong, and likes to fight," he said. "Get your sick fucking hands off her," Dragon growled. "Don't worry Dragon. You know I don't like girls. Not like you used to. I just liked to watch you with them. You'd give them what they wanted and then you'd give them what they deserved. Be honest now. Tell her how much fun that was." He shoved Raven at Dragon then.

Dragon went crazy then. He snapped and howled at Ng, fighting the chains with all the rage he had ever had inside him. "Ng!! You fucking sick piece of shit!!" he raged. "Those were innocent girls. They didn't want anything!!! They didn't 'deserve' anything!!! You drugged me and made me do that!! He was spitting at him, veins about to burst. "I'm going to kill you. Kill you for everything you did to me!!! Everything you made me do that I can't forget no matter what!!!"

Ng made a maniacal grin at her and Dragon, then shoved her back to Tran who pushed her to kneel, as he stood behind her with a 9 mm pistol against her throat.

She was truly scared then, scared seeing him pushed over the limit. "Dragon! Dragon stop! Don't let him do this to you," she said. Ng stepped up close to Dragon. "Shut her up, Dragon. I don't like girls, especially mouthy ones."

Dragon heard her in his mind and tried to calm down. She went quiet and played along, pretending to be compliant, waiting for Dragon to tell her what to do. Easy baby, Dragon said to her in his mind. I'm alright now. We need to get out of this. Sensei is coming, so be ready.

"I want to see my friends? We've overstayed our welcome, and I'm really craving the sight of you being dead," Dragon said. He glared at Ng, knowing somehow that he would turn the tables and finally get his peace.

Ng looked amused. "Dragon, really? We have done this before and it takes me down memory lane, but because you mean so much to me, I must caution you to be realistic," Ng said. "You know how it always ends with us. I enjoyed you the most this way, don't you remember?" He eyed Dragon hanging, thinking of the things he used to do.

Dragon tried to shut it out and not let him destroy what was left of him now, feeling Raven's anger about to take over her ability to control herself as well.

"Where are my friends?" Dragon hissed at him. "Your friends are fine, very nice as well I might add. A little old for me though. I wish I'd found them much sooner," Ng said. He made Dragon hate him anew.

Ng moved to touch him again. Dragon could see he couldn't resist. He touched Dragon's face, his lips, then down his chest, all the way to the top of his pants. He stopped there but his breath caught as he remembered what was there. He went behind Dragon then and reached up his shirt at the back, pulling it up so he could see the dragon. He hugged Dragon's body to him lovingly, laying his face against the dragon, pressing his entire body against Dragons.

Dragon let him do it so he could see more clearly into his mind.

Ng sighed and held Dragon to him like a long lost love. "I really have missed you. Maybe when we take our little boat ride, I can relive some of my favorite memories of us before we finally say goodbye for good," he said. "It's going to be sad for me Dragon."

Dragon wanted to be physically sick as he endured Ng's assault, again tolerating his unwanted touch, his unwanted sexual desire and his unwanted ownership. He pushed the images of what he was talking about away from his mind, along with the overwhelming need to vomit.

"My friends, where are they?" he managed. It broke Ng out of his reverie and he released him. "They're fine, they will be joining us, have no fear," Ng said. He moved away, trailing his fingers off of Dragon as if he hated to let go.

Dragon could see the weak moment and intended to use it against Ng. Everything that was happening now had to count for something, Dragon thought. He had been given his chance and he was going to take it. He needed to act and it came to him what to do. Raven flashed her eyes at Dragon then, spurring him to do it. She wasn't tied so she was capable of anything and they had no idea.

Hey eyed her, showing her. 'Get Tran's gun, I'll grab Chang, shoot them both, get me down, leave Ng to me.' She let him know she was ready in her mind, and he nodded to her, 'now baby,' he said.

She moved then, lightening fast, grasping Tran's gun and turning it into his groin, using his own finger to pull the trigger. The gun went off removing his genitals at close range. He fell screaming as she grasped the gun away from him, getting instantly to her feet. She shot him in the face to shut him up, angry at him for hitting her when she was drugged.

Simultaneously Dragon had used his abdominal muscles to pull his legs up and wrap Chang in a scissor hold around his neck dragging him to the ground. Raven spun from Tran, shooting Chang between the eyes, as Dragon swung back trying to stay himself.

Ng had taken it all in and was running.

She took aim and shot the chain, freeing Dragon. Taking off after Ng he ran. Raven had kicked off her shoes and followed Dragon running. Dragon could hear a helicopter on the roof but it wasn't a Blackhawk.

Ng had disappeared into the stairwell ahead of them. He climbed the stairs, issuing orders on his phone as he went. He had burst out onto the roof, just as Sensei and Damascus and his team appeared from another rooftop stairwell with Sarge and Wax.

Damascus and Jacob had gotten them from the room they were in, killing the guards and freeing them, moving onward to find Sensei. They were all heavily armed now. There were four stairwell exits onto the roof and as they ran they covered them, looking for Ng's men to appear.

Dragon was running full out after Ng now, gaining on him as he headed for his helicopter that had been waiting for him. As he ran past Wax and Sarge who had come from a side angle to join him, he yelled to them to cover him, seeing one of Ng's men in the helicopter doorway taking aim on him.

Sensei intercepted Raven grabbing her from a full out run, which toppled them to the rooftop, as they tangled in a heap. She was struggling, fighting him. "No Dragon!!" She screamed through the rotor noise, as he ran straight into the gun sights.

Gunfire erupted everywhere now as Ng's man fired. Wax had taken aim and his shot met him in the forehead, killing him instantly. Sarge hit the pilot in the chest, shooting through the windscreen.

Not stopping, Dragon staggered, losing his momentum twisting back left as the bullet hit him. Raven screamed again as Sensei picked her up around the waist, turning her away, gunfire exploding all around them. Damascus and his team surrounded them, as Ng's men began to appear from the stairwells.

As Damascus and his team unloaded in a deafening blast of automatic gunfire, the Blackhawk rose up from below the edge of the rooftop like a monster from a sci-fi movie, roaring it's defiance, cannons, missiles and guns ready, rotors pulsing. It hovered, tilting forward like an alien invader eyeing them, its lights hunting them, blurred in the smoke and dust. Tom-Tom held it, waiting for Chekov's orders.

Dragon reached Ng in the deafening roar, pulling him backwards to the ground. He was on him then and he saw Ng's fear, saw his own rage and felt it overflowing. He wrapped the foot or so of dangling chain around his right hand and eyeing Ng with absolute hatred, he plowed him into oblivion with his chain covered fist. He beat him to death then, smashing his skull in, removing his face and not stopping even though there was nothing left of him he just kept hitting him.

He wasn't aware of Raven screaming, Wax pulling him backwards to the ground, throwing Ng's lifeless bloody body into his helicopter. The Blackhawk, was just a beating pulse in the background compared to the noise in his head.

Damascus' guns had gone quiet as there was nothing left of anyone. It was a death scene, a war zone. Sensei had shoved Raven into Damascus' arms as he needed to get to Sarge who lay motionless. Damascus went to his knees, shouldering his gun and held her while the rest surrounded him, eyeing everywhere, adrenalin pumping.

She had gone catatonic, seeing Dragons' thoughts as he beat Ng, seeing Sarge hit and fall. She had departed from reality.

Damascus pulled her hair away from her face and willed her to stay, much as she had done for him, not so long ago. She had heard him on some level and turned into him and clung to him, holding into him with everything she had. He knew he had to get her out of there, all of them, and he laid into her in an embrace of his whole body, all he could give her then, to protect her and make her feel safe until it was over.

"Sensei, I looked behind me like you said," Sarge said. "Good boy son, it saved you, it saved you," Sensei said.

He held Sarge's head to his chest, seeing how close he had come to losing another son. A shot had hit him in the side of his head above his ear, bone deep, stunning him, deafening him. He had shot the pilot and suddenly knew to look behind him, Sensei's warning coming to him instinctively. Moving suddenly, the shot grazed him deeply, instead of making it through the back of his head like it would have if he hadn't turned.

"Come, get up, we need to go," Sensei said. He urged him to move.

They made it to Tom-Tom then who had set down lightly, just enough for them to climb aboard. Wax had pulled Dragon, mostly by his shirt because he couldn't take either of his arms and now held him propped against him. Damascus pulled the door shut and they lifted off, in an eerie gloom, the rooftop lights illuminating the smoky aftermath of bodies and blood and death. Ng's pilot was apparently not dead and had begun to lift off shakily.

"Tom-Tom, take him out, get him over the water and eliminate him." Chekov ordered. "Affirmative," Tom-Tom said. They all sat in silence as Tom-Tom went after Ng's pilot. He chased him over the harbor where the debris would not harm anyone and sent a missile into the fuel tanks blowing it into thousands of pieces. It and everyone inside would be gone, ending in the ocean, falling from existence leaving a trail of negative energy. It went silent but for the noise in all their minds as Tom-Tom veered sharply to escape the explosion and took them away.

Sensei took charge. They were headed to the airport; Simon had been summoned and was waiting. They would fly immediately to Munich, Dragon and Sarge needing urgent medical attention. Tom-Tom would flee to Thailand with Damascus and wait while his team completed their mission. Sensei prioritized things and decided to give his attention to Damascus then. Damascus still held Raven, holding her to him with the love he clearly still had for her.

She lay with glazed eyes. Sensei took her and laid her against Dragon, who was also only half with them. He lay against the far wall on the floor, propped against Wax who held him semi upright, under his arms. Sensei laid her against Dragon's bloody chest, but he was only able to partially hold her as his left shoulder had a gunshot wound and his right hand was a smashed bloody pulp of broken bones, still wrapped in chain. Wax helped hold her against him, and Dragon rested his face on the top of her head.

Sensei had no idea what he was going to do with all that faced him, but he directed his attention to Damascus. "Son, you must go, I understand you are worried but all of you did everything you could here. You need to keep doing your job, and get through it. We will wait for you at HQ until you get back. You will only be a few extra days. I won't leave without you." Sensei reassured him. Damascus looked at Sensei, his dark eyes trying to find the comfort he was offering. "Thank you for everything," Sensei told them. "You saved their lives. I am proud of the men you have become. Be safe and I will see you in a few days," he said. He was trying to be positive with them, as Tom-Tom set them down beside the DLI jet.

They all nodded, and Sensei hugged Damascus to him, before taking Raven in his arms and leaving the Blackhawk for the jet. Damascus was proud of them too and he would take this in stride and deal with his anxiety at being separated from them. He and his team sat silent as Tom-Tom lifted off again, taking them off on a new journey.

Sensei carried Raven, and Wax had Dragon on one side and Sarge on the other, as they made their way to the jet. He shoved Dragon ahead of him up the stairs and pulled Sarge behind him. Sensei carried Raven past the gaping Simon, followed by Dragon who looked like a creature from a horror movie. He was bloody, everywhere, chains dangling from his wrists, bloody and dripping. He seemed unaware, not even noticing Simon.

"Mr Li!" Simon gasped. "Let's go Simon, we need medical attention. There was an incident with some business associates, we need to leave immediately," Sensei said. "Of course," Simon said. He pulled the stairs in, secured the doors and latched himself into his cockpit, knowing never to ask questions.

Dragon sat and allowed Wax to strap him in. "Son," Sensei said. "Are you alright for the moment?" Dragon nodded and let his eyes fall to Raven.

The seat belt was around her tiny hips. She had managed to curl into a fetal position on the seat in-between Sensei and Sarge. She was vacantly holding the gold diamond encrusted Dragon that was still somehow around her neck. Her knees and elbows were crusted with blood, her pony tail was half down and her face was dirt streaked with dried tears.

He sought her with his mind, weakly trying to reach her. He could 'see' that in her mind she was on the patio in Hawaii by the pool on a chaise, braiding Lily's hair. Dragon's tears for her came then, an uncontrollable reaction to seeing her lost from him at that moment and how her pain had taken her to a safer place. Wax turned and put his arms around his shoulders. He let his face rest against Wax's neck and his sobs wracked him into Wax's shoulder. Wax's own tears fell silently as his heart broke for his friends' anguish.

Sarge took Raven's smaller hand in his, trying to get her to look at him, tracing little lines on her palm. He was seeing if he could amuse her, something willing him to keep his own composure.

She reacted then, slightly, eyeing him from under her lashes, like she used to when she was little. She still touched the Dragon necklace but eyed his bloody hair. He looked at her with his serene blue eyes, looking to her like he did when they were younger. She had digressed with her only ability to protect her sanity. The cognitive part of her mind had told her he was dead.

"Raven, hey, can you fix my head for me?" he asked. "You can shave my hair off." She reached to him then and curiously moved his hair to see the wound in his scalp. "I thought you died," she whispered. Her tears were coming then, as she risked reality. "No." Sarge shook his head at her. "Me die? Uh Uh," he said. He smiled to her, letting his blue pools soothe her. "I'm right here, and I think I need you to stitch up this cut." She looked at him trying to believe what he was saying. "See," he said. He kissed her fingers of the hand he still held. "We're all here." She looked at them all then, stopping her gaze on Dragon.

"Baby," he said weakly. "You went somewhere, but can you come back now, I need you," he said.

He had control back almost but tears still wouldn't stop rolling down his face. She looked at him, then Sensei and then seemed to look nowhere at all, while her mind decided what place it was safe to be in. Her hands went to her seat belt then and she went to him, kneeling down between his knees, seeing his condition. Using his left hand he winced but managed to brush her cheek with his fingertips.

"I need you," he said. "Baby," she said. She was gradually coming back because he asked her to, but not wanting to see what was there.

It was killing Sensei and he felt he may actually lose it for the first time in his life. The seat belt sign flashed off then as they reached their cruising altitude, and he was on his feet.

"Wax, help me get him to the bed. Raven, bring some Vodka and a bowl if you can find one," he said.

Dragon's head lolled now, his blood loss, his pain level and his emotional state finally taking him down. She hurried to the bar as Wax and Sensei laid Dragon on the bed. Sensei had pulled his shirt off and undid his belt and the top of his jeans. She brought Sensei the Vodka and a bowl.

"Towels and whatever cloths are in the bathroom," he said. She went and got as many as were there. "Here Papa," she said. He handed her a face cloth. "Cold water, clean his face my dear. Wax, lift his shoulder and put this towel under it," Sensei said.

He handed Wax a thickly folded white towel. Dragon winced as Wax moved his shoulder, placing the towel under the wound. It appeared the bullet had gone right through, there was a hole in the front and an exit wound in the back. Sensei poured the Vodka onto it and into it. He was hoping to run the alcohol through the hole and have it run out the back, cleansing as best he could with what he had. Dragon cringed at the sting of it, gasping through the pain.

"Sorry son," Sensei said. "I can put you out?" "No, I'm Ok," he said. His eyes followed Raven as she tried to help him cope with the pain. She gently smoothed his hair back off his forehead, cleaning the sweat and spattered blood off his face. "Baby," he whispered. "SShhh," she said. "If Sensei wasn't here I'd do something that would make you feel a lot better." He closed his eyes and imagined it. Sensei grinned at her, loving her.

"OK, Wax, you need to go and get ice, crush it up and get it into something and put it against Sarge's head and don't let him sleep. Give him a drink, keep him talking. Get me one too actually he said, I don't give a fuck what," Sensei said. Wax nodded. "You're getting one too baby girl, and don't argue with me," Wax said. "And Wax can you bring ice in here too, use this bowl," Sensei said.

His attention turned to the cuffs still on Dragon's wrists. He unbuckled them one at a time. He freed Dragon's left wrist, then gently worked on the right one. Wax returned with the ice and some Scotch's for them. "Thanks Waxy, now stay with Sarge, he can't sleep. Ok?" Sensei said. "I'll be right out here if you need me," Wax said. He went to entertain Sarge.

"Papa, look at his hand," Raven said. As Sensei pulled the final cuff off the damage became evident. The chain had made nasty open wounds on the knuckles which were now crusted with dried blood. They needed stitching, but had swollen badly into gaping open flesh. Broken bones too numerous to count were evident even without an x-ray.

"All we can do on this plane is ice it, clean it and wait to get to Munich. An x-ray will show, but this will need to be redone surgically. I can only hope there is no nerve damage, or he won't use a bow or shoot again unless he becomes left-handed," Sensei said. "I'm here, hello," Dragon said weakly.

Raven kissed him. "Baby, don't worry OK, Papa will fix it. He fixed Wax's leg, remember?" she said. Dragon gave her a soft smile, trying not to wince as Sensei wrapped the damaged hand carefully so the displaced bones wouldn't move any further. He then covered it in ice.

"You can kiss me some more," Dragon said.

She gave him a sweet sexy smile and touched her lips gently to his, and he let her tongue soothe him. Sensei looked him over and decided it was all he could do for the moment unless he wanted pain relief. "Dragon, I can put you out if the pain is too much," Sensei said. "I'll be ok," he said. He knew Sensei would know if he was suffering with it too much.

Sensei rose then. "I'll give you a bit of privacy while I tend to Sarge, but Raven, he needs his energy for other things right now. Do you understand me?" He eyed her, giving her his warning look. "Yes Papa, don't worry." She smiled to him and drank her Scotch. Sensei downed his and went out.

"Baby, what do you want?" she asked. "Just kiss me," he said. So she did. She lay beside him as best she could, so as not to touch anything that would hurt him and she kissed him gently and passionately. Eventually he was straining the zipper of the jeans and she undid it to give him more room. "Just let me feel your warm hand on me baby," he said. "Are you sure?" she asked. She gently traced her fingers over his length. "Mmmm uh huh," he said, nodding his approval.

When Sensei came in later to check on them he sighed, as his love overwhelmed him. She had crawled against his chest, finding the remaining area of his body that wasn't injured and they were asleep. He hated to wake them but it was time to land. He touched Dragon's forehead, drawing him awake.

Dragon focused, now feeling his pain again, as he tried to move, not strong enough to pull himself up without the use of his arms. Sensei woke Raven and helped her up.

"Go little one and get Wax to help me," he said. Gently he fixed her hair away from her sleepy face. She went to get Wax.

Seeing her weak disheveled look Wax took her and gently sat her with Sarge who pulled her into him, closing the seat belt around her.

"Come here, let me hold you ok," he said. He was worried about her. She had seen a lot and it had hit her hard. She curled into his warmth, lying against his chest. "How are you Sarge?" she asked. "I have a headache," he said. "Wax wouldn't shut up and let me sleep." She smiled into his chest. "You aren't supposed to sleep when you have a head injury." "Well I can't stay awake forever," he pouted. "Papa will hook you up to some machine and then you can sleep. He will be able to tell everything about you, when you are sleeping, like even when you get a hard-on," she said. He squeezed her into him, smiling. "That's all you think about, isn't it."

CHAPTER THIRTY THREE
REACTION TO ACTION

Munich was just rising to a new dawn. "There's a new doctor at HQ, a woman," Sensei said. "Competent from what I'm told and she has an impressive resume. I don't know where the General finds these people? At any rate she may be able to help me." He was trying to stay positive, remembering Schultz.

He distracted himself then, wondering about the media fall out and how it was going to be handled. Chekov would likely have his hands more than full with this one. He took a deep breath, recalling his faith, the ever turning cause and effect, his understanding of reality.

They touched down in Munich safely, and sat silently as they taxied to the DLI hangar and yet another Blackhawk. A young pilot awaited them and lifted off as soon as they were secured. He had been instructed to get them back to HQ as fast as he could.

Chekov and the General awaited them when they stepped out of Wendy's care to head to the infirmary. "Come, this way," Chekov said. "We've moved the location, it's much larger now." They went through two large sliding doors into the new world of medicine that existed there now. The new doctor awaited them. "Dr. Yung," Chekov said. She nodded, but instantly turned to the task at hand, eyeing Dragon's condition, and Sarge's head. "This way," she said. She turned, expecting them to follow. There were four curtained bays. She motioned for them to use two of the beds and pulled the dividing curtain away so they could work together on both of them at once. "Sensei, please, what have we got?" She turned to him professionally, wanting his assessment.

"This is Dragon. You can see a gunshot wound and broken bones in his hand. This is Sergeant Willis," he said. He pulled Sarge's hair away, exposing the gaping laceration and bone damage to the side of his skull. "Ok, let's stabilize them," she said.

She pointed out where things were and Sensei and Raven assisted her in setting IV lines. Blood pressure and heart monitors adorned them and finally Morphine to start with for Sarge. Dr. Yung produced a synthetic pain killer that Sensei didn't like but realized was necessary, known as Fentanyl, several times stronger than morphine, inducing sleep in patients suffering from severe pain. She dosed Dragon with it, knowing when it came to examining his hand he would need it. He drifted away with it nearly immediately.

To distract herself and leave them clear to do what they needed to do for Dragon, Raven busied herself attending to Sarge who was drifting in and out. She found some scissors and did what she could to delicately trim the hair around his wound so it could be administered to without ruining all his hair. She cleaned his face. She then cut away his bloodied shirt, then everything else. She cleaned any blood from his chest and body, washed his hands and dried him, then covered him with a clean sheet and a blanket. She turned his head comfortably on the side so his neck wouldn't get sore.

"Papa?" she said. Dr. Yung was carefully examining the gunshot wound in Dragon's shoulder, so he gave her his attention. "Do you think I can simply stitch this closed?" she asked. Sensei put on clean gloves and carefully touched the wound. "Irrigate it for bone fragments first my dear then let us see it again," he said. She lined toweling under his head and around, and using a bottle of sterile fluids she rinsed it thoroughly. It was unnerving, as small pieces of bone fell loose and washed away. He had been closer than they had realized initially when she had gotten it fully exposed.

Sensei and Dr. Yung paused to evaluate it at that point. "He's a lucky man," Dr. Yung said. "I would staple that closed. The bone will repair itself. I will do a CT scan and an MRI anyway, but as far as the outer wound goes, that's all it needs I think," she said. She looked at Sensei, for his opinion.

"Go ahead dear," Sensei said to Raven. "Papa, I've never stapled anything before," she said. Dr. Yung smiled. "Here, it's easy," she said. Taking the devise she deftly pulled the skin to meet in a neat seam and pressed a staple over it. "Okay?" she asked. Raven nodded to her. "It's just Sarge's head, what could go wrong?" she said.

Wax laughed then, knowing Sarge would appreciate her humor.

Carefully and tentatively she completed the task, closing a nearly five inch tear in his scalp. It covered the grazed bone but he would have an indent. Antibiotics and pain medication would handle the rest and tests would be able to clear him of internal brain injury. She carefully brushed his hair back and secured it off the staples allowing the air to keep it dry and clean. He slept evenly then, as she lay his hands by his sides.

Dr. Yung and Sensei decided Dragon's shoulder wound would have to close itself. An MRI could determine if there was any damage to the tendons, but it would drain and clear itself, infection being the biggest initial hurdle to overcome. Antibiotics would help and they would have to wait. They moved on to the issue of his hand. An X-ray revealed the gruesome news and they stood analyzing it, deciding what approach to take. There were several broken bones, in the fingers and hand and two in the wrist. They decided on a two part treatment which consisted of setting and immobilizing the hand and finger bones and then using screws they could set and heal the wrist bones.

The massive tissue damage caused by the use of the chain only complicated things. They couldn't just set the bones and cast it because of the open flesh. Dr. Yung suggested an intricate surgery, gaining access from the already open tissue, setting the bones one by one using tiny screws and plates, and then stitching the wounds closed. A changeable dressing could be applied and 2 pins would protrude from his wrist bones for a four week period before they could be removed, then the wrist cast traditionally. With any luck there would be little or no nerve damage but that would remain to be seen. Sensei agreed to her approach and they prepared him.

He told Raven to remove Dragons' clothes, to give her something to do as he could tell she was not happy about the news and was struggling to stay strong for him. She nodded and went about it, as Dr. Yung gave her some privacy, stepping away to have a word with the General about their findings. Dragon lay unaware, soundly drugged, breathing evenly. Raven trembled with worry for him as he lay finally naked. She covered him up to his waist in a sheet and blanket, avoiding his injured hand that was nearly impossible to look at. His left arm was secured across his body in a bandage, keeping his shoulder from moving too much as it drained clear reddish fluids. She had to content herself with brushing his hair back from his face, and kissing his forehead.

Dr. Yung returned shortly, ready to begin. "The General and Chekov left to attend to things but wish to be notified as soon as we are through here," she said. Sensei nodded, anxious to move on with it.

Wax had slid to the floor and was sitting waiting by Sarge's bed. Raven thought she had never really seen Wax look unhappy until just then. Sensei, ever aware of them, spoke to Wax then.

"Son, take her and look after her, maybe a bath, some clothes and come back in a couple of hours. We should be nearly done and can wake him up then for her," Sensei said. Raven panicked. "Papa no, I have to stay with him," she said. She looked pleadingly at him, her tears falling then.

Sensei's heart was breaking for her and Dr. Yung spoke then, trying to help. "Raven, he's in wonderful hands here and I'm worried about you. Go with your friend and take a minute to yourself, he will be right here," she said.

Wax had stood and had her hand, ready to pick her up if he had to. "Come on kid, they're right," he said.

She eyed Sensei for reassurance and he flooded her mind with affirmations that he would look after Dragon while she was gone for just a bit. She allowed Wax to take her, not even realizing she had no shoes on, the dress from what seemed like forever ago, that was dirty and torn from her tangle with Sensei on the roof, blood from Dragon or who knew covered her and touching her hair then she realized she wanted all of it off her and away from her.

Wax took her to her and Dragon's usual room and Wendy let them in. She was lost now. She had never been in the room without Dragon and she waited for Wax to take care of her. He unzipped the dress for her, while the water filled the tub. He untied her hair from the now fallen disheveled pony tail and she took his hand and followed him to the bath in just her panties.

"I'll wait out here," Wax said. "No, stay with me Ok Waxy," she said.

She slid the panties off and was standing looking at him. She looked so vulnerable and he realized she really didn't have any idea how she affected people. He took a deep breath and used the self control he prided himself for. No wonder Dragon was such a mess all the time, he thought to himself.

"Come on then," he said. He made her get in the tub, while he sat on the tiled surface beside her. "Wet your hair, wash all this shit away, ok?" he said. She looked up at him from the bubbles and he caught her expression. "Come on??" Wax said. He ran a hand through his dreads. "He washes your hair for you?" She nodded. He realized it was not the time to make fun of her or Dragon, so he picked up a bottle, reading the label to see it was shampoo.

"This isn't in the Kama Sutra," he mumbled. She managed a giggle then. "Waxy not everything we do is from the Kama Sutra. Girls need other things sometimes," she said. He took her hair and poured shampoo through it for her. "Ok, if you say so," he said. He fell into a relaxed comfortableness with her as he made sure he did a good job for her. "Why do you have so much hair?" he complained eventually. He was trying to rinse it thoroughly for her and it seemed unending. "This is fucking ridiculous," he said.

He eventually finished with her hair deciding she looked perfectly clean. "Ok, you're done kid, now come and take this towel from me, I want to go shower quick," Wax said. He stood and held it for her to wrap around herself.

She did as he asked, and he stood her there, covering her in it and doing his best to gather her hair and dry it as well.

"Are you showering here?" she said. "No, I need clean clothes, can you wait here and I will be back in a few minutes? I'm just across the hall," Wax said. He looked at her face to see if she was OK. "Ya, I'll wait here, hurry though," she said.

She crawled onto her and Dragon's bed, and wrapped herself up in a ball inside the towel. He eyed her, not sure. She looked at him and again he was floored by her vulnerability.

"Do you have clothes to wear?" he said. She was trying not to cry, not wanting to do it to him. "Waxy, Dragon does all this, please just find me whatever and I'll put it on," she said. "I don't know what's wrong with me right now, I can't figure anything out." She gave up and finally started to cry. "Hey, it's Ok," he said. He felt terrible for her and went to her, pulling her against him and holding her. "Ok, I'll find you some stuff to wear and fix your hair; I'll make it look just like mine," he said. He made her smile then. "You can come with me after and wait for me in my room while I shower and change. Then we'll go see Dragon and Sarge, OK?" Wax said.

Even though they had been in each other's lives for years he had always seen her as strong and independent. He had no idea of the side of her that needed Dragon for more than their obvious sexual dependency.

Looking up at him as he held his hand for her to come with him, she asked him. "You shot that guy in the helicopter, the one that shot Dragon?" "Yup," Wax said. "That man, Richard Ng, it was him," she said. "Yup," Wax said. He didn't want to say much else. The whole thing was a nightmare as far as he was concerned. "Dragon beat him to death," she said. It was as if she needed to say it out loud to be sure she really saw what she saw. "Yes he did," Wax said. "Let it go baby girl, it's over and we're all here, that's what's important." "He's really dead? Right?" she said. Wax took her then and held her into him. "Tom-Tom blew them into oblivion, remember?" he said.

He took her chin and made her look into his eyes. She nodded to him then and allowed him to dress her, thinking how lucky it was to have Waxy. His expert shooting had saved them numerous times.

He pulled her into the usual HQ uniform, really the only thing he could find for her in the room, other than one of Dragon's T shirts. She found him the stuff that detangled her hair and he ran it through her mane, finally able to pull a brush through it.

"There baby girl. Did I do good?" he said. She eyed herself. "Toothbrush!" she said. They found it, and he put toothpaste on it and handed it to her, much as Dragon did for her all the time. She brushed her teeth while he waited.

"Ok Waxy, thanks, let's go fix you up now," she said. She tried a smile for him. "So Dragon does all this stuff for you?" Wax asked. "Ya, I guess he does," she said. "Well, we do it together. He likes it I suppose and now I'm used to it. And he knows if he didn't get me to wear things I wouldn't wear anything at all, maybe one of his shirts." Wax smiled at her. "You have to put something on baby girl, we're guys around here," he said. "I guess so," she said.

"When I was a little girl, you know, before, all I ever had to wear was an old T-shirt, or nothing. It didn't matter to me, I was just a kid and we never had anything. Like my Mom did drugs and had sex for money," she said. She was remembering it from her past and from what Sensei had told her. "Sometimes my mom would get extra money if the men got to look at me," she said. "Sensei told me that it was good he found me because soon they would have done more than just looked." She shrugged and looked at him as if it was simply neither here nor there.

Wax shook himself, understanding her more than he ever had; her simplicity about some things, her vulnerability and lack of sexual boundaries. Dragon had filled those blanks for her and taken care of the things she had never been taught. Sensei had protected her first and now Dragon did. Her early childhood had left her without basics and even now, she only performed them because she was told to.

"You're safe now, you know that don't you?" Wax said, holding her then. "We're all safe now, Dragon is safe now." He was thinking grateful thoughts of his own then. "Waxy, the things they did to him, I saw in Ng's mind," she said. She looked to Wax then, and he could see her pain. "What happened to me was nothing compared to what he lived like." Her tears were falling again now. "I know baby girl, I've heard it from his own mouth, but he needs us now, to move on from it, and help him," Wax said. "It explains a lot about why he is who he is and why we love him so much."

He felt his mind caving in nearly at the thought of such things. She just stood looking at him, vulnerable and innocent. It made him mentally thank whatever powers that be, that she was with them and not back there, that Dragon was free, that they were all where they were now and not where they had been. Her words also eased him out of any guilt he occasionally retained after every time he had pulled the trigger.

He gently touched her bruised cheek, becoming aware of the love he had for her that they sometimes took for granted between them. He gathered himself then, and pulled his own clothes off right in front of her and headed to the shower. When he emerged from the bathroom, drying himself she was still standing right where he left her. He decided he should just hurry and dress, as she seemed at the limit of what she could emotionally manage for one day. He quickly dressed in the same uniform as she and went to her, taking her by the shoulders. She unglazed momentarily, focusing on him. He led her out the door.

When they arrived back in the infirmary, Sensei was just completing the dressing on Dragon's hand and wrist. Dr. Yung was clearing away instruments and disposing of bloodied gauze and things they had used. Sarge was how she had left him and Dragon lay still, deeply under and unaware. She went to Sensei and questioned him with her mind. He let her move to the top of the bed so she could kiss Dragon's face and just feel him. She looked at Sensei then, a million questions surfacing. Dr. Yung intercepted, knowing she needed answers.

"Raven, he will be fine. We did a lot of work to his hand, his shoulder will become more painful as the next 24 hours pass, but other than some inconveniences he will be up and about fairly soon." Raven smiled shyly at her, looking at Sensei for reassurance again. "Please, if it's Ok now, can you wake him?" Raven said. She desperately needed to see his eyes and talk to him. She had never in her whole life with him seen him like this. He had always been indestructible.

"Yes I think he's ready," Dr. Yung said. Sensei rechecked his vital signs, and then nodded. "He's very healthy Raven, he should be fine in no time," she said. She made small talk while they waited. Sensei stepped away then, letting Dr. Yung tend to it and checked on Sarge.

Moments passed and Dragon began to surface. Raven wanted nothing more than to feel his arms around her but that wouldn't be possible and she felt uncertain about not being able to have his touch on her. She waited until he slowly opened his eyes. She had her hand on his left elbow, staying on that side of his bed, keeping clear of his right side for the moment. She squeezed it gently and he turned towards her instinctively, seeing her, both with his eyes and also with his mind.

She could feel his mind clear, an understanding of things coming back to him. She gently reached and touched his face with her fingertips. In his mind he wanted her kiss, not able to find words yet. She leaned over him as best she could without disturbing anything and touched his lips with her now trembling ones.

"Baby," she said. She needed so badly to be closer to him, if not in his arms, he in hers. "Papa!" she said. And he knew loud and clear what she wanted. "I need to hold him, please??" She begged out loud now.

Dr. Yung looked taken by her adoration of Dragon and eyed the situation, wanting to help. "Would you wake Sergeant Willis please?" Sensei asked. "Wax will take care of him now." "Of course Sensei," she said. Sensei turned to Dragon and looked into his eyes and his mind. "Dragon, Wax and I are going to help you sit up, OK?" he said.

Dragon nodded that he agreed. So Wax and Sensei, very carefully and with much finesse helped Dragon sit on the side of the bed. Sensei had Raven tie the white sheet around his waist so he could make it to their room. She did so and he stood then, finding his balance. The only place Wax could hold him was his waist and upper right arm, but they managed and left the infirmary.

Sarge had woken as Wax had returned to take him. "Come on man, let's get you going. You're a little out of it but let's pretend we're leaving the bar," Wax said. He helped him up and he stood weaving. Wax tied the sheet so he could cover up and get to their room. "Cover your junk man or Erika's dick radar will detect you and then you'll be sorry," Wax said. "Shit no kidding, good idea man," Sarge slurred.

Wax paused for a moment, turning to Dr. Yung. She had turned her back momentarily pretending to be reading a chart while he got Sarge up, giving them some privacy.

"Thanks Doc," he said. "Wish we could have met under different circumstances." She nodded to Wax, suddenly aware of him, involuntarily fixing her errant hair, realizing she had a surgical cap over it and then not knowing where to look. "Sure," she said. She was not very good with social skills at the best of times. "We're normally a lot of fun to be around," Wax said. "I'm sure," she said. "Maybe another time," she tried.

Wendy closed the door behind them, as Wax steadied Sarge in the hallway. "Nice try," Sarge said. He was groggy but aware. "Just shut up and walk," Wax said. He was grinning, propping Sarge up as they went. "They scanned your brain and there was nothing there," he said. "Just the way I like it," Sarge slurred. His Morphine was still helping him along.

Dragon had been able to stand briefly on his own and she had wrapped her arms around his waist and lay against him as much as she could then, kissing every part of his skin that she could get to without hurting him. Sensei had pulled the duvet back and then came to help him to the bed. She removed the sheet from him so he could be comfortable, trying to keep her eyes off his body. They propped his hand under a pillow, extending his arm out far enough for her to curl herself into his right side, up against him. Sensei put a folded towel under his draining shoulder and then checked his blood pressure.

She pulled her clothes off and crawled into him, kissing his chest and neck. She was able to put her head on his right shoulder without affecting his hand and he turned so he could kiss her.

"Ok now?" Sensei asked, covering them. "Better Papa," she said. Dragon didn't speak because he was using his lips to kiss her everywhere he could reach without moving. "Ok I'm going to check on Sarge, and then I will be back. I have to stay here with you while we sleep, you understand that Raven?" he said. "Yes Papa, I want you to stay. But go see Sarge because I need to know he's ok too," she said. Finally physically connected to him again she was feeling dreamily tired now.

"Baby," Dragon said. "Stay right here with me now." His eyes were somewhat unfocussed from the drugs but he could see her and he smiled, wanting to reassure her but needing her touch on him. "I will baby," she said. "We'll figure this out. I'm going to miss your hands on me." It made him smile. "You can put your hands on me," he said. She smiled into his chest. "I will touch you baby, all you want me to. Now that you're kind of helpless I can spoil you," she said. She hugged him harder. "Soon," he said. He was relaxing into thoughts of it, which made Sensei smile as he came back into the room then.

"Sarge is just fine, Wax got him to bed and they are both out cold now, my dear," he said. He brushed her hair off her face for her, taking in her serenity then. "Papa you should rest now too," she said. He pondered for a moment, wanting to see the General. "Maybe I will, just for awhile, get things clearer before I see the General," he said. He found a spot below them at the bottom of the bed.

When Sensei woke her, it was noon. She became aware instantly, worrying for Dragon, his pain overwhelming. "Dragon, son, I need you to sit up," he said. "You have to swallow two of these pills, OK?" Sensei said. "Raven, help me."

They helped Dragon push himself up so he could lean against pillows. He swallowed the pills for Sensei, as he held water for him to drink to get them down. He eyed Raven, now kneeling beside him again, her tiny frame naked and soft. He so badly wanted to touch her.

"Sensei, untie my left arm, I need to have one free hand at least," he said. He eyed Sensei and let him know he meant it. "Alright son, but easy, OK," Sensei said. Sensei and Raven could not feel the exact pain he had but rather the unsettling energy and tension in his mind that it was causing.

"The pain in my hand is overriding everything Sensei. My shoulder feels like nothing compared to it," Dragon said. Sensei listened as he untied Dragon's shoulder. "You had eight fractures which we corrected with screws and as you can see, there are two temporary ones in your wrist." Sensei said.

Dragon eyed his right hand, bound up and unrecognizable as a hand at all. He leaned his head back against the wall, looking at the ceiling, wondering how he would possibly cope with it.

Dr. Yung had arrived just then. "How is Sarge's head today? Have you seen him?" Raven asked. Sensei raised his eyebrows also wanting to know. "I have, and he is well. He and your friend Wax, I believe, are anxious to see Dragon," she said.

Raven caught the thought from her mind when she mentioned Wax's name that the demure Dr. Yung found him quite delightful to look at. Sensei warned her in her mind to stop match making, especially when it came to 'lady killer' Wax. The General would not approve of Wax bedding and then laying an emotional trashing on his new doctor. She giggled at Sensei's analogy of Waxy.

"Papa, can you get them?" she said, wanting to see them both badly then. "Yes my dear, that's sounds like a good idea." Sensei said.

She sat looking at Dragon, wanting to distract him from his discomfort while they waited. "Baby, I stapled Sarge's head together with this gun thing," she said. "He must have been out cold," Dragon said.

He reached with his now free left hand, to touch her face. She took his hand, as he brushed her cheek and kissed his fingers, longing for them in her mind. He eyed her, warning her to keep her thoughts off of things or he would have a big problem in front of the new doctor.

Dr. Yung suddenly felt that she wasn't sure she should still be standing there. She realized Raven was wearing nothing at all. Their sexuality was overwhelming and the desire they had for one another was obvious. She had heard rumors about it around HQ. Chekov in particular had warned her, using discreet words that she should be prepared for anything. She also was quite curious to know who 'Damascus' was. Many of the girls never seemed to stop talking about him.

She decided to ask Raven, seeing as they had a moment. "Where is Damascus? Was he not with you in Hong Kong?" she asked. Raven smiled, 'seeing' the reason for the question. "He and his team had a mission to do in Thailand. He'll be here in a few days I think. Why?" she asked. She wasn't able to help herself from playing a teasing game. "Oh, I was hoping to meet him as well, he's um, 'well liked around here' shall I say," Dr. Yung said. She tried to sound nonchalant.

"Really," Dragon said. He was also finding it amusing. "Well liked. Is that how his sexual conquests are referring to him?" He stated the obvious just to make her more uncomfortable. Raven eyed him, and giggled. "Baby, stop it." "Um, I'm not allowed to repeat what girls, I mean patients tell me," Dr. Yung said. She tried to hold her composure under Dragon's directness. "I would think the more accurate statement would be that he is 'well missed'. He and Jacob, all of them from what I gather," Dragon said. "Yes, I don't know, actually, is what I mean," Dr. Yung said. She was sorry she had mentioned it at all but even more eager now to see who they were. She was more than relieved when Wendy let Sensei in with Sarge and Wax in tow.

"Hey, come here you," Sarge said to Raven.

He was happy to see her looking more herself as he recalled her traumatized face from the plane yesterday. Dr. Yung watched curiously as Raven jumped into Sergeant Willis' arms, still unclothed. He hugged her tightly to him, and she leaned against him, hugging him back.

He released her to kneel on Dragon's bed. "You look much better," he said. He held her back so he could see her face then. "So do you, Sarge," she said. She gave him a quick kiss on his lips. "You taste good too. Let me see," she said. She tilted her head and looked at the wound hidden by his hair now. "Can't even tell now," he said. He smiled his beautiful sweet smile at her. "I stapled you," she said. "Yes, I heard that. And I survived," he said.

"Dr. Yung helped Sensei fix Dragon," Raven said. "Yes I heard, and she did a CT scan of my head and according to Wax there was nothing there," Sarge said. "Well we didn't need a scan to know that," Raven said.

Sensei cleared his throat, signaling them to avoid their familiar path for the moment. "Ok you two, this could go south, so no more," he said. He shifted his eyes to Dr. Yung and back to Raven, handing her one of Dragon's T shirts to put on.

"Hey, you look totally shitty," Wax said. He gave Dragon a glance up and down. "There's a bunch of screws in my hand that I'm going to leave an imprint on your face with as soon as I get a chance," Dragon said. "Fair enough," Wax said. "Just heal up fast, because someone here needs a lot of help with things," he said. He nodded toward Raven and she winked at him.

"Waxy had to help me yesterday baby. He washed my hair for me and he untangled it and brushed it and got me some clothes. I think it traumatized him to have to do something with a girl that wasn't in the Kama Sutra," she said. Sarge and Sensei laughed at him and Dragon just smiled in amusement.

Wax shrugged. "I don't know anything about girl stuff and you were all like incapable or something, I had to help you," Wax said. "And now I know why you're stunned senseless most of the time buddy."

"Come here baby," Dragon said. He was thinking she was adorable and wanting her beside him again. "Thanks Waxy, I remember seeing her when I woke up and I could smell her hair and it was soft and everywhere. If you ever decide to put your gun away for good, you could do hair," Dragon said. "And you need to shut the fuck up," Wax said. He tried to sound polite about it, grinning at him.

"Boys," Sensei said. He wanted them to watch their frat house behavior in front of the doctor.

Dr. Yung had found it very amusing and was glad she had been warned about them being 'different'. She found it charming, much as the General did. "Excuse me, I should be going, but Dragon, come to the infirmary later so I can check your shoulder and re-do the dressing on your hand," she said. He eyed her and nodded, now distracted by Raven and thoughts of her in the bath tub. "Sergeant Willis, I would like to see you as well, I want to also check your vitals and you need another shot of antibiotics. Does your head ache at all?" she asked. She took another look at the wound, even though she had just seen to it about half an hour ago. "Just a bit, better though," he said. He was not comfortable being administered to. "Ok, whenever is fine, but if you start to get worse or have blurred vision, come right away," she said.

Raven couldn't resist. "Sarge gets blurred vision all the time and then he can't come at all. It's been happening since 1942," she said. Sensei turned away hiding a grin, and Wax and Dragon just burst out laughing. "That's right," Sarge said. "It happens all the time." Dr. Yung blushed but let a smile show on her face as she moved towards the door. "Very well," she said. "But no alcohol for a few more days please, for either of you."

"Of course," Sensei said. He made a serious face, trying to project some sort of decency. "Fuck that," Sarge said. He waited until she was out of the room, getting them all laughing again. Sensei just ran a hand through his hair. "Raven, honestly," he said. "Papa, I'm sorry but I couldn't let that go," she said.

Dragon entered Raven's thoughts, to distract her, wanting her to run the bath for them. She eyed him and leaned to carefully kiss him.

"Please baby, I need you," he said. He spoke out loud, not caring if they knew his intentions. She got up and went and turned the water on. "Papa can you help us?" she asked. She eyed Wax. "Someone else could but he might die of it."

Wax just eyed her back and grinned, pointing at her and nodding. "Keep it up, keep it up. You're getting closer and closer baby girl," Wax said. She giggled, thinking he was almost as fun as Sarge to bug. "Are you going to go all Sarge on me Waxy?" she said. "If I need to," he said. "You obviously want some 'Hollywood,' so maybe you'll finally get some." She shrugged, giving him a disappointed look. "You could have given me some yesterday." Wax eyed Sarge, respecting his pain all these years.

"Ok you," Dragon said. "Leave Wax alone or he won't do your hair ever again." Wax rolled his eyes at Sarge. "Fuck, I'm out of here, maybe I'll just shoot myself. It would be quicker," Wax said. He hoped Sarge would get better soon and take back his role.

"Ok Waxy, I'm sorry" Raven said. She went to him and pulled him around by his arm into her hug. "You're right; I can't wait until you give me some big time 'Hollywood!' I'm jealous that every other girl gets some and I don't," she said. She gave him a wet kiss on his lips as he smiled down at her. "Ok, easy baby girl, I got enough to go around if you know what I mean." "I know you do, remember Mexico? My little pink dress wanted to fall all off by itself," she said. He smiled, winking at her. "Go mess up Daddy there, he's waiting," Wax said. He saluted Dragon as he went out the door, shoving Sarge ahead of him.

They sat in the bath water together then, like they had done so many times before. They both moaned as they fell together finally. Dragon's right hand was supported on a thick folded towel along the side of the bath tub and he lay back as she moved over him and put him inside her. He let his breath out as the feel of her eased him.

He traced the fingers of his left hand, all he had in terms of touch, all over her. In her hair, on her face, her breasts, he couldn't touch her enough. She loved him with her eyes, her body and every single part of her, knowing what he needed to feel. His pain from his injuries was bad but having her was the best thing for him and it soothed him more than any drug could. His head fell back in the pleasure of her feel around him. She coaxed him into moving himself against her. In spite of his pain, his body craved her and he got what he needed.

She lay against him, not needing anything else in the whole world then. She felt that something had changed in him with the departure of Richard Ng. She could sense that there was vacant space inside him, left empty from the release of the fear and the hatred and the memories that died with Ng. She wanted to fill that space for him, with her, with them and the people they loved. Make new memories and move on with their lives together. He eyed her lovingly as he caught her thoughts.

"You are right," he said. "It's done, and we have to move on." "Baby, I just want to forget what I saw in your mind," she said. "Then forget it angel," he said. He spoke softly to her, kissing her gently. He knew she had experienced it with him, never leaving him through the horror of it and wanted them both to be free of it now. "I want to go home, and stay home baby," she said. She could feel tears brimming.

Dragon kissed her eyes to make them stop. "We will then. I know Sensei is done, I can 'see' it in him," Dragon said. "Yes, it's kind of scary, he actually seems defiant or something," she said. "Don't worry baby," he said. "Sensei will sort it out, and all I want or need right now is you." He touched her gently where she liked it most and she squirmed as he made her breathless. He refueled his want for her, moving inside her again.

Sensei waited for them, and reflected over their lives, everything. He didn't know. It had to stop. He knew now deep down that their vigilante life wouldn't work forever. He was going to tell the General that their days of killing were over. Things had come full circle and it was time to stop.

He would not lose any of them and not live with any of them losing one another. He would lead them on a path; continue with the General's work but without the violence. He wasn't sure how yet but he would see to it. He would wait for Damascus to come, and then they would all go home.

Sensei meditated on his knowledge of Karma, the reaction of life to Wholesome Actions and Unwholesome Actions, and the balance between them. He recalled a specific teaching that had come into his mind, relevant to them. It examined evil as a characteristic, suggesting that when other people are thought to be evil it becomes possible to justify doing them harm. And in that thinking are the actual seeds of evil itself. He didn't know how he could ever explain this to the General, in terms he would embrace. Sensei remembered what he needed to know to move them forward, that evil was something created, not something people are, or some outside force that infects people.

Had they in fact created evil, he wondered. Dragon had been given the chance of revenge, which he had exacted. And as with every action there is a reaction and he had incurred it, with what was going to be a painful and slow rehabilitation of his body, his mind and his being. There had been many reactions in their pasts, bringing Sensei to the path that he felt they needed to be on now. Two young members of Damascus's team, two beings he considered his own children were dead, Raven had lost her choice to carry a child for them. Damascus had nearly lost his life and bore the physical scars of it. He had nearly disintegrated emotionally; trying to be something he couldn't be, unable to find himself at one point. Sergeant Willis had come so close it was disturbing, his loyalty and devotion would have led him to it. Had Sensei not paid attention to his visions, Sarge would have been killed on the last mission.

And these were only some of the physical reactions they had experienced. It didn't even take into consideration the random injuries, the mental images and scars from the things they had done, some of the emotional sacrifices they had made. Wax could take a life; he specialized in it, and devoted himself to doing it, without a second thought. Dragon had pushed himself into roles he fuelled with memories from his past and the others had played along. Sensei cringed now at what he could see had been eroding to them, whether they were aware of it or not, admitted to it or not. Had something evil been toying with them, right in front of him, all along, the reaction to their actions?

CHAPTER THIRTY FOUR
THE FOUR NOBLE TRUTHS

Sensei was done, stopped in the momentum, no longer able to take a step forward and he knew what needed to change. He summoned his Buddhist background for guidance and had come to the knowledge of what he needed to do, based on the beliefs and the core philosophies. The Four Noble Truths would lead them out of this and that was what he needed to do.

They had all suffered the first truth, the obvious physical and mental suffering associated with birth, life, and dying. Everything that had happened to each of them had been a part of life that all humans went through. The varying degrees didn't matter now, he realized. Whether you grew up with all you wanted, or died a little each day at the hands of a tormentor. It didn't matter now and on another level it didn't matter then either, because everything is temporary. That was the first truth.

The second was that of ignorance and the misunderstanding of the nature of reality. A delusional state involving a fear of getting what one doesn't want and not getting what one does want. There was also attachment; the human desire to achieve pleasurable things. The human condition could be a fearful thing. Sensei felt they were beyond it within themselves, because of how he had raised them, none of them cared for things so much, and he didn't want that to ever change.

The third truth which Sensei wanted to focus on with them all was Cessation, the end of the cycle. It was the hamster wheel of things that they needed to get off of. Freedom lay within that concept, how to stop it, but how to continue on and how to not have them where they were right now. It lay within him from his upbringing and he would teach it to them. That was what he had for them besides his love. He needed to guide them and he needed to figure it out.

The fourth noble truth was where he needed to lead them. It was the path to cessation, the Eightfold Path, the essence of Buddhist practice. It involved the mental, spoken and bodily acts, operating in dependence of one another. Taken together they defined a complete path, or way of living. He had been taught, 'Know the cause of your suffering and simply remove it'. That was what he knew he had to do. Buddha had said, "If an arrow is sticking out from your side, don't argue about where it came from or who made it, just pull it out."

He was then taken away from his thoughts as Wendy announced the General and Chekov had arrived. Sensei mentally advised Dragon they were there, quietly closed the bathroom door, and then admitted them.

"I hope you don't mind the intrusion Sensei, but I understand from Dr. Yung that things went well and I wanted to reassure myself in person," the General said. Sensei could tell he was taxed and weary. Chekov stood patiently, not seeming to have a lot to say at the moment.

Raven had dried Dragon, and wrapped a towel around his waist, and after she had somewhat done something with their hair she had tied one around herself upon Dragon's insistence, because Chekov and the General would be standing there. She just smiled at him, happy that he seemed much more himself then. He had wanted more of her, but as Sensei had advised them they had company, he would have to wait. They had already decided that it was going to be fun to see how he could please her without much use of his hands for awhile. She had used her mouth on him to give him some idea of what she thought would work for her. She opened the door and staying stuck to him they joined Sensei.

"Sit son," Sensei said. "General," Dragon said. He smiled to him as he allowed Sensei to make him sit on the bed and fuss over his shoulder. "How are you Dragon?" the General asked. The kindness and concern in his eyes was evident.

Raven curled into Dragon, letting his right hand rest on her. The tips of his fingers were free of the dressing and he felt the warmth of her thigh, the feel of it curiously mixing with the pain.

"It's Ok General, it is what it is, as you can see," Dragon said. He was trying to give the General a genuine impression that he was fine aside from a few unpleasant issues that would be temporary.

"How are you General," Raven said. She was concerned for his health. He smiled at her. "My dear, it is sweet of you to ask, but let us concern ourselves with the well-being of Dragon and Sergeant Willis, shall we," he said.

He had not wanted to answer her question. She found it curious, and eyed Chekov, wanting to lose her temper and shake information out of him. Dragon eyed her, amused at her flash of anger and wanting to see her do it. Sensei sent them both a word, ending their distraction.

"Dragon, please, if there is anything you need or wish for while you are here, just ask Chekov," the General said. "I am deeply sorry for the turn of events in Hong Kong and Chekov is following up with everything he has to investigate Richard Ng." Dragon eyed Chekov, who shifted uncomfortably. "Chekov, don't waste your energy on my account. I killed the man and it's done as far as I'm concerned. What's to know? He saw me, he recognized me, he lured me and he's dead now, along with anyone else there. I'm all for calling it a success and moving on," he said. He eyed them as they looked at him. "What?" he said. He didn't really get the big deal.

"Very well, Dragon," Chekov said. "We haven't quite finished analyzing issues regarding your past. We don't know who else may still be alive that knows who you really are. It may be that we will never be certain and it will always be a threat," he said. "I aborted the mission because I could not tell what Tran was saying when he went behind the wall. Had I been able to, none of this would have happened. We are working on a lip reading program but it is not ready yet."

Dragon just nodded, recalling Chekov's orders to abort, before it all went crazy. "You caught it in time Chekov and all of our other fail-safes were in place, so we are all still here. Don't sweat it," Dragon said.

Chekov nodded and shuffled nervously about something. "I have a few unpleasant questions for you. If now isn't a good time…" he said. He eyed Raven in the bath towel, realizing they had intruded on something. Dragon eyed him, then Raven, who was alert with a slight anxiety then.

"Go ahead Chekov," Dragon said. He settled her with his thoughts. Chekov took a deep breath and continued. "Can you recall anyone; names, faces, ages, male or female?" he asked. "Not really," Dragon said. "Ok, um, Richard Ng had a daughter, the one married to Tran. She has contacted us and wants to meet you," he said.

Dragon just smiled in a resigned way, and shook his head. "Everyone wants to meet me, until they do," he said. He turned his gaze away and Chekov shuffled some more. "I haven't responded yet. Do you know of her?" he asked.

Dragon stood then and paced, trying to remember. "No," he said. He shook his head, trying to think back. "It's not completely clear to me because I was wasted out of my face for the last two years I was there. There was only ever an old woman, other children, and men. Ricky, 'Richard Ng', and a few others, that varied. He'd use them to out-number me because he couldn't handle me himself. Randomly, there were many. Some were repeat customers, some came only once. I never paid attention and eventually because of the Heroin I couldn't anyhow. Any of them would have seen the dragon. I can't even begin to tell you how many."

Raven had gotten up and moved to him, gently holding his waist, running her hand up his chest to draw his eyes down to her. "You don't have to do this," she said. With his loose left hand he brushed her cheek and smiled to her, loving her. "It's Ok baby, what difference does it make now," he said. Sensei stood quietly waiting, prepared to stop it if he caught any sign that Dragon was suffering.

Chekov had gone pale and was visibly shaken. "They paid to um?" he whispered. Dragon saw him breaking up and appreciated his feelings. "Yes Chekov, they paid for that and more. But Chekov, it's why we're all here, right? It's why I need you to keep doing what you do. So we can all keep doing what we do. It's important Chekov," he said.

Chekov swallowed hard and gathered himself, forcing himself to look at Dragon. Look at him with a new respect. "Well, I can send some photos to Sensei's laptop. Take a look at them whenever it suits you. I want to know if you recognize her before I reply," he said.

Dragon paced away with his back to them, thinking. "What does all this mean Chekov? And give it to me straight," Dragon said.

Chekov looked at the dragon on his back when he was facing away, actually seeing it for the first time. It was stunning yet frightening. He knew of the unfortunate way that it had come to exist, yet somehow it suited Dragon and seemed to belong on him, two entities creating the one. Seeing Dragon shirtless in front of him now, his dominant size and stature, his confident demeanor and unwavering eye contact, it dawned on him what a formidable player he had been in their little games.

He did his best then to answer the question for him. "We need to protect you and we need to protect the persona of David Li. I need to respond to the daughter, a piece of the puzzle we need to complete the picture. It is unknown at this time if there will ever be an end to this," he said.

"The likelihood is that she knows exactly who I am," Dragon said. "Find her and I'll kill her." Chekov, Sensei and the General eyed each other, as Dragon turned away again. The General simply nodded to Chekov.

"I'll get back to you then Dragon," Chekov said. "By the way, your stock purchase in Tran International was completed, causing a significant rise in its value, due to investor interest in DLI's involvement. It is holding solid with the recent turn of events." Dragon just shrugged. "Are you richer?" he asked. "Yes, as are you," Chekov said.

Dragon just turned away again nodding, finding the concept surreal, gently feeling Raven with his free left fingertips, needing her against his pain now. Chekov nodded to the General and Sensei and turned to leave, presumably to see to his communication with Tran's widow.

"Well Dragon, you seem to be on your game. Does nothing faze you son?" the General said.

Dragon turned to smile affectionately at the older man. He thought of telling the General that broken bones and bloody wounds were a way of life and he had learned to tune them out a long time ago. He touched Raven's hair, thinking about how he liked to tune them out now, much different from then.

Instead he answered from his heart. "This is temporary General, just like everything else. I have given it enough of my time and energy. I have moments with my wife that overshadow anything and it is those that I live for and are what 'fazes' me as you put it." To this the General smiled and his eyes had a sparkle that had been absent initially.

He nodded at Dragon, thinking him remarkable beyond words. He smiled to Raven, taking her hand and kissing the back of it. "You just keep fazing him my dear and we shall all live to see another day, which as Sensei keeps reminding us, is a gift," he said. Dragon grinned at them all then, as Raven blushed into his chest. "You heard the man," he said.

The General winked at Dragon and brought an end to their conversation. "Very well then, we shall wait to hear from Chekov. Sensei I believe you and I need to take a walk," he said. "Let's leave these two alone I think now." He placed his hand on the opaque panel. "General." Wendy commented formally, allowing him out of the room. "Wendy," he replied politely.

Sensei followed him out, sending Raven a little thought of what she may want to do to Dragon while they were gone. It made her jaw drop slightly and the warmth return between her thighs.

Dragon turned to her when they had gone, eyeing her with a deep glowing look in his eyes that disarmed her so strongly she blushed under his gaze. "Don't think I didn't catch Sensei's thought," he said. His sexy grin was pushing her off the ledge she was barely managing to stay on at that moment.

Sensei had sent her the image of the practice of Tantric love, which involved hours of prolonged orgasm suspension, creating extreme sexual pleasure, unavailable by traditional love making. In the Buddhist belief, it was a close replica to Nirvana.

"Try me," Dragon said.

Catching her thoughts, pushing her, making her want it, he took a step closer. She was dying then to spend hours with him that way, needing it with him. He moved in on her. "Ok baby," he said. He was moving against her and edging her closer. "Sensei's wisdom is at work here. Just let me love you." She let him back her onto the bed as she pulled her towel away, nearly there for him already.

EPILOGUE

The ocean moved them gently as the Dream Weaver drifted; her engines silent. The land had faded from their sight and they sat in the hot breeze, the calm ocean making no sound around them. Sensei stood watching. Dragon and Raven sat together on the stern deck padding. She was cocooned into herself, her knees drawn up, arms wrapped around them, leaning against him as his arm draped her, relaxed and serene. She looked up to him then, feeling at peace. Sensing her loving eye he looked down at her, his sexy smile coming to his lips then. The breeze blew tendrils of their hair about their faces, their tanned skin glowing. She adored him, as always and forever. He looked as if he wanted to say something to her, ask her what she was looking at, something like that; still smiling to her like they had a secret.

Wax stood at the side of the yacht, as they watched. Sarge sat, waiting for his friend. Damascus stood out on the bow deck, watching and eyeing the beautiful blues in the ocean, the breeze blowing his spikes away, his sunglasses reflecting. The boys sat around him, taking in the serenity and beauty of where they were and the peace of where life had gotten them to. It was silent except for a song from Wax's IPod, a moving ballad, deep and meaningful to each in its own way, almost surreal.

Wax was nearly done. He stood now with the Desert Eagle only, all that was left. He held it, allowing some memories to come to him and with them he raised it in his left handed grasp and with all his strength threw it. In a slow motion release, finally from all that they were and had been, it spiraled through the air, taking with it the past. Wax turned away from it, the breeze moving his hair back, the sun glowing on his skin and his beautiful smile of freedom bringing them all happiness. One love, One life...

Printed in the United States
By Bookmasters